U0154515

宋雷◆編著　楊智傑、朱芃臻◆校訂

法律英語

同義・近義法律用語辨析

翻譯指南

前言

　　在英美法漫長的發展和演變歷程中，法律語言（the Language of Law）創制和衍生出大量同義或近義的術語。這些術語的區分和辨析，是法律翻譯中最令人頭疼和最容易出錯的事。筆者在歷時 8 年的《英漢法律用語大辭典》編寫過程中，發現在法律英語翻譯過程中（甚至包括在一些權威詞典中）術語翻譯的錯誤之多，真可謂是「種種舛誤，令人吃驚」。

　　譯者混淆同義或近義法律術語的原因多種，有些錯誤是翻譯中望文生義所導致的，如 final judgment，譯者想當然地便將它譯為「終審判決」，並由此以訛傳訛，導致幾乎所有的英漢或漢英詞典全都由此錯下去，全然不顧或不知它與真正的「終審判決」，即 judgment of last resort 具有天壤之別。

　　有些錯誤則是因為譯者懶惰或粗心所致。一詞多義本是語言的普遍現象，但不少人在翻譯時常滿足於知道它的一兩個一般含義，而不願再花力氣去查詞典，尤其是查英英法律詞典進行辨析。如 summons，不少人只知道它的「傳票」的含義，而不知道它還有「起訴狀」（originating process）的含義；同樣，不少譯者只知道 amendment 是「修正案」，而不知道也不願接受它為「修正條款」〔如 Amendment to Constitution（《聯邦憲法》修正條款）〕。有些混淆則是因法律文化差異導致的。有些分歧甚至是源於英英法律詞典之間的歧義，如在 defalcation 和 embezzlement 的定義問題上，

Black's Law Dictionary 的解釋便與 *Merriam Webster's Dictionary of Law* 等詞典相悖。

　　此外，從詞源學的觀點來看，法律英語除包含不少古英語辭彙外，其還從拉丁語、法語等中吸收了許多術語。因而，就同一法律術語而言，除表示類概念的上義詞（supper ordinate）外，還經常存在一些表示種概念的下義詞（hyponym）。如 killing（殺人）為表示類別的通用術語；而表示具體的特殊術語則有：homicide（他殺）、murder（謀殺）、manslaughter（非謀殺）。至於法律規定的，與之相關的同義或近義的術語就更多。同理，decision 是「裁判」或「判決」的上義詞，而 award、finding、judgment、sentence、verdict、decree、ruling 和 disposition 則為下義詞；defamation 為「毀謗」的上義詞，而 slander 和 libel 則為下義詞。讀者在翻譯時，務必要知道術語含義的差別。

　　法律翻譯最重要的標準是準確，但不能辨別近義或同義術語，準確只能是奢望。

　　本書旨在用最簡潔的語言和方式，對常用的一些同義或近義法律術語進行辨析，幫助讀者儘快瞭解法律術語的差別，以期為國內的法律翻譯工作更上一個臺階做一點微薄的貢獻。

　　鑒於法律術語辨析和翻譯所涉及的領域和知識太多，太深奧，儘管筆者竭盡全力，遺漏和謬誤在所難免，望廣大讀者不吝賜教。

宋雷

使用說明

一、用索引查詢

如要找到你想查詢的法律術語或單詞,請首先參閱本書後面的索引。索引中的術語按字母順序排列,主要分為兩種。

1. *220* **final judgment**(條目)

該索引的 final judgment(條目)部分表示 final judgment 這個術語被用作為本書一段短文的標題。其前面的數字 220 為書頁數碼,表示讀者可在本書的第 220 頁中找到對該片語的解釋和辨析:

Final judgment

該片語常被誤認為是「終審判決」,目前幾乎所有流行的英漢(法律)詞典或相關工具書都難逃此錯[①]。依定義,「終審判決」即法院對訴訟案件進行最後一級審判時所作的判決,終審判決一經宣布,即為發生法律效力的判決,不能再行上訴[②]。從此意義上講,final judgment(最終判決)決非終審判決,因為 final judgment 本身的含義剛好與此相反,其是指初審法院對案件實體(merits)審理後作出的可上訴的判決(故它也稱為 final appealable judgment、final appealable order 等),其與法院的審級完全無關[③]。final judgment rule 對此作有專門規定:a party may appeal only from a district court's final judgment that ends the litigation on the merits[4]。而我們所說的不能再行上訴的終審判決應是 judgment of court of last resort 或 judgment of last resort 才對[5]。

注

① Cf.《英漢法律詞典》，法律出版社（1999），第 311 頁；陳慶柏等（翻譯），《英漢雙解法律詞典》，世界圖書出版公司（1998），第 221 頁；薛波，《漢英法律詞典》，外文出版社（1995），第 912 頁；《漢英法律詞典》，中國商業出版社（1995），第 997 頁。

② Cf. 周振想，《法學詞典》，上海辭書出版社（1980），第 484 頁。

③ "A court's last action that settles the rights of the parties and disposes of all issues in controversy, except for the award of costs and enforcement of the judgment. Also termed final appealable judgment; final decision; final decree; definitive judgment; determinative judgment; final appealable order." Cf. Bryan A. Garner, *Black's Law Dictionary*, 7th Edition, West Group (1999), at P. 847.

④ *Id.* at P. 644.

⑤ Cf. Philip R. Bilancia, *Dictionary of Chinese Law and Government*, Stanford University Press (1981), at P. 121.

2. finder Cf. broker

在該索引中，finder 表示它是被本書列為比較的一個法律術語。

Cf. broker 等同 Confer broker，表示在本書中，broker 是本書一段短文的標題，而有關 finder 的論述可參照 broker 為標題的短文。

有些術語具有多種重要的意思，必須用幾篇短文論述其不同的含義。在此種情況下，索引中的標題單詞或片語後面參見兩個或以上的單詞或片語。如：

felony Cf. treason; high crime; non-arrestable offense; crime ﹐

此種索引表示本書中多篇短文均有與 felony 相關的辨析內容說明。讀者可參見本書以 treason 為標題的短文；以 high crime 為標題的短文；以 non arrestable offense 為標題的短文以及以 crime 為標題的短文進行查閱。

二、注釋說明

注釋是術語辨析的有機組成部分，其中許多英文引自英美法權威原版詞典，因而在每一條目下接排注釋，未採用頁下注的傳統注釋形式，方便讀者查閱。

1. 短文注釋中的符號：

Cf. = Confer 參見
Id. = Idem 同前，同上
P. = page 頁

2. 注釋中所指的參考書目資料內容順序排列一般為引文內容—作者—書名（為斜體字）—出版社—年代—頁碼。例如：

"A court's last action that settles the rights of the parties and disposes of all issues in controversy except for the award of costs and enforcement of the judgment. Also termed final appealable judgment; final decision; final decree ; definitive judgment ; determinative judgment; final appealable order." Cf. Bryan A. Garner, *Black's Law Dictionary*, 7th Edition, West Group (1999), at P. 847.

3. 有時一條注釋所指的參考書目有幾本，此時其排列情況見下列例文：

① Cf.《英漢法律詞典》，法律出版社（1999），第 311 頁；陳慶柏等（翻譯），《英漢雙解法律詞典》，世界圖書出版公司（1998），第 221 頁；薛波，《漢英法律詞典》，外文出版社（1995），第 912 頁；《漢英法律詞典》，中國商業出版社（1995），第 997 頁。

目次

Abandon ▸ Relinquish ▸ Renounce

三個單詞均有拋棄及放棄的含義。abandon 主要指因挫折、氣餒、厭倦、厭惡等原因而放棄或中止某事（包括權利或義務），或遺棄財產（to denote a complete giving up, especially of what one has previously been interested in or responsible for）[1]，且有永遠不再主張之含義[2]。包括 to abandon a crime（中止犯罪）；to abandon a contract（撤銷契約）（Cf. abandonment）。在家事法上，尤指「離棄」配偶或家庭成員（有離開而不再歸來的含義，Cf. abandonment），如 to abandon a child（離棄子女）[3]。relinquish 含義最廣，可用於指權利或財產等的放棄[4]，常表示自願（雖然有時也表示被迫），故常無暴力行為或強烈情感相伴隨[5]。renounce 則指自願或正式宣布放棄某事，如：to renounce one's claim, right, authority, principle 等[6]。

注

[1] Cf. The Editors of the Reader's Digest, *Use the Right Word*, The Reader's Digest Association Proprietary Ltd. (1971), at P. 335.

[2] "to give up with the intent of never again asserting or claiming an interest in (a right or property)", Cf. Linda Picard Wood, J.D., *Merriam Webster's Dictionary of Law*, Merriam-Webster, Incorporated, Springfield, Massachusetts (1996), at P. 1.

[3] "*Family law*, to leave a spouse or child willfully and without an intention to return." Cf. Bryan A. Garner, *Black's Law Dictionary*, 7th Edition, West Group (1999), at P. 2.

④ "To abandon, to give up, to surrender, to renounce some right or thing." Cf. The Publisher's Editorial Staff, *Black's Law Dictionary*, Abridged 6th Edition, West Publishing Co. (1991), at P. 895.

⑤ "a word wide in meaning, usu. does not suggest forceful action or strong feeling in dropping, desisting, renouncing; it sometimes suggests regret at giving up or delay in the process", Cf. Philip Babcock Grove, Ph.D., *Webster's Third New International Dictionary of the English Language Unabridged*, G & C Merriam Co. (1976), at P. 1918.

⑥ "Renounce means to declare against or give up formally and definitively." Cf. The Editors of the Reader's Digest, *Use the Right Word*, The Reader's Digest Association Proprietary Ltd. (1971), at P. 487.

Abandonment ▸ Desertion ▸ Waiver

上述三個單詞均有「放棄」的含義。其中，abandonment 爲通用詞，可用於放棄訴訟、財產、各種權利、理由等；家事法上指「離棄」配偶或子女，主要強調離開且不準備返回之行爲，有一去不復返的含義①。desertion 常用作指放棄應當履行的責任或義務，尤指不服兵役或遺棄配偶或家庭成員；在遺棄配偶等時主要強調未盡責任義務而非一定有離開之實際行爲（如 constructive desertion，只要終止同居行爲即可構成 desertion），故爲「遺棄」，也稱爲 "gross neglect of duty" ②。waiver 通常用於表示對某種權利的放棄③。

注

① "The act of leaving a spouse or child willfully and without an intent to return." Cf. Bryan A. Garner, *Black's Law Dictionary*, 7th Edition, West Group (1999), at P. 2.

② "Separation of one spouse from the other, with a deliberate intention and, without reasonable cause and the other spouse's consent, to end cohabitation permanently." Cf. Daphne A. Dukelow, *The Dictionary of Canadian Law*, Thomson Professional Publishing Canada (1991), at P. 276.

③ "The renunciation, repudiation, abandonment, or surrender of some claim, right, privilege, or of the opportunity to take advantage of some defects, irregularity, or a legal wrong." Cf. The Publisher's Editorial Staff, *Black's Law Dictionary*, Abridged 6th Edition, West Publishing Co. (1991), at P. 1092.

Abandonment ▸ Rescission

　　兩者均可用作指契約的「撤銷」，尤其是在土地買賣契約中。區別在於 abandonment 僅指契約一方接受另一方當事人所造成的債務不履行之情況（merely the acceptance by one party of the situation that a nonperformance party has caused），另一方所導致的違約後果並不嚴重。而 rescission 則指契約一方當事人在有充足理由，如因另一方嚴重違約（material breach）而終止或解除所有契約責任和義務①；它是無過失當事人（non breaching party）最常尋求的一種衡平法上的救濟（equitable judicial remedy）和保護方法，其可使得雙方當事人回復到契約之前的狀況（restore the parties to their pre-contractual positions）②。

① "In the context of contracts for the sale of land, as if it were synonymous with *rescission*, but the two should be distinguished. An abandonment is merely the acceptance by one party of the situation that a nonperformance party has caused. But a rescission due to a material breach by the other party is a termination or discharge of the contract for all purposes." Cf. Bryan A. Garner, *Black's Law Dictionary*, 7th Edition, West Group (1999), at P. 2.

② "A rescission amounts to the unmaking of a contract, or an undoing of it from the beginning, and not merely a termination, and it may be effected by mutual agreement of parties, or by one of the parties declaring rescission of contract without consent of other if a legally sufficient ground therefore exists, or by applying to courts for a decree of rescission." Cf. The Publisher's Editorial Staff, *Black's Law Dictionary*, Abridged 6th Edition, West Publishing Co. (1991), at P. 905.

Abate ▶ Curtail ▶ Diminish ▶ Lower ▶ Reduce

上述單詞均有減輕和減少的含義。其中，reduce 最為通用，可指在體積、數量、金額、程度及範圍等方面的減少，如 to reduce expenses（labor force, acreage of property, means, etc.）以及 to reduce, to letting rooms, private 等①。abate 在法律英語中常用作及物動詞，多指在強度或程度上減輕或全部及部分廢除，常用於減價及稅收、遺產或騷擾的減少等②。curtail 一般用作指突然減少或徹底除去原來並不計畫或打算的事務，多指抽象而非具體的東西③。diminish 常指部分刪減，如責任、人口、數量等，所刪減部分有時並非無價值④。lower 多指價值、等級及程度的減少和降低，其強調程度和所指的精確程度不及 reduce⑤。

注

① "Reduce has a wider range of connotations than the other word and is also the most general. It means to make less in size, amount, number, extent or intensity." Cf. The Editors of the Reader's Digest, *Use the Right Word*, The Reader's Digest Association Proprietary Ltd. (1971), at P. 484.

② "To break down, destroy or remove; to lower the price." Cf. Daphne Dukelow, *The Dictionary of Canadian Law*, Thomson Professional Publishing Canada (1991), at P. 1; "Abate means to reduce, as in strength or degree, usually from an excessive intensity or amount." Cf. The Editors of the Reader's Digest, *Use the Right Word*, The Reader's Digest Association Proprietary Ltd. (1971), at P. 485.

③ "Curtail is to reduce abruptly and radically, as by cutting off or cutting short than was originally intended. The word is used chiefly of non-material things and conveys the idea of the unexpected." Cf. The Editors of the Reader's Digest, *Use the Right Word*, The Reader's Digest Association Proprietary Ltd. (1971), at P. 485.

④ "Diminish is a more accurate word than reduce when one wishes to stress the idea of removing part of something so that there is a manifest and sometimes progressive lessening, but not to the point of total disappearance. The word may suggest either the loss of something valuable or a lessening of that which is undesirable." *Id.* at P. 485.

⑤ "Lower is to make less, especially in value, degree or level. It is not as emphatic or precise a word as reduce in this sense, although fairly close in meaning." *Id.* at P. 485.

Abdicate ► Renounce ► Resign ► Cede ► Relinquish ► Surrender ► Yield

這些單詞均有放棄（權利或職位等）的含義。其中，abdicate 主要是指放棄某種法定職位，如君主正式放棄其王位等，有時也指放棄某種特權（prerogative）[1]。renounce 常與 abdicate 互換使用，多指放棄某種權利、權利要求、資格或慣例（right, claim, title, practice），且有作出某種犧牲的含義[2]。resign 多指正式通知辭去從上級或其他人處所獲的某種職位或未滿任期[3]。cede 指正式放棄權利，常用於法律上的轉讓及根據條約割讓領土等[4]。relinquish 最為通用，可表示自願或非自願的放棄[5]，如 to relinquish control over sth 或 to relinquish a claim 等。surrender 多指被迫，或在感情或權勢的影響下的放棄[6]。yield 類同 surrender，但相比之下，其所受的壓力或所受到的情感的影響小於後者[7]。

注

[1] "To refuse or renounce a thing, a person in office to renounce it or give it up voluntarily." Cf. Daphne A. Dukelow, *The Dictionary of Canadian Law*, Thomson Professional Publishing Canada (1991), at P. 2.

[2] "To give up or abandon formally (a right or interest); to disclaim." Cf. Bryan A. Garner, *Black's Law Dictionary*, 7th Edition, West Group (1999), at P. 1299.

[3] "To give up a possession, office or claim." Cf. Daphne A. Dukelow, *The Dictionary of Canadian Law*, Thomson Professional Publishing Canada (1991), at P. 922.

[4] "to yield or grant usu. by treaty", Linda Picard Wood, J.D., *Merriam Webster's Dictionary of Law*, Merriam-Webster, Incorporated,

Springfield, Massachusetts (1996), at P. 71.

⑤ "Relinquish is the most general and neutral term in the group. It can indicate no more than the release of one's grasp. It can denote the letting go from one's direction or possession, usually voluntarily but sometimes reluctantly." Cf. The Editors of the Reader's Digest, *Use the Right Word*, The Reader's Digest Association Proprietary Ltd. (1971), at P. 487.

⑥ "Surrender means to give up under compulsion to any person, passion, influence or power." *Id.* at P. 487.

⑦ "Yield is close to surrender, but implies milder compulsion and therefore some softness, concession, respect or even affection on the part of the person who yields." *Id.* at P. 487.

Abduct ▸ kidnap ▸ Hijack

　　三者均有劫持及綁架的含義。在英國或普通法中，abduct 主要是指誘拐或挾持婦女，即在普通法上指「挾持婦女罪」，主要指以婚姻、賣淫、非法性行爲等爲目的，用誘騙或武力脅迫方式，違反婦女意志而拐走 16 或 18 歲以下的或有精神障礙的少女以及婦女；在美國成文法中，其爲「挾持罪」，多與受害人的性別無關①。kidnap 主要是指爲索取贖金的綁架或劫持人質的行爲，其爲「綁架」，古時也稱爲 manstealing②。hijack 則是指爲達到某種目的而「劫持」飛機等運輸工具③。與以上三個單詞相對應的名詞 abduction、kidnapping 和 hijacking 也有如此差別。

注

① Cf. Bryan A. Garner, *A Dictionary of Modern Legal Usage*, Oxford University Press (1995), at P. 4.

② "To seize and take away a person by force or fraud, often with a demand for ransom." Cf. Bryan A. Garner, *Black's Law Dictionary*, 7th Edition, West Group (1999), at P. 874.

③ "to seize possession or control (of a vehicle) from another person by force or threat of force, esp., to seize possession or control of an aircraft", Cf. Linda Picard Wood, J.D., *Merriam Webster's Dictionary of Law*, Merriam-Webster, Incorporated, Springfield, Massachusetts (1996), at P. 226.

Abet ▶ Encourage ▶ Incite ▶ Instigate ▶ Provoke

以上單詞均有煽動和慫恿的含義。abet（教唆，尤指教唆罪）指鼓勵、教唆他人犯罪，常含有協助並參與犯罪之意，如 abet 他人犯 murder 罪，則包括命令、促使、協商、鼓勵、誘惑、幫助殺人等屬於知情、共謀、協助或參與犯罪的情節行為①。encourage 則多指鼓勵、支持或勸告某人幹某事②。在刑法中，incite 幾乎與 abet 同義，此外，在表示激勵或鼓動時，incite 所導致的後果可好可壞，造成的影響也可大可小③。instigate 指唆使或鼓動某人犯罪，常涉及一些極端行為，如 to instigate an assassination 或 to instigate a plot to seize control of a government 等④。provoke 也可指挑唆或煽動，但此種行為不必一定且經常不是經有意識策劃，故常用作指一些激情或衝動性質的行為⑤。

注

① "To encourage and assist someone, esp. in the commission of a crime; to support (a crime) by active assistance." Cf. Bryan A. Garner, *Black's Law Dictionary*, 7th Edition, West Group (1999), at P. 4.

② "In criminal law, to give courage to; to inspirit; to embolden; to raise confidence; to make confident; to help; to forward; to advise." Cf. The Publisher's Editorial Staff, *Black's Law Dictionary*, Abridged 6ᵗʰ Edition, West Publishing Co. (1991), at P. 364.

③ "Incite means to spur to action, any may be applied to measures leading to salutary as well as deplorable results, to minor as well as profound changes." Cf. The Editors of the Reader's Digest, *Use the Right Word*, The Reader's Digest Association Proprietary Ltd. (1971), at P. 294.

④ "Instigate usually suggests the setting in motion of events that in some way threaten or upset the status quo. It will therefore convey a negative or unfavorable connotation to the extent that one deplores violent change. It suggests an insidious design to bring about some drastic action." *Id.* at P. 294.

⑤ "to excite; to stimulate; to arouse", Cf. Bryan A. Garner, *Black's Law Dictionary*, 7ᵗʰ Edition, West Group (1999), at P. 852; "Provoke, as here considered, can be used, like instigate, to point to a variety of results, but it does not necessarily or even commonly imply conscious design. It may on the contrary imply spontaneous reaction." *Id.* at P. 295.

Ability ▸ Faculty ▸ Capacity

　　三個單詞均有能力的含義。ability 為通用詞，指天生或後天所得的做好某事的能力，尤指實施法律行為的權力（power to carry out a legal act）①，如 the ability to enter into an agreement with others。相比之下，faculty 則主要指某種特殊行為的天賦能力，在離婚案件中可指丈夫對妻子提供贍養費的能力②。capacity（也稱為legal capacity）多表示在法律或其他意義上的一種地位或資格③。

注

① "The capacity to perform an act or service; esp. the power to carry out a legal act." Cf. Bryan A. Garner, *Black's Law Dictionary*, 7th Edition, West Group (1999), at P. 4.

② "In the law of divorce, the capability of the husband to render a support to the wife in the form of alimony, whether temporary or permanent, including not only his tangible property, but also his income and his ability to earn money." The Publisher's Editorial Staff, *Black's Law Dictionary*, Abridged 6th Edition, West Publishing Co. (1991), at P. 411.

③ "the legal ability or qualification to perform an act having legal consequences, such as entering into a contract, making a will, suing or being sued, committing a crime, or getting married", Cf. James E. Clapp, *Random House Webster's Dictionary of the Law*, Random House (2000), at P. 69.

Able ▸ Capable ▸ Competent ▸ Qualified

　　上述四個形容詞均有「有能力的」或「有資格的」含義。able 多指做某事的才能或能力，如 able to make payment，且有形容人多才多藝的含義。capable常用來指滿足一般要求的能力，以及解決具體和實際問題的能力①。competent 和 qualified 多強調滿足特殊規定或要求的能力；其中，qualified 常指從事某一職業或做某事所需的諸如學歷、證明等資格，如 a qualified voter。而 competent 則有「能幹」的含義，指是否有充分滿足某種要求或勝任某項職務或工作的能力。因而，a qualified lawyer 有時並非一定是 a competent lawyer②。

注

① "Able suggests versatility and resourcefulness and capable a practical, problem solving approach." Cf. The Editors of the Reader's Digest, *Use the Right Word*, The Reader's Digest Association Proprietary Ltd. (1971), at P. 106.

② "Qualified stresses the possession of required skill and is generally applied to professions or trades for which a minimum of schooling or training is required. A qualified teacher has completed the academic training prescribed, but is not necessary competent." *Id*. at P. 106.

Abolish ▸ Abrogate ▸ Annul ▸ Rescind ▸ Revoke ▸ Repeal

以上單詞均有廢止和取消的含義。abolish 指完全廢除制度、風俗、習慣等[①]，如 to abolish slavery, ignorance。abrogate 主要指對下屬機構簽發的命令、規則的廢除，或經立法廢除法規或習俗等，如 to abrogate certain privileges[②]。annul 指終止某事務的存在或宣布其無效或從未真正存在過，如 to annul the marriage[③]。rescind 常用於契約的撤銷，以及經同級或上級機構予以撤銷或廢除規定等，如to rescind an order[④]。revoke 主要指以收回或撤銷以往授予或准予事項的方式予以廢除或廢止，或廢除遺囑效力，如 to revoke a charter[⑤]。repeal主要指以立法方式撤銷或廢除法規、命令、許可等，如 to repeal an amendment[⑥]。

注

① "To do away with wholly. Applies particularly to things of a permanent nature, such as institutions, usages, customs, as the abolition of slavery." Cf. The Publisher's Editorial Staff, *Black's Law Dictionary*, Abridged 6th Edition, West Publishing Co. (1991), at P. 3.

② "To annul or repeal an order or rule issued by a subordinate authority; to repeal a former law by legislative act, or by usage." *Id.* at P. 4.

③ "To annul is either to end something existing or to declare that it never really existed." Cf. The Editors of the Reader's Digest, *Use the Right Word*, The Reader's Digest Association Proprietary Ltd. (1971), at P. 665.

④ "With respect to a contract, for one or more parties to end it." Cf. Daphne Dukelow, *The Dictionary of Canadian Law*, Thomson Professional Publishing Canada (1991), at P. 916; "to make void by the same or by a superior authority", Cf. Linda Picard Wood, J.D., *Merriam Webster's Dictionary of Law*, Merriam-Webster, Incorporated, Springfield, Massachusetts (1996), at P. 427.

⑤ "To annul or make void by recalling or taking back." Cf. The Publisher's Editorial Staff, *Black's Law Dictionary*, Abridged 6th Edition, West Publishing Co. (1991), at P. 915.

⑥ "to abrogate an existing law by legislative act", Cf. Bryan A. Garner, *Black's Law Dictionary*, 7th Edition, West Group (1999), at P. 1301.

Abortion ▶ Miscarriage

　　兩者均有墮胎和終止妊娠的含義。abortion（也稱為 procuring an abortion）常指有意的而非自然流產，且多在妊娠 12 周內進行的「墮胎」行為，在過去的普通法及制定法上，其可算作一種犯罪（輕罪）①。miscarriage 除用於指妊娠最後 3 個月內的有意「墮胎」行為外，其與 abortion 的區別在於它常用於指自然的非人工行為的「流產」②。

注

① "With respect to human beings, however, abortion has long been used to refer to an intentionally induced miscarriage as distinguished from one resulting naturally or by accident." Cf. Rollin M. Perkins & Ronald N. Boyce, *Criminal Law*, 3rd Edition (1982), at P. 187.

② "The expulsion of a fetus, usually in the final third of a pregnancy." Cf. F. A. Jaffe, *A Guide to Pathological Evidence*, 2nd Edition, Toronto, Carswell (1983), at P. 180.

Abrogation ▸ Derogation ▸ Antiquation

　　三個單詞均有取消或廢除的含義。abrogation 表示正式經授權取消或廢除下級機關頒布的某部法律、命令、規則等，常等同 cancellation 或 annulment①。derogation 則表示廢除一部法律的某一部分，故其應爲「部分廢除」②。antiquation 多指用新法置換過時舊法的方式廢除或取消某部法規③。

注

① "Annulment; repeal of a law." Cf. Daphne Dukelow, *The Dictionary of Canadian Law*, Thomson Professional Publishing Canada (1991), at P. 3.

② "The partial repeal or abrogation of a law by a later act that limits its scope or impairs its utility and force." Cf. Bryan A. Garner, *Black's Law Dictionary*, 7th Edition, West Group (1999), at P. 455.

③ "to make obsolete by replacing with something newer or better", Cf. Jess Stein, *The Random House College Dictionary*, Revised Edition, Random House, Inc. (1979), at P. 60.

Absolute majority ▸ Simple majority

兩片語常用於選舉或投票中，其區別在於 absolute majority（絕對多數）指以占參加選舉或投票之人數的 2/3 或以上的票數。而 simple majority（簡單多數）僅指 1/2 或以上之票數。

Absolve ▸ Exonerate ▸ Pardon ▸ Forgive ▸ Vindicate ▸ Exculpate

以上單詞均有免罪或免除責任或懲罰的含義。absolve 主要指免除對某行為的責任或義務，如 absolved from his promise，以及經裁定免除因未履行此責任或義務而應受的懲罰[①]。exonerate 主要指解除對侵權等不法行為的指控或指責，並強調消除今後的嫌疑[②]。pardon 指赦免罪行，免除刑罰，如 prisoner was pardoned by the governor[③]。forgive 指因同情或憐憫，個人放棄本應要求懲罰的權利，或去掉所厭惡或復仇的念頭或情感[④]。vindicate 指透過提供指控或指責不公平的證據而使受指控或指責者免除責任或罪過[⑤]。exculpate 指免去指控或懲罰，或證明無辜或無過失，它與 exonerate 的主要區別在於其適用範圍較廣，可適用於所有的罪行，即不管是否提起過指控，也不管受指控的行為是否合法[⑥]。

注

① "to set free or release from some obligation or responsibility; to determine to be free of fault, guilt, or liability", Cf. Linda Picard Wood, J.D., *Merriam Webster's Dictionary of Law*, Merriam-Webster, Incorporated, Springfield, Massachusetts (1996), at P. 3.

② "Exonerate means to free from accusation or blame, and stress freedom from future suspicion." Cf. The Editors of the Reader's Digest, *Use the Right Word*, The Reader's Digest Association Proprietary Ltd. (1971), at P. 197.

③ "to release a person from penalties for a past offense or alleged offense", Cf. James E. Clapp, *Random House Webster's Dictionary of the Law*, Random House (2000), at P. 318.

④ "Forgive is to pardon with compassion, usually on a directly personal level." Cf. The Editors of the Reader's Digest, *Use the Right Word*, The Reader's Digest Association Proprietary Ltd. (1971), at P. 420.

⑤ "to clear of suspicion, blame, or doubt", Cf. The Publisher's Editorial Staff, *Black's Law Dictionary*, Abridged 6th Edition, West Publishing Co. (1991), at P. 1085; "to clear from censure or suspicion by means of demonstration", Cf. Bryan A. Garner, *Black's Law Dictionary*, 7th Edition, West Group (1999), at P. 1564.

⑥ "Exculpate means to free from blame or prove innocent of guilt. Unlike exonerate, it does not necessarily imply that a formal charge was made nor that the blameworthy act was illegal or illicit. It may apply to any culpable action." Cf. The Editors of the Reader's Digest, *Use the Right Word*, The Reader's Digest Association Proprietary Ltd. (1971), at P. 198.

Abstain ▸ Forbear ▸ Refrain

　　三個單詞均有克制和約束的含義。abstain 主要是指自我約束以放棄某項權利或戒除某項行為，尤指不當或不健康的行為①。refrain 多指暫時或短時間的一種克制或約束行為，或克制衝動②。forbear 則常指出於忍耐或慈善而實施的自我克制行為③。

注

① "to hold oneself back voluntarily, especially from something regarded as improper or unhealthy", Cf. James E. Clapp, *Random House Webster's Dictionary of the Law*, Random House (2000), at P. 4.

② "Refrain has to do with withholding an action temporarily, or checking a momentary desire." Cf. The Editors of the Reader's Digest, *Use the Right Word*, The Reader's Digest Association Proprietary Ltd. (1971), at P. 2.

③ "Forbear is, in its intransitive sense, to exercise self-control, often out of motive of patience, or charity." *Id.* at P. 2.

Abstract ▸ Abridgement ▸ Digest ▸ Brief ▸ Summary

　　以上單詞均有「摘要」的含義。abstract 多指著述或法院紀錄等法律文件的簡短書面說明，常作爲正文的一種索引，其多爲原作者以外的人所寫①，如 an abstract of the proposed legislation。abridgement 和 digest 都常用來指某一法律文件或案例等的摘錄，其中，abridgement 爲「節本」或「節略」，其多保留原文的章節順序，且有時可能僅作很少的刪節或改動，在很大程度上保留了原文作者的詞語和風格，如 an abridgement in which passages involving sexual frankness were omitted。相比之下，digest 爲「摘要」，其所作的改動較大，除對原文的章節進行改寫外，常在體例及安排等上均有變更②。brief 和 summary 均指對所考慮事項的主要觀點的簡要陳述，如 the brief of a legal argument，相比之下，summary 所指的摘要更爲概括扼要，可完全不考慮原文的風格及措辭③。

注

① "Summary or epitome, or that which comprises or concentrates in itself the essential qualities of a larger thing or several things." Cf. The Publisher's Editorial Staff, *Black's Law Dictionary*, Abridged 6th Edition, West Publishing Co. (1991), at P. 5.

② *Id.* at P. 313.

③ "The word implies a pithy paraphrase, with no attempt to catch the style of the original." Cf. The Editors of the Reader's Digest, *Use the Right Word*, The Reader's Digest Association Proprietary Ltd. (1971), at P. 595.

Abuse ► Maltreatment ► Mistreatment ► Persecution ► Wrong

五個單詞均有「虐待」或「濫用」的含義。其中，abuse 為最常用，可指所有誹謗中傷或有害言詞或行為，不管是否故意，常用於濫用特權、權力、法律程序、毒品以及虐待兒童、婦女等①，如 a policeman abusing his authority by searching the house without a warrant。maltreatment 和 mistreatment 十分近義，均指有卑劣動機的行為。相比之下，mistreatment 的虐待程度較 maltreatment 輕，且其不一定具有身體上的虐待或故意傷害②；而 maltreatment 則通常以精神上的虐待為主③。persecution 多指因種族、宗教或信仰等原因而施加的迫害或虐待④。wrong 主要指在無正當理由或原因的情況下受到不公正或有害的待遇，或自己的權利受到侵犯⑤。

注

① "Abuse, the most general term in this group, covers all injurious use or treatment by word or act. It does not always connote a deliberate act." Cf. The Editors of the Reader's Digest, *Use the Right Word*, The Reader's Digest Association Proprietary Ltd. (1971), at P. 689.

② "Mistreatment is thus more general than maltreatment and need not imply physical abuse or even the desire to harm." *Id.* at P. 689.

③ "Maltreat, however, suggests harsher or more consciously cruel treatment than mistreatment, which can apply to acts whose chief effect is psychological rather than physical." *Id.* at P. 689.

④ "punishment or harassment usu. of a severe nature on the basis of race, religion, or political opinion in one's country or origin", Cf. Linda Picard Wood, J.D., *Merriam Webster's Dictionary of Law*, Merriam-Webster, Incorporated, Springfield, Massachusetts (1996), at P. 362.

⑤ "treat with injustice", *Id.* at P. 539.

Access right ▸ Right of way

兩片語經常被人混淆。儘管access 本身有「進入、透過」等含義（to enter, approach, pass to and from a place, a landowner's legal right to pass from her or his land to a highway and to return without being obstucted①），但 access right 卻是家事法上的術語，指離婚父（母）對不屬於他（她）監護的子女的「探視權」或「探望權」（A right, granted in an order or agreement, of access to or visitation of a child. Family Orders and Agreements Enforcement Assistance Act, R.S.C. 1985, c. 4, s. 2②），而非有些詞典中所說的「出入權」或「通行權」。真正的「通行權」是 right of way，其屬於地役權（easement）的一種，指在他人擁有的土地上通行經過的權利（A person's legal right, established by usage or by contract, to pass through grounds or property owned by another③）。

注

① Cf. Linda Picard Wood, J.D., *Merriam Webster's Dictionary of Law*, Merriam-Webster, Incorporated, Springfield, Massachusetts (1996), at P. 6.

② Cf. Daphne Dukelow, *The Dictionary of Canadian Law*, Thomson Professional Publishing Canada (1991), at P. 788.

③ Cf. Bryan A. Garner, *Black's Law Dictionary*, 7th Edition, West Group (1999), at P. 1588.

Accessory before the fact ▶ Accessory after the fact

　　以上片語均有策劃、鼓勵、協助或唆使他人犯重罪，即具有「從犯」（accessory）的含義。按傳統，「從犯」曾包括 accessory before the fact（事前從犯）和 accessory after the fact（事後從犯）兩類。accessory before the fact 和 principal（正犯）的區別在於前者未出現而後者則出現在犯罪現場，目前美國多數州的法規已經廢除此種區分而將 accessory before the fact 當作共犯歸類爲 principal①。accessory after the fact 則是指明知有人犯重罪而協助、庇護該罪犯以逃避司法懲處之從犯，現多數州已不再籠統使用此術語，而將其分爲若干具體的犯罪，如干擾司法罪 "obstructing justice" 等②。

注

① "The traditional distinction between accessories before the fact and principals, that accessories were not present and principals were present at the commission of the crime, is not recognized under most modern state statutes. Accessories before the fact are usually considered principals", Cf. Linda Picard Wood, J.D., *Merriam*

Webster's Dictionary of Law, Merriam-Webster, Incorporated, Springfield, Massachusetts (1996), at P. 6.

② "Many state statutes now omit the term accessory after the fact and instead characterized the accessory as having committed a particular offense, such as obstructing justice", *Id.* at P. 6.

Accidental ▸ Chance ▸ Contingent ▸ Incidental ▸ Fortuitous ▸ Casual

上述單詞均有偶然和意外的含義。accidental 主要指未曾預料的不幸事件或災難，其無任何規律性，雖無故意或預謀，但後果影響常常卻較嚴重①。chance 為非正式用語，多指巧合或不屬已知的自然法則調整的事件②。contingent 經常表示無法預見或不可控制的緊急情況，如某些不可抗力等③。incidental 多指附帶發生的未曾計畫或預料的事件，其多少都具有一些價值④。fortuitous 指某事未經策劃，其原因不明，在指事件時，可表示該偶發事件非常不幸（以往多將該詞誤用作 fortunate 的同義詞而認為其結局一般較好）⑤。casual 指無規律、不正規、無計畫或不可預測，且常用於指附帶發生的無關緊要的小事等⑥。

注

① "Employed in contradistinction to willful… produced by mere chance, or incapable of being traced to any cause." Cf. Daphne Dukelow, *The Dictionary of Canadian Law*, Thomson Professional Publishing Canada (1991), at P. 6.

② "Chance is least formal of these. On one hand it can indicate coincidence, on the other hand, it can suggest an occurrence that is governed by no known physical laws." Cf. The Editors of the Reader's Digest, *Use the Right Word*, The Reader's Digest Association

Proprietary Ltd. (1971), at P. 77.

③ "Possible, but not assured; doubtful or uncertain; conditional upon the occurrence of some future event which is itself uncertain, or questionable. This term, when applied to a use, remainder, devise, bequest, or other legal right or interest, implies that no present interest exists, and that whether such interest or right ever will exist depends upon a future uncertain event." Cf. The Publisher's Editorial Staff, *Black's Law Dictionary*, Abridged 6th Edition, West Publishing Co. (1991), at P. 222.

④ "Depending upon or appertaining to something else as primary; something necessary, appertaining to, or depending upon another which is termed the principal; something incidental to the main purpose." *Id.* at P. 523.

⑤ "Occurring by chance. A fortuitous event may be highly unfortunate. Literally, the term is neutral, despite its common misuse as a synonym for *fortunate*." Cf. Bryan A. Garner, *Black's Law Dictionary*, 7th Edition, West Group (1999), at P. 664.

⑥ "Occurring without regularity, occasional; impermanent, as employment for irregular periods. Happening or coming to pass without design and without being foreseen or expected; unforeseen, uncertain; unpremeditated." Cf. The Publisher's Editorial Staff, *Black's Law Dictionary*, Abridged 6th Edition, West Publishing Co. (1991), at P. 150.

Accomplice ▸ Abettor ▸ Accessory ▸ Confederate

　　上述單詞具有共犯或從犯的含義。其中，accomplice 和 confederate 的含義相近，在美國，其有雙重含義：一是「共犯」，指與他人一起共同實施犯罪，不論其身分是正犯或從犯[1]；二是「從犯」[2]，此時其主要指在策劃或實施階段，協助他人犯罪或故意不履行法定阻止義務而旨在加速或促進犯罪的實施者，因此，一個accomplice 或 confederate 可能但不必一定親自作案[3]，此時其等同accessory。abettor 則指直接參與犯罪者，故其應為「共犯」[4]，如：A look-out is an abettor in a bank robbery（銀行搶劫案中的把風者是該案的共犯）。abettor 也可拼寫為 abetter，其也稱為 principal in the second degree（二級正犯）。相比之下，accessory 則為「從犯」，與正犯（principal）相對，主要指協助重罪犯犯罪者；其分為兩類，如果此種協助是在犯罪預備時進行，其也被稱為 an accessory before the fact（事前從犯）；如果是在罪犯之後協助罪犯脫逃，其也被稱為 an accessory after the fact（事後從犯）[5]（有關此種分類的區別，參見條目 accessory before the fact）。

注

① "a person who is in any way concerned with another in the commission of a crime, whether as principal in the first or second degree or as a accessory", Cf. Bryan A. Garner, *Black's Law Dictionary*, 7th Edition, West Group (1999), at P. 16.

② "a person knowingly, voluntarily, and intentionally unites with the principal offender in committing a crime and thereby becomes punishable for it", *Id.* at P. 16.

③ "Person is liable as an accomplice to the crime of another if he gave assistance or encouragement or failed to perform a legal duty to prevent it with the intent thereby to promote or facilitate commission of the crime." Cf. The Publisher's Staff, *Black's Law Dictionary*, Abridged 6th Edition, West Publishing Co. (1997), at P. 10.

④ "An abettor is an accomplice or confederate who is present and who participates in the execution of a crime." Cf. The Editors of the Reader's Digest, *Use the Right Word*, The Reader's Digest Association Proprietary Ltd. (1971), at. P. 3.

⑤ "a person who is not actually or constructively present but with criminal intent contributes as an assistant or instigator to the commission of a felony, also called accessory before the fact"; "a person who knowing that a felony has been committed aids, assists, or shelters the offender with the intent to defeat justice, also called accessory after the fact", Cf. Linda Picard Wood, J.D., *Merriam Webster's Dictionary of Law*, Merriam-Webster, Incorporated, Springfield, Massachusetts (1996), at P. 6.

Accumulation ▸ Aggregation ▸ Collection ▸ Conglomeration

以上單詞均有聚積或集合的含義。accumulation 主要指同類事物，如金錢、資本、收益等的逐漸積累，而非一下或突然的聚集，且此種積累多爲無序或無組織關聯①。collection 常可與 accumulation 交替使用，但它所指的累積則常指一種有序或有組織的聚合②，如：An accumulation of many specimens is needed when one is preparing a scientific collection。aggregation 常指具有一定凝聚力的某種集合體，但其關聯性卻趕不上 collection③，如 An industrial empire is often an aggregation of unrelated enterprises。conglomeration 則常指許多不同來源或不同地區甚至矛盾的事物的集合體④，如：a conglomeration of many different kinds of people from various countries and cultures。

注

① "Increase by continuous or repeated additions, or, if taken literally, means either profit accruing on sale of principal assets, or increase derived from their investment, or both." Cf. The Publisher's Editorial Staff, *Black's Law Dictionary*, Abridged 6th Edition, West Publishing Co. (1991), at P. 15.

② "Collection and accumulation are often used interchangeably, but collection frequently implies a high degree of selection and organization in the mass collected." Cf. The Editors of the Reader's Digest, *Use the Right Word*, The Reader's Digest Association Proprietary Ltd. (1971), at P. 4.

③ "Aggregation always denotes a mass brought together that forms, in some sense, a coherent whole, but one that has a less degree of organization than does a collection." *Id.* at P. 4.

④ "Conglomeration implies that many different and sometimes even incongruous things are brought together from widely scattered sources or regions." *Id.* at P. 4.

Accuse ▶ Charge ▶ Impeach ▶ Incriminate ▶ Indict

　　這些單詞均有指控某人犯罪的含義。accuse 指刑事指控，爲通用詞，可表示正式或非正式，官方或個人指控①，如：to accuse sb. of murder（指控某人犯謀殺罪）。charge 一般指向法院提起的正式指控，如：to charge sb. with murder（指控某人犯謀殺罪）；此外，它還可表示譴責某人違背某些行爲準則等②。impeach 爲「彈劾」，多指因公共官員犯了內亂外患罪或其他嚴重罪行而對其提起的指控③；在英國，此種指控多由下議院提起，由上議院審理。incriminate 用於刑事犯罪，可指直接控告罪犯，如：He was incriminated in the conspiracy（他被指控參與共謀）；也可指某人因不利證詞而受牽連，而後一用法更爲常見，如 to incriminate oneself（自證其罪）。

indict 主要用於刑事犯罪，且多用於對罪行較爲嚴重的罪犯的正式指控，在美國，尤指由大陪審團直接透過 indictment 而提起的控訴④，如性質較輕的 summary offences 則不用該單詞表示起訴或指控。

注

① "To charge with a crime." Cf. Daphne Dukelow, *The Dictionary of Canadian Law*, Thomson Professional Publishing Canada (1991), at P. 8; "To charge (a person) judicially or publicly with an offense, to make an accusation against." Cf. Bryan A. Garner, *Black's Law Dictionary*, 7th Edition, West Group (1999), at P. 22.

② "to take proceedings or lay an information against a person believed to have committed an offense", Cf. Daphne Dukelow, *The Dictionary of Canadian Law*, A Carswell Publication (1991), at P. 150; "to accuse sb. formally of having committed a crime", Cf. P. H. Collin, *English-Chinese Bilingual Law Dictionary*, 2nd Edition, Peter Collin Publishing Ltd. (1998), at P. 85.

③ "to charge with a crime or misconduct, specifically, to charge (a public official) before a competent tribunal (as the US Senate) with misconduct in office", Cf. Linda Picard Wood, J.D., *Merriam Webster's Dictionary of Law*, Merriam-Webster, Incorporated, Springfield, Massachusetts (1996), at P. 235.

④ "To charge (a person) with a crime by formal legal process, esp. by grand-jury presentation." Cf. Bryan A. Garner, *Black's Law Dictionary*, 7th Edition, West Group (1999), at P. 776.

Accused ► Convicted

兩者（加上定冠詞 the）均用於刑事案件中，指被告或罪犯。

其區別在於 the accused 是指因違法行為而受到起訴者，在此階段，按無罪推定原理其還不應被稱為罪犯，只有在被定罪，即 convicted of guilty 時，其才可被稱為罪犯，故 the accused 只應為「刑事被告」[1]。而 the convicted 指被法院裁定有罪者（a person to be found guilty of a criminal offense），其自然便可被譯為「罪犯」，至於其是否被判刑、翻案或被赦免等則是後話。此外，在外國法中，the convicted 一般不包括犯藐視法庭罪（contempt of court）而被指控和受罰者，而 the accused 則包括此類人員[2]。

注

[1] "a person who has been arrested for or formally charged with a crime; the defendant in a criminal case", Cf. Linda Picard Wood, J.D., *Merriam Webster's Dictionary of Law*, Merriam-Webster, Incorporated, Springfield, Massachusetts (1996), at P. 6.

[2] Cf. Daphne A. Dukelow, *The Dictionary of Canadian Law*, A Casewell Publication (1991), at P. 216.

Acknowledge ▸ Admit ▸ Concede ▸ Confess

上述單詞均有「承認」的含義。acknowledge 指承認責任或義務，所指的承認常帶有不自願或尷尬的色彩[1]。admit 多指對過去否認或躲避的問題的承認，有自願的含義[2]。concede 是指在充分證據的情況下，被迫對最不願承認的事實的承認[3]。confess 多指認罪或承認指控等[4]。

注

[1] "One *acknowledges* something embarrassing or awkward, and usually not voluntarily; more often, the acknowledgement is extracted from

one more or less unwillingly." Cf. The Editors of the Reader's Digest, *Use the Right Word*, The Reader's Digest Association Proprietary Ltd. (1971), at P. 5.

② "to make a voluntary acknowledgement by a party of the existence of the truth of certain facts which are inconsistent with his claims in an action." Cf. The Publisher's Editorial Staff, *Black's Law Dictionary*, Abridged 6th Edition, West Publishing Co. (1991), at P. 31.

③ "One *concedes*, usually because of overwhelming evidence, something which he has been very reluctant to admit." Cf. The Editors of the Reader's Digest, *Use the Right Word*, The Reader's Digest Association Proprietary Ltd. (1971), at P. 5.

④ "to admit (as a charge or allegation) as true, proven, or valid." Cf. Linda Picard Wood, J.D., *Merriam Webster's Dictionary of Law*, Merriam-Webster, Incorporated, Springfield, Massachusetts (1996), at P. 94.

Acquisition ▸ Consolidation ▸ Merger

　　三個單詞均指公司之間的相互整合或合併。準確地講，acquisition 應譯為「收購」，merger 應當譯為「合併」，而 consolidation 則應譯為「合組新公司」。以 acquisition 方式進行的收購，多指一個公司以收購某公司股份的方式進行接管或達到控股的目的（the obtaining of controlling interest in a company①），其結果是兩個法人實體地位在交易之後仍可同時存在，鑒於收購所需資金關係，故此種方式多用作收購小公司。相比之下，merger 所指的是一個公司對另一個的合併，其多以被合併公司的消亡形式進行，但有時也可保留被合併的公司的名稱，或合併公司成為被合併公司的控股公司，但此時被合併公司已失去其法人身分，不再是獨立的商務實體（An amalgamation of two corporations pursuant to statutory provision in which one of the corporations survives and the other disappears. The absorption of one company by another, the former losing its legal identity, and the latter retains its own name and identity and acquiring assets, liabilities, franchises, and powers of the former, and absorbed company ceasing to exist as separate business entity[2]）。目前流行的公司之間的「併購」，則指 merger and acquisition，略爲 MA，指用收購方式進行的合併。consolidation 常用於大公司的合併，在合併時多有新資本注入，其與 merger 和 acquisition 的主要區別在於 consolidation 是把兩個或兩個以上的公司合併成爲一家新公司，而原有的諸公司都得宣布解散（Merger differs from a consolidation wherein all the corporations terminate their existence and become parties to a new one[3]）。

注

① Cf. Linda Picard Wood, J.D., *Merriam Webster's Dictionary of Law*, Merriam-Webster, Incorporated (1996), at P. 10.
② Cf. The Publisher's Editorial Staff, *Black's Law Dictionary* (with Pronunciations), Abridged 6th Edition, West Publishing Co. (1991), at P. 682.
③ *Id.* at P. 682.

Acquit ▸ Absolve

兩者均有宣告無罪的含義。區別在於 acquit 多爲因證據不足等原因經審判裁定無罪或因證據不足而不予起訴或撤訴[1]。absolve 除有此種含義之外，還多用於表示有罪但卻予以赦免或免罪[2]。

注

① "to find not guilty", Cf. Daphne A. Dukelow, *The Dictionary of Canadian Law*, Thomson Professional Publishing Canada (1991), at P. 10; "to release a criminal defendant from a charge, either upon a finding of not guilty by the jury or because the court or the prosecution determined that the trial should not go forward after the trial was commenced", Cf. James E. Clapp, *Random House Webster's Dictionary of the Law*, Random House (2000), at P. 11.

② "to free of guilt or suspicion", Cf. James E. Clapp, *Random House Webster's Dictionary of the Law*, Random House (2000), at P. 4; "To free from the penalties for misconduct." Cf. Bryan A. Garner, *Black's Law Dictionary*, 7ᵗʰ Edition, West Group (1999), at P. 8; "To pardon; to acquit of a crime." Cf. Daphne A. Dukelow, *The Dictionary of Canadian Law*, Thomson Professional Publishing Canada (1991), at P. 3.

Act ▸ Law ▸ Statute ▸ Bill ▸ Legislation

　　上述單詞均有法律或法規的含義。act 主要是指由立法機關所制定的法律（the formal product of a legislative body①），該單詞常用作單一的法律的名稱，翻譯時可譯爲○○法，如 Criminal Law Act（《刑法法》）、Anti-competitive Act（《反不當競爭法》）等。相比之下，law 可用作指單部法律或法規，如：a law或 laws，又可用作表示一般和抽象的含義（the law），但它一般不用作某個特定的法律命令的名稱，如 Uniform Law on the International Sale of Goods 則不應譯爲《統一國際商品銷售法》，而只能譯爲《國際商品銷售統一法規編纂》，這樣可避免人們將其誤認爲是一部具體的

法規（事實上，它是歐洲共同體的一部示範性法典）。同理，如
《中華人民共和國婚姻法》不應翻譯爲 Marriage Law of the People's
Republic of China（此種譯法容易被人誤認爲其是一部論述中國的婚
姻法的論著，或一部涵蓋所有有關婚姻的法律法規的法規彙纂），
而應譯爲 Marriage Act of the People's Republic of China。statute 主要
指「制定法」，與判例法相對，因而，作爲立法機關制定的 act 既
可稱作 a law，也可成爲 a statute。bill 除有時可指「頒布的成文法」
（an enacted statute）②之外（如在 Bill of Rights 中），其主要指提交
議會審議的「議案」或「法案」，一般情況下，a bill 經議會透過生
效後，即成爲 an act（A legislative proposal offered for debate before its
enacted③），因而，act 只能譯爲「法」、「法律」、「法令」等，
而決不能譯爲本應由 bill 表示的「法案」。legislation 主要指「立
法」，即具有立法權力的機關或人所頒布的法律④，在這個意義上
講，其與 statute 相似，一般說來，legislation 又可分爲本位立法和次
位立法兩種（primary and secondary legislations）。

注

① Cf. Linda Picard Wood, J.D., *Merriam Webster's Dictionary of Law*,
   Merriam-Webster, Incorporated (1996), at P. 10.

② Cf. Bryan A. Garner, *Black's Law Dictionary*, 7ᵗʰ Edition, West Group
   (1999), at P. 157.

③ *Id.* at P. 157.

④ "the enactment of statue of a legislature", Cf. James E. Clapp, *Random
   House Webster's Dictionary of the Law*, Random House (2000), at P.
   268.

Act ▸ Action ▸ Deed ▸ Performance

以上單詞均有「行為」的含義。act 多指按自己的意願已經完成的行為[1]。除指已完成的行為外，action 還表示正在進行的行為或者指完成行為的程序[2]。deed 常指需極大勇氣、情操、智慧、力量或技能所取得的成就行為[3]。performance 所指的行為常與行為人作為時的方式相關[4]。

注

[1] "Something done or performed." Cf. Bryan A. Garner, *Black's Law Dictionary*, 7th Edition, West Group (1999), at P. 24; "An act, in the sense considered here, is something that is done." Cf. The Editors of the Reader's Digest, *Use the Right Word*, The Reader's Digest Association Proprietary Ltd. (1971), at P. 5; "something done by a person in accordance with his or her free will", Cf. Linda Picard Wood, J.D., *Merriam Webster's Dictionary of Law*, Merriam-Webster, Incorporated (1996), at P. 10.

[2] "thing which has been done", Cf. P. H. Collin, *Dictionary of Law*, 2nd Edition, Peter Collin Publishing Ltd. (1993), at P. 8; "Action refers to the accomplishing of something or the process by which it is accomplished." Cf. The Editors of the Reader's Digest, *Use the Right Word*, The Reader's Digest Association Proprietary Ltd. (1971), at P. 5.

[3] "*Deed*, while sometimes used to connote any *act*, is usually in meaning an achievement of great courage, nobility, intelligence, strength or skill." Cf. The Editors of the Reader's Digest, *Use the Right Word*, The Reader's Digest Association Proprietary Ltd. (1971), at P. 5.

[4] "the performance of a person is the manner in which he carries out the

acts that are part of his job's routine" *Id.* at P. 6.

Action ► Litigation ► Suit ► Proceedings ► Procedure

上述單詞均有訴訟的含義。action、litigation 和 proceedings 都爲一般術語,可指各種訴訟案件。但 action 則逐漸演變,現在多用於指民事訴訟了,因而有 action is a mode of proceeding[1]的說法。如果要表示刑事訴訟,多應在 action 前面加 criminal 予以區分。litigation 除了指訴訟之外,還有訴訟程序的含義[2],如 Civil Litigation便爲《民事訴訟程序》,是一本有關英國民事訴訟程序的專著。suit 是 lawsuit 的簡略形式,主要用於指民事訴訟。傳統上,action 和 suit 之間的差異在於 action 指普通法法院的訴訟,其程序到法院判決(judgment)即終止;而 suit 則爲衡平法法院的用語,其程序包括判決和執行(judgment and execution)[3]。在美國,這兩個單詞的差異因衡平法法院和普通法法院的合併已經不再存在。procedure 主要是指訴訟程序,如 criminal procedure code(刑事訴訟法典)等。

注

① Cf. Bryan A. Garner, *A Dictionary of Modern Legal Usage*, 2nd Edition, Oxford University Press (1995), at P. 20.

② "The process of carrying on a lawsuit." Cf. Bryan A. Garner, *Black's Law Dictionary*, 7th Edition, West Group (1999), at P. 944.

③ "When the jurisdictional distinction existed, an action ended at judgment, but a suit in equity ended after judgment and execution." Cf. Bryan A. Garner, *A Dictionary of Modern Legal Usage*, 2nd Edition, Oxford University Press (1995), at P. 20.

Actual fraud ▸ Constructive fraud

兩片語之間的差異在於 actual fraud（事實詐欺）具有事實上的故意，由此給他人帶來傷害，其也被稱爲 fraud in fact、positive fraud 以及 moral fraud①。相比之下，constructive fraud（推定詐欺）雖然無詐欺故意和虛假陳述，但後果卻與前者相同，且它常用作針對公共利益，其也稱爲 legal fraud、fraud in contemplation of law 和 equitable fraud，表明其是依據法律所推定成立的②。

注

① "A concealment or false representation through a statement or conduct that injures another who relies on it in acting." Cf. Bryan A. Garner, *Black's Law Dictionary*, 7th Edition, West Group (1999), at P. 671.; "fraud committed with the actual intent to deceive and thereby injure another", Cf. Linda Picard Wood, J.D., *Merriam Webster's Dictionary of Law*, Merriam-Webster, Incorporated (1996), at P. 203.

② "conduct viewed by a court as having the same effect as actual fraud though not involving any false representation of fact", Cf. James E. Clapp, *Random House Webster's Dictionary of the Law*, Random House (2000), at P. 193; "conduct that is considered fraud under the law despite the absence of an intent to deceive because it has the same consequences as an actual fraud would have and it is against public interests", Cf. Linda Picard Wood, J.D., *Merriam Webster's Dictionary of Law*, Merriam-Webster, Incorporated (1996), at P. 203.

Actual performance ▸ Specific performance

兩者均與債或義務的履行相關。actual performance 爲「實際履

行」，爲債的履行原則之一，指債的雙方當事人應當按債所規定的
標的履行，不能由其他標的代替履行，也不可折合成金錢代償。
special performance（也稱爲 specific relief）主要用於契約事項，指
由法院簽發命令，強制某人按其允諾履行某契約義務，因其極具強
制性，故爲「強制履行」，須注意的是該術語經常被人混淆成 actual
performance 而譯爲「實際履行」。

注

"Special performance: A court-ordered remedy that requires precise
fulfillment of a legal or contractual obligation when monetary damages
are inappropriate or inadequate, as when the sale of real estate or a rare
article is involved." Cf. Bryan A. Garner, *Black's Law Dictionary*, 7th
Edition, West Group (1999), at P. 1407.

Adaptation ▸ Adjustment

　　兩個單詞均有作某種修改或變更以適應新情況或環境所需的含
義。相比之下，adaptation 所作的變更較大且爲必須[①]；而 adjustment
僅指較細微的修正或變更[②]。

注

① "Adaptation involves considerable change to meet new requirements."
　 Cf. The Editors of the Reader's Digest, *Use the Right Word*, The
　 Reader's Digest Association Proprietary Ltd. (1971), at P. 6.
② "Adjustment implies a minor change in contrast with adaptation." *Id.*
　 at P. 6.

Adjective law ▸ Procedural law

兩片語均有「程序法」的含義,意思相同,指為保證實體法所規定的權利義務關係的實現而制定的訴訟程序的法律,與「實體法」(substantive law)相對。只是 procedural law 為一般用語,而 adjective law(也稱為 adjectival law)則學究氣較濃,多為法學家們所用。

注

Cf.《法學詞典》,上海辭書出版社(1980),第688頁。

Adjudicative fact ▸ Legislative fact

兩者之間的差別在於 adjudicative fact(判決事實)是指訴訟,尤其是行政訴訟中與當事人具體相關的事實,如個人動機、故意等,其為個案屬性[1]。而 legislative fact(法定事實)則泛指與案件具體當事人的個人問題無關,即不屬於個案性質而屬於法律規定的具有一般屬性的社會、經濟、科技等的事實問題[2]。

注

[1] "Factual matters concerning the parties to an administrative proceeding as contrasted with legislative facts which are general and usually do not touch individual questions of particular parties to a proceeding." The Publisher's Editorial Staff, *Black's Law Dictionary* (with Pronunciations), Abridged 6th Edition, West Publishing Co. (1991), at P. 26.

[2] "A fact that explains a particular law's rationality and that helps a court or agency determine the law's content and application." Cf.

Bryan A. Garner, *Black's Law Dictionary*, 7th Edition, West Group (1999), at P. 611.

Admiralty court ▶ Naval court

兩片語均指與海洋相關事項的法院。區別在於 admiralty court 主要是對有關海事的契約、侵權、傷害和犯罪行使管轄權的法院，故其為「海事法院」，也稱為 admiralty 或 maritime court[①]。值得注意的是在英國，儘管 admiralty 有「海軍部」或「與海軍相關」的含義[②]，但 admiralty court 卻決非「海軍法院」或「海軍軍事法庭」[③]，而是道地的「海事法院」，儘管在 1340 年初建時，「最初看起來設置這些法庭的目的是預防和懲罰海盜行為」，並「是海軍大臣助理主審的法院」[④]。事實上，「海軍軍事法院或法庭」應該是 naval martial-court，其是實施管轄海軍的法律規則（naval law）的法院（庭）[⑤]。相比之下，naval court 中儘管也有 naval 一詞，但其卻應是「海事事故法庭」（與軍事法庭無關，至於 naval 一詞，大概與先前英國的船舶管理均屬於準軍事化規定有關），此種法庭由國外停泊的船舶的船長或使館官員組成，專門負責處理船主或貨主（owner of ship or cargo）提出的緊急調查申訴或船舶被遺棄、沉沒、滅失等意外事故案件[⑥]。

注

① "A court that exercises jurisdiction over all maritime contracts, torts, injuries, or offenses." Cf. Bryan A. Garner, *Black's Law Dictionary*, 7th Edition, West Group (1999), at P. 47.

② "*Brit.* the executive department or officers having jurisdiction over naval affairs generally"; "of or belonging to British naval affairs or officials" Cf. Philip Babcock Grove, Ph.D., *Webster's Third New*

International Dictionary of the English Language Unabridged, G & C Merriam Co. (1976), at P. 28.

③ 「admiralty court：海軍法院，（大寫）(英) 海軍軍事法庭」，Cf.《英漢法律詞典》，法律出版社（1985），第 29 頁。

④ Cf.《牛津法律大辭典》，光明日報出版社（1989），第 22 頁。

⑤ *Id.* at P. 632.

⑥ *Id.* at P. 632; "naval court: Any officer who commands a ship belonging to Her Majesty on any foreign station or any consular officer may hold such a court when a complaint which requires immediate investigation arises, when the owner's interest in any Canadian ship or cargo seems to require it or when a Canadian ship is abandoned, wrecked or lost." Cf. R. M. Fernandes & C. Burke, *The Annotated Canada Shipping Act*, Toronto, Butterworths (1988), at P. 213.

Admissibility ▸ Relevance ▸ Weight ▸ Sufficiency

證據的 admissibility（可採性）、relevance（相關性）、weight（說服性）以及 sufficiency（充分性）均是有關證據規則（rules of evidence，指適用於庭審時證據提交的標準）相關的一些法律原則問題。admissibility 指能否被允許接受作為聽證會、審判或其他程序之證據的特性或狀況（The quality or state allowed to be entered into evidence in a hearing, trial, or other proceeding①）。relevancy 主要指相關性質或狀況（the quality or state of being relevant②）。weight 指證據說服力的一種比較（the persuasiveness of some evidence in comparison with other evidence③）。sufficiency 則指證據的充足性（whether enough evidence exists to justify the fact④）。

在英美法的證據規則中，admissibility 處於核心地位，確定一個證據是否應予採用，主要依據其實質性（materiality）、證明性（probativeness）和有效性（competency）而定。而實質性和證明性合在一起則構成證據的相關性。美國證據法在證據價值的評斷和運用證據證明案件事實上賦予法官和陪審員極大的自由裁量權，因此美國的證明制度屬於自由心證（free proof）範疇，而不屬於規制證明或法定證明（regulated proof）範疇。

注

① Cf. Bryan A. Garner, *Black's Law Dictionary*, 7th Edition, West Group (1999), at P. 48.
② Cf. Linda Picard Wood, J.D., *Merriam Webster's Dictionary of Law*, Merriam-Webster, Incorporated, Springfield, Massachusetts (1996), at P. 418.
③ Cf. Bryan A. Garner, *Black's Law Dictionary*, 7th Edition, West Group (1999), at P. 1588.
④ *Id.* at P. 1447.

Admission ▸ Confession ▸ Staement

　　三個單詞均與被告招認違法或犯罪事實有關。confession 多限於刑事犯罪領域（在加拿大民事訴訟程序中，其可等同於 formal admission），指刑事被告完全承認其被指控的犯罪及有關定罪所需的所有事實，或至少是主要事實，並承認有罪（acknowledgement of guilt），有供認不諱的含義，陪審團根據其招供則可作出有罪裁定，故爲「供認、自白」①。相比之下，admission 常用作指對民事責任行爲的承認。在刑事領域，admission 多指對無犯罪故意的刑事責任行爲的招認，多表示承認一個或數個事實，此種招供遠沒有達到足以定罪的程度；與 confession 相比，admission 主要的區別在於被告無認罪表示（an admission is a confession that an allegation or factual assertion is true without any acknowledgement of guilt with respect to the criminal charges, whereas a confession involves an acknowledgement of guilt as well as of the true of predicate factual allegations[②]），故 admission 應譯爲「供述」，而不能譯爲「供認、自白」，因其沒有「認」，即認罪的含義。在刑事訴訟中，statement 主要是指警方在偵破犯罪過程中對某人，尤指嫌疑犯的招供所作的紀錄和報告（an account of a person's (usually a suspect's) acknowledgement of a crime, taken by the police pursuant to their investigation of the offense[③]），故應譯爲「供述紀錄」。

注

① 有關 confession 的各種定義："a criminal acknowledgement suspect's of guilt, usually in writing and often including details about the crime", Cf. Bryan A. Garner, *Black's Law Dictionary*, 7th Edition, West Group (1999), at P.293; "a written or oral statement by an accused party acknowledging the party's guilt (as by admitting commission of a crime)." Cf. Linda Picard Wood, J.D., *Merriam Webster's Dictionary of Law*, Merriam-Webster, Incorporated, Springfield, Massachusetts (1996), at Ps.94－95; "a statement made by an accused person, whether before or after he is accused of an offense, that is completely or partially self-incriminating with respect to the offense of which he is accused." Cf. Daphne Dukelow, *The Dictionary of Canadian Law*, A Carswell Publication (1991), at P. 195.

② Cf. James E. Clapp, *Random House Webster's Dictionary of the Law*, Random House, New York (2000), at P. 29.

③ Cf. Bryan A. Garner, *Black's Law Dictionary*, 7th Edition, West Group (1999), at P. 1416.

Adolescent ▸ Youth

　　兩者均有青少年的含義。adolescent 一般指青春期至成年前階段的青少年，各國規定不一致，如加拿大規定為 16 至 18 歲，英國為 14 至 17 歲。youth 包括的範圍則較廣，如在美國，其包括 children 和 young persons。而在加拿大，在不同的法規中，其有不同的界定，如在《勞動安全法》中，其為 14 至 16 歲，在《防止青少年犯罪法》中，其為 14 至 25 歲。

注

Cf. Daphne Dukelow, *The Dictionary of Canadian Law*, A Carswell Publication (1991); Cf. Linda Picard Wood, J.D., *Merriam Webster's Dictionary of Law*, Merriam-Webster, Incorporated (1996); Cf. The Publisher's Editorial Staff, *Black's Law Dictionary* (with Pronunciations), Abridged 6th Edition, West Publishing Co. (1991).

Adult ▸ Minor

　　兩詞之間的區別似乎很明顯，前者為「成年人」，後者為「未成年人」。這是按法定年齡（an age specified by law）而區分的，然而有時候此種概念並非完全正確。在法律領域，該單詞所指的範疇有時也以婚姻狀況區分①。如在美國一些州，凡已經結婚的未達法定年齡者都可被視為成年人，即：A person who is below the statutory age but married will usually be considered an adult②，因此，法定年齡有時並非是確定成年人或未成年人的唯一標準，其有例外。

注

① "An individual who is married or has attained the age of eighteen years." Cf. Daphne Dukelow, *The Dictionary of Canadian Law*, A Carswell Publication (1991), at P. 21.

② Cf. Linda Picard Wood, J.D., *Merriam Webster's Dictionary of Law*, Merriam-Webster, Incorporated, Springfield, Massachusetts (1996), at P. 76.

Advertisement ▶ Commercial

上述兩詞均有廣告的含義。commercial 主要指在電視或廣播節目中插入的商業或促銷產品的廣告①。而 advertisement 則含義較廣，除主要用於指報刊或雜誌上以書面印刷形式刊登的廣告外，也可用於指電視節目廣告等②。

注

① "a television or radio advertisement", Cf. Della Thompson, *The Concise Oxford Dictionary*, 9th Edition, Oxford University Press (1995), at P. 265.

② "Any representation by any means whatever for the purpose of promoting directly or indirectly the sale or disposal of any product. Includes: 1) an advertisement in a newspaper, magazine or other publication or circular; 2) advertisement shown on a billboard sign, handbill or similar item that is located elsewhere than on the business premises of the credit grantor on whose behalf the advertisement is being made; 3) a message broadcast by television or radio." Cf. Daphne A. Dukelow, B.Sc., LL.B., LL.M., *The Dictionary of Canadian Law*, Thomson Professional Publishing Canada (1991), at P. 23.

Advice ▸ Counsel

兩者均有諮詢及顧問的含義。advice 爲通常用語，大小事件都可適用，如無修飾詞界定，advice 多表示是 adviser 對某些個人性質事項直接所作的帶個人傾向的意見。而 counsel 則含有 solemn advice 之意，一般表示對比較重要的諸如公務等事件所作出的正式、權威且非個人性質的諮詢意見[*]。

注

[*] "Advice and counsel mean an opinion or a judgment given by one person to another urging him either to do something or not to do it. Advice, the more general term, may be given on serious matter or relatively trivial ones, but counsel suggests solemn advice given in an official or authoritative capacity about a matter of some importance, at least to the person seeking it. Advice, unless qualified by an adjective suggesting otherwise, often implies that the adviser has a direct and more or less personal interest in the person advised; the subject of advise is thus often personal in nature. Counsel, on the other hand, suggests a detached, impersonal view on the part of the person giving it; and the subject of counsel is often of a business nature." Cf. The Editors of the Reader's Digest, *Use the Right Word*, The Reader's Digest Association Proprietary Ltd. (1971), at P. 9.

Affiant ▸ Deponent

兩單詞均有「宣誓作證者」的含義，且有時兩個單詞可以互換使用，但兩者仍有一定差異。區別在於前者爲自願提供有關事實之宣誓書（affidavit）者[①]；而後者指對在質詢和詰問下提供口供宣誓書（deposition）者[2]。

注

① "Affiant is the person who makes and subscribes an affidavit. The word is used, in this sense, interchangeably with deponent. But the latter term should be reserved as the designation of one who makes a deposition." Cf. The Publisher's Editorial Staff, *Black's Law Dictionary*, Abridged 6th Edition, West Publishing Co. (1991), at P. 36.

② "a person who gives a deposition", Cf. Linda Picard Wood, J.D., *Merriam Webster's Dictionary of Law*, Merriam-Webster, Incorporated (1996), at P. 133.

Affidavit ▶ Deposition

　　兩者均有口供書的含義。其區別在於 affidavit（宣誓證明書）是一種宣誓文件，為不經盤問而自願所作的口供的筆錄，當證人無法親自出庭時，affidavit 可被法庭作為證言接受[1]。deposition（證明筆錄）則是宣誓後在正式質詢下所作口頭證明的筆錄，是接受詰問的一種產物[2]。在法律程序中，按規定，向法庭提供 deposition 的當事人必須向另一方當事人通知，並給予另一方當事人對證人進行交互詰問（cross-examination）的機會[3]；相比之下，affidavit 則無如此之規定。

注

① "A written or printed declaration or statement of facts, made voluntarily, and confirmed by the oath or affirmation of the party making it, taking before a person having authority to administer such oath or affirmation." Cf. The Publisher's Editorial Staff, *Black's Law*

Dictionary, Abridged 6th Edition, West Publishing Co. (1991), at P. 36.

② "a statement that is made under oath by a party or witness (as an expert) in response to oral examination or written questions and that is recorded by an authorized officer", Cf. Linda Picard Wood, J.D., *Merriam Webster's Dictionary of Law*, Merriam-Webster, Incorporated (1996), at P. 134.

③ "Depositions are distinguished from affidavits by the requirement that notice and an opportunity to cross examine the deponent must be given to the other party." *Id*. at P. 134.

Affiliate ▸ Subsidiary ▸ Branch ▸ Division ▸ Office

以上單詞均有分公司或附屬公司的含義。其中，affiliate 和 subsidiary 都是指具有法人地位的子公司。affiliate 含義較廣，其可指與母公司聯繫鬆散，主要特徵是參股，直接或間接擁有 5% 或以上具有表決權的股份，不為母公司控股的公司，即我們所稱的「聯姻公司」或「橫向聯合分公司」①；其也可用作指與另一公司有聯繫的公司，即「關係企業」，此時其既可指 parent company，也可指 subsidiary、branch 或 division，甚至同為一母公司子公司的「姊妹公司」（sister corporation）②。而 subsidiary（也稱為 subsidiary corporation）與母公司聯繫較緊密，多受母公司控股，是嚴格意義上的子公司③。branch 和 office 一般是指不具備法人地位的稱為分公司的一種分支機構；division 則常用於美國，可略為 div.。

注

① Cf. 宋雷，《也談「公司」一詞的翻譯》，《中國翻譯》，1994 年第 5 期，第 57 頁。

② "a corporation that is the *parent company or subsidiary* of another corporation, or under common ownership with another corporation, as in the case of *sister corporation*", Cf. James E. Clapp, *Random House Webster's Dictionary of Law*, Random House (2000), at P. 19.

③ "a corporation in which a parent corporation has a controlling share", Cf. Bryan A. Garner, *Black's Law Dictionary*, 7ᵗʰ Edition, West Group (1999), at P. 345.

Affirm ▸ Reverse ▸ Remand

　　以上單詞是指上訴法院對上訴案件處理方式的最基本的三個術語。affirm 爲「維持原判」，指上訴法院維持下級法院判決（to uphold the judgment or actions of a lower court[①]），值得注意的是該單詞的搭配一般爲 judgment，如：The trial court's judgment was affirmed 這種用法正確。The trial court was affirmed 非正規用法[②]。reverse 爲「撤銷原判」，指上訴法院因下級法院的一些錯誤而撤銷其判決（of an appellate court, to nullify the judgment of a lower court in a case on appeal because of some errors in the court bellow[③]），如 to reverse a judgment or reverse a decision。remand 則是案件的「發回重審」，指上訴法院將案件發回原審法院，要求下級法院按自己的指示重新審理（to send a case back from an appellate court to the lower court from which it was appealed, for further proceedings in accordance with the appellate court's instructions[④]）。其後的搭配一般是 case，如 to remand a case[⑤]。

注

① Cf. Linda Picard Wood, J.D., *Merriam Webster's Dictionary of Law*, Merriam-Webster, Incorporated (1996), at P. 17.

② Cf. Bryan A. Garner, *A Dictionary of Modern Legal Usage*, Oxford

University Press Ltd. (1995), at P. 35.

③ Cf. James E. Clapp, *Random House Webster's Dictionary of the Law*, Random House, New York (2000), at P. 377.

④ Cf. Bryan A. Garner, *A Dictionary of Modern Legal Usage*, Oxford University Press Ltd. (1995), at P. 369.

⑤ *Id.* at P. 17.

Agency by estoppel ▸ Agency in fact

　　兩個片語的區別在於 agency by estoppel（表見代理）（也稱爲 agency by operation of law、apparent agency 或 ostensible agency）並不存在眞正的代理關係（actual agency），即委託人和代理人之間並無代理約定存在，只是因委託人的行爲讓第三人合理地認爲他與代理人之間確有代理關係，且第三人因此種確認作爲受到傷害，此時由法院依據法律推定成立而委託人不得否認的一種代理關係[①]。相比之下，agency in fact（事實代理）所表示的代理關係則是由委託人和代理人經約定事實確立的，其與前者正好相對[②]。

注

① "An agency created by operation of law and established by a principal's actions that would reasonably lead a third party to conclude that an agency exists." Cf. Bryan A. Garner, *Black's Law Dictionary*, 7th Edition, West Group (1999), at P. 62.

② "An agency created voluntarily, as by a contract. Agency in fact is distinguishable from an agency relationship created by law, such as agency by estoppel." *Id.* at P. 62.

Aggression ▸ Assault ▸ Attack ▸ Offensive

上述單詞均有侵犯和攻擊的含義。aggression 多指無故違反聯合國憲章規定的戰爭行爲，如侵略別國的行爲[1]。attack 多指企圖傷害或消滅他人[2]，常在他人無防備或準備情況下進行攻擊。assault 爲猛烈攻擊，尤指近距離的身體接觸和暴力[3]，常針對某個人或少數人，且常帶有因嫉妒、怨恨等個人情感，其突然性和出其不意性往往比 attack 更強，因此 attack 能用 surprise 修飾，而用 surprise 去修飾 assault 則爲累贅。offensive 有時可與 attack 互換使用，有時則指一種大規模的軍事進攻行動[4]。

注

[1] "the use of armed force by a state against the sovereignty, territory integrity, or political independence of another state, or in any other manner inconsistent with the Charter of the United Nations", Cf. James E. Clapp, *Random House Webster's Dictionary of Law*, Random House (2000), at P. 20.

[2] "to try to hurt or harm someone", Cf. P. H. Collin, *Dictionary of Law*, Peter Collin Publishing (1993), at P. 37.

[3] "Assault typically suggests close physical contact and extreme violence, especially against one or a few people." Cf. The Editors of the Reader's Digest, *Use the Right Word*, The Reader's Digest Association Proprietary Ltd. (1971), at P. 20.

[4] "In some contexts it is interchangeable with attack, but in others it applies to a large-scale co-ordinated military campaign of men and materiel." *Id.* at P. 11.

Aggrieved party ► Injured person ► Victim

乍看上去，上述單詞或片語似乎均有「受害人」的含義，但究其內涵差異卻極大。首先是 aggrieved party，因單詞 aggrieve 在表示「傷害」或「不公正對待」時，只適用於法律場合情況下的傷害[1]，故在法律英語中，aggrieved party（也稱爲 party aggrieved 或 person aggrieved）專指在司法或準司法程序中其合法權益受到傷害或不公正對待者，即受到認爲不公正的判決、命令或懲處者，按規定，此種人具有上訴或申訴之權利地位（standing as an appellant or a petitioner or a complaint）[2]。爲與其他「受害人」相區別，最好將其譯爲「受屈人」[3]或「權益受侵害人」或不服判決、命令等的「上訴人」或「申訴人」[4]。因此，the aggrieved party in a case 便應爲「案件受屈人」，指在案件中的受到不公正待遇者，或「案件申（上）訴人」，指案件中的 plaintiff 或 petitioner[5]，而不應是有些詞典中的「案件中受害的一方」或「被害人」[5]。injured person 和 victim 則是指其權利、財產或人身等受到其他當事人傷害者，injured party 指法律訴訟中的曾受到另一方當事人行爲傷害的「受害人」，即原告[6]。victim 尤指犯罪、侵權或其他過錯行爲之受害人[7]。

注

① "Aggrieve: (to bring grief to; to treat unfairly) is now used almost exclusively in legal contexts, and almost always in the form of a past participle", Cf. Bryan A. Garner, *A Dictionary of Modern Legal Usage*, 2nd Edition, Oxford University Press Ltd. (1995), at P. 39.

② "a party with a legally recognized interest that is injuriously affected, esp. by an act of a judicial or quasi-judicial body and that confers standing to appeal", Cf. Linda Picard Wood, J.D., *Merriam Webster's Dictionary of Law*, Merriam-Webster, Incorporated (1996), at P.

354; "one whose right has been directly and injuriously affected by action of court. One whose pecuniary interest in subject matter of an action is directly and injuriously affected or whose right of property is either established or divested by complained of decision." Cf. The Publisher's Editorial Staff, *Black's Law Dictionary*, Abridged 6th Edition, West Publishing Co. (1991), at P. 775.

③ Cf.《英漢法律辭彙》，香港律政司（1998），第44頁。

④ Cf. 田中英夫，《英米法辭典》，東京大學出版會（1996），第38頁。

⑤ Cf. 陸谷孫，《英漢大詞典》，上海譯文出版社（1995），第62頁；《英漢法律詞典》，法律出版社（1999），第34頁。

⑥ "party in a court case which has been harmed by another party", Cf. P. H. Collin, *Dictionary of Law*, 2nd Edition, Peter Collin Publishing Ltd. (1993), at P. 279.

⑦ "A person harmed by a crime, tort, or other wrong." Cf. Bryan A. Garner, *Black's Law Dictionary*, 7th Edition, West Group (1999), at P. 1416.

Agreement ► Contract

　　兩者均指表達兩個或以上之當事人合意（mutual consent）之文件。在英美法中，agreement（協議）經常被作為 contract 的同義詞，但其內涵比 contract（契約）要廣（agreement is in some respects a broader term than contract）①，它還常用作指不具備契約要素或要件，即無對價（consideration）的某些協議。而契約總是含有對價的。總體說來，所有契約均是一種協議，而協議卻未必一定是契約②。要使協議成為契約，其必須符合契約的要件規定（only if it meets the requirements of a Contract），有時還需當事人在交易過程中透過語言或經交易過程或商業慣例等的默示予以補償條件。

注

① Cf. The Publisher's Editorial Staff, *Black's Law Dictionary*, Abridged
6ᵗʰ Edition, West Publishing Co. (1991), at P. 44.

② "Agreement may refer either to an informal arrangement with
no consideration or to a formal legal arrangement supported by
consideration. Contract is used only in this second sense." Cf. Bryan
A. Garner, *A Dictionary of Modern Legal Usage*, Oxford University
Press Ltd. (1995), at P. 40.

Aid ▸ Assistance

　　兩個單詞均有協助和幫助的含義，兩個單詞都較 help 正式。aid
和 assistance 所指的是向行為人本身在實施過程中遇到困難或麻煩
的事情提供援助，相比之下，aid 比 assistance 所提供的幫助更為主
動，且所滿足的需要更為迫切。

注

Cf. The Editors of the Reader's Digest, *Use the Right Word*, The Reader's
Digest Association Proprietary Ltd. (1971), at P.264.

Alcoholic ▸ Drunk ▸ Drunkard ▸ Inebriate

　　這些單詞均有「酗酒者」的含義。其中，alcoholic 和 drunkard
為通用詞；相比之下，alcoholic 指酒精中毒病人或酗酒成性者，其
比 drunkard 更為正式和中性，多從醫學角度指無法控制其酒量者，
故為更常用的法律辭彙①。drunkard 則常帶有譴責的含義，指經常過

度飲酒的醉鬼②。drunk 為 drunkard 的縮寫，因而更不正式，同時其
譴責和鄙視的程度也就更多③。inebriate 為一技術性術語，指當時正
處於醉酒狀態者④，該術語現已顯得有些過時守舊，多被 alcoholic
所取代。

注

① "A person who suffers from the illness of alcoholism." Cf. *Alcoholism
and Drug Abuse Amendment Act* (Canada), S.A. 1985, c. 6, s. 3.

② "Drunkard carries a tone of condemnation and can apply justly only
to someone who frequently drinks past the point of sobriety." Cf. The
Editors of the Reader's Digest, *Use the Right Word*, The Reader's
Digest Association Proprietary Ltd. (1971), at P. 11.

③ "Drunk is, of course, a shortening of drunkard, having greater
informality than the latter and a tone of even greater contempt." *Id.* at
P. 11.

④ "A person under the influence of or addicted to the use of intoxicating
liquors." Cf. The Publisher's Editorial Staff, *Black's Law Dictionary*,
Abridged 6th Edition, West Publishing Co. (1991), at P. 535.

Alias summons ▶ Pluries summons

兩片語均為「追加的傳票」，所傳喚的都是當事人，區別在於
alias summons 為「第一次追加傳票」，作用是取代最初的傳票①。
pluries summons（也稱為 pluries 或 pluries writ）則是「第二次追加
傳票」，其是在 original 和 alias summons 未生效而簽發的傳票②。

注

① "A second summons issued after the original summons has failed for some reason." Cf. Bryan A. Garner, *Black's Law Dictionary*, 7th Edition, West Group (1999), at P. 1450.

② "Process that issues in the third instance, after the first and the alias have been ineffectual." Cf. The Publisher's Editorial Staff, *Black's Law Dictionary*, Abridged 6th Edition, West Publishing Co. (1991), at P. 1176.

Alimony ▶ Maintenance ▶ Palimony ▶ Galimony

　　以上單詞均有「扶養費用」的含義。alimony 爲「贍養費」，指夫妻雙方在分居、婚姻訴訟或離婚時法院命令一方配偶向另一方配偶支付的維持生活等費用，也稱爲 spousal support、maintenance 或 estover[①]。相比之下，alimony 爲過去所用詞，現在法院更常用 maintenance 或 spousal support 作爲其替代。palimony 則爲法院判處的同居者分手後一方支付給另一方的扶養費，其爲 pal（同居夥伴，即 live-in partner）和 alimony 混成（blending）而得的一個新詞，在美國，一些州在特定情況下曾有過此種「扶養費」判給的先例[②]。galimony 指同性同居者分手後一方支付給另一方的扶養費，其爲 gal 與 palimony 混成的新詞[③]。

注

① "A court-ordered allowance that one spouse pays to the other spouse for maintenance and support while they are separated, while they are involved in a matrimonial lawsuit, or after they are divorced." Cf. Bryan A. Garner, *Black's Law Dictionary*, 7th Edition, West Group (1999), at P. 73.

② "an alimony-like financial provision upon the breakup of an unmarried couple who lived together. The courts in some states have expressed a willingness to make such awards in limited circumstance." Cf. James E. Clapp, *Random House Webster's Dictionary of the Law*, Random House (2000), at P. 317.

③ Cf. Gail J. Koff, *Practical Guide to Everyday Law*, Simon & Schuster, Inc. (1985), at P. 217.

Allegation ▸ Affirmation

　　兩者均有「聲稱」或「斷言」的含義。其中，allegation 主要指訴辯狀或證詞中關於事實的陳述[①]；在教會法中，其還可指在作為原告人控訴之後的任何抗辯，包括應答抗辯、反對抗辯或例外抗辯等。affirmation 多指正式嚴肅的聲明，表示聲明人不願用誓詞，而願用效力等同誓言的聲明提供真實情況，對某事進行確認[②]。

注

① "an assertion that one intends to prove at trial, especially such an assertion as set forth formally in a complaint, indictment, or the like", Cf. James E. Clapp, *Random House Webster's Dictionary of the Law*, Random House (2000), at P. 25.

② "A solemn declaration with no oath. A person who objects to taking an oath may affirm, and the affirmation has the same effect as an oath." Cf. *Citizenship Act*, R.S.C. 1985, c. C-29, Schedule.

Allegiance ▸ Fealty ▸ Fidelity ▸ Loyalty

　　這些單詞均有效忠的含義。相比之下，allegiance 多指義務上的忠誠，如公民效忠其國家或王國[①]，如 oath of allegiance；同時其也用於表示政治或原則等方面的忠誠。fealty 則專門用於封建王朝封臣或奴隸等對封建主的效忠[2]。fidelity 常表示一種強烈的奉獻精神，有依附和固執的含義[3]，如：His fidelity to the principles of justice never wavered。比較之下，loyalty 則更多帶有個人關係色彩，表示強烈的個人承諾，具有熱愛和獻身的含義，常用於對個人、事業、責任或政府的忠誠[4]。

注

① "Obedience owed to the sovereign or government." Cf. Daphne Dukelow, *The Dictionary of Canadian Law*, A Carswell Publication (1991), at P. 37.

② "In feudal law, fidelity; allegiance to the feudal lord of the manor; the feudal obligation resting upon the tenant or vassal by which he was bound to be faithful and true to his lord, and render him obedience and service." Cf. The Publisher's Editorial Staff, *Black's Law Dictionary*, Abridged 6th Edition, West Publishing Co. (1991), at P. 422.

③ "fidelity implies a strong and faithful dedication", Cf. The Editors of the Reader's Digest, *Use the Right Word*, The Reader's Digest Association Proprietary Ltd. (1971), at P. 11.

④ "Faithfulness or allegiance to a person, cause, duty, or government." Cf. Bryan A. Garner, *Black's Law Dictionary* 7th Edition, West Group (1999), at P. 959.

Allision ▶ Collision

在海商法中 allision 和 collision 均有「船舶碰撞」的含義，其區別在於 allision 是指行進中的船舶與靜止的物體（stationary object），如下錨的船舶或橋墩等相撞[1]。而 collision 的含義則廣一些，既指船舶與靜止物體相撞，即等同 allision，又指兩隻行進中的船舶相互碰撞，即 crashing together of two vessels；兩詞在指車輛碰撞時也同理②。

注

① "The sudden impact of a vessel with a stationary object such as an anchored vessel or a pier." Cf. Bryan A. Garner, *Black's Law Dictionary*, 7th Edition, West Group (1999), at P. 75.

② "Striking together of two objects, one of which may be stationary. The term implies an impact or sudden contact of a moving body with an obstruction in its line of motion, whether both bodies are in motion or one stationary and the other, no matter which, in motion." Cf. The Publisher's Editorial Staff, *Black's Law Dictionary*, Abridged 6th Edition, West Publishing Co. (1991), at P. 181.

Ambassador ► Envoy ► Minister ► Legate ► Nuncio ► Plenipotentiary

以上單詞均有國家首腦或政府的外交使節（diplomat）的含義。ambassador 為「大使」，指由一個國家任命的駐其他國家的最高級別外交代表①。minister 為「公使」，級別比 ambassador 低一級②。凡附有特殊使命的 minister 或 ambassador 則稱為 envoy，即「特命全權公使」或「特命全權大使」③。legate 和 nuncio 均可指梵蒂岡國或羅馬教皇派出的使節，legate 等同其他國家派出的 ambassador④；nuncio 則等同 envoy⑤。plenipotentiary 為「全權使節」，其可是 ambassador、envoy 或 minister，但該單詞多指 plenipotentiary minister，儘管其級別低於大使，但仍可以其政府的名義全權處理國家的各項重要事項⑥。

注

① "A diplomatic officer of the highest rank, usu. designated by a government as its resident representative in a foreign state." Cf. Bryan A. Garner, *Black's Law Dictionary*, 7th Edition, West Group (1999), at P. 79.

② "A diplomatic representative, esp. one ranking below an ambassador." *Id.* at P. 1011.

③ "A diplomat of the rank of minister or ambassador sent by a country to the government of a foreign country to execute a special mission or to serve as a permanent diplomatic representative." Cf. The Publisher's Editorial Staff, *Black's Law Dictionary*, Abridged 6th Edition, West Publishing Co. (1991), at P. 370.

④ "An ambassador of the Pope." Cf. Daphne Dukelow, *The Dictionary of Canadian Law*, Thomson Professional Publishing Canada (1991), at P. 572.

⑤ "the Pope's envoy", *Id.* at P. 703.

⑥ "A minister ranking below ambassador but possessing full power and authority as a governmental representative, esp. as an envoy of a sovereign ruler." Cf. Bryan A. Garner, *Black's Law Dictionary*, 7th Edition, West Group (1999), at P. 1011.

Amens ▶ Demens

　　兩者均與精神狀況有關。區別在於 amens 為「心神喪失者」（與之相對的形容詞「心神喪失」則為 amentia），指精神完全失常的瘋子①。demens 為「癡呆者」，指弱智或癡呆病人（與之相對的「癡呆症」則為 dementia ②）。

注

① "*Demens* indicate one whose mental faculties are enfeebled; one who has lost his mind; distinguished from amens, one totally insane." Cf. The Publisher's Editorial Staff, *Black's Law Dictionary*, 5th Edition, West Publishing Co. (1979), at P. 387.

② "Unalterable mental deterioration." Cf. F. A. Jaffe, *A Guide to Pathological Evidence*, 2nd Edition, Toronto, Carswell (1983), at P. 174.

Amnesty ▶ Pardon

　　兩個單詞均有「赦免」罪犯的含義。amnesty 指取消罪名或對罪行忽略不計，多適用於侵犯國家主權的犯罪或政治犯，由於其常用於針對一群人或一個階層的人，故也稱為 general pardon，即「大赦」①，其可經行政命令或立法予以頒布②。pardon 多用於指寬恕某個罪犯的罪行，常適用於那些危害國家治安的罪犯，由於 pardon 通常只能由國家行政長官，如總統或州長等的恩准（For federal offenses a pardon can be issued only by President; for state offenses, usu. only by the governor）③，故其也稱為 executive pardon④。此外，pardon 並非等同 quashing a conviction，即罪犯的罪行雖然可以赦免，但其犯罪紀錄仍然存在⑤。

注

① "amnesty: A pardon extended by the government to a group or class of persons, usu. for a political offense. Unlike an ordinary pardon, amnesty is usu. addressed to crimes against state sovereignty." Cf. Bryan A. Garner, *Black's Law Dictionary*, 7th Edition, West Group (1999), at P. 83.

② "Amnesty may be granted either by executive decree or by legislative act." Cf. James E. Clapp, *Random House Webster's Dictionary of the Law*, Random House (2000), at P. 27.

③ *Id.* at P. 318.

④ "A pardon is usu.granted by the chief executive of a government." Cf. Bryan A. Garner, *Black's Law Dictionary*, 7th Edition, West Group (1999), at P. 1137.

⑤ "Pardon bars any further prosecution or punishment, but it does not remove a conviction from one's record." Cf. James E. Clapp, *Random House Webster's Dictionary of the Law*, Random House (2000), at P. 318.

Amotion ▸ Disfranchisement ▸ Expulsion

上述單詞均有驅逐或取消的含義。在公司法中，amotion 是指按普通法之程序，經股東大會同意解除公司某高級官員職務，如因故解除某人董事職務①，但其仍然可保留公司成員資格。而 disfranchisement 和 expulsion 則都是指取消某人作為公司成員的資格②。

注

① "In corporation law, the common law procedure by which a director may be removed for cause by the shareholders." Cf. The Publisher's Editorial Staff, *Black's Law Dictionary*, Abridged 6th Edition, West Publishing Co. (1991), at P. 55.

② "The act of disfranchising. The act of depriving a member of a corporation his right as such, by expulsion. It differs from amotion, which is applicable to the removal of an officer from office, leaving him his rights as a member." *Id*. at P. 324.

Answer ▸ Reply ▸ Rejoinder

三個單詞均有當事人在法庭審判時的答覆或辯駁的含義。answer 爲「答辯」，是最通用辭彙，在司法程序中，指被告對原告指控的第一次答辯或提出相反陳述。在一般訴訟中，其可指答覆書面質詢的正式書面陳述；在離婚訴訟中爲被告人對離婚請求的答辯；在宗教法院中其被稱爲申辯，但也要求有本人的答辯①。reply 也爲「答辯」，用於指原告對被告答辯時提出的問題或反訴所作的答覆和反駁，或對第三方當事人的辯護的答覆和反駁②。rejoinder 爲「第二次辯護」，指普通法訴訟中被告對原告之 reply 的辯駁③。

注

① "A defendant's first pleading that addresses the merits of the case, usu. by denying the plaintiff's allegations. An answer usu. sets forth the defendant's defense and counterclaims." Cf. Bryan A. Garner, *Black's Law Dictionary*, 7th Edition, West Group (1999), at P. 90.

② "In its general sense, the plaintiff's answer to a defendant's set-off or counterclaim. Under Fed. R. Civil P. 7 (a), a reply is only allowed in two situations: to a counterclaim denominated as such, or, on order of court, to an answer or a third-party answer." Cf. The Publisher's Editorial Staff, *Black's Law Dictionary*, Abridged 6th Edition, West Publishing Co. (1991), at P. 901.

③ "The defendant's answer to the plaintiff's reply (or replication)." Cf. Bryan A. Garner, *Black's Law Dictionary*, 7th Edition, West Group (1999), at P. 1291.

Appendant ▸ Appurtenance ▸ Appurtenant

上述單詞均有「從屬權」的含義。區別在於 appendant 所指的權利有時效限制，繼承後只能使用一定期限。而 appurtenance 和 appurtenant 所指的從屬權則無此種限制。

注

"Appendant differs from appurtenance in that appendant must ever be by prescription, i.e., a personal usage for a considerable time, while an appurtenance may be created at this day, for if a grant be made to a man and his heirs, of common in such a moor for his beasts levant or couchant upon his manor, the appurtenance to the manor, and the grant will pass them." Cf. The Publisher's Editorial Staff, *Black's Law Dictionary*, Abridged 6th Edition, West Publishing Co. (1991), at P. 64.

Appoint ▸ Assign ▸ Designate ▸ Name

以上單詞均有不經選舉程序而任命委派的含義。其中，appoint 多指由官方或正式負有職責的人進行的任命。在這一點上，name 最不正式，其多半強調結果，對任命者或任命方式一般都予忽略。相比之下，designate 則是所有辭彙中最正式的一個。assign 的含義主要不在於挑選某人完成某項任務，其主要在於將某項任務指派給某人去完成。

注

Cf. The Editors of the Reader's Digest, *Use the Right Word*, The Reader's Digest Association Proprietary Ltd. (1971), at P. 18.

Appraisal ▸ Evaluation

兩者均有評估或評價的含義。appraisal 除可用作對資產、商標等的評估，對工程項目而言，appraisal 多指項目進行前對項目可行性等所作的評估。evaluation 則多指項目完成後對項目所作的總結評價。

Apprehension ▸ Arrest ▸ Attachment ▸ Seizure

這些單詞均有逮捕或拘捕的含義。其中，apprehension 和 arrest 都是指刑事拘捕，可互換使用；apprehension 是指將罪犯抓獲並予以拘禁[1]，arrest 則指對正在實施犯罪的人或被懷疑實施了犯罪的人進行的實際管束，尤指將某人拘押以送警察局進行刑事指控[2]。attachment 多用於民事上的拘押，常指對債務人的人身進行拘捕以迫使其到庭解決債務糾紛[3]。Seizure 所指的拘捕有兩種含義，一是達到 arrest 的程度，另一種則是短時間拘提以訊問或調查（等同stop）。根據憲法規定，兩種情況對逮捕令（warrant）的要件要求也就不同[4]。

注

① "Capture a person on a criminal charge." Cf. Daphne Dukelow, *The Dictionary of Canadian Law*, Thomson Professional Publishing Canada (1991), at P. 53.

② "Any significant deprivation of an individual's freedom of action, especially the taking of an individual into custody for the purpose of transporting him to a police station and charging him with a crime." Cf. James E. Clapp, *Random House Webster's Dictionary of the Law*, Random House, New York (2000), at P. 35.

③ "The arrest of a person who either is in contempt of court or is to be held as security for the payment of a judgment." Cf. The Publisher's Editorial Staff, *Black's Law Dictionary*, Abridged 6ᵗʰ Edition, West Publishing Co. (1991), at P. 123; "the taking into custody of a person to hold that person as security for the payment of a judgment", Cf. Bryan A. Garner, *A Dictionary of Modern Legal Usage*, 2ⁿᵈ Edition, Oxford University Press (1995), at P. 88.

④ "The seizure of a person (as for arrest or investigation). Not all seizures, however, require a warrant.A seizure that constitutes an arrest requires probable cause to be reasonable, and a stop usu. requires reasonable suspicion of the particular person or persons stopped, although stops like those at drunk driving checkpoints may be justified by a plan that places explicit and neutral limitations on the conduct of police officers with no requirement of individualized suspicion." Cf. Linda Picard Wood, J.D., *Merriam Webster's Dictionary of Law*, Merriam-Webster, Incorporated, Springfield, Massachusetts (1996), at P. 448.

Approval ▸ Approbation ▸ Sanction

　　以上單詞均有批准、同意的含義。其中，approval 爲通常用語，多用於指同意承擔一任務等情況①。sanction 較 approval 正式，一般用於正式行文中②。需要注意的是 sanction 同時又具有制裁的含義，故應當隨時分清其用法。approbation 爲最正式的單詞，常表示宗教意義上的權威性批准③。

注

① "Approval is the most general and least formal of these. In the official context, it usually means the giving of permission to undertake a task." Cf. The Editors of the Reader's Digest, *Use the Right Word*, The Reader's Digest Association Proprietary Ltd. (1971), at P. 19.

② "explicit or official approval", Cf. The Publisher's Editorial Staff, *Black's Law Dictionary*, Abridged 6th Edition, West Publishing Co. (1991), at P. 442.

③ "Approbation, the most formal of these, refers to the giving of authoritative approval, especially in an ecclesiastical context." Cf. The Editors of the Reader's Digest, *Use the Right Word*, The Reader's Digest Association Proprietary Ltd. (1971), at P. 19.

Arbiter ▸ Arbitrator ▸ Judge ▸ Referee ▸ Umpire

　　以上單詞均有裁決或裁判者的含義。其中，儘管 judge 可指很多場合中的裁決者，如 judge of the diamond at the show 及 judge of the cars 等，但在法律語言學中，嚴格說來，judge 唯一的含義即是「法官」，不論其是經指定還是選舉而獲得職位的[①]。arbiter 和 arbitrator 均可用作指「仲裁員」，但在這種含義上，後者比前者通用。arbiter 屬於書面語，更常用於指無正式授權或職務，而憑藉威望以作裁決或制定標準者。從裁決的方式上看，arbiter 受制於法律規則，而 arbitrator 則可按自己的判斷行使自由裁量權[②]（但 Arthur A. Leff 卻對此區別持異議[③]）。在羅馬法中，arbiter 還可用作指被授予自由裁量權的法官，或經裁判官（praetor）指定按衡平法規則審理屬於善意動機類案件（bona fidei）者。referee 和 umpire 也可用作指 arbitrator。此外，referee 還常用作指由法院命令或指定，就未決案件作額外的調查、取證、聽審當事人且提交相關報告的專家（或律師）。此種 referee 的指定可不需有關當事人的同意，此時，其為「託查官（人）」（即能對未決事項進行聽審且將結果報告法院的準司法官，通常爲律師，經法官任命以處理某事項，源於委託，因其處理之事項是法院專門「委託」的）④。在用作指仲裁時，umpire則常表示在兩個或多個仲裁人意見不和時，被指定作終局裁決的「首席仲裁人」⑤。

注

① "A public official appointed or elected to hear and decide legal matters in court." Cf. Bryan A. Garner, *Black's Law Dictionary*, 7th Edition, West Group (1999), at P. 844; "a public official vested with authority to hear, determine, and preside over legal matters brought in court", Cf. Linda Picard Wood, J.D., *Merriam Webster's Dictionary of Law*, Merriam-Webster, Incorporated, Springfield, Massachusetts (1996), at P. 267.

② "Arbiter: A person chosen to decide a controversy. A person bound to decide according to the rules of law and equity, as distinguished from an arbitrator, who may proceed wholly at his own discretion, so that it be according to the judgment of a sound man." Cf. The Publisher's Editorial Staff, *Black's Law Dictionary*, Abridged 6th Edition, West Publishing Co. (1991), at P. 69.

③ "Sometimes a distinction in sought to be made between an arbiter, who decides according to rules, and an arbitrator, who is free to settle matters in his own sound discretion. But the distinction doesn't hold; arbiter often have huge moments of discretionary power, and more important, most arbitrators today proceed according to elaborate rules, both procedural and substantive." Cf. Arthur A. Leff, *The Leff Dictionary of Law*, 94 Yale L.J. 1855, 2050 (1985).

④ "Person who is appointed by court to exercise certain judicial powers, to take testimony, to hear parties, and report his findings. He is an officer exercising judicial powers, and is an arm of the court for a special purpose." Cf. The Publisher's Editorial Staff, *Black's Law Dictionary*, Abridged 6ᵗʰ Edition, West Publishing Co. (1991), at P. 886.

⑤ "a person having authority to decide finally a controversy or question between parties, as one appointed to decide between disagreeing arbitrators", Cf. Linda Picard Wood, J.D., *Merriam Webster's Dictionary of Law*, Merriam-Webster, Incorporated, Springfield, Massachusetts (1996), at P. 510.; "An impartial person appointed to make an award or a final decision, usu. when a matter has been submitted to arbitrators who have failed to agree." Cf. Bryan A. Garner, *Black's Law Dictionary*, 7ᵗʰ Edition, West Group (1999), at P. 1525.

Argue ▸ Debate ▸ Dispute ▸ Reason

這些單詞均有爭辯或辯論的含義。argue 爲最常用單詞,主要用於說服他人接受某項結論或支持、證明某項結論,其有時措辭較激烈,有接近爭吵之嫌;argue 也可指在法庭上陳述案情[①]。debate 通常指正式的 argue,雙方陳述觀點,過程受裁決人的控制,且按一定的規則進行,尤指議會對議案進行討論等[②],如:The House of Representatives debate the proposal for two days。dispute 則常指感情多於理性的 argue,且常帶有一種派系觀點[③]。reason 多指謹慎和煞費苦心進行的爭辯,目的在於勸導或作某課題上深層次的探討[④]。

注

① "to give reasons for or against a matter in dispute; to present a case in court", Cf. Linda Picard Wood, J.D., *Merriam Webster's Dictionary of Law*, Merriam-Webster, Incorporated, Springfield, Massachusetts (1996), at P. 31.

② "discussion leading to a vote, especially the discussion of a motion in Parliament", Cf. P. H. Collin, *Dictionary of Law*, 2ⁿᵈ Edition, Peter Collin Publishing Ltd. (1993), at P. 153.

③ "Dispute, in this context, means to argue with more passion than logic, often from a factional point of view." Cf. The Editors of the Reader's Digest, *Use the Right Word*, The Reader's Digest Association Proprietary Ltd. (1971), at P. 20.

④ "Reason means to argue or discuss in a careful and painstaking manner in order to persuade or explore a subject in depth." *Id*. at P. 20.

Arms ► Armament ► Arsenal ► Deterrent ► Munitions ► Weapon

　　上述單詞均有武器裝備的含義。其中，arms 和 weapon 爲一般常用語，多數情況下均可互換使用，arms 更傾向指士兵個人所擁有的武器，如刀、槍、箭等，而weapon 則範圍更廣，隨手碰到的任何東西，如石頭、棍棒等均可成爲weapon。此外，arms還可指一個國家的整體軍事能力①，如：Both countries bankrupted themselves in their race to manufacture arms。在指國家的軍事能力方面，armament 比 arms 更爲常用，指用於戰爭的所有武器和裝備，包括飛機、軍艦、坦克等②。munitions 通常泛指裝備而不只是武器，尤指彈藥③。arsenal 和 deterrent 目前常用作指核武器，arsenal 表示裝備有核彈頭的武器庫④，而 deterrent 則爲核武器庫的一種委婉用詞。

注

① "Arms and weapon are general terms, nearly interchangeable, for the

67

instruments of combat. Of the two words, arms is more frequently restricted in use to these weapons that an individual soldier can wield, whereas weapons are anything used in the fight, from the chance sticks and stones to hydrogen bombs." Cf. The Editors of the Reader's Digest, *Use the Right Word*, The Reader's Digest Association Proprietary Ltd. (1971), at P. 20.

② *Id.* at P. 20.

③ "Arms, ammunition, implements of war, military stores of any articles deemed of being converted thereunto or made useful in the production thereof." Cf. *Official Secret Act*, R.S.C. 1985, c. 5, s. 2.

④ "Arsenal and deterrent have come into fairly recent use to refer to a country's nuclear arms. Arsenal indicates a stockpile of nuclear warheads. Deterrent is almost a euphemistic word for a nuclear arsenal." Cf. The Editors of the Reader's Digest, *Use the Right Word*, The Reader's Digest Association Proprietary Ltd. (1971), at P. 21.

Arson ▸ House-burning

　　兩者均與縱火焚燒房屋或財產有關。它們之間的區別在於 arson（也稱爲 statutory arson）有兩種含義：⑴指普通法上規定的有意和有預謀地縱火焚燒他人住宅的犯罪，侵犯他人居住安全或占用財產之權利，稱爲「縱火焚宅罪」；⑵指制定法上規定的有意違法縱火焚燒他人財產（其內涵大於住宅）或自己之財產（如爲騙保費）之犯罪，爲廣義的「縱火罪」 ① 。相比之下，house-burning（也稱爲 combustio domorum）則是指有意焚燒自己的房屋，由此對他人房屋導致威脅（但並非眞正造成損害）之犯罪，其屬於普通法上的輕罪（misdemeanor），該罪名於 1968 年被 Statutory burglary 所取代，現只在蘇格蘭保留，故其爲「焚宅罪」 ② 。

① "At common law, the malicious burning of the house of another. This definition, however, has been broadened by state statutes and criminal codes. For example, the Model Penal Code, Art. 220.1(1), provides that a person is guilty of arson, a felony of the second degree, if he starts a fire or causes an explosion with the purpose of (a) destroying a building or occupied structure of another; or (b) destroying or damaging any property, whether his own or another's, to collect insurance for such loss. Other situations include the destruction of property by other means; e.g. explosion." Cf. The Publisher's Editorial Staff, *Black's Law Dictionary*, Abridged 6ᵗʰ Edition, West Publishing Co. (1991), at P. 73.

② "The common-law misdemeanor of intentionally burning one's own house that is within city limits or that is close enough to other houses that might be in danger of catching fire, although no actual damage to them results." Cf. Bryan A. Garner, *Black's Law Dictionary*, 7ᵗʰ Edition, West Group (1999), at P. 744.

Assert ▶ Affirm ▶ Allege ▶ Aver ▶ Avouch ▶ Avow ▶ Maintain ▶ Testify

　上述單詞均有「宣稱」或「斷言」等含義。其中，assert 指有力地且具有說服力地陳述和要求，以求得（法庭等的）認可①。affirm 指主動、莊嚴和正式地宣稱或陳述某事屬實，故主要表示確認，如上級法院對下級法院判決的確認，以及聲稱其沒有宗教信仰，或聲稱契約有效、某訴辯事實屬實等②。allege 表示在尚未提供證據的情況下的聲稱，其聲稱的事實需要經過證實或得到否決，故其經常具有「指控」的含義③；此外，其還可用作等同 aver。aver 指在訴辯狀（pleading）之辯護中引例證明，用簡短事實說明，故爲「立證」④。avouch 指一種擔保或確認，尤指確認或證明一行爲⑤。avow 指在訴辯狀中公開宣稱或承認，或證明已實施的行爲正當等⑥，如 avow one's guilt。maintain 多指違背事實對以前的陳述進行堅持，或就事實作相反爭辯，如：In spite of circumstantial evidence pointing to his guilt，the accused maintained that he was innocent。testify 主要指作爲證人以提供證據的方式陳述和確認⑦。

注

① "to present and demand recognition", Cf. Linda Picard Wood, J.D., *Merriam Webster's Dictionary of Law*, Merriam-Webster, Incorporated, Springfield, Massachusetts (1996), at P. 34.

② "To ratify, uphold, approve, make firm, confirm, establish, reassert; to make a solemn and formal declaration or asseveration." Cf. The Publisher's Editorial Staff, *Black's Law Dictionary*, Abridged 6th Edition, West Publishing Co. (1991), at P. 37.

③ "to sate without proof or before proving", Cf. Linda Picard Wood, J.D., *Merriam Webster's Dictionary of Law*, Merriam-Webster, Incorporated, Springfield, Massachusetts (1996), at P. 23.

④ "to sate (as a fact) in a pleading", *Id.* at P. 23.

⑤ "To maintain or justify an act." Cf. Daphne Dukelow, *The Dictionary of Canadian Law*, Thomson Professional Publishing Canada (1991), at P. 77.

⑥ "In pleading, to acknowledge and justify an act done." Cf. The Publisher's Editorial Staff, *Black's Law Dictionary*, Abridged 6th Edition, West Publishing Co. (1991), at P. 92.

⑦ "To give evidence under oath or affirmation at a trial, hearing, or deposition." Cf. James E. Clapp, *Random House Webster's Dictionary of the Law*, Random House, New York (2000), at P. 428.

Assistant ▸ Subordinate

二者均有助手或協助人的含義。二者的主要區別在於 subordinate 有時強調一種等級差異，有屈就甚至蔑視的情感，而 assistant 則沒有此種含義。

注

"Subordinate emphasizes the inferiority of a helper or assistant, and its greater formality does not always mitigate an overtone of condescension, sometimes extending even to contempt." Cf. The Editors of the Reader's Digest, *Use the Right Word*, The Reader's Digest Association Proprietary Ltd. (1971), at P. 24.

Associate ▸ Ally ▸ Partner

上述單詞均有表示與職業或工作相關的同事或夥伴的含義。 associate 為「聯合者」或「合夥者」，是其中最通用的單詞，多表示職業或商事關係，這種關係也可能是選擇、機遇或需要的結果①。 ally為「同盟者」，常表示一種選擇關係，主要用於指在戰爭中站在同一邊的國家②。partner 則常用於指選擇和契約關係，共同參與冒險事業，為「合夥人」，尤指合夥性質的律師事務所（law firm）的共同所有人③。

注

① "Associate is the least specific of these; its formality would suggest a business or professional context. While it implies close connection, the relationship might be the result of choice, chance or necessity." Cf. The Editors of the Reader's Digest, *Use the Right Word*, The Reader's Digest Association Proprietary Ltd. (1971), at Ps. 24－25.

② "A nation which has entered into an alliance." Cf. Daphne A. Dukelow, *The Dictionary of Canadian Law*, Thomson Professional Publishing Canada (1991), at P. 40.

③ "one of two or more persons associated as joint principals in carrying on a business for the purpose of enjoying a joint profit, a member of a partnership, specific: a partner in a law firm", Cf. Linda Picard Wood, J.D., *Merriam Webster's Dictionary of Law*, Merriam-Webster, Incorporated, Springfield, Massachusetts (1996), at P. 352.

Assurance ▶ Insurance

　　二者均有保險的含義。區別在於 assurance 主要爲英式英語，多指人壽保險、生命險等①。而 insurance 則爲美式英語，多用於指海上、財產和其他險種②。

注

① "Same as insurance, term used in Canada and England." Cf. The Publisher's Editorial Staff, *Black's Law Dictionary*, Abridged 6th Edition, West Publishing Co. (1991), at P. 82; "Assure and Assurance are used in Britain for insurance policies relating to something which will certainly happen (such as death or the end of a given period of time), for other type of policy use insure and insurance." Cf. P. H. Collin, *Dictionary of Law*, Peter Collin Publishing (1993), at P. 37.

② "An agreement by which one party (the insurer) commits to do something of value for another party (the insured) upon the occurrence of some specified contingency; esp. an agreement by which one party assumes a risk faced by another party in return for a premium payment." Cf. Bryan A. Garner, *Black's Law Dictionary*, 7th Edition, West Group (1999), at P. 802.

Attorney-law ▸ Attorney in fact

二者均有法律事務代理人的含義，attorney-at-law 主要指具有律師資格[①]，且註冊登記而從事法律事務代理者（licensed to practice law）。而 attorney in fact 則是指經授權委託書（power of attorney）授權主要從事非訴訟活動者，多在庭外處理委託事務，其不一定必須具有律師資格[②]。

注

① "A person who practices law; lawyer." Cf. Bryan A. Garner, *Black's Law Dictionary*, 7th Edition, West Group (1999), at P. 802.

② "an attorney who may or may not be a lawyer who is given written authority to act on another's behalf esp. by a power of attorney", Cf. Linda Picard Wood, J.D., *Merriam Webster's Dictionary of Law*, Merriam-Webster, Incorporated, Springfield, Massachusetts (1996), at P. 38.

Avoid a tax ▸ Dodge a tax ▸ Evade tax

以上片語都有力圖不繳納稅收之含義。其中，avoid a tax 指透過合法途徑巧妙規避稅收，故爲「避稅」或「規避賦稅」[①]。而 evade tax（偷稅，逃稅）則指非法的「偷稅漏稅」[②]。tax avoidance 與 tax

evasion 也有此種差別,即前者為合法規避,後者則為一種犯罪。
dodge a tax 等同 evade tax,但從嚴格意義上講,其並不是一個正式
法律術語③。

注

① "to prevent the occurrence of or responsibility for tax, esp. through lawful means", Cf. Linda Picard Wood, J.D., *Merriam Webster's Dictionary of Law*, Merriam-Webster, Incorporated, Springfield, Massachusetts (1996), at P. 40.

② "to unlawfully fail to pay (taxes) through fraudulent or deceptive means", *Id.* at P. 171.

③ "to evade responsibility or a duty, esp. by trickery or deceit", Cf. Philip Babcock Gove, Ph.D., *Webster's Third New International Dictionary of the English Language*, G & C Merriam Co. (1976), at P. 667.

B

Bail ▸ Trust

二者的區別在於前者爲「寄託」或「寄存」，且多指動產的寄託（存）（to place personal in someone else's charge），動產受託人（bailee）在此無替他人處置財產的義務和權利；後者爲「信託」，其有三要素：(1)受託人（trustee），其持有信託財產，且負有爲他人利益處理財產的衡平法上的義務；(2)受益人（beneficiary），受託人對其負有爲他處理受託財產的衡平法上的義務；(3)受託財產（trust property），即受託人爲受益人所持有的財產。

注

參見以下條目 Bailment 和 Trust。

Bailment ▸ Trust

二者均用於表示一種財產的代管方式。bailment 爲「寄託」，是指根據明示或默示契約把動產交付給某人的行爲。構成寄託，必須由特定動產的所有者或委託人把實際的或推定的占有權轉移給另一人（bailee 受寄託人），以便後者按要求方式進行處置，然後要返回原物，或以改變了的形式進行返回[1]。而 trust 爲「信託」，指財產或法定權利的所有人（即信託人）將財產或權利交給另一個或另幾個人，後者據此爲另一方（受益人）、其他人或爲某一特定目的或幾個目的而持有財產和行使權利[2]。信託應由明示建立，其方式如下：由法律建立、由生前宣布而建立、由遺囑建立或由法律的實施而產生，後者又包括推定信託和結果信託兩種。

① "an arrangement in which one person transfers possession (but not ownership) of personal property to another for storage. The legal rights and duties of the parties depend upon the purpose and terms of the bailment. The bailee may be storing the bailor's goods for a fee." Cf. James E. Clapp, *Random House Webster's Dictionary of the Law*, Random House (2000), at P. 46.

② "Any arrangement whereby property is transferred with intention that it be administered by trustee for another's benefit. A fiduciary relationship in which one person is the holder of the title to property subject to an equitable obligation to keep or use the property for the benefit of another." Cf. The Publisher's Editorial Staff, *Black's Law Dictionary*, Abridged 6th Edition, West Publishing Co. (1991), at P. 1047.

Banishment ▸ Deportation ▸ Exile ▸ Expatriation ▸ Relegation

　　以上單詞均有流放或放逐的含義。exile 指長期離開祖國或家鄉，其可是自願的，如為執行公務、躲避危險、壓迫等原因，也可以是一種強制性懲罰，作為刑罰，其多有一定期限①。banishment 則指被流放或逐出國境，即流放國外，其常指喪失國籍，永久被流放②；現也用於強迫離開（forcible removal）。deportation 主要是指將不受歡迎的外國人驅逐出境③。expatriation 多指某人自願稱自己為他國公民而放棄對祖國的效忠；用作流放時④，則指強迫某人離開祖國且使其放棄國籍。relegation 可指羅馬法中的放逐，其類似流放刑，但比流放刑輕，被放逐者仍可保持其公民權；在英格蘭，其也多指暫時的司法放逐⑤。

注

① "Expulsion from a country, esp. from the country of one's origin or longtime residence." Cf. Bryan A. Garner, *Black's Law Dictionary*, 7th Edition, West Group (1999), at P. 595.

② "Expulsion from a nation; loss of nationality." Cf. Daphne A. Dukelow, *The Dictionary of Canadian Law*, Thomson Professional Publishing Canada (1991), at P. 82.

③ "The removal under this Act of a person from any place in Canada to the place whence he came to Canada or to the country of his nationality or citizenship or to the country of his birth or to such country as may be approved by the Minister under this Act, as the case may be." Cf. *Immigration Act*, R.S.C. 1970, c. 1-2, s. 2.

④ "The voluntary act of abandoning or renouncing one's country, and becoming the citizen or subject of another." Cf. The Publisher's Editorial Staff, *Black's Law Dictionary*, Abridged 6th Edition, West Publishing Co. (1991), at P. 399.

⑤ "Banishment or exile, esp. a temporary one." Cf. Bryan A. Garner, *Black's Law Dictionary*, 7th Edition, West Group (1999), at P. 1293.

Bankrupt ▶ Insolvent ▶ Broke

三者均有「破產的」含義。在英國，insolvent 主要用於指公司的破產，為「資不抵債」（公司破產為 winding-up），指債務人無法向債權人清償債務，由法院正式宣布其 insolvent，故處於破產狀況，接下方是接管、清算等程序。在英國，個人破產則多用bankrupt。在美國，一般則無此區別，兩者均可作為破產，也可作爲「資不抵債」，且均可用於個人或公司。過去美國各州都制定有各自的 insolvency law。目前，這些 insolvency laws 基本上都被美國《聯邦破產法》（Federal Bankruptcy Act）所取代。此時，insolvency 則僅是《聯邦破產法》所規定的破產程序之一。broke 爲非正式用語。

注

"Insolvent and Insolvency are general terms, but are usually applied to companies; individuals are usually described as bankrupt once they have been declared by a court." Cf. P. H. Collin, *Dictionary of Law*, 2nd Edition, Peter Collin Publishing (1993), at P. 281.

Bar association ► Law society

　　二者均有律師協會的含義。在英國，因律師分爲「巴律師」和「沙律師」（參見 lawyer），因而 bar association 是指英格蘭和威爾士的「巴律師協會」，bar 在此是指 barrister。而 law society（也稱爲 society of solicitors）則指英格蘭和威爾士的「沙律師協會」。蘇格蘭的律師協會自成體系，其沙律師協會爲 Law Society of Scotland，而蘇格蘭的沙律師則被稱爲 law agent；蘇格蘭的巴律師協會則是 Faculty of Advocates[1]。美國的律師的劃分與英國不同，其沒有沙、巴律師之分，因而在美國，律師協會只用 bar association 來表示。美國各州的律師協會被稱爲 state bar association，全美律師協會則被稱爲 American Bar Association（略爲 ABA「美國律師協會」），需注意的是 ABA 爲一種自願的業務發展傾向的組織，相比之下，各州的律師協會則常有權規範律師業務，如處分律師、對違規違法者提起訴訟等[2]。中國的律師既不屬於 barrister 體系，也不屬於 solicitor 系列，故將中國的律師協會翻譯爲 bar association 或 law society 均不恰當。目前，有人將中國的律師協會翻譯爲 All China Lawyers' Society（「中華全國律師協會」），筆者認爲此種翻譯還是較爲貼切的。至於今後，如果中國律師的學歷結構、執業慣例以及中國的司法考試等規定發生較大變化，中國的律師協會是否可譯爲 CBA，即 China Bar Association，目前尚不知此問題的答案。

注

① Cf. 李榮甫、宋雷，《法律英語教程》，法律出版社（1999），第41－44頁。

② Cf. The Publisher's Editorial Staff, *Black's Law Dictionary*, Abridged 6th Edition, West Publishing Co. (1991), at P. 53.

Barter ► Exchange ► Swap ► Trade

以上單詞均可用於指不經金錢而直接交換商品或服務等，稱爲「易貨貿易」。其中，barter 爲最正式和典型術語，常指不使用任何具抽象價值的仲介物，也不用任何中間人，自己直接以物換物，如農夫用糧食交換靴子（barter grain for boots）①。倘若農夫不是爲自己使用而換取靴子，而是用靴子交換其他物品或用於其他目的，此時則可以說他是想 trade the boots with sb. else for sth. he really wants②。在 bartering 和 trading 中，人們必須 exchange one item for another。swap 可用作等同 barter，但其沒有 barter 正式③。

注

① "Barter is the most formal and most specific of these. It means a system of exchange in which goods and services are traded without the use of money as a medium of exchange." Cf. Douglas Greenwald, *The Concise McGraw-Hill Dictionary of Modern Economics*, McGraw-

Hill, Inc. (1983), at P. 23.

② Cf. The Editors of The Reader's Digest, *Use the Right Word*, The Reader's Digest Association Proprietary Ltd. (1971), at P. 37.

③ *Id.* at P. 37.

Bawd ▶ Panderer ▶ Pimp

三者均指參與婦女賣淫活動者。其中，bawd（「鴇婆」或「鴇公」）用於指為妓女拉客者（尤指婦女），其為舊用語（archaic word），現已鮮見[1]。panderer則為「組織賣淫嫖娼者」，專指招募妓女或為他人安排場所賣淫嫖娼者（recruiting prostitutes or arranging a situation for another to practice prostitution）[2]。pimp則為「皮條客」，指替妓女拉客且從中分得該妓女賣淫所得中的一定利益者（soliciting customers for a prostitute in return for a share of the prostitute's earnings）[3]。

注

① "A person, usu. a woman, who solicits customers for a prostitute." Cf. Bryan A. Garner, *Black's Law Dictionary*, 7th Edition, West Group (1999), at P. 146.

② Cf. Linda Picard Wood, J.D., *Merriam Webster's Dictionary of Law*, Merriam-Webster, Incorporated, Springfield, Massachusetts (1996), at P. 349.

③ Cf. Bryan A. Garner, *Black's Law Dictionary*, 7th Edition, West Group (1999), at P. 1168.

Behavior ▶ Conduct ▶ Demeanor

　　以上單詞均有行為舉止儀態的含義。其中，behavior 為最常用辭彙，可用作指人們的一切行為，包括單獨或集體，其可為精神病學者、社會學家、人類學家研究的對象，常指積極或消極的社會行為活動[①]。conduct 也可用作指個人行為活動，不論是以作為或不作為的方式予以表示[②]，但從技術含義上講其沒有 behavior 強烈，其修飾的行為範疇比 behavior 窄，常暗示遵循或違反一種固定的規則，如：a prison sentence commuted for good conduct。此外，conduct 還有一種用倫理或道德標準來衡量 behavior 的含義。demeanor 常指具體的個人在特定的時間的外在行為舉止，含有對該人的服飾、聲音、手勢、態度及表情的一種評價，陪審團可用作判斷證人的信譽[③]。

注

① "Behavior is the most general of these; at its most technical, it refers to all activity of people, singly or collectively, that might be studied by psychologists, sociologists or anthropologists." Cf. The Editors of The Reader's Digest, *Use the Right Word*, The Reader's Digest Association Proprietary Ltd. (1971), at P. 41.

② "The word conduct... covers both act and omissions... In cases in which a man is able to show that his conduct, whether in the form of action or inaction, was involuntary, he must not be held liable for any harmful result produced by it." Cf. J. W. Cecil Turner, *Kenny's Outlines of Criminal Law*, 13 n. 2 (16th Edition, 1952), at P. 24.

③ "Outward appearance or behavior, such as facial expressions, tone of voice, gestures, and the hesitation or readiness to answer questions. In evaluating a witness's credibility, the jury may consider the witness's demeanor." Cf. Bryan A. Garner, *Black's Law Dictionary*, 7th Edition,

West Group (1999), at P. 442.

Bench warrant ▶ Arrest warrant

二者之間的區別在於 arrest warrant爲「逮捕狀」（也稱爲 warrant of arrest），指由相關的權力機構，如法官或地方行政官所簽發授權逮捕某人或搜查某地的命令[1]。bench warrant 則爲「法庭拘提令」，指由法院簽發授權拘提某人的令狀，其多在蔑視法庭、證人拒絕接受傳喚或收到刑事起訴書不出庭等情況適用[2]。此處的 bench 等同 court considered in its official capacity。

注

[1] "a warrant issued to a law enforcement officer ordering the officer to arrest and bring the person named in the warrant before the court or magistrate", Cf. Linda Picard Wood, J.D., *Merriam Webster's Dictionary of Law*, Merriam-Webster, Incorporated, Springfield, Massachusetts (1996), at P. 530.

[2] "A warrant issued directly by a judge to a law-enforcement officer, esp. for the arrest of a person who has been held in contempt, has been indicted, has disobeyed a subpoena, or has failed to appear for a hearing or trial." Cf. Bryan A. Garner, *Black's Law Dictionary*, 7th Edition, West Group (1999), at P. 1579.

Beneficiary ▶ Trustee

二者均與信託有關。在信託中，財產，尤其是不動產的權益一般分爲普通法上的權益和衡平法上的權益[1]。trustee（受託人）屬普通法上的財產權益所有人，其持有法律名義上的財產所有權[2]。而

beneficiary（信託受益人）則被視爲是獲得信託眞正好處的衡平法上的權益所有人，其應享有財產的收益權、用益權等實際權利[3]。

注

① "A fiduciary relationship in which one person is the holder of the title to property subject to an equitable obligation to keep or use the property for the benefit of another." Cf. The Publisher's Editorial Staff, *Black's Law Dictionary*, Abridged 6th Edition, West Publishing Co. (1991), at P. 1047.

② "One who, having legal title to property, holds it in trust for the benefit of another and owes a fiduciary duty to that beneficiary." Cf. Bryan A. Garner, *Black's Law Dictionary*, 7th Edition, West Group (1999), at P. 1519.

③ "A trust is a fiduciary relationship in which one party (trustee) holds legal title to another's property for the benefit of a party (beneficiary) who holds equitable title to the property." Cf. Linda Picard Wood, J.D., *Merriam Webster's Dictionary of Law*, Merriam-Webster, Incorporated, Springfield, Massachusetts (1996), at P. 503.

Benefit ▸ Favor ▸ Gain ▸ Profit

以上單詞均有「利益」的含義。其中，benefit 爲最常用辭彙，可指任何種類的利益，包括物質的或其他類別，不論用什麼方式獲得[1]。favor 可指在競爭中獲得之益處，如裁定原告勝訴（rule in favor of the plaintiff），更多卻指經他人許可而產生的 benefit[2]。gain 有時可指在無任何人受損的情況下獲得或得到某種無形財產，如 an act that results in a clear gain for civil liberties，但其更常用作指獲得物質上的利益[3]，如 capital gains 等。相比之下，profit 則更常用作指投資、企業或交易所獲得的物質或金錢上的利益或收穫④。

注

① "Benefit is the most general of these, referring to any kind of good, however acquired, material or otherwise." Cf. The Editors of The Reader's Digest, *Use the Right Word*, The Reader's Digest Association Proprietary Ltd. (1971), at P. 45.

② "The word, however, most often refers to benefit that results from securing the approval of others." *Id*. at P. 46.

③ "More commonly, however, the word suggests material acquisition." *Id*. at P. 46.

④ "financial gain from an investment, enterprise, or transaction", Cf. James E. Clapp, *Random House Webster's Dictionary of the Law*, Random House (2000), at P. 345.

Bequeath ▶ Devise

二者均有「遺贈」的含義。bequeath 多指「動產遺贈」（especially to give personal property by will），如：John bequeathed his shares to his nephew（約翰將其股份贈與了他的侄兒）。而 devise 則專門用於指「不動產遺贈」（to give real property by will）。應注意的是此種傳統的區別現正在逐漸消失，如立遺囑人在遺囑中明文規定 bequeath 與 devise 同義，bequeath 有時也可表示不動產遺贈（but sometimes of real property①）。而美國的《統一遺囑檢驗法典》則用 devise 指所有的遺贈（The Uniform Probate Code uses devise to refer to any gifts made in a will②）。

注

① Cf. Linda Picard Wood, J.D., *Merriam Webster's Dictionary of Law*, Merriam-Webster, Incorporated, Springfield, Massachusetts (1996), at P. 49.

② *Id.* at P. 137.

Bestiality ▸ Buggery ▸ Crime against nature ▸ Pederasty ▸ Sodomy

以上單詞或片語均是法律語言中指違反自然的性行為的術語。首先是 crime against nature，其含義最廣，指所有刑法中規定禁止的有悖自然的性行為，包括肛交、口交、獸姦等①；在普通法中，該片語包括：bestiality 和 sodomy 兩種含義。其中，bestiality 主要指兩性中任何一方與動物發生性交②；sodomy 則多指男人之間或兩性之間的肛交，此時它可與 buggery 替換使用；在美國它還可指口交、獸姦③。buggery 多指從肛門進行性交，即雞姦，也可指用肛門或陰道與動物發生性交④。pederasty 則指一成年男人與一男童進行肛交，此種行為在美國各州均被視為非法⑤。

注

① "Deviate sexual intercourse per os or per anum between human beings who are not husband and wife and any form of sexual intercourse with an animal; crime of buggery or sodomy." Cf. The Publisher's Editorial Staff, *Black's Law Dictionary*, Abridged 6th Edition, West Publishing Co. (1991), at P. 258.

② "sexual contact between a human being and an animal", Cf. James E. Clapp, *Random House Webster's Dictionary of the Law*, Random

House, New York (2000), at P. 52.

③ "the crime of oral or anal sexual contact or penetration between persons or of sexual intercourse between a person and an animal; esp. the crime of forcing another person to perform oral or anal sex." Cf. Linda Picard Wood, J.D., *Merriam Webster's Dictionary of Law*, Merriam-Webster, Incorporated, Springfield, Massachusetts (1996), at Ps. 459－460.

④ "A carnal copulation against nature; a man or a woman with a brute beast, a man with a man, or man unnaturally with a woman. This term is often used interchangeably with sodomy." Cf. The Publisher's Editorial Staff, *Black's Law Dictionary*, Abridged 6th Edition, West Publishing Co. (1991), at P. 134.

⑤ "Anal intercourse between a man and a boy. Pederasty is illegal in all states." Cf. Bryan A. Garner, *Black's Law Dictionary*, 7th Edition, West Group (1999), at P. 1152.

Bid and asked ▸ Bids and offers

　　二者均為證券買賣報價時常使用的術語，bid and asked 為「買進出價和賣出喊價」，bids and offers 則為「買價和賣價」，差異在於前者尤指證券的場外買賣①。在兩術語中，bid 都是指買受人所出的最高應買價，而 asked 與 offers 則指出賣人所給出的最低賣價，這兩者之間的差額則為 spread。在證券買賣中，經紀人一般對一種證券要報出兩個價格任客戶選擇，較低的一個價格是經紀人買入價，較高的則是經紀人的賣出價，其差額就是經紀人的利潤②。

注

① "A notation describing the range of prices quoted for securities in an over-the-counter stock exchange." Cf. Bryan A. Garner, *Black's Law Dictionary*, 7th Edition, West Group (1999), at P. 1152.

② Cf. 倪克勤，《證券交易與銀行業務術語詞典》，四川人民出版社（1992），第 46－47 頁。

Bigamy ▸ Digamy ▸ Monogamy ▸ Polygamy ▸ Polygyny ▸ Polyandry

以上單詞均可用於表示某人的婚姻狀況。其中，bigamy 爲「重婚罪」，指兩種情況：(1)有效婚姻存續期間與另一人結婚的犯罪行爲（notifiable offense of going through a ceremony of marriage to someone when you are still married to someone else[①]）；(2)在知道對方爲有夫之婦或有婦之夫時，仍與其同居的犯罪行爲（Sometimes, the crime of cohabiting with a person with knowledge that one or the other of the cohabiting parties is married to someone else[②]）。重婚罪在英國等地屬於嚴重犯罪（serious offense），重婚罪犯則被稱爲 bigamist。digamy 是指因第一次婚姻無效或離婚或配偶死亡後的「再婚」（a second marriage after the death of, or annulment or divorce from the first spouse[③]），其也稱爲 deuterogamy 和 digama。monogamy 爲「一夫一妻制」，其爲多數國家認可（the marriage of one wife to one husband, a custom prevalent in most modern cultures[④]）。polygamy 爲多配偶制，指一個人同時可有兩個或以上配偶（the state of being simultaneously marriage to more than one spouses[⑤]），其包括 polygyny（一夫多妻制，the condition or practice of having more than one wife[⑥]）和 polyandry（一妻多夫制，the condition or practice of having more than one husband[⑦]）兩種形式。在加拿大或英國等地，polygamy 被視爲一種犯罪，其包括同時與多人同居（an offense to practice or enter into or in any manner agree or consent to practice or enter into any form of polygamy, or any kind of conjugal union with more than one person at the same time, whether or not it is by law recognized as a binding form of marriage[⑧] ）。

注

① Cf. P. H. Collin, *Dictionary of Law*, 2nd Edition, Peter Collin Publishing (1993), at P. 54.

② Cf. James E. Clapp, *Random House Webster's Dictionary of the Law*, Random House, New York (2000), at P. 53.

③ Cf. Bryan A. Garner, *Black's Law Dictionary*, 7th Edition, West Group (1999), at P. 461.

④ *Id.* at P. 1023; Cf. Daphne Dukelow, *The Dictionary of Canadian Law*, Thomson Professional Publishing Canada (1991), at P. 651.

⑤ Cf. Bryan A. Garner, *Black's Law Dictionary*, 7th Edition, West Group (1999), at P. 1180.

⑥ *Id.* at P. 1180.

⑦ *Id.* at P. 1180.

⑧ Cf. Daphne Dukelow, *The Dictionary of Canadian Law*, Thomson Professional Publishing Canada (1991), at P. 788.

Bilboes ▸ Stocks

　　兩者均指古時候的一種刑具。bilboes 為「腳手枷」，多在船上使用，指在一塊木板上鑽四個洞用以枷住犯人的手腳[①]。而 stocks 則指同時用兩塊木板，分別鑽洞後枷夾犯人的手和腳，故稱為「手枷和腳枷」[②]。

注

① "A device for punishment at sea consisting of a board with holes that secure an offender's hands and feet", Cf. Bryan A. Garner, *Black's Law Dictionary*, 7th Edition, West Group (1999), at P. 155.

② "A punishment device consisting of two boards that together form holes for trapping an offender's feet and hands", *Id.* at P. 1431.

Bill of attainder ▸ Bill of pains and penalties

二者均為《美國聯邦憲法》所禁止的法律，都屬於剝奪犯有嚴重罪行，如 treason 或 felon 等罪犯公民權利的一種專門立法，對法令規定之犯罪者可不經審判即處以懲罰。區別在於 bill of attainder（極刑懲處法，也稱為 act of attainder）規定不經審判即可適用死刑①；而 bill of pains and penalties（嚴刑懲治法）規定的處罰則相對較輕，不包含死刑②。《美國聯邦憲法》是將 bill of pains and penalties 歸併在 bill of attainder 中一起加以禁止的。

注

① "A special legislative act prescribing capital punishment, without a trial, for a person guilty of a high offense such as treason or a felony." Cf. Bryan A. Garner, *Black's Law Dictionary*, 7th Edition, West Group (1999), at P. 159.

② "An act is *a bill of attainder* where the punishment is death and *a bill of pains and penalties* when the punishment is less severe; both kinds of punishment fall within the scope of the constitutional prohibition." Cf. The Publisher's Editorial Staff, *Black's Law Dictionary*, Abridged 6th Edition, West Publishing Co. (1991), at P. 114.

Board of directors ▸ Board of trustees

二者均可指公司的董事會,即由股東選舉的負責確定公司的方針政策、任命經理人、制定主要業務和金融決策之機構。區別在於 board of directors 是指一般公司的董事會[①];而 board of trustees 則多指慈善公司等(charitable company)之董事會[②],包括校董事會等[③]。

注

① "The governing body of a corporation elected by the stockholders, usually made up of officers of the corporation and outside (non-company) directors." Cf. The Publisher's Editorial Staff, *Black's Law Dictionary*, Abridged 6th Edition, West Publishing Co. (1991), at P. 119.

② "Board of directors is also termed, esp. in charitable organizations, board of trustees." Cf. Bryan A. Garner, *Black's Law Dictionary*, 7th Edition, West Group (1999), at P. 166.

③ "The board of trustees of a school district." Cf. Daphne Dukelow, *The Dictionary of Canadian Law*, Thomson Professional Publishing Canada (1991), at P. 100.

Bodily harm ▸ Bodily injury

二者的含義常被視為等同(Cf. *Merriam Webster's Dictionary of Law* 等)。如一定要加以區別,可以認為 bodily harm(身體損害)是一個界定十分含混的術語,其除指身體的一般傷害(impairment),痛苦(physical pain)外,也可指因傷害引起的心理、精神等疾病(illness),有時甚至可指交通事故受害人的衣服損壞[1]。而 bodily injury（身體傷害）則主要指肉體的傷害（physical damage to one's body），其也稱爲 physical injury，如性質嚴重則稱爲 great bodily injury（嚴重身體傷害）或 grievous bodily harm（嚴重身體損害），屬於刑法或侵權法上的術語[2]。

注

① "Physical pain, illness, or impairment of body." Cf. Bryan A. Garner, *Black's Law Dictionary*, 7th Edition, West Group (1999), at P. 722.
② "physical harm to an individual's body", Cf. James E. Clapp, *Random House Webster's Dictionary of the Law*, Random House, New York (2000), at P. 238.

Bond ▸ Debenture

　　二者均有「債券」的含義。bond 爲通用語，但與 debenture 在一起時（debenture bond）多指具有抵押擔保的「擔保債券」，其償還期限一般較長，常爲國家或政府（包括外國）等機構發行[1]。公司也可發行 bond，如公司發行的債券是無擔保或抵押的債券（unsecured bond）時其則被稱爲 debenture[2]。由此可知，debenture 是一種不具備抵押擔保，屬於無擔保債務票據（unsecured debt instruments）之承諾債務的憑證，故有人也將其譯爲「信用債券」或「無抵押擔保債券」。在美國，debenture 通常只能由三種公司發行〔具有部分有形資產的服務公司（service corporation）、大的藍籌股公司（large, blue-chip companies）、以其所有資產爲按揭抵押之公司（corporations that have mortgaged all their available assets）〕[3]；但有時 debenture 也可以由任何個人發行，故其不宜純粹譯爲「公司債券」。debenture 常可轉換爲公司的股票[4]。

注

① "A long-term, interest-bearing debt instrument issued by a corporation or governmental entity usu. to provide for a particular financial need; esp., such as instrument in which the debt is secured by a lien on the issuer's property." Cf. Bryan A. Garner, *Black's Law Dictionary*, 7th Edition, West Group (1999), at P. 172.

② "Corporation bonds may be unsecured (debenture) or secured by the assets of the corporation." Cf. Douglas Creenwald, *The Concise McGraw-Hill Dictionary of Modern Economics*, 3rd Edition, McGraw-Hill Book Inc. (1984), at P. 29.

③ *Id.* at P. 89.

④ "Debentures are often convertible to stocks." Cf. Linda Picard Wood, J.D., *Merriam Webster's Dictionary of Law*, Merriam-Webster, Incorporated, Springfield, Massachusetts (1996), at P. 122.

Border ▶ Boundary ▶ Frontier

三個單詞均有邊界的含義。相比較，border 強調地區分界，多含有邊境特徵，如河流或山川，其含義粗略，沒有 boundary 所指的精確，且由於河流或山川的改變，border 也可能發生變化①，如：cross the border into Canada。而 boundary 則多指領土所能達到的最遠之疆界劃分，其相當精確，可經條約在文件或地圖上進行修改，常強調一種理論上的分界②，如 By international agreement, the boundary of each nation fronting a body of water extends exactly three miles from the coastline。frontier 為一國際法術語，常指兩國邊界，指某國沿著另一國 border 那部分的領土區域，因此可以說它是從一種內部的角度去理解和看待 border，包括了比作為「邊界線」的 boundary 更廣泛的區域③。

注

① "Border often suggests a territorial feature, such as a river or mountain range, and hence is not as precise as boundary." Cf. The Editors of The Reader's Digest, *Use the Right Word*, The Reader's Digest Association Proprietary Ltd. (1971), at P. 61.

② "a theoretical line that marks the limit of an area of land", Cf. Linda Picard Wood, J.D., *Merriam Webster's Dictionary of Law*, Merriam-Webster, Incorporated, Springfield, Massachusetts (1996), at P. 58.

③ "In international law, that portion of the territory of any country which lies close along the border line of another country, and so fronts or faces it. The term means something more than the boundary line itself, and includes a tract of strip of country, of indefinite extent, contiguous to the line." Cf. The Publisher's Editorial Staff, *Black's Law Dictionary*, Abridged 6th Edition, West Publishing Co. (1991), at P. 461.

Boss ▸ Chief ▸ Head ▸ Leader ▸ Master

以上單詞均有首領或領導的含義。其中，boss 起源於美國口語，原指工頭或作爲雇主的老闆，現擴大適用到所有管理、監督者或直接上司，或對某事物具有控制權者。chief 的含義最廣，可泛指許多群體或組織之最高權威者。head 與 chief 相似，也爲一般術語，它所指的人所居地位一般較低，如 head of the telephone office 以及 head of a boys' school 等。leader 一般指因能力等關係爲眾人所推選並自願追隨者。master 多指被授予權力以使人服從者，但並不一定含 leader 所具有的那種內在的讓人自願服從的能力。

Cf. The Editors of The Reader's Digest, *Use the Right Word*, The Reader's Digest Association Proprietary Ltd. (1971), at Ps. 58—59.

Bounds ▸ Confines ▸ Limit

以上三者均有界限的含義。bounds可用作比喻，指超過某種界限，如 His impudence exceeds all bounds；片語 out of bounds 常作軍事用語，指禁止某人進入某一區域；此外，其還可用於指一片土地之邊界[①]。confines 常等同 bonds，也指某種界限，也常用作比喻，相比較，它與地理或區域因素的聯繫更少一些[②]。limit 為通用詞，幾乎可指任何界限或分界[③]，如 to pass beyond the city limits。

[②]

① "As a noun, it denotes a limit or boundary, or a line inclosing or marking off a tract of land." The Publisher's Editorial Staff, *Black's Law Dictionary*, Abridged 6th Edition, West Publishing Co. (1991), at P. 128.

② "Confines, like bounds, defines the extent of an area without reference to what lies beyond, but confine is less consistently restricted to the description of geographical limits." Cf. Laurence Urdang, *The Dictionary of Confusable Words*, Facts on File Publications (1988), at P. 61.

③ "Point at which something ends or point where you can go no further." Cf. P. H. Collin, *Dictionary of Law*, 2nd Edition, Peter Collin Publishing (1993), at P. 323.

Brand ▸ Tradmark ▸ Trade name

以上單詞和片語均用作指商業、商品或服務的名稱,但它們並非同義(儘管有些人把它們都當作「商標」)。差異在於 brand(品牌)主要指已經樹立的,經常是著名的且用於廣告的商品名稱,其不是正式的法律術語,一般不具備法律上的排他權[①]。brand mark 或 brand name 爲「商品商標」,常指同一企業生產或銷售的一系列產品或提供的服務的名稱,如「長虹」便是 the brand name of a line of household appliances。與 brand 相比較,trademark(商標)爲典型的法律術語,表示經登記註冊之商標,具有排他權,未經同意使用則構成侵權,其可以是詞語、符號等,爲製造商或商人所採用以將自己的商品與他人的商品加以區別[②]。trade name(商號)是指用於區分業務或職業的名字或標記,有時也可當作商標使用,與 trademark 一樣,其也受到法律的保護,其多用於表示經營某種業務的公司、企業、團體等實體的名稱的區分等[③]。

注

① "A word, mark, symbol, design, term, or a combination of these, both visual and oral, used for the purpose of identification of some product or service." Cf. The Publisher's Editorial Staff, *Black's Law Dictionary*, Abridged 6th Edition, West Publishing Co. (1991), at P. 130.

② "A word, phrase, logo, or other graphic symbol used by a manufacturer or seller to distinguish its product or products from those of others." Cf. Bryan A. Garner, *Black's Law Dictionary*, 7th Edition, West Group (1999), at P. 1500.

③ "a name or mark that is used by a person (as an individual proprietor or a corporation) to identify that person's business or vocation and that may also be used as trademark or service mark. Like a trademark or service mark, a trade name is protected by law against infringement." Cf. Linda Picard Wood, J.D., *Merriam Webster's Dictionary of Law*, Merriam-Webster, Incorporated (1996), at P. 499.

Broker ▸ Intermediary ▸ Jobber ▸ Finder ▸ Middleman

這些單詞均有「中間人」或「居間人」的含義，但各自有一些差異。其中，broker 爲「經紀人」，主要是指以收取傭金（commission）爲目的而代表他人直接參加談判、議價、進行買賣交易者，故其更接近買賣代理人的含義，其可參與多種交易，如不動產買賣、證券、股票交易等[①]。intermediary 爲「居間人」或「調停人」，主要是指在分歧雙方或談判雙方之間進行斡旋，起聯繫或談判作用者[②]。jobber 主要是指商品買賣交易中的中間人[③]。finder 則是指爲他人尋找商機或介紹客戶且因此而領取傭金者，但他卻不直接參與交易談判或運作[④]。middleman 所包括的含義較廣，其可指僅將當事人撮合一塊兒讓他們自己簽約者，也可具有 broker、jobber 或 intermediary 等的含義[⑤]。

注

① "a person or entity that puts together a buyer and seller of property or services, acting as an agent for one or both of the parties and taking a commission on the transaction. Examples include a broker who arranges insurance coverage for people or companies, a broker who arranges sales of real property, an a broker who arranges purchases and sales of stocks and bond." Cf. James E. Clapp, *Random House Webster's Dictionary of the Law*, Random House, New York (2000), at P. 64.

② "A mediator or go-between; a third party negotiator." Cf. Bryan A. Garner, *Black's Law Dictionary*, 7th Edition, West Group (1999), at P. 820.

③ "Someone who buys and sells goods wholesale and handles goods on commission." Cf. G. H. L. Fridman, *Sales of Goods in Canada*, 3rd Edition, Toronto, Carswell (1986), at P. 493.

④ "An intermediary who contracts to find, introduce and bring together parties to a business opportunity, leaving ultimate negotiations and consummation of business transaction to the principals." The Publisher's Editorial Staff, *Black's Law Dictionary*, Abridged 6th Edition, West Publishing Co. (1991), at P. 437.

⑤ "An agent between two parties; an intermediary who performs the office of a broker or factor between a seller and buyer, producer and consumer, land-owner and tenant, etc." *Id.* at P. 685.

Bull ▸ Signature ▸ Brief

三個單詞在宗教法上均有教皇的命令或通告的含義。其中，bull 是指「教皇詔書」，其因文書上的鉛印印記而得名，最常用於法律 事項①。brief 所指的文書的級別一般要低於 bull，蓋教皇戒指印鑒， 在宗教法中稱爲「教皇通諭」或「教廷通牒」②。signature 爲「教皇 手諭」，或許是因其是以簽名而非蓋印而得名。

注

① "In ecclesiastical law, an instrument granted by the Pope of Rome, and sealed with a seal of lead, containing some decree, commandment, or other public act, emanating from the pontiff. Bull, in this sense, corresponds with edict, or letters patent from other governments.

There are three kinds of apostolical rescripts: the brief, the signature, and the bull; which last is most commonly used in legal matters." The Publisher's Editorial Staff, *Black's Law Dictionary*, 5th Edition, West Publishing Co. (1979), at P. 177.

② "a papal letter that is less formal than a bull and is signed by the secretary of briefs and sealed with a pope's ring", Cf. Philip Babcock Gove, Ph.D., *Webster's Third New International Dictionary*, G&C Merriam Company, Publishers (1971), at P. 277.

Burden of proof ▸ Burden of production ▸ Burden of persuasion

以上片語均和當事人對證據的責任相關，以往不少人將它們都籠統譯爲「舉證責任」，其實，在英美法中，它們原本是有一定差異的。事實上，burden of proof 應爲「證明責任」（也稱爲 *onus probandi*），其包含有 burden of production 和 burden of persuasion 兩術語的含義，即既「舉證」又「說服」。此便是當事人必須承擔的用證據證明指控或斷言的眞實性的責任；廣義上講，其也等同 burden of persuasion①。而 burden of production 則是「證明責任」的一部分，爲「舉證責任」，指當事人必須就訴爭問題提供充足證據以供事實裁定人作出正確裁決②，其也稱爲 burden of going forward with evidence、burden of producing evidence、production burden 或 degree of proof。而 burden of persuasion 也是「證明責任」的一部分，其爲「說服責任」，指當事人應說服事實裁定人相信自己所舉事實的責任③，其也稱爲 persuasion burden、risk of non-persuasion、risk of jury doubt；廣義上講，其也可等於 burden of proof。

注

① "A party's duty to prove a disputed assertion or charge. The burden of proof includes both the burden of persuasion and the burden of production." Cf. Bryan A. Garner, *Black's Law Dictionary*, 7th Edition, West Group (1999), at P. 190.

② "the requirement that a party to a case introduce evidence to support a claim or defense in order to have that issue considered by the judge or jury", Cf. James E. Clapp, *Random House Webster's Dictionary of the Law*, Random House, New York (2000), at P. 64.

③ "A party's duty to convince the fact-finder to view the facts in a way that favors that party. In civil cases, the plaintiff's burden is usu. by a preponderance of the evidence, while in criminal cases the prosecution's burden is beyond a reasonable doubt." Cf. Bryan A. Garner, *Black's Law Dictionary*, 7th Edition, West Group (1999), at P. 190.

Business company ▸ Business corporation ▸ Business firm

上述片語都是有關公司的術語，它們所指的公司性質十分廣泛，其包括所有爲營利目的而設立的公司或實體，包括法律、新聞、印刷、娛樂、金融等各業，因而不能簡單譯爲商業（商業公司應爲 commercial company/corporation）或貿易公司（貿易公司應爲 trading company/corporation），而應爲「商事公司」①。business corporation 除作「商事公司」講解外，還用作指「企業法人」，即從事生產經營，以創造社會財富，擴大社會積累，以營利爲目的的法人，如工廠、商店、各種生產經營、服務性的合作組織、公司等。其與非生產性、非營利性的「非企業法人」（non-profit corporation 或 not-for-profit corporation[2]）相對。business firm 則主要指性質屬於合夥的商事公司或商事企業（參見 company 與 firm 之區別）。

注

① "Business corporation: One formed for the purpose of transacting business in the widest sense of that term, including not only trade and commerce, but manufacturing, mining, banking, insurance, transportation, and practically every form of commercial or industrial activity where the purpose of the organization is pecuniary profit; contrasted with religious, charitable, educational, and other like organizations, which are sometimes grouped in the statutory law of a state under the general designation of corporation not for profit." Cf. The Publisher's Editorial Staff, *Black's Law Dictionary*, Abridged 6th Edition, West Publishing Co. (1991), at P. 237.

② "A corporation organized for some purpose other than making a profit, and usu. afforded special tax treatment." Cf. Bryan A. Garner, *Black's Law Dictionary*, 7th Edition, West Group (1999), at P. 343.

Buy ▸ Purchase

　　二者均有「購買」的含義。buy 爲通用詞，不甚正式，但可適用於幾乎所有的買賣交易①。相比之下，purchase 更正式，常指數量較大，且在較好的商店所進行的購買活動；此外，不動產交易一般都使用 purchase②。

注

① "As a verb, buy is the ordinary word, purchase the more formal word." Cf. Robert Hendrickson, *Business Talk*, (1984), at P. 61.

② "Traditionally, however, purchase has been the proper word for real property." Cf. Bryan A. Garner, *A Dictionary of Modern Legal Usage*, 2nd Edition, Oxford University Press (1995), at P. 125.

C

Cadaver ▸ Corpse

兩單詞均有「屍體」的含義。區別僅在於前者爲美式英語，後者則爲英國人通用。

注

"cadaver: US dead body. Note: GB English is corpse", Cf. P. H. Collin, *Dictionary of Law*, 2nd Edition, Peter Collin Publishing (1993), at P. 71.

Calendar call ▸ Trial calendar

以上兩片語均與審判日程安排相關。calendar call 指法庭舉行的安排備審案件的審判日程的會議，故爲「審判日程安排會」[1]；而 trial calendar 則是指經會議決定的法院所有的「待審案件的日程安排表」，也稱爲 docket、court calendar 或 cause list[2]。

注

[1] "A court session given to calling the cases awaiting trial to determine the present status of each case and commonly to assign a date for trial." Cf. The Publisher's Editorial Staff, *Black's Law Dictionary*, Abridged 6th Edition (1991), at P. 140.

[2] "Comprehensive list of cases awaiting trial and containing the dates for trial, names of counsel, expected time required for trial, etc." *Id.* at P. 1046; "A schedule of pending cases." Cf. Bryan A. Garner, *Black's Law Dictionary*, 7th Edition, West Group (1999), at P. 495.

Canon law ▸ Ecclesiastical law

二者均與宗教或寺院相關，但它們之間卻有一定的差異。canon law 範圍較窄，只有兩含義，一是指「教會法」，尤指 12 至 14 世紀編纂的羅馬天主教教會法，以及其他基督教教派的教會法，主要有關寺院的內部規則（internal rules of the Roman Catholic Church, or a similar body of religious rules in certain other Christian denominations），其也稱為 *corpus juris*、*canonici*、papal law 或 *jus canonicum*；二是指「寺院法」，指某特定宗教所發展起來的一整套規則法律[①]，其也稱為 church law 或 canonical law。相比之下，ecclesiastical law 的含義較寬[②]，涉及所有有關寺院的法律，其除有「寺院法」的含義，即有關特定教派的學說、原則等的法律外，還指「宗教法」，即指英國法律史上有關寺院具有管轄權事項之法律，其包括結婚、離婚、遺囑（marriage, divorce, will）等，到 19 世紀，這些事項被移交到民事法院管轄（transferred to the jurisdiction of the civil courts），在這種意義上，其也被稱為 *jus ecclesiasticum* 或 law spiritual。

注

① Cf. Bryan A. Garner, *Black's Law Dictionary*, 7th Edition, West Group (1999), at P. 198.

② "Although these generic terms overlap a great deal, ecclesiastical law broadly covers all laws relating to a church, whether from state law, divine law, natural law, or societal rules; canon law is more restricted, referring only to the body of law constituted by ecclesiastical authority for the organization and governance of a Christian church." Cf. Bryan A. Garner, *A Dictionary of Modern Legal Usage*, 2nd Edition, Oxford University Press (1995), at P. 303.

Careless driving ▸ Reckless driving

二者均有在駕駛機動車過程中沒有盡到應有的注意和小心的含義。其區別在於 careless driving 僅為一種較輕微的過失，故為「疏忽駕駛」①。而 reckless driving 則較嚴重，可能對他人生命、安全或權利造成實質性和不公正的危險，且有時還帶故意和放肆，其為一種刑事犯罪，故為「莽撞駕駛機動車輛罪」②。

注

① "Driving a vehicle on a highway without due care and attention or without reasonable consideration for other person using the highway." Cf. *The Highway Traffic Act*, (Canada) S.M. 1985—1986, c. 3, s. 188(1).

② "The criminal offense of operating a motor vehicle in a manner that shows conscious indifference to the safety of others." Cf. Bryan A. Garner, *Black's Law Dictionary*, 7th Edition, West Group (1999), at P. 1277.

Case law ▸ Common law

二者均可譯為「判例法」，但實際上它們卻有一定區別。嚴格地講，case law（也稱為 decisional law、adjudicative law、jurisprudence 或 organic law）包括法官解釋制定法時所創制的新規則（new rules）和司法判決（judicial decisions）兩部分內容。而 common law 則多在與制定法（statute）相對時可譯為「判例法」，但其只包括司法判決（court decision）部分而不包括法官解釋制定法時所創制的新規則部分①。故可以說 case law 是在 common law 基礎上發展起來的，其內容比 common law 的含義更廣②。此外，最初與

「專門法」special law 相對而得名的 common law 在不同的場合和不同對象面前還有另外一些譯法，如在與 written law（成文法）相對時，common law 多譯爲「不成文法」；與 civil law（大陸法）相對時，common law 譯爲「英美法」；與 equitable law（衡平法）相對時，其爲「普通法」。

注

① "Strictly speaking, the term *common law* is confined to rules which have been developed entirely by judicial decisions. It excluded new rules made by judges when they interpret statutes. The term case law covers both kinds of new rules." Cf. Li Rong-fu/Song Lei, *A Course Book of Legal English*, *judge-made law*, Law Press, China (1999), at P. 23.

② "Case law is a development of the common law brought about through the process of time." Cf. Li Rong-fu/Song Lei, *A Course Book of Legal English*, *Bases of Legal system*, Law Press, China (1999), at P. 9.

Casebook ► Hornbook

二者均指英、美等國家法學院所使用的法學教科書。casebook 爲「案例選編」或「判例教科書」，指一種包含法院主要判例及其評論和說明，以供學生學習討論的教科書，收集的多爲上訴法院判例，且有作者注釋①。而 hornbook 則爲「法學基礎」或「法學基礎理論教科書」，主要包含某領域法律的基本原則或學說（rudimentary principles or doctrines of an area of law）②。同理，casebook method和hornbook method的區別也在於前者爲「判例教學法」，也稱爲 case method、case system 以及 Langdell method，主要在英美法系國家流行；而後者則是以法學原理和學說爲主的「法學基礎理論教學法」，也稱爲 lecture method，主要在大陸法系國家使用，且主要集中於諸如程序法或證據法等法律領域之教學③。

注

① "Type of book used in law school containing text of leading court decisions in particular field of law (e.g., contracts, torts), together with commentary and other features useful for class discussion and further understanding of subject as prepared by author." Cf. The Publisher's Editorial Staff, *Black's Law Dictionary*, Abridged 6th Edition (1991), at P. 148.

② "A book explaining the basic, fundamentals or rudiments of any science or branch of knowledge. The phrase hornbook law is a colloquial designation of the rudiments or general principles of law." *Id.* at P. 507.

③ "The hornbook method predominates in civil-law countries, and in certain fields of law, such as procedure and evidence." Cf. Bryan A. Garner, *Black's Law Dictionary*, 7th Edition, West Group (1999), at P. 742.

Charge ▶ Mortgage ▶ Pledge ▶ Lien ▶ Hypothecation

以上各個單詞均有債務人將其財產作抵押擔保的含義。在英美法中，擔保（security）包括人的擔保（personal security）和物的擔保（real security）兩種。其中物的擔保可分爲三種類型：一爲由債權人取得對擔保物的所有權，而不依賴於對物的占有的擔保；二是債權人不享有對擔保物的所有權，但依賴於對物的占有的擔保；三是既不依賴取得對物的所有權，也不依賴對物的占有的擔保。屬於第一種類型的擔保爲 mortgage（按揭）；屬於第二種類型的擔保有

pledge（質押）和lien（留置）；屬於第三種類型的擔保有 charge 和 hypothecation。charge 和 mortgage 經常用於不動產的擔保中，它們在實務上儘管區別不大，但在理論上，尤其是房地產抵押上仍存在較大差異。charge 是指房地產所有者將某些權益賦予債權人，作為償還債務或履行責任的擔保，一旦抵押人無力償還債務或履行責任，債權人即可行使這些權益，處置該抵押的房地產以獲得清償。charge 包括的範圍很廣，涉及所有土地負擔[①]，有時在實施時不涉及房地產所有權的權益，而只是賦予債權人對房地產的某些權益，包括占有權益，故此時 charge 等同大陸法系中的「抵押」，當然也有人主張將其譯為「財產負擔」。而 mortgage 在香港則被譯為「按揭」，指房地產按揭人將其房地產的產權（業權）移轉給債權人，作為償還債務的擔保，但實際占有權卻仍然為債務人所有。在按揭期間，債權人即成為按揭房地產的產權所有人，如債務人不履行債務或有其他違約行為，債權人可以按按揭房地產所有權人的名義起訴，取消按揭人的回贖權，從而取得按揭房地產的包括占有權在內的絕對產權（title）[②]。過去中國大陸多將 mortgage 譯為抵押，但鑒於該單詞的內涵與大陸法系的抵押含義有一定差異，且目前中國大陸已開始使用「按揭」這個術語（儘管從法的角度上看，內地現仍從大陸法系的抵押觀念來認識按揭），從翻譯角度上講，筆者認為最好能將 mortgage 翻譯為「按揭」。pledge 為「質押」或「質權」，指動產（包括代表無形財產產權的證券等）的占有權而非所有權因債務擔保的轉移[③]。而 lien 則為「留置」，多指在商業領域，根據雙方協定尤其是依據法律產生的對貨物（goods）的一種擔保物權（security interest），以迫使對方清償債務或履行其他義務[④]。hypothecation 來源於羅馬法中的 hypotheca，債權人通常不實際占有抵押物或其產權（title）[⑤]，在英美法中，其常用作指海商法中的船隻或貨物的「抵押」。

① "Includes every encumbrance on land given for the purpose of securing the payment of a debt or the performance of an obligation." *Court Order Enforcement Act*, R.S.B.C. 1979, c. 75. s. 42.

② "A legal transfer of ownership but not possession of property from a debtor to a creditor. The transfer becomes void upon payment of the debt for which the property has been put up for security. Thus, certain property is conditionally transferred when a debt is incurred, but ownership is regained upon completion of all obligations." Cf. John P. Wiedemer, *Real Estate Finance*, 3rd Edition, Reston Publishing, Reston, Va. (1980).

③ "a deposition of personal property, or of document (such as stock certificates) representing intangible property, with a lender or other person as a security for a loan or other obligation", Cf. James E. Clapp, *Random House Webster's Dictionary of the Law*, Random House, New York (2000), at P. 331.

④ "a charge or encumbrance upon property for the satisfaction of a debt or other duty that is created by agreement of the parties or esp. by operation of law", Cf. Linda Picard Wood, J.D., *Merriam Webster's Dictionary of Law*, Merriam-Webster, Incorporated (1996), at P. 294.

⑤ "Generally, there is no physical transfer of the pledged property to the lender, nor is the lender given title to the property; though he has the right to sell the pledged property upon default." Cf. The Publisher's Editorial Staff, *Black's Law Dictionary*, Abridged 6th Edition (1991), at P. 510.

Charter ▶ Articles of association
▶ Certificate of incorporation ▶ Articles of amendment
▶ Memorandum of association ▶ By-laws

　　上述單詞或片語均有公司「章程」的含義。對於這些術語，美國與英國和加拿大等國的用法有一定差異。如在美國，articles of association（在許多州也稱爲 articles of incorporation）爲公司的「組織大綱」或「公司簡章」，一般是指組建公司時向有關政府當局提交的公司簡章，其內容簡單，通常只包括公司名稱、公司存在的時間、經營目的、股份數額、股票種類、董事姓名地址等內容①。而在公司被批准成立後，公司內部管理等許多具體事項則由 by-laws 或 articles of amendment 予以規定，故 by-laws 和 articles of amendment 在美國即等同「公司章程細則」或「公司內部管理規章」②（在英國或加拿大等，articles of amendment 指「更改公司體制之規章」③）。儘管 by-laws 或 articles of amendment 也是按州法規定制定，但它們卻是另外的獨立的文件。在英國及加拿大等地，articles of association 則指含公司章程細則或內部管理規則④；而 memorandum of association 則等同組建公司時向有關部門提交的公司簡章⑤。certificate of incorporation 在美國有些州也用作指公司章程，但其多用於不發行股票的公益公司或慈善公司⑥。charter（也稱爲 corporate charter）也可用作指章程，它和 articles of association 的區別在於它是指經君主或立法機關特許成立（未作爲公司登記註冊）的公司的章程，如英國原先的「東印度公司」（East Indian Company）的章程等⑦。相比之下，中國的一般公司的章程是將公司組織大綱或簡章和章程細則（或內部管理規章）合併組成的一個文件，統稱爲「公司章程」，因而，中國意義上的「公司章程」實際上等同於 articles of association 加上 by-laws。故筆者認爲，按美式英語，中國公司的「公司章程」的準確翻譯應爲：Articles of Association & By-laws；按英式英語，其應爲：Memorandum of Association & Articles of Association。

① Cf. Attorney Anthony Mancuso, *How to Form Your Own California Corporation*, 8ᵗʰ Edition, at Appendix, Nolo Press, Berkeley (1994); "Basic instrument filed with the appropriate governmental agency on the incorporation of a business. It sets forth the purposes of the corporation, its duration, the rights and liabilities of the shareholders and directors, classes of stock, etc." Cf. The Publisher's Editorial Staff, *Black's Law Dictionary*, Abridged 6ᵗʰ Edition (1991), at P. 74.

② "A rule of administrative provision adopted by an association or corporation for its internal governance. Corporate by-laws are usu. enacted apart from the articles of association." Cf. Bryan A. Garner, *Black's Law Dictionary*, 7ᵗʰ Edition, West Group (1999), at P. 193; "Terms and conditions of corporate management enacted subsequent to articles of incorporation." Cf. The Publisher's Editorial Staff, *Black's Law Dictionary*, Abridged 6ᵗʰ Edition (1991), at P. 73.

③ "A document which changes the capital structure or the constitution of a company and is ordinarily authorized by a special resolution of the shareholders." Cf. H. Sutherland, D. B. Horsley & J. M. Edmiston, eds, *Franser's Handbook on Canadian Company Law*, 7ᵗʰ Edition, Toronto, Carswell (1985), at P. 453.

④ "articles of association or U.S. articles of incorporation = document which regulates the way in which a company's affairs are managed", Cf. P. H. Collin, *Dictionary of Law*, 2ⁿᵈ Edition, Peter Collin Publishing (1993), at P. 32.

⑤ "legal document setting up a limited company and giving details of its aims, capital structure, and registered office", *Id.* at P. 346.

⑥ "in some states, same as articles of association", Cf. James E. Clapp, *Random House Webster's Dictionary of the Law*, Random House, New York (2000), at P. 74.

⑦ "a certificate of incorporation or other documents issued by the state granting corporate status to an entity", *Id.* at P. 78; "document from the Crown establishing a town or a corporation or a university or a company", Cf. P. H. Collin, *Dictionary of Law*, 2nd Edition, Peter Collin Publishing (1993), at P. 86.

Civil court ▸ Civil custody ▸ Civil prison ▸ Civil prisoner

首先應注意的是 civil court，該片語除在英、美等國指「民事法院」①外，在其他地區，如在加拿大，它可用作指具有一般管轄權（包括具有簡易審判程序）的刑事法院，其與民事無任何關係，civil 在此等同 ordinary②，故應譯為「普通刑事法院」。同樣，civil custody 也是指警方或其他相關民政當局「對一般罪犯所作的拘留或關押」（普通監獄"civil prison"或教養所"penitentiary"的關押均包括在內）③。civil prison 則可指任何關押由普通刑事法院（civil court）經簡易審判程序（summary procedure）審判的罪行較輕，刑期在 2 年以下罪犯之監獄（包括 jail 和其他場所），故為「普通監獄」④。由此可知，civil prisoner 則是指由 civil court 所判處的被 civil prison 關押的刑期為 2 年以下的「普通服刑犯」。對於 civil prisoner 而言，《英漢法律詞典》的新版本更正了其第一版將該術語譯為「民事犯」之謬誤，將其譯為了「普通犯」⑤，然而該詞典援引的《法窗譯話》之解釋，即「普通犯」是「與政治犯、國事犯、軍事犯、戰犯等對稱時用」的解釋卻仍然為一謬誤，這裡的「普通」兩字，實則應為「罪行較輕」的含義。

注

① "A court with jurisdiction over non-criminal cases." Cf. Bryan A. Garner, *Black's Law Dictionary*, 7th Edition, West Group (1999), at P. 357.

② "A court of ordinary criminal jurisdiction in Canada and includes a court of summary jurisdiction." Cf. Daphne Dukelow, *The Dictionary of Canadian Law*, Thomson Professional Publishing Canada (1991), at P. 162.

③ "The holding under arrest or in confinement of a person by the police or other competent civil authority, and includes confinement in a penitentiary or civil prison." *Id*. at P. 162.

④ "Any prison, jail or other place in Canada in which offenders sentenced by a civil court in Canada to imprisonment for less than two years can be confined, and, if sentenced outside Canada, any prison, jail or other place in which a person, sentenced to that term of imprisonment by a court having jurisdiction in the place where the sentence was passed, can for the time being be confined." Cf. *Canada National Defense Act*, R.S.C. 1985, c. N.5, s. 2.

⑤ Cf.《英漢法律詞典》，Revised Edition，法律出版社（1999），第 131 頁。

Commencement

該單詞可用作指「訴訟的開始」。按美國《聯邦民事訴訟法典》的規定，民事訴訟多以向法院提交 complaint 開始①；而在英國高等法院則以收到 statement of claim 開始。在美國，刑事訴訟（criminal action）多從向治安法官（magistrate）提交 preliminary complaint（自訴案件）或線人向其提交 information，且據此簽發逮捕令狀時算起。刑事起訴（指公訴）criminal prosecution 則以：⑴治安法官收到線人提交的檢舉狀（information）且簽發逮捕狀，或⑵大陪審團認定被告有罪且提交訴狀（indictment）時算作開始[2]。

注

① "Civil action in most jurisdictions is commenced by filling a complaint with the court." Cf. Fed. R. Civil P. 3.

② "Criminal action is commenced within statute of limitations at time preliminary complaint or information is filled with magistrate in good faith and a warrant issued thereon. A criminal prosecution is commenced 1) when information is laid before magistrate charging commission of crime, and a warrant of arrest is issued, or 2) when grand jury has returned an indictment." Cf. The Publisher's Editorial Staff, *Black's Law Dictionary*, Abridged 6th Edition (1991), at P. 183.

Commercial law ▸ Business law

二者均有「商法」的含義。二者之間的差別在於 commercial law 多指法院等實際實施的由立法機關頒布的法律[1]。而 business law 則指法學院所開設的課程名稱或學者們所進行的理論討論的法則[2]。如《商法雜誌》便多稱爲 Business Law Journal 而不是 Commercial Law Journal。

注

① "A phrase used-to designate the whole body of substantive jurisprudence applicable to the rights, intercourse, and relations of persons engaging in commerce, trade, or mercantile pursuits." Cf.

The Publisher's Editorial Staff, *Black's Law Dictionary*, Abridged 6th Edition (1991)，at P. 185.

② Cf. David M. Walker, *The Oxford Companion to Law*, Oxford University Press (1980), at P. 120.

Commission merchant ▸ Factor ▸ Merchandise broker

以上單詞或片語均有代理銷售商的含義。其中，factor 和 commission merchant 爲同義詞，均指實際或技術意義上占有他人商品或物品以供銷售，且常以自己的名義予以銷售，其應譯爲「代銷商」①。而 merchandise broker 則指權力有限，只負責商品銷售談判，不實際占有或控制商品者，其應譯爲「銷售經紀人」②。

注

① "One whose business is to receive and sell goods for a commission, being entrusted with the possession of the goods to be sold, and usually selling in his own name." Cf. The Publisher's Editorial Staff, *Black's Law Dictionary*, Abridged 6th Edition (1991), at P. 186.

② "One who negotiates the sale of merchandise without possessing it. A merchandise broker is an agent with very limited power." Cf. Bryan A. Garner, *Black's Law Dictionary*, 7th Edition, West Group (1999), at P. 188.

Commutation ▸ Good time

二者均有假釋的含義，差別在於 commutation 是法院判刑後，經行政機關命令削減懲罰。其與有條件特赦（conditional pardon）不同，它並未免除法律眼中的罪過，結果是其並不像特赦一樣起到恢復公民權利的作用[①]。good time 爲「因服刑表現好而假釋」，其與 commutation 的差異在於，commutation 所指的行政機關假釋並未以罪犯在監獄服刑的表現爲依據，而 good time 所指的假釋則是指監獄的獄政管理機構根據服刑人員的表現好壞決定的刑期縮減。美國目前的 good time 法規之規定一般如下，「根據假釋法規，監獄委員會可以依據罪犯在監獄的良好行爲而提前將其釋放出獄。一般說來，每良好服刑 1 個月便可減免幾天刑期。通常的程序是第一年行爲符合規範可假釋 1 個月，第二年可假釋 2 個月，以此類推，直到第六年及以後每服刑 1 年假釋 6 個月。由此，如表現良好，3 年刑期則可假釋爲 2 年零 6 個月；10 年徒刑可減爲 6 年零 3 個月。儘管是否假釋由一個監獄委員會裁定，但卻由立法機關決定假釋時間安排。」[②] good time 還可分爲幾種，除一般服刑人員稱爲的「法定假釋」（statutory good time）之外，在一些州的監獄，罪犯還可以透過非凡行爲獲得「業績假釋」（merit good time），以及參加監獄工廠勞動而得到「工業假釋」（industrial good time）[③]。

注

① "Commutation of sentence is a reduction of the penalty by executive order. Commutation differs from conditional pardon in that it does not wipe away guilt in the eyes of the law, and consequently does not restore civil rights as does a pardon. Massachusetts governors commuted to life imprisonment 50 percent of the death sentences imposed by juries and courts from 1947 to 1971." Cf. H. L. A. Hart, *Punishment and Responsibility*, Clarendon Press, 1982, at P. 89.

② "Under good-time laws a prison board may release prisoners before they have served their full sentences if they have maintained good conduct in prison. Generally, for every month of satisfactory conduct, a certain number of days is deducted from the inmate's sentence.

A usual procedure is to deduct one month from the first year of satisfactory conduct, two months for the second year, and so on, up to six months for the sixth and each succeeding year. A three-year sentence can thus be reduced to two years and six months by good behavior, a ten-year sentence can be reduced to six years and three months. A prison board determines whether or not the prisoner has earned the reduction in time, but the legislature makes the schedule of reductions in time. Granting "time off for good behavior" differs, in this respect, from commutation of sentence by executive order, in which the sentence is shortened because the inmate's behavior has been good, or for other reasons." *Id*. at P. 91.

③ In addition to "statutory good time," as the general system is called by inmates, prisoners in some states may earn"merit good time" for extraordinary behavior and "industrial good time" for participation in the prison industries. *Id*. at P. 91.

Companies act ▸ Company law ▸ Corporations act ▸ Corporation Law

四者均為「公司法」，但其用法有一些差別。一般說來，companies act用於指立法機關制定的一部具體法規①，如《英國公司法》（Companies Act of UK）等，此時 companies 為複數形式。而 company law 則用於泛指某國或某管轄區的所有有關公司法的法規、條例、慣例、案例等②（參見 act 與 law 的用法區別），此時 company 為單數形式。美國公司法中的「公司」一詞有時也用 corporation 來表示（更多時候用 corporate），但其規則也如上。具體法規多用 corporations act 表示（美國歷史上曾有過一部 Corporation Act，但它卻與公司法毫不相干，是美國歷史上即 1661

年的一部有關宣誓效忠的法規③），如《加利福尼亞州公司法》（Corporations Act of California），此時 corporation 習慣用複數形式；統稱時則為 corporation law（或corporate law），此時 corporation 習慣用單數形式。

注

① "Act of the British Parliament which states the legal limits within which a company may do business." Cf. P. H. Collin, *Dictionary of Law*, 2nd Edition, Peter Collin Publishing Ltd. (1993), at P. 279.

② "Laws which refer to the way companies may work." *Id*. at P. 109.

③ "Corporation Act: *Hist*. A 1661 English statute prohibiting the holding of public office by anyone who would not take the Anglican sacrament and the oaths of supremacy and allegiance." Cf. Bryan A. Garner, *Black's Law Dictionary*, 7th Edition, West Group (1999), at P. 345.

Company ▶ Corporation ▶ Firm

　　三個單詞均有「公司」的含義。鑒於在英國公司法被稱作 company law（參照 companies act），因此在英國，company 常用作指已經登記註冊的正式公司，包括大公司在內①。而在美國，公司法被稱作 corporate law 或 corporation law，因而美國人多視 corporation 為按公司法正式註冊登記成立的大公司，而視 company 為規模較小或不甚正式的公司②，故我們對 company 和 corporation 的理解應依照英、美兩國不同的國情而定。以往，firm 多指合夥企業或未按公司法規定的程序而正式成立的商事實體或企業③，其多不是具有完全法人資格的獨立實體，這在破產法上尤為重要，儘管現在其也常被用於指 company。

注

① "Any body corporate; A body corporate with share capital." Cf. Daphne A. Dukelow, *The Dictionary of Canadian Law*, Thomson Professional Publishing Canada (1991), at P. 186.

② "At common law, the technical term for an entity having a legal personality was corporation. The word company could refer to a partnership or other unincorporated association of persons." Cf. Bryan A. Garner, *A Dictionary of Modern Legal Usage*, 2nd Edition, Oxford University Press (1995), at P. 182.

③ "Traditionally, this term referred to a partnership, as opposed to a company. But today it is frequently used in reference to a company." Cf. Bryan A. Garner, *Black's Law Dictionary*, 7th Edition, West Group (1999), at P. 649.

Competence ▶ Competency

　　在法律英語中二者均有「能力」的含義。其區別在於 competence 是指「證人作證的能力或資格」，即 basic or minimal ability to testify①，如 competence of a witness。而 competency 則主要是指被告的精神承受能力，尤指刑事被告（criminal defendant）承受審判的能力（ability to stand trial），包括明白訴訟的含義，能正常與律師進行諮詢，並在辯護中起協助作用等②。

注

① "A basic or mental ability to do something; qualification, esp. to testify." Cf. Bryan A. Garner, *Black's Law Dictionary*, 7th Edition, West Group (1999), at P. 278.

② "The mental ability to understand problems and make decision; a criminal defendant's ability to stand trial, measured by the capacity to understand the proceedings, to consult meaningfully with counsel, and to assist in the defense." *Id*. at P. 278.

Composition ▶ Accord

　　二者均有和解性「債務償付協議」的含義。區別在於 accord 是債務人和一個債權人之間達成的清償部分債務之協定，用以避免訟爭①；而 composition 則是一債務人和所有或至少是大部分債權人之間所達成的協定②。

注

① "An agreement between two persons, one of whom has a right of action against the other to settle the dispute. In a debtor/creditor relationship, an agreement between the parties to settle a dispute for some partial payment." Cf. The Publisher's Editorial Staff, *Black's Law Dictionary*, Abridged 6th Edition (1991), at P. 10.

② "an agreement among a debtor and her creditors that each creditor will take less than the full amount owed so that the debtor will be able to pay at least some portion of the amount due to each creditor", Cf. James E. Clapp, *Random House Webster's Dictionary of the Law*, Random House, New York (2000), at P. 94.

Concurrent negligence ▶ Joint negligence ▶ Comparative negligence ▶ Contributory negligence

以上片語均為侵權法中的術語。concurrent negligence 為「並存過失」，指兩個或兩個以上侵權行爲人（被告）獨立（不一定同時）對一個受害人（原告）加害，造成同一傷害或損失而負有過失責任[1]。joint negligence 爲「共同過失」，其與 concurrent negligence 很相似，差別在於其是指兩個或兩個以上的侵權行爲人同時而非獨立加害而導致一個傷害之過失責任[2]。comparative negligence 爲「比較過失」或「相對過失」，主要用在賠償金的確認上，即按行爲人（被告）的過失大小決定其承擔的賠償金的比例，而受害人（原告）也會因其自身的過失而減少索賠所得[3]。contributory negligence 多爲「混合過失」或「與有過失」（現有不少英漢詞典將其當作「共同過失」，此純屬一種錯誤[4]），指傷害或損失是因加害人和受害人，即原告和被告共同責任所致[5]。目前美國很多州有關 contributory negligence 的法則已經被 comparative negligence 的法則所替代。

注

① "The negligence of two or more parties acting independently but causing the same damage."Cf. Bryan A. Garner, *Black's Law Dictionary*, 7th Edition, West Group (1999), at P. 1056.

② "The negligence of two or more persons acting together to cause an accident." *Id*. at 1057.

③ "the modern doctrine that as between a plaintiff and a defendant in a tort case, and sometimes as among several defendants, fault (and liability for damages) should be allocated in proportion to each party's contribution to the injury or loss complained", Cf. James E. Clapp, *Random House Webster's Dictionary of the Law*, Random House, New York (2000), at P. 297.

④ Cf. 《英漢法律詞典》，Revised Edition，法律出版社（1999），第 182 頁；陸谷孫，《英漢大詞典》，上海外文出版社

（1995），第 682 頁；陳慶柏等翻譯，《英漢雙解法律詞典》，世界圖書出版公司（1998），第 129 頁；《牛津法律大辭典》，光明日報出版社（(1983），第 207 頁。

⑤ "a negligence by a plaintiff contributing to the injury or loss that is the subject of a tort case, as when a plaintiff sues over an automobile accident that was primarily caused by the defendant but was also partly caused or made worse by inattentiveness on the part of the plaintiff", Cf. James E. Clapp, *Random House Webster's Dictionary of the Law*, Random House, New York (2000), at P. 297.

Confidential ▸ Private confidential ▸ Strict confidential

　　以上單詞或片語均可用作文件等封套上用語，表示文件的機密程度，其一般分為三等：即⑴機密（confidential），⑵極機密（private confidential），⑶絕對機密（strict confidential）。

注

Cf. Chen Bai-chu, *English-Chinese Business Dictionary*, 中國商業出版社 (1994), at P. 361.

Conflict of laws ▸ Private international law

　　二者都是國際法中的術語，均指不同國家私法之間的衝突。差別在於 conflict of law（法律衝突法）多為英美法系國家採用，尤其是美國，除指國家之間的法律衝突之外，還可用於指美國各州之間的法律衝突。private international law（國際私法）最初主要用於大陸法系國家，後才逐漸為英美法系國家普遍接受。

"In most countries conflict of laws is primarily a branch of international law, but because law in the United States is a patchwork of more than fifty independent legal systems, conflict-of-laws problems pervade all areas of American law." Cf. James E. Clapp, *Random House Webster's Dictionary of the Law*, Random House, New York (2000), at P. 99.

Conspirator ▸ Plotter

兩個單詞均有「陰謀者」的含義。差別在於 conspirator 多指參與一群人共同秘密進行的違法活動者，常用作指參與嚴重犯罪，特別是叛國罪者①。相比之下，儘管 plotter 所參與的活動的目的也陰險邪惡，且有時難於策劃和實施，但其性質總的說來較爲輕微②。

注

① "Conspirators are those who take part in a conspiracy, which is a legal term denoting an intention to violate the law by a group of people acting in concert; in general use, it is applied to major crimes and even more particularly to treason." Cf. The Editors of The Reader's Digest, *Use the Right Word*, The Reader's Digest Association Proprietary Ltd. (1971), at P. 3.

② "Plotters are implicated in an activity which has a sinister purpose, but which, even though it is difficult to plan and execute, may be petty in scope." *Id.* at P. 3.

Contempt ▸ Contumacy

在法律英語中，contempt 爲「藐視法庭罪」（也稱爲 contempt of court），指故意不服從法庭命令或有意干擾法庭程序的行爲[1]。藐視法庭罪一般分爲兩種，即「直接藐視」（direct contempt）和「推定藐視」（constructive contempt）〔也稱爲「間接藐視」（indirect contempt）〕[2]。直接藐視法庭是指在法庭上的言行冒犯，如咆哮公堂等，其也稱爲「刑事藐視」（criminal contempt）[3]（值得注意的是「刑事藐視」更多的是與 civil contempt 相對）。「推定藐視」或「間接藐視」法庭之行爲主要指不執行或拒絕服從合法的裁判[4]。以往推定藐視也被稱爲 consequential contempt，此術語現偶爾也還在使用[5]。藐視法庭罪也可分類爲「刑事藐視」（criminal contempt）〔也稱爲「普通法上的藐視法庭罪」（common-law contempt）〕和「民事藐視」（civil contempt）兩種[6]。刑事藐視是指不尊重法庭或阻撓審判工作的順利進行[7]；民事藐視是指拒不執行法院已生效的判決或裁定[8]。contumacy 也有藐視法庭的含義，其主要指拒不出庭或在法庭上不服從裁定或指示，拒不出庭的情況稱爲推定藐視法庭（行爲）（presumed contumacy），在法庭上不服從裁定或指示稱爲事實上的藐視法庭（行爲）（actual contumacy）[9]。

注

① "a judicial finding of willful disobedience of an order, or other willful disrupting the procedures of a court. Unless otherwise specified, contempt alone usually means contempt of court", Cf. James E. Clapp, *Random House Webster's Dictionary of the Law*, Random House (2000), at P. 103.

② "Contempts are, generally, of two kinds, direct and constructive." Cf. The Publisher's Editorial Staff, *Black's Law Dictionary*, Abridged 6th

Edition, West Publishing Co. (1991), at P. 221.

③ "Contempt that is committed in open court, as when a lawyer insults a judge on the bench." Cf. Bryan A. Garner, *Black's Law Dictionary*, 7th Edition, West Group (1999), at P. 313; "They are also called criminal contempts, but that term is better used in contrast with civil contempts." Cf. The Publisher's Editorial Staff, *Black's Law Dictionary*, Abridged 6th Edition, West Publishing Co. (1991), at P. 221.

④ "Contempt that is committed outside of court, as when a party disobeys a court order." Cf. Bryan A. Garner, *Black's Law Dictionary*, 7th Edition, West Group (1999), at P. 313.

⑤ "constructive contempts were formerly called consequential contempt, and this term is still in occasional use", Cf. The Publisher's Editorial Staff, *Black's Law Dictionary*, Abridged 6th Edition, West Publishing Co. (1991), at P. 221.

⑥ "Contempts are also classed as civil or criminal." *Id.* at P. 221.

⑦ "contempt consisting of conduct that disrupts or opposes the proceedings or power of the court", Cf. Linda Picard Wood, J.D., *Merriam Webster's Dictionary of Law*, Merriam-Webster, Incorporated (1996), at P. 101.

⑧ "The failure to obey a court order that was issued for another party's benefit." Cf. Bryan A. Garner, *Black's Law Dictionary*, 7th Edition, West Group (1999), at P. 313.

⑨ "Contempt of court ﹕ the refusal of a person to follow a court's order or direction." Cf. Bryan A. Garner, *Black's Law Dictionary*, 7th Edition, West Group (1999), at P. 331; "The refusal or intentional omission of a person who has been duly cited before a court to appear and defend the charge laid against, or, if he is duly before the court, to obey some lawful order or direction made in the cause. In the former case it is called *presumed* contumacy; in the latter, actual." Cf. The Publisher's Editorial Staff, *Black's Law Dictionary*, Abridged 6th Edition, West Publishing Co. (1991), at P. 221.

Convoy ▸ Escort

兩個單詞均有護送的含義。一般說來，convoy 是指對船隻的護航，其目的主要是保護船隻[①]。escort 的含義則較廣，除用作指保護性質的護衛外，還可以指禮儀上的護送，如新船處女航時其他船隻可 escort[②]。此外，在軍事行動中，convoy 多指水上護衛，而 escort 則多用於陸路護衛。

注

① "Ships of war sent by a country in wartime to escort and protect merchant ships which belong to that country." Cf. Daphne Dukelow, *The Dictionary of Canadian Law*, Thomson Professional Publishing Canada (1991), at P. 216.

② "one or more persons, vehicles, ships, etc. accompanying a person, vehicle, etc. esp. for protection or security or as a mark of rank or status", Cf. Della Thompson, *The Concise Oxford Dictionary*, 9th Edition, Oxford University Press (1995), at P. 460.

Cooling-off period ▸ Cooling time

二者的區別在於 cooling-off period（爭議緩和期）為民商法上的術語，指貨物銷售或罷工中，爭議雙方當事人所需進一步考慮或談判，從而不採取任何具體衝突行為之時間[①]。cooling time（神智平

息期）則爲刑法術語，常用作指情感受刺激或挑釁後的一種激情或
憤怒之平息時間，以對其行爲後果作正確判斷等②。《英漢雙解法律
詞典》③將他們列爲同義術語，說前者是英式英語，而後者爲美式英
語，此種說法是否正確，望讀者謹慎。

注

① "An opportunity to resile from a contract and cancel it within a
specified time period." Cf. G.H.I. Fridman, *Sale of Goods in Canada*,
3rd Edition, Toronto, Carswell (1986), at P. 492; "The time before a
strike or lock-out may begin." Cf. *Labor Management Regulation Act*,
s. 2.

② "time in which to become calm following provocation. If a court
finds that the cooling time was sufficient or reasonable, a defendant
may not use provocation to reduce a murder charge to involuntary
manslaughter", Cf. Linda Picard Wood, J.D., *Merriam Webster's
Dictionary of Law*, Merriam-Webster, Incorporated (1996), at P. 106.

③ 世界圖書出版社，第 132 頁。

Coroner ▸ Medical examiner

　　二者均有驗屍人員之含義。coroner 源於英格蘭，指一公共
官員，其可爲醫生、律師或其他司法人員，對因暴力或有疑義
之突然死亡原因進行調查（whose duty is to investigate the causes
and circumstances of any death that occurs suddenly, suspiciously, or
violently），以往幾乎所有的詞典均將 coroner 譯爲「驗屍官」①，
此種翻譯很不準確，首先，驗屍必定包括解剖屍體等，其必定是法
醫或至少是醫生的職責，但 coroner 多不是醫生；其次，coroner 的
責任也決非只是檢驗屍體②。故筆者建議將其譯爲「死因調查員」

（香港將其譯爲「死因裁判官」[③]），與其相應的 coroner's court 也就應爲「死因調查法庭」，而非以往的「驗屍官法庭」。medical examiner 也爲公共官員，負責對有疑點的死亡原因進行調查，包括決定是否必要進行屍檢等，故其才是「驗屍體官」[④]，美國很多州現已用 medical examiner 替代了 coroner[⑤]。

注

① Cf. 《英漢法律詞典》，Revised Edition，法律出版社（1999），第 187 頁；陸谷孫，《英漢大詞典》，上海外文出版社（1995），第 701 頁；陳慶柏等翻譯，《英漢雙解法律詞典》，世界圖書出版公司（1998），第 134 頁；《牛津法律大辭典》，光明日報出版社（1983），第 211 頁。

② "a public officer whose principal duty is to inquire by an inquest into the cause of death when there is reason to think the death may not be due to natural causes", Cf. Linda Picard Wood, J.D., *Merriam Webster's Dictionary of Law*, Merriam-Webster, Incorporated (1996), at P. 107.

③ Cf. 香港律政司，《英漢法律辭彙》，第三版，政府印務局（1998），第 222 頁。

④ "a public officer who determines the necessity of any conducts autopsies to find the cause of death", Cf. Linda Picard Wood, J.D., *Merriam Webster's Dictionary of Law*, Merriam-Webster, Incorporated (1996), at P. 310.

⑤ "Medical examiners have replaced coroners in many states." Cf. Bryan A. Garner, *Black's Law Dictionary*, 7th Edition, West Group (1999), at P. 996.

Corpse ▸ Cadaver

二者含義相同，都有「屍體」的含意。區別僅在於前者為英式英語，後者為美式英語。

注

"GB body of a dead person. Note: US English is cadaver." Cf. P. H. Collin, *Dictionary of Law*, 2nd Edition, Peter Collin Publishing Ltd. (1993), at P. 135.

Corroborating evidence ▸ Cumulative evidence

二者之間的區別在於 corroborating evidence（確認證據、認證證據）是指另外提供的一種獨立的、不同來源的附加證據，使得已經提供的證據更為有力和肯定[1]。而 cumulative evidence（複證、累積證據）則是指與已經提供的證據屬於同一類別，目的在於補充或增強前一證據力度的證據，或為加強各部分之間的可靠性的證據[2]。

注

① "Evidence supplementary to that already given and tending to strengthen or confirm it. Additional evidence of a different character to the same point. In some jurisdictions, corroborating evidence of an accomplice to the crime is given much weight." Cf. The Publisher's Editorial Staff, *Black's Law Dictionary*, Abridged 6th Edition, West Publishing Co. (1991), at P. 240.

② "Additional or corroborative evidence to the same point. That which goes to prove what has already been established by other evidence." *Id.* at P. 264.

Costs

該單詞可用作指「訴訟費」。在英、美等國，訴訟費主要包括兩種：(1)法院收取的各種開支和費用，包括立案費、陪審團費、庭審費用、判例彙編費等，也稱為「法庭費用」（court costs）[1]，這部分費用有些類似中國法律領域中所說的訴訟費、裁判費；(2)訴訟、刑事檢控或其他法律活動的開支費用，尤指經法院判決由一方當事人支付給另一方當事人的費用，也稱為「訴訟費用」（litigation costs）[2]，該部分費用在英美法系國家通行，而在中國法律中尚無規定。在西方，當人們說：the case was dismissed with costs 時，即表示「該案件被駁回，且敗訴方應向勝訴方支付訴訟費用」；而當人們說：the claim was dismissed without costs 時，則表示「訴訟主張雖然被駁回，但敗訴方不必向勝訴方支付訴訟費用」。按照 costs 評定和估算的方式，其可分為四類：即「評定訴訟費」（taxed costs）、「協定訴訟費」（agreed costs）、「估定訴訟費」（assessed costs）以及「規定訴訟費」（fixed costs）。總體說來，taxed costs 是最常用方式，而後三類應當屬於特殊情況（special cases）。taxed costs 是指「當事人有權得到的由法院的訴訟費評估官員所評估並批准的當事人在訴訟中所發生的開支費用」[3]。由於評定訴訟費的程序本身既費時又費錢（The taxation of costs is an expensive and time consuming process）[4]，所以不少律師轉而尋求由雙方當事人「協定訴訟費用」。但 agreed costs 的適用卻受到一定限制，如在涉及法律援助的案件或在有些涉及未成年人或精神病患者的訴訟中便不能適用此種方式[5]。除實際「評定」訴訟費之外，法院還可用大略「估定」的方式，確定一筆具體數額的費用判定給當事人。儘管估定的費用通常要比評定的費用少一些，但基於種種原因，尤其是兩者的差額也不會太懸殊，因而「估定訴訟費」在訴訟實踐中也不鮮見[6]。按規定，有些案件只能適用 fixed costs 而非 taxed costs，其中包括追索固定款額的不須進行事實審的案件（recovery of a liquidated sum without a trial），以及申請執行的案件（enforcement proceedings）[⑦]等。

注

① "The charges or fees taxed by the court, such as filing fees, jury fees, courthouse fees, and reporter fees. Also termed court costs." Cf. Bryan A. Garner, *Black's Law Dictionary*, 7th Edition, West Group (1999), at P. 350.

② "The expenses of litigation, prosecution, or other legal transaction, esp. those allowed in favor of one party against the other. Also termed litigation costs." *Id.* at P. 350.

③ "taxed costs, i.e. that part of the party's expenditure which is assessed and approved by the taxing officer of the court", Cf. (Brit.) *Rules of Supreme Court Order* 62, r. 3(4); *County Court Rules* 38, r. 1.

④ Cf. John O'Hare & Robert N. Hill, *Civil Litigation*, 5th Edition, Longman Group UK Ltd. (1990), at P. 530.

⑤ "This is not possible in legal aid cases or sometimes in cases involving minors and mental patients." *Id.* at P. 530.

⑥ "The amount given by way of assessed costs (the sum is assessed there and then at the hearing) will often less than that which could have been obtained on a taxation. Nevertheless, assessed costs are frequently encountered in practice in various reasons." *Id.* at P. 530.

⑦ *Id.* at P. 531.

Counterclaim ▸ Cross-claim ▸ Cross action

以上三者是各不相同但卻最容易混淆的法律術語，目前流行的很多詞典把它們都當作一個概念，即「反訴」對待，而事實上三者的含義差別極大。首先是 counterclaim 和 cross claim，它們的區別在於前者是指在同一訴訟中針對另一方當事人，即被告方對原告方提出的訴訟主張，故其應爲「反訴」，其也稱爲 counteraction、countersuit 或 cross-demand[①]。而後者則是指同一訴訟中的共同方當事人，即共同被告或共同原告之間相互所提出的訴訟主張，故其應爲「共同訴訟人之間的訴訟主張」或「交叉訴訟主張」而非「反訴」[②]。而 cross-action 的區別則在於該術語是指被告就同一有爭議的訴因對案件中的原告或共同被告所提出的另一獨立訴訟（separate action）[③]（此訴訟如在中國應當另案處理），故其也非「反訴」而應是「交叉訴訟」。

注

① "A defendant's assertion in the main action of a right or claim against the plaintiff." Cf. Daphne A. Dukelow, *The Dictionary of Canadian Law*, Thomson Professional Publishing Canada (1991), at P. 226; "a cause of action or claim for relief asserted by a defendant against the plaintiff in a civil case", Cf. James E. Clapp, *Random House Webster's Dictionary of the Law*, Random House (2000), at P. 112.

② "Cross claim: a claim or cause of action against one or more of the other defendants. For example, in a tort case against several people alleged to have harmed the plaintiff jointly, the defendants often assert cross-claims against each other, each claiming a right of contribution (要求對方分擔損失賠償) from the others. In rare cases, a cross-claim might be asserted by one plaintiff against another in the same case." Cf. James E. Clapp, *Random House Webster's Dictionary of the Law*, Random House (2000), at P. 119.

③ "An independent suit brought by defendant against plaintiff of co-defendant." Cf. The Publisher's Editorial Staff, *Black's Law*

Dictionary, Abridged 6th Edition, West Publishing Co. (1991), at P. 162; "an action brought by a defendant in an existing action against a plaintiff or co-defendant", Cf. Linda Picard Wood, J.D., *Merriam Webster's Dictionary of Law*, Merriam-Webster, Incorporated (1996), at P. 115.

Counterfoil ▸ Stub

二者均有票據存根的含義，區別僅在於前者為英式英語，後者為美式英語。

Cf. Della Thompson, *The Concise Oxford Dictionary*, 9th Edition, Oxford University Press (1995), at P. 306.

County court

英國目前的 county court（郡法院，其在美國被譯為「縣法院」）體制始建於 1846 年，其取代了舊有的郡法院和 court of request。現在英國共有 288 個郡法院，其管轄權受訴訟標的和地域的限制，如其能受理標的在 5,000 英鎊以下的契約和侵權案件，土地稅率在 1,000 英鎊以下的不動產占有案件，標的在 30,000 英鎊以下的衡平法案件。地域管轄權則依訴訟提起地或案由發生地而定。除正式審理案件的法官外，county court 中負責處理訴訟中期事項的司法官員（judicial officials in charge of interlocutory matters）有 circuit judge（巡迴法官）和 registrar（司法常務官）兩種。前者由 Lord Chancellor 任命，同時也在 Crown Court 中任職，其可從具有 10 年律師資格的巴律師或從任律師 10 年且任過 3 年 recorder（「特委法官」，即 Crown Court 的業餘法官）的沙律師中挑選；後者則從具有 7 年律師經歷的沙律師中挑選，其職權主要在於處理訴訟中期請求、小額案件、破產、離婚或海事等訴爭，其判決和命令可向法官上訴或由法官復審。此外，郡法院的 chief clerk（總書記員）主要處理各種行政管理事務，如傳票和文件的送達安排，命令起草和監督其簽署等；bailiff 則主要負責送達傳票和簽署判決書和命令等。

注

Cf. John O'Hare & Robert N. Hill, *Civil Litigation, Introduction*, Longman Group UK Ltd. (1990).

Courts in England & Wales

英格蘭和威爾士的司法機構有 (the) county court、the magistrates' court、the high court、the crown court、the court of appeal、the house of lords、the privy council、the European Court of Justice、industrial tribunals 和 courts-martial 等。

其中，the magistrates' court（也稱為 court of petty sessions 或 court of summary jurisdiction）為「治安法院」，有對刑事案件和民事案件的初審管轄權，適用普通法或制定法，負責審理輕罪、收養、親子關係確認、扶（撫）養、監護、家庭暴力、特許等事宜[1]。the county court 為「郡法院」，負責審理標的在 5,000 英鎊之內的地方民事案件[2]。the high court（也稱為 high court of justice）為「高等法院」，為英國最高法院組成部分，是英格蘭和威爾士的主要民事法院，其分為 3 個庭：王座法庭、大法官法庭、家事法庭，負責受理標的在 5,000 英鎊以上的民事案件[3]。the crown court 為「刑事法院」，也是最高法院的組成部分，為郡法院之上的高級刑事法院，負責巡迴審理重大刑事案件，此外還有有限的民事上訴管轄權[4]。

the court of appeal 爲「上訴法院」，也是最高司法法院組成部分，分民事和刑事兩庭，各負責受理來自高等法院、郡法院之民事案件的上訴以及來自刑事法院的刑事案件之上訴⑤。the house of lords 爲「上議院」，是國家的最高上訴法院，受理來自上訴法院的民事案件的上訴，對某些重大案件也有初審權⑥。the privy council 爲「樞密院」，其實是指 judicial committee of the Privy Council（樞密院司法委員會），其負責受理英格蘭和威爾士的某些上訴和來自大英國協國家的上訴⑦。the European Court of Justice 爲「歐洲法院」，負責審理與歐洲共同體立法事項之上訴⑧。此外，英國還有 industrial tribunals（勞資爭議法庭）和 courts martial（軍事法庭），它們均屬專門法庭，前者負責有關就業問題的爭議⑨，後者負責審理違反軍紀的案件⑩。

注

① "A court with limited jurisdiction over minor criminal and civil matters." Cf. Bryan A. Garner, *Black's Law Dictionary*, 7th Edition, West Group (1999), at P. 359.

② "One of the types of court set up in England and Wales which bears local civil cases." Cf. P. H. Collin, *Dictionary of Law*, 2nd Edition, Peter Collin Publishing Ltd. (1993), at P. 139.

③ "main civil court in England and Wales", *Id.* at P. 258.

④ "court, above the level of the magistrates' court, which has centers all over England and Wales and which bears criminal cases", *Id.* at P. 147.

⑤ Cf. David M. Walker, *The Oxford Companion to Law*, Oxford University Press (1980), at P. 219.

⑥ "The upper chamber of the British Parliament, of which, the 11-member judicial committee provides judges who serve as the final court of appeal in most civil cases." Cf. Bryan A. Garner, *Black's Law*

Dictionary, 7th Edition, West Group (1999), at P. 744.

⑦ "an appeal court for appeals from courts outside the UK, such as the courts of some Commonwealth countries", Cf. P. H. Collin, *Dictionary of Law*, 2nd Edition, Peter Collin Publishing Ltd. (1993), at P. 430.

⑧ "court responsible for settling disputes relating to European Community law, and also acting as a last Court of Appeal against laws in individual countries", *Id.* at P. 204.

⑨ "court which decides in disputes between employers and trade unions", *Id.* at P. 276.

⑩ "courts which tries someone serving in the armed forces for offenses against military discipline", *Id.* at P. 141.

Court of appeals ▶ Supreme court

在美國，court of appeals（在有些州也稱爲 court of appeal）可指聯邦中級法院或州中級法院①。如在加州和路易斯安那州，其是指中級法院，這些州的高級法院稱爲 supreme court；而在哥倫比亞特區、馬里蘭和紐約州，court of appeal 是指州高級，即州最高法院，這些州的 supreme court 反而成了州的中級法院②。在英格蘭，court of appeal 是最高司法法院"Supreme Court of Judicature"的一個分院，譯爲「上訴法院」③。

注

① "An intermediate appellate court, also termed (as in California and England) *court of appeal*." Cf. Bryan A. Garner, *Black's Law Dictionary*, 7th Edition, West Group (1999), at P. 357; Cf. Linda Picard Wood, J.D., *Merriam Webster's Dictionary of Law*, Merriam-Webster, Incorp (1996), at P. 112.

② "A supreme court is an appellate court existing in most states, usu. as the court of last resort. In New York, a court of general jurisdiction with trial and appellate divisions. The Court of Appeals is the court of last resort in New York." Cf. Bryan A. Garner, *Black's Law Dictionary*, 7th Edition, West Group, at P. 1454.

③ "An England court of civil and criminal appellate jurisdiction established by the Judicature Acts of 1873 and 1875." *Id.* at P. 362.

Crib death ▸ Cot death

二者均指 3 至 12 個月大的原本健康的嬰兒的猝死[①]，差別僅在於前者爲美式英語，後者多爲英式英語[②]。

注

① "Crib death: Sudden infant death syndrome; the sudden death of an apparently well infant, who is usually between three and twelve months old." Cf. F. A. Jaffe, *A Guide to Pathological Evidence*, 2nd Edition, Toronto, Carswell (1983), at P. 173.

② 陸谷孫，《英漢大詞典》，上海譯文出版社（1995）。

Crime

該單詞可用作指「犯罪」，其有很多種分類方法。在美國，最常見的是將犯罪分爲重罪（felonies）和輕罪（misdemeanors）兩種。其他分類包括：⑴本身不道德或有過錯之犯罪（*crime mala in se*）與本身並無道德過錯因素，只是因制定法規定禁止之犯罪（*crime mala prohibita*）；⑵處監禁且剝奪公民權利之犯罪（infamous crime）和不處監禁且不剝奪公民權利之犯罪（crimes which are not infamous）；⑶涉及道德敗壞之犯罪和不涉及道德因素之犯罪（crime involving moral turpitude or not involving moral turpitude）；⑷惡性犯罪（major crime）和輕微犯罪（petty crime）；⑸普通法上的犯罪（common law crimes）和制定法上的犯罪（statutory crimes）[①]。在英格蘭和威爾士，犯罪可按性質分爲 7 類：⑴侵犯人身罪（crime against the person），其包括：謀殺（murder）、謀殺以外的殺人（manslaughter）、暴力脅迫人身（assault）、毆打（battery）、傷害（wounding）、嚴重傷害身體（grievous bodily harm）、誘拐（abduction）等罪；⑵侵犯財產罪（crime against property），其包括：盜竊（theft）、搶劫（robbery）、夜間入室盜竊（burglary）、詐騙（obtaining property or service or pecuniary advantage by deception）、敲詐勒索（blackmail）、銷贓（handling stolen goods）、預備竊盜（going equipped to steal）、刑事損害（criminal damage）、侵占且圖謀損害或破壞財產（possessing something with intent to damage or destroy property）、僞（變）造（forgery）等罪；⑶性犯罪（sexual offences），其包括：強姦（rape）、雞姦（buggery）、重婚（bigamy）、猥褻（indecency）等罪；⑷政治罪（political offence），包括：叛國罪（treason）、製造恐怖罪（terrorism）、煽動叛亂（sedition）、洩露官方機密（breach of the official secrets）等罪；⑸妨礙司法罪（offence against justice），其包括：協助罪犯（assisting an offender）、共謀（conspiracy）、僞證罪（perjury）、藐視法庭（contempt of court）、破壞審判（perverting the course of justice）等罪；⑹破壞公共秩序罪（public order offence），其包括：妨礙員警公務（obstruction of the police）、非法集會（unlawful assembly）、淫穢（obscenity）、私藏武器（possessing weapons）、濫用毒品（misuse of drugs）、破壞治安（breach of the peace）等罪；⑺公路交通犯罪（road traffic offence），其包括：粗心或魯莽駕

車（careless or reckless driving）、酒後駕車（drunken driving）、無
照或無保險駕車（driving without a license or insurance）[②]。

注

① Cf. The Publisher's Editorial Staff, *Black's Law Dictionary*, Abridged
   6th Edition, West Publishing Co. (1991), at P. 256.
② Cf. P. H. Collin, *Dictionary of Law*, Peter Collin Publishing (1993), at
   Ps. 144—145.

Criminal assault ▸ Civil assault

二者均指以暴力脅迫人身（有時伴有毆打）。相比之下，
criminal assault 性質惡劣嚴重，故屬於犯罪範疇，爲「暴力脅迫
罪」[①]。Civil assault 情節較輕，屬於侵權範疇，爲「民事脅迫行
爲」[②]。需注意的是與 wrong 可同時屬於刑事範疇及侵權範疇一樣，
assault 也可同時既爲 criminal assault 也爲 civil assault 範疇[③]。

注

① "An assault considered as a crime and not as a tort." Cf. Bryan A.
   Garner, *Black's Law Dictionary*, 7th Edition, West Group (1999), at
   P. 110.
② "An assault considered as a tort and not as a crime." *Id*. at P. 110.
③ "An assault may be both a criminal assault and a civil assault." Cf.
   Linda Picard Wood, J.D., *Merriam Webster's Dictionary of Law*,
   Merriam-Webster, Incorporated (1996), at P. 34.

Cross examination ▸ Direct examination ▸ Redirect examination ▸ Recross examination

　　以上片語均是指法庭上當事人對證人的詰問。一般說來，當事雙方在法庭上對宣誓證人的「詰問」（examination）[1]共有四次，雙方各有兩次機會。按規定是由提供證人的當事人或其代理人對代表己方證人首先詰問，此即為 direct examination，譯為「直詰」，其也被稱為「主詰問」（examination-in-chief）[2]。主詰問的目的在於透過己方證人的證言使自己獲得最大的優勢[3]。通常，重大問題不准在主詰問中提出，除非證人被證實不友善。在此之後為他方當事人或其代理人對該證人的詢問，即 cross examination，譯為「反詰問」。反詰問的內容範疇一般在主詰問內容範疇之內或有關證人的信譽事項，但法院也可自由裁量批准就重大問題向證人進行詰問[4]。此後又是提供證人的當事人或其代理人對己方證人的詰問，此第二次詰問即 redirect examination，譯為「覆主詰問」[5]。在此之後是對方當事人或其代理人再次對該證人的詰問機會，此次詰問為 recross examination，譯為「覆反詰問」[6]。在非正式情況，「主詰問」、「反詰問」、「覆主詰問」以及「覆反詰問」均可省略其中的 examination 而簡稱為 direct、cross、redirect 以及 recross[7]。

注

[1] "examination: the questioning of a witness under oath", Cf. Bryan A. Garner, *Black's Law Dictionary*, 7th Edition, West Group (1999), at P. 581.

[2] "The first questioning of a witness in a trial or other proceeding, conducted by the party who called the witness to testify." *Id.* at P. 472.

[3] Cf. Renstrom, P.G., *The American Law Dictionary*, ABC-Clio (1998), at P. 156.

④ "In accordance with Rule 611 of the Federal Rules of Evidence, cross examination should only refer to matters that were covered during direct examination or that are relevant to the witness's credibility." Cf. Linda Picard Wood, J.D., *Merriam Webster's Dictionary of Law*, Merriam-Webster, Incorporated (1996), at P. 116.

⑤ "examination of a witness again after cross examination", *Id.* at P. 413.

⑥ "A second cross-examination, after redirect examination." Cf. Bryan A. Garner, *Black's Law Dictionary*, 7th Edition, West Group (1999), at P. 1281.

⑦ "Informally, these stages are called direct, cross, redirect, and recross, without the word *examination*." Cf. James E. Clapp, *Random House Webster's Dictionary of the Law*, Random House (2000), at P. 168.

Crown Court ▶ Magistrate's court

　　二者均是英國 England 和 Wales 地區審理刑事案件的法院。一般說來,凡是案情較輕微,屬於 summary offenses 的犯罪僅可在 magistrate's court(治安法院)中審理①。而案情嚴重,須經 indictment 予以起訴之案件則只能在 Crown Court(刑事法院)中審理②(因 Crown Court 也作初審法院審理案件,故筆者認為有人將其譯為「刑事上訴法院」的翻譯不甚妥當)。此外大量的案件,如 theft 及多數 burglaries 等犯罪,則屬於 "triable either way",即「兩種法院均可審理」之案件。此時,被告既可選擇接受 Crown Court 中由一名法官和陪審團進行的審判,其也可選擇在 magistrate's court 審理。但治安法官則可作出「此案因過於嚴重而應移送到 Crown Court 予以審理之裁定」(the magistrate may decided that the case is so serious that it should be committed to the Crown Court for trial)。

注

① "The magistrate's court bears cases of petty crime." Cf. P. H. Collin, *Dictionary of Law*, 2nd Edition, Peter Collin Publishing Ltd. (1993), at P. 333.

② "A Crown Court is formed of a circuit judge and jury, and bears major criminal cases." *Id.* at P. 147; "An English court having jurisdiction over major criminal cases." Cf. Bryan A. Garner, *Black's Law Dictionary*, 7th Edition, West Group (1999), at P. 384.

Currency depreciation ► Currency devaluation

　　二者均有「貨幣貶值」的含義。區別在於前者指的是透過市場上供求關係所引起的匯率下降，後者則指國家對貨幣價值的調整，指貨幣官方匯率的下降。

注

Cf. 倪克勤，《證券交易與銀行業務術語詞典》，四川人民出版社（1992），第 119 頁。

Curriculum vitae ► Resume

　　二者均有個人簡歷或履歷表的含義，區別只在於前者為英式英語，後者為美式英語。

注

Cf. P. H. Collin, *Dictionary of Law*, Peter Collin Publishing (1993), at P. 148.

Custom ▶ Usage

二者意思相近，區別在於 usage（慣例）爲一反覆行爲，而 custom（習俗）爲因此種行爲而在某特定行業或專業導致產生的法律或總規則。實踐中，存在有 usage 而無相關 custom 的情況，卻不存在有 custom 但無導致其產生或出現的相關 usage 的情況。

"Usage is a repetition of acts, and differs from custom in that the latter is the law or general rule which arises from such repetition." Cf. The Publisher's Editorial Staff, *Black's Law Dictionary*, Abridged 6th Edition, West Publishing Co. (1991), at P. 1072.

D

Damage ▶ Damages

　　通常情況下，damage 和其複數形式 damages 的區別應當較大。一般說來，單數形式的 damage 爲損害，指對人身、財產或名譽等的傷害[1]；而 damages 則爲損害賠償（金），指在民事訴訟中法院判處的責令侵權人等對一受害當事人所受損害的金錢補償[2]。但逐漸地，damages 也經常在英文詞典或著述中被用作當「損失」或「滅失」，即有望得到損害賠償金補償的損失或滅失，其等同 losses for which damages are recoverable，儘管 *Black's Law Dictionary* 仍對 damages 作較嚴格界定，說其是 "compensation in money for a loss or damage"，但就在該詞典內，仍有諸如 "diminution of damages" 和 "mitigation of damages" 等片語，其中的 damages 均爲「損失」或「損害」[3]。筆者認爲，儘管很多英、美人士將這兩個術語混用，但讀者在做漢譯英時，還是應遵循其區別原則[4]。

注

[1] "loss or harm resulting from injury to person, property, or reputation", Cf. Linda Picard Wood, J.D., *Merriam Webster's Dictionary of Law*, Merriam-Webster, Incorporated (1996), at P. 119.

[2] "the money awarded to a party in a civil suit as reputation for the loss or injury for which another is liable", *Id.* at P.119.

[3] 這兩術語同義，它們具有兩種定義，一是「輕損失責任學說」，在此含義中，damages 的含義爲「損失」；另一定義爲「減少對傷害人懲處的損害金」，在此含義中，damages 的含義是「損害賠償金」。Cf. The Publisher's Editorial Staff, *Black's Law*

Dictionary, Abridged 6th Edition, West Publishing Co. (1991), at
P. 693.

④ "The word damage, meaning loss, injury, or deterioration, is
to be distinguished from its plural, —damages—which means
a compensation in money for a loss or damage." Cf. American
Stevedores, *Inc. v. Porello*, 530 U.S. 446, 450 n.6 (1947)(quoting
Blacks).

Damages

damages〔損害賠償（金）〕①的種類很多，但最常見的有
compensatory damages、punitive damages、nominal damages 以及
aggravated damages 四種。其中 compensatory damages、punitive
damages 和 nominal damages 均爲金錢賠償（pecuniary damages），
即均屬於賠償金範疇；只有 aggravated damages 爲非金錢賠償（non-
pecuniary damages），即嚴格意義上不屬於賠償金。compensatory
damages（也稱爲 actual damages）爲「補償性賠償金」，指根據實
際損失的多少予以的賠償②。punitive damages（也稱爲 exemplary
damages, vindictive damages, added damages, punitory damages,
presumptive damages, speculative damages, imaginary damages, smart
money, punies）爲「懲罰性賠償金」，指因過錯人所犯過失惡劣等
故而處的超出實際損失數量之賠償，一般用於侵權而非違約之訴③。
nominal damages 爲「象徵性賠償金」，指證明被告有過錯但卻無
法證明實際損失時所處的數額很少的一種賠償金④。而 aggravated
damages 則爲加重的損害賠償，指如受害人受傷害太深而無法用金錢
補償時所科處的除金錢之外的其他補償，其中包括如賠禮道歉、契
約的強制履行（specific performance）等⑤。

注

① "the money awarded to a party in a civil suit at reparation for the loss or injury for which another is liable", Cf. Linda Picard Wood, J.D., *Merriam Webster's Dictionary of Law*, Merriam-Webster, Incorporated (1996), at P. 119.

② "damages awarded to compensate for the harm resulting from the defendant's wrong, including actual financial loss and intangible harm such as pain and suffering. These are the damages to which a plaintiff is normally entitled upon proving her case", Cf. James E. Clapp, *Random House Webster's Dictionary of the Law*, Random House (2000), at P. 123.

③ "damages awarded in cases of serious or malicious wrong doing to punish or deter the wrongdoer or deter others from behaving similarly", Cf. Linda Picard Wood, J.D., *Merriam Webster's Dictionary of Law*, Merriam-Webster, Incorporated (1996), at P.120.

④ "A trifling sum awarded when a legal injury is suffered but when there is no substantial loss or injury to be compensated." Cf. Bryan A. Garner, *Black's Law Dictionary*, 7th Edition, West Group (1999), at P. 396.

⑤ "Non-pecuniary damages awarded to mitigate a plaintiff's feelings when the defendant's misbehavior has been hurtful." Cf. Daphne Dukelow, *The Dictionary of Canadian Law*, Thomson Professional Publishing Canada (1991), at P. 29.

Date of expiration ▶ Date of maturity

二者均有「到期日期」的含義，區別在於前者指到期失效，而後者指到期生效，結果剛好相反。

注

參見本書條目expiration。

Death benefit ▶ Death grant

二者均指給死者之受益人的費用。區別在於 death benefit 是指 (1)由雇主向死亡雇員家屬或受益人支付的津貼或指根據《社會保險法》提供的撫恤金，稱爲「死亡撫恤金」；(2)因投保（如人身意外保險或年金保險等）人死亡由保險公司向受益人賠付的費用，有些類似人壽保險金，稱爲「死亡保險金」[①]。death grant 則是指由政府提供給死者家屬等專用於支付喪葬開支之費用，應爲「喪葬費」[②]。現在有的英漢詞典將 death benefit 譯爲「喪葬福利金」，而把 death grant 譯爲「死亡補助金」[③]，這些譯法似乎都不準確。

注

[①] "Amount paid under insurance policy on death of insured. A payment made by an employer to the beneficiary or beneficiaries of a deceased employee on account of the death of the employee." Cf. The Publisher's Editorial Staff, *Black's Law Dictionary*, Abridged 6th Edition, West Publishing Co. (1991), at P. 277.

[②] "state grant to the family of a person who has died, which is supposed to contribute to the funeral expenses", Cf. P. H. Collin, *Dictionary of Law*, Peter Collin Publishing (1993), at P. 152.

[③] Cf. 《英漢法律詞典》，Revised Edition，法律出版社（1999），第 215 頁。

Death duty/tax ▶ Estate tax ▶ Inheritance tax ▶ Succession duty/tax ▶ Legacy tax

以上這些片語均與遺產有關，目前，不少英漢詞典對這些術語的譯法多有一些問題。實際上，在國外，尤其是在美國，這幾種稅收有較明顯的區別。準確地講，estate tax 應當譯爲「遺產稅」，其是針對死者遺留的大宗財產所徵的稅，其稅率一般很高，以遺產淨值爲計徵依據，向遺產繼承人徵收[1]。而 inheritance tax 則應譯爲「繼承稅」，它是針對繼承人的繼承權所徵的稅收，其屬於特權稅（excise）的範疇[2]。death duty（or tax）爲通用語，其是指對死者的財產及財產轉讓所徵收的一切賦稅，其既包括 estate tax 又包括 inheritance tax，故應當譯爲「遺產繼承稅」[3]。succession duty（or tax）和 legacy tax 均爲就遺囑所指定遺贈產的繼承權所徵之稅，也爲一種特權稅（excise），從某種意義上講等同 inheritance tax，故應譯爲「遺贈產繼承權稅」或「遺贈產繼承稅」[4]。

注

[1] "a tax imposed on large estate left by decedents, based upon the value of the estate and required to be paid out of estate funds before the estate is distributed to heirs or takers under a will", Cf. James E. Clapp, *Random House Webster's Dictionary of the Law*, Random House (2000), at P.164.

[2] "Tax imposed in some states upon the privilege of receiving property from a decedent at death as contrasted with an estate tax which is imposed on the privilege of transmitting property at death. A tax on the transfer or passing of estates or property by legacy, devise, or intestate succession; not a tax on the property itself, but on the right to acquire it by descent or testamentary gift." Cf. The Publisher's Editorial Staff,

Black's Law Dictionary, Abridged 6th Edition, West Publishing Co. (1991), at P. 539.

③ "An estate tax or inheritance tax." Cf. Bryan A. Garner, *Black's Law Dictionary*, 7th Edition, West Group (1999), at P. 1469.

④ "An excise on privilege of taking property by will or inheritance or by succession on death of owner." Cf. The Publisher's Editorial Staff, *Black's Law Dictionary*, Abridged 6th Edition, West Publishing Co. (1991), at P. 618.

Decentralization ▸ Devolution

　　二者均有中央政府將權力下放地方政府的含義，區別在於前者所下放的權力要少於後者。在實行 devolution 的國家，地方當局幾乎等於是自治區政府①，而在實行 decentralization 的國家則不然。如翻譯「聯邦政府將警察權下放各州」時便應使用 devolution 而非 decentralization②。

注

① "Devolution involves passing more power than decentralization. In a devolved state, the regional authorities are almost autonomous." Cf. P. H. Collin, *Dictionary of Law*, Peter Collin Publishing (1993), at P. 169.

② Cf. Bryan A. Garner, *Black's Law Dictionary*, 7th Edition, West Group (1999), at P. 463.

Deception ▸ Deceit ▸ Fraud

　　三個單詞均有詐欺、哄騙的含義，且三者用法經常被混淆。其中，deceit 多爲一種可予起訴的民事侵權行爲，指故意以虛假陳述或因無知傳播虛假陳述使他方當事人相信，從而導致他方當事人遭受損失之違法行爲，其應爲「欺騙」[1]。deception 本身雖然不是罪行，但卻有多種罪行與之相關，如詐騙財產、保險單、年金契約，以詐騙行爲獲取報償性工作，詐騙他人放棄債權或使自己免於債務等；其在英國法上指一種犯罪，指不誠實地獲得他人財產，或利用語言或行爲或意思表達以獲得金錢上的好處，或故應譯爲「詐騙」[2]。fraud 被譯爲「詐欺」，其涉及內容極廣，多爲民事侵權行爲，但也可以是犯罪[3]，指爲獲得物質利益而透過陳述或行爲所作的虛假表示。在民法上，受詐欺人可視其爲不法侵權行爲而提起損害賠償之訴，值得注意的是一個以詐欺爲由而提起的侵權之訴也可稱爲欺騙之訴（an action of deceit）；在刑法上，詐欺是指蓄意的詐騙行爲，爲許多犯罪成立的要素。

注

① "A fraudulent and deceptive misrepresentation, artifice, or device, used by one or more persons to deceive and trick another, who is ignorant of the true facts, to the prejudice and damage of the party imposed upon." Cf. The Publisher's Editorial Staff, *Black's Law Dictionary*, Abridged 6th Edition, West Publishing Co. (1991), at P. 281.

② Cf. David M. Walker, *The Oxford Companion to Law*, Oxford University Press, New York (1980), at P. 245.

③ "A knowing misrepresentation of the truth or concealment of a material fact to induce another to act to his or her detriment. Fraud is usu.a tort, but in some cases (esp. when the conduct is willful) it may be a crime." Cf. Bryan A. Garner, *Black's Law Dictionary*, 7th Edition, West Group (1999), at P. 670.

Decision ▸ Award ▸ Finding ▸ Judgment ▸ Sentence
▸ Verdict ▸ Decree ▸ Ruling ▸ Disposition

以上單詞均有裁定、裁決或判決的含義。它們之間的區別在於：decision 爲通用辭彙，可指任何類別的裁判或判決，如 arbitral decision（仲裁判斷）或 judicial decision（司法判決）等[1]。award（也稱爲 arbitrament）專指仲裁判斷或陪審團有關損害賠償金的裁決[2]。finding（finding of fact 也常簡稱爲 finding）多用於指對事實的裁定[3]。judgment 多指法院對訴訟案件的最終判決（final decision），可指民事判決，也可用於指刑事判決，尤其是指結果爲赦免、撤銷原判、駁回上訴等不科處刑罰之判決[4]。而與之相對，sentence 的中心含義爲科刑（inflicting punishment on the convicted），故其只限於指刑事判決，且爲處以刑罰之目的的判決[5]；如無罪開釋則應用其他詞，如 decision 或 judgment 等來表示。verdict 是指陪審團作出的有關事實等的陪審裁決[6]。decree 是指法院根據衡平法上的權利所作的裁定，故多用於指衡平法院、海事法院以及繼承和離婚法院所作的判決或裁定[7]。ruling 多指在訴訟中就動議所作出的裁定，以及爲解釋法律、法令、法規、條例等而作出裁定[8]。disposition 在民事上多指法官就某事項或動議的裁定，等於 judge's ruling；其更多用於刑事案件方面，指科刑，如 probation is often a desirable disposition；此外，其還常用作對未成年罪犯的判決，指科刑或給予其他所規定的對待和處理。

注

① "an authoritative determination (as a decree or judgment) made after consideration of facts or law." Cf. Linda Picard Wood, J.D., *Merriam Webster's Dictionary of Law*, Merriam-Webster, Incorporated (1996), at P. 123.

② "A final judgment or decision, esp. one by an arbitrator or by a jury assessing damages." Cf. Bryan A. Garner, *Black's Law Dictionary*, 7th Edition, West Group (1999), at P. 132.

③ "A decision upon a question of fact reached as the result of a judicial examination or investigation by a court, jury, referee, coroner, etc." Cf. The Publisher's Editorial Staff, *Black's Law Dictionary*, Abridged 6th Edition, West Publishing Co. (1991), at P. 437.

④ "a court's final decision in a case, or occasionally on a particular aspect of a case", Cf. James E. Clapp, *Random House Webster's Dictionary of the Law*, Random House (2000), at P. 255.

⑤ "a court's judgment imposing a penalty upon a person convicted of an offense, or the penalty imposed, such as imprisonment, a fine, community service, or death", *Id.* at P. 393.

⑥ "A jury's finding or decision on the factual issues of a case." Cf. Bryan A. Garner, *Black's Law Dictionary*, 7th Edition, West Group (1999), at P. 1554.

⑦ "A judicial or administrative interpretation of a provision of a statute, order, regulation, or ordinance." Cf. The Publisher's Editorial Staff, *Black's Law Dictionary*, Abridged 6th Edition, West Publishing Co. (1991), at P. 927.

⑧ "The final judgment of a matter, and with reference to decisions announced by court, judge's ruling is commonly referred to as disposition, regardless of level of resolution.In criminal procedure, the sentencing or other final settlement of a criminal case." *Id.* at P. 326.

D

Defalcation ▶ Embezzlement

二者均與委託保管款項有關。區別在於 defalcation 是指無法說

明委託保管資金去向或無法交付委託保管款，其並非一定為犯罪或
瀆職或怠忽職守行為①，故不能簡單譯為「貪污公款」或「挪用公
款」，而應譯為「虧空委託保管款項」。相比之下，embezzlement
更具有反面性，指故意詐欺性地侵占、轉換、使用因職務、僱傭或
地位關係而所託付之金錢或財產之犯罪行為，故可譯為「侵吞或挪
用公款罪」以及「侵占信託財產罪」②，在此點上，其與 defalcation
不能等同（儘管有些法律詞典也認為這兩個術語基本等同，如第 7
版的 *Black's Law Dictionary*）。

注

① "failure to account for or pay over money that has been entrusted
to one's care; also: an instance of such failure. Defalcation does not
necessarily involve culpability or misconduct", Cf. Linda Picard
Wood, J.D., *Merriam Webster's Dictionary of Law*, Merriam-Webster,
Incorporated (1996), at P. 127; "misuse, misappropriation, or loss
of funds over which one has fiduciary responsibility as a trustee, a
corporate of public official, or the like", Cf. James E. Clapp, *Random
House Webster's Dictionary of the Law*, Random House (2000), at
P. 129; "Includes any fraudulent act or omission of a public officer
that occasions loss in money or property to a) Her Majesty; or b)
persons other than Her Majesty when such money or property was in
the custody of the public officer in the course of his official duties,
whether such loss is recovered or not." Cf. *Public Officers Guarantee
Regulations*, C.R.C., c. 723, s. 2.

② "the crime of converting to one's own use property of another that is
lawfully within one's possession. The usual case involves the taking
of money over which one exercises control in the course of one's job",
Cf. James E. Clapp, *Random House Webster's Dictionary of the Law*,

Random House (2000), at P. 156.

Dafamation ▶ Libel ▶ Slander

　三個單詞均有誹謗或侵犯名譽的含義。其中，defamation（毀譽）是通用的法律概念，指透過向第三者傳播虛假事實而致使他人（申訴者）名譽受損。其可包含兩種形式的名譽誹謗，即 libel 和 slander[1]。前者，即 libel 爲「書面誹謗」，指以書寫的、印刷的、電影的、廣播的或其他可永久保留的形式對他人的名譽進行的誹謗[2]。而 slander 則爲「口頭誹謗」，主要指用口頭的，或其他無法保留的形式的言論破壞他人的名譽[3]。在英、美、加拿大等國，誹謗一般屬於侵權責任範疇，但依據普通法規定，如書面誹謗，即 libel 的內容屬褻瀆、猥褻、煽動性質，則可視爲犯罪被起訴[4]。相比之下，slander 無論如何也構不成犯罪，此外，對 slander 提起侵權之訴多須旁證證明的確造成事實損害等方可[5]。

注

[1] "the negligent, reckless, or intentional communication to a third person of a falsehood that is injurious to the reputation of a living individual, or of a corporation or other organization. Defamation is the basis for the torts of libel and slander", Cf. James E. Clapp, *Random House Webster's Dictionary of the Law*, Random House (2000), at P. 129.

[2] "A defamatory statement expressed in a fixed medium, esp. writing but also a picture, sign, or electronic broadcast." Cf. Bryan A. Garner, *Black's Law Dictionary*, 7th Edition, West Group (1999), at P. 927.

[3] "A defamatory statement expressed in a transitory form, esp. speech." *Id.* at P. 1392.

④ "libel is not merely an actionable tort, but also a criminal offense", Cf. The Publisher's Editorial Staff, *Black's Law Dictionary*, Abridged 6th Edition, West Publishing Co. (1991), at P. 1393.

⑤ "Libel is in all cases actionable *pe se*; but slander is, save in special cases, actionable only on proof of actual damage." *Id*. at P. 1393.

Defendant ▸ Respondent ▸ Accused ▸ Defender ▸ Libel(l)ee

上述這些單詞均有「被告」的含義。其中，defendant 為通用語，可用於一般民事或刑事案件的初審中，與其相對的原告為 plaintiff[①]。respondent 用於上訴審（此時也稱為 appellee）及申請獲得特別命令或離婚、遺囑驗證等衡平法案件中，與其相對的原告（或上訴人）有 appellant、petitioner、applicant 等[②]。accused 專指刑事被告[③]，與之相對的原告有 plaintiff（刑事自訴人）或 prosecution（公訴方）。defender 則是蘇格蘭專門用語，與其相對的原告為 pursuer[④]。libel(l)ee 則專指海事或離婚案件的原告，與其相對的原告為 libel(l)ant[⑤]。

注

① "the party against whom a criminal or civil action is brought", Cf. Linda Picard Wood, J.D., *Merriam Webster's Dictionary of Law*, Merriam-Webster, Incorporated (1996), at P. 128.

② "The party against whom an appeal is taken. At common law, the defendant in an equity proceeding." Cf. Bryan A. Garner, *Black's Law Dictionary*, 7th Edition, West Group (1999), at P. 1313.

③ "a person or persons arrested, indicted, or otherwise formally charged with a crime; the defendant(s) or prospective defendant(s) in a criminal case", Cf. James E. Clapp, *Random House Webster's Dictionary of the Law*, Random House (2000), at P. 10.

④ "Scots law: a party defendant in a legal proceeding—opposed to pursuer", Cf. Philip Babcock Gove, Ph.D. and the Merriam-Webster Editorial Staff, *Webster's Third New International Dictionary*, G & C Merriam Co. (1976), at P. 591.

⑤ "The party against whom a libel has been filed in admiralty or ecclesiastical court." Cf. Bryan A. Garner, *Black's Law Dictionary*, 7th Edition West Group (1999), at P. 928.

Delegated legislation ▸ Primary legislation

二者專指不同分類的兩種立法。primary legislation 爲「本位立法」或「最高立法」，多指由議會直接制定的法律，在英國，其還包括根據皇家特權經樞密院令形式所頒布的法律①。delegated legislation 則爲「受權立法」（與授權法相區別），也可稱爲「次位立法」（secondary legislation），指經議會法令，即「母法」（parent act）授權的人或機構在限定的範圍內制定的法律②。

注

① "Bills proposed in Parliament become Acts. These Acts may either be general or personal and local. Both of these are sometimes known as primary legislation." Cf. Li Rong-fu/Song Lei, *A Course Book of Legal English*, Law Press, China (1999), at P. 16.

② "orders, which have the power of Acts of Parliament, but which are passed by a minister to whom Parliament has delegated its authority", Cf. P. H. Collin, *Dictionary of Law*, 2nd Edition, Peter Collin Publishing Ltd. (1993), at P. 160.

Delict ▸ Tort

二者均可指侵權行為，區別在於適用大陸法系法律的州或地區多用 delict 表示侵權，如在美國路易斯安那州便通用該詞[1]，故人們說大陸法系中的 delict 是英美法系中 tort 的對應詞（Delict is the civil law equivalent of the common law tort）[2]。

注

① Cf. Linda Picard Wood, J.D., *Merriam Webster's Dictionary of Law*, Merriam-Webster, Incorporated (1996), at P. 130.
② *Id.* at P.130.

Delinquent child

該片語很容易被人誤譯為「犯罪兒童」或「犯罪少年」，甚至不少英漢（法律）詞典都作這樣的翻譯[1]。實際上，此處的 child 決非兒童（10 歲以下者）且範圍大於少年（10 歲左右到 15 至 16 歲的階段[2]），其是指 a person below an age specified by law，為未成年人，等同 juvenile 或 infant，常為 12 至 18 歲者[3]，故應將其理解為「違法犯罪的未成年人」才對。

注

① Cf. 《英漢法律詞典》，法律出版社（1999），第 226 頁；陳慶柏等翻譯，《英漢雙解法律詞典》，世界圖書出版公司（1997），第 161 頁；陸谷孫，《英漢大詞典》，上海譯文出版社（1995），第 825 頁；《新英漢詞典》，上海譯文出版社（1979），第 309 頁。
② Cf. 《現代漢語詞典》，商務印書館（1988），第 286、1009 頁。

③ 英國或加拿大一般認爲 child 等同 minor，其年齡段各司法管轄區各自不同。而在美國，似乎各司法管轄區之規定也不一致，如 *Black's Law Dictionary* 給 delinquent child 的定義是：A legal infant, who has either violated criminal laws or engaged in disobedient or indecent conduct，而該詞典給予 infant 的年齡定義則是：An infant in the eyes of the law is a person under age of twenty one years。

Demurrer ► Plea ► Exception ► Confession and avoidance

以上均爲普通法上的術語，有「抗辯」的含義。在普通法中，demurrer 爲訴辯狀呈送程序（pleadings）中就訴狀或反訴中的指控提交的答辯書，主要指被告方雖承認所控事實，但卻以其法律依據不足以使訴訟成立爲由而進行的抗辯①，其可分爲普通抗辯（general demurrer）、特殊抗辯（special demurrer）和陳述性抗辯（speaking demurrer）三種。而 confession and avoidance（也稱爲 avoidance、plea in confession and avoidance 或 plea of confession and avoidance）則是承認所控事實，但卻提出新的附加事實以迴避應負的責任②。如同時提出混合過失（contributory negligence）以迴避自己應當負的部分責任的抗辯則可稱爲 confession and avoidance。相比之下，plea 則主要指對所控事實或訴因進行反駁而作的抗辯，尤指在民事訴訟中被告呈送的首次 pleading③。exception 作抗辯講時，常指 exceptions for insufficiency of a pleading，表示一種以訴狀要件不完善或有缺陷爲由的抗辯。根據現行《美國聯邦訴訟法典》的規定，demurrers、pleas 和 exceptions for insufficiency of a pleading 均已被廢除，代之以 motion 和 answer，但在有些州上述抗辯仍在使用。

注

① "A pleading stating that although the facts alleged in a complaint may be true, they are insufficient for the plaintiff to state a claim for relief and for the defendant to frame an answer." Cf. Bryan A. Garner, *Black's Law Dictionary*, 7ᵗʰ Edition, West Group (1999), at P. 448.

② "a common-law plea in which a party confesses an allegation but alleges additional facts to avoid the intended legal effect of the original allegation", Cf. Linda Picard Wood, J.D., *Merriam Webster's Dictionary of Law*, Merriam-Webster, Incorporated (1996), at P. 95.

③ "In common law a pleading; any one in the series of pleadings. More particularly, the first pleading on defendant." Cf. The Publisher's Editorial Staff, *Black's Law Dictionary*, Abridged 6ᵗʰ Edition, West Publishing Co. (1991), at P. 797.

Deposit ▸ Earnest (money) ▸ Down payment

　　以上詞語被不少詞典譯為「定金」，但實際上它們之間是有較大差異的。其中，deposit（也稱為security deposit）是「履約保證金」，擔保契約的履行，如違約，則將喪失此筆保證金①；契約一方收到 deposit 後，一般不能先動用；deposit 也可作為押金，如圖書館借書所繳納的押金，如不歸還所借之書，押金則會被沒收；其也可等同購物前所繳納的「定金」②。earnest（也稱為 earnest money、bargain money、caution money、hand money）多指在買賣中的「購貨定金」，起源於動產買賣，其現在常用於不動產交易，且經常交由第三人代管（in escrow），如違約不買，也會被沒收③。down payment 多指締結契約時約定付款中的「首付款」或「頭款」④，其與 deposit 有區別的是契約一方收到 down payment 後，即可動用，且

down payment 不具有定金所含的如果違約則應雙倍償還的性質。

注

① "Money placed with a person as earnest money or security for the performance of a contract. The money will be forfeited if the depositor fails to perform." Cf. Bryan A. Garner, *Black's Law Dictionary*, 7th Edition, West Group (1999), at P. 451.

② "money given in advance so that the thing which you want to buy will not be sold to someone else", Cf. P. H. Collin, *Dictionary of Law*, 2nd Edition, Peter Collin Publishing Ltd. (1993), at P. 164.

③ "A deposit paid (usu. in escrow) by a prospective buyer (esp. of real estate) to show a good-faith intention to complete the transaction, and ordinarily forfeited if the buyer defaults." Cf. Bryan A. Garner, *Black's Law Dictionary*, 7th Edition, West Group (1999), at Ps. 525—526.

④ "The portion of a purchase price paid in cash (or its equivalent) at the time the sale agreement is executed." *Id.* at P. 1150; "A sum of money, the value of a negotiable instrument payable on demand, or the agreed value of goods, given on account at the time of the contract." Cf. Daphne A. Dukelow, *The Dictionary of Canadian Law*, Thomson Professional Publishing Canada (1991), at P. 304.

Depositary ▶ Depository

　　這兩個單詞的含義有些混淆。美國 *Black's Law Dictionary*（第 6 版）專門告誡讀者不能將兩詞用錯，該詞典說前者是指人或機構，及受託人或公司等；而後者專指地方，即存放處、儲存地，且說在美國其專指經挑選和指定銀行①。但其他許多文獻及法律詞典，包括許多英文詞典卻視兩詞可以互換②。如 *Black's Law Dictionary*（第

6 版）中的 depository bank 在其第 7 版版本以及 *Merriam Webster's Dictionary of Law* 中便成了 depositary bank。本書編者認爲 depositary 和 depository 雖爲一個詞的兩種不同拼寫，且兩者也可互換，但在指「受託人」或「受託機構」時，可遵循 *Black's Law Dictionary* 的說法，將 depositary 作爲首選詞。相反的，在指「寄存地」或「保存地」時，可將 depository 作爲首選。

注

① "One with whom anything is lodged in trust, as depository is the place where it is put… *Depositary* should not be confused with *depository* which is the physical place of deposit." Cf. The Publisher's Editorial Staff, *Black's Law Dictionary*, Abridged 6th Edition, West Publishing Co. (1991), at P. 302.

② Cf. Daphne Dukelow, *The Dictionary of Canadian Law*, Thomson Professional Publishing Canada (1991), at Ps. 272—273; Cf. Linda Picard Wood, J.D., *Merriam Webster's Dictionary of Law*, Merriam-Webster, Incorporated (1996), at P. 134.

Depositary bank ▶ Remititng bank

　　二者均指與票據託收相關的銀行。區別在於 depositary bank（保管銀行）是指首先接收予以託收之票據的銀行（the first bank to which an item is transferred for collection①）。而 remitting bank（託收銀行或受託銀行）則指支付或轉讓票據之支付行或居間銀行（a payor or intermediary bank that pays or transfers an item②）。

注

① Cf. The Publisher's Editorial Staff, *Black's Law Dictionary*, Abridged

6th Edition, West Publishing Co. (1991), at P. 303.

② Cf. U.C.C. §4-105(f)

Depreciation ▸ Depletion ▸ Amortization

D

三者均可用作指財產價值之逐漸減少。其中，depreciation 多用於指有體財產（tangible property），尤指固定資產的貶值，強調資產質量或使用價值的降低①。amortization 為攤銷，表示資產帳面價值的減少或任何金額在一定期限內的逐漸消減，如債券溢價、債券折扣的定期減計等，多用於指無體（intangible assets）資產。depletion 用於指因自然資源，如土地價值、石油、天然氣、其他礦產、森林等的耗竭，強調物質數量的減少②。

注

① "the gradual decline in the value of tangible property that occurs because of wear and tear and obsolescence", Cf. James E. Clapp, *Random House Webster's Dictionary of the Law*, Random House (2000), at P. 134.

② "A decrease in the value of land or other natural resources due to the extraction of minerals or other natural wealth. Depletion resembles depreciation in that both are reduction in the value of fixed assets. Whereas depreciation is a reduction in the quality and usefulness of an asset because of physical deterioration, depletion is the reduction of the physical quantities of a fixed asset." Cf. Douglas Greenwald & Associates, *The Concise McGraw-Hill Dictionary of Modern Economics*, McGraw-Hill Book Co. (1984), at P. 95.

Depreciation reserve ▶ Allowance for depreciation ▶ Accumulated depreciation

以上三個片語均與因資產折舊而減稅有關。其中，depreciation reserve（資產的「折舊估價額」）最容易被誤譯爲「折舊儲備金」，事實上，此處的 reserve 並非指一筆基金，其只是帳面上一種「折舊費用累計」（valuation of a reserve），其目的是爲折舊減稅提供依據①。鑒於 depreciation reserve 經常被人誤解，目前不少人開始用諸如 allowance for depreciation（資產的「折舊減稅額」）或 accumulated depreciation（資產的「累計折舊值」）一類的術語替代它②。值得注意的是 allowance for depreciation 中的 allowance 等同 deduction 而非「津貼」，因此，depreciation allowance 應爲「因折舊而減稅」而非「折舊津貼」（不少詞典有此種錯誤譯法）。

注

① "A valuation-reserve account used to record depreciation charges. The use of the word reserve does not mean that a fund of cash has been set aside; rather, the word is employed to stand for a valuation reserve, in which credits are made to show the reduced valuation of a asset." Cf. Harold Bierman. Jr., and Allan R. Drebin, *Managerial Accounting*, 3rd Edition, Dryden Press, Hinsdale, Ill. (1978).

② "Because of the common misinterpretation of the term reserve, terms such as allowance for depreciation and accumulated depreciation are coming into use." Cf. Douglas Greenwald & Associates, *The Concise McGraw-Hill Dictionary of Modern Economics*, McGraw-Hill Book Company (1984), at P. 96.

Depression ▶ Recession

二者均可用於指經濟的不景氣，差別在於前者情況比後者更為嚴重，故 depression 為「經濟蕭條」[1]。recession 為「經濟衰退」[2]。美國歷史上最嚴重的兩次大蕭條（Great Depression）為1873至 1879（時間共 65 個月）以及 1929 至 1933（共 45 個月），而其二戰後的經濟衰退一般時間只為 11 個月。

注

[1] "A protracted period in which business activity is far below normal and the pessimism of business and customers is great. It is characterized by a sharp curtailment of production, little capital investment, a contraction of credit, falling prices, mass unemployment and low employment, and a very high rate of business failures." Cf. Douglas Greenwald & Associates, *The Concise McGraw-Hill Dictionary of Modern Economics*, McGraw-Hill Book Co. (1984), at P. 97; "In economic parlance, a depression is more severe than a recession." Cf. The Publisher's Editorial Staff, *Black's Law Dictionary*, Abridged 6th Edition, West Publishing Co. (1991), at P. 304.

[2] "A decline in overall business activity. In the United States, the average post World War II recession has lasted about eleven months." Cf. Douglas Greenwald & Associates, *The Concise McGraw-Hill Dictionary of Modern Economics*, McGraw-Hill Book Co. (1984), at P. 291.

Detective

美國的偵探可分為私人偵探（private detective）以及屬於警察

的偵探（one who is a member of a police force）[1]。在英國警方中，detective 的級別從高至低分爲 6 級：探員（detective constable）、探長（detective sergeant）、偵探督察（detective inspector）、偵探督察長（detective chief inspector）、偵探總監（detective superintendent）和偵探總監長（detective chief superintendent）[2]。

注

① Cf. The Publisher's Editorial Staff, *Black's Law Dictionary*, Abridged 6th Edition, West Publishing Co. (1991), at P. 310.
② Cf. P. H. Collin, *Dictionary of Law*, Peter Collin Publishing (1993), at Ps. 167—168.

Detention ▸ Attachment ▸ Garnishment ▸ Capture ▸ Levy ▸ Seizure ▸ Distress

以上單詞均有扣押財產的含義。其中，detention 多指非法扣押他人財產，與 detainer 同義，常爲一種違法（wrongful）行爲①。attachment 是指得到法院的命令且由法庭官員予以執行的對債務人財產的扣押，如防止被告轉移財產或迫使其到庭解決債務糾紛等②。garnishment 是指對第三人保管的債務財產之扣押，包括對債務人的工資的扣押，目的是用其償還債務③。capture 爲「捕獲」，多用於國際法中，指交戰國扣押敵國或載有應予沒收貨物的中立國船舶的權利，以及交戰國對陸地上非私人財產（即戰利品）的扣押；在民法中，其指捕獲不屬於他人的魚類、飛禽和野獸從而獲得該財產的一種方式④。levy 是指執行判決扣押債務人之動產或不動產，同時拍賣以償還債務（也稱爲 levy of execution）⑤。seizure 則是指因違法或執行判決等扣押財產的行爲⑥，其與 capture 的區別在於 capture 是由軍隊實施的，而 seizure 則是由文官政府實施的⑦。distress 是指扣押債務人之動產（goods）以還債，尤指地主（房東）扣押財產以求佃戶（房客）償還租金[8]。

注

① "wrongfully holding goods which belong to someone else", Cf. P. H. Collin, *Dictionary of Law*, Peter Collin Publishing (1993), at P. 168.

② "The seizing or freezing of property by court order in order to subject the property to the jurisdiction of the court, either so that a dispute as to ownership of it can be resolved or so that it will be available to satisfy a judgment against the owner." Cf. James E. Clapp, *Random House Webster's Dictionary of the Law*, Random House (2000), at P. 41.

③ "a remedial device used by a creditor to have property of the debtor or money owed to the debtor that is in the possession of a third party attached to pay the debt to the creditor", Cf. Linda Picard Wood, J.D., *Merriam Webster's Dictionary of Law*, Merriam-Webster, Incorporated (1996), at P. 137.

④ "In international law, the taking or wresting of property from one of two belligerents by the other. Also a taking of property by a belligerent from an offending neutral." Cf. The Publisher's Editorial Staff, *Black's Law Dictionary*, Abridged 6th Edition, West Publishing Co. (1991), at P. 145.

⑤ "seizure of property in accordance with legal authority; esp. attachment or seizure of property of a judgment debtor in order to satisfy a judgment", Cf. C. R. B. Dunlop, *Creditor-Debtor Law in Canada*, Toronto, Carswell (1981), at P. 424.

⑥ "A species of execution in which a sheriff executes a writ of fi. fa. by taken possession of the chattels of the debtor." Cf. Daphne A.

D

Dukelow, *The Dictionary of Canadian Law*, Thomson Professional
Publishing Canada (1991), at P. 971.

⑦ "Capture, in technical language, is a taking by military power; a
seizure is a taking by civil authority." Cf. The Publisher's Editorial
Staff, *Black's Law Dictionary*, Abridged 6th Edition, West Publishing
Co. (1991), at P. 145.

⑧ "The seizure of another's property to secure the performance of a duty,
such as the payment of overdue rent." Cf. Bryan A. Garner, *Black's
Law Dictionary*, 7th Edition, West Group (1999), at P. 487.

Detinet ▸ Detinuit

　　二者均是指普通法上與動產被非法扣留相關的訴訟的術語。區
別在於 detinet 爲「追索非法扣押錢財之訴」，指訴訟主體即原告錢
財爲被告所扣押，原告的目的是要求索回財產①。而 detinuit 則爲
「追索動產產權之訴」，指在提起訴訟時，訴爭財產已經爲原告所
占有，原告提起訴訟的目的是使占有合法化或要求得到因財產被非
法扣押而導致的損害賠償②。

注

① "a common law action alleging that the defendant is withholding
money or items owed (as under a contract)", Cf. Linda Picard Wood,
J.D., *Merriam Webster's Dictionary of Law*, Merriam-Webster,
Incorporated (1996), at P. 137.

② "An action of replevin is said to be in the detinuit when the plaintiff
acquires possession of the property claimed by means of writ. The
right to retain is, of course, subject in such case to the judgment of
the court upon his title to the property claimed." Cf. The Publisher's

Editorial Staff, *Black's Law Dictionary*, 5th Edition, West Publishing Co. (1979), at P. 405.

Devisee ► Legatee

在英漢或漢英法律詞典中，兩個單詞均有「受遺贈人」的含義，指經遺囑饋贈而非經法定繼承（inheritance）而獲得財產者。區別在於 devisee 指接受不動產遺產者[1]，legatee 則多指接受動產遺贈者[2]。

注

[1] "person who receives freehold property in a will", Cf. P. H. Collin, *Dictionary of Law*, 2nd Edition, Peter Collin Publishing Ltd. (1993), at P. 169.

[2] "commonly it refers to one who takes personal property under a will", Cf. The Publisher's Editorial Staff, *Black's Law Dictionary*, Abridged 6th Edition, West Publishing Co. (1991), at P. 623.

Digest ► Abridgement

在法律英語中，digest 有「判例摘要」的含義，指英美國家法院出版的一種判例摘要彙編[1]。其與 abridgement（節本、節略）之間的差異在於 abridgement 所含的內容單一，編輯者只需將原著進行併縮即可。而 digest 則內容廣泛，具有自己的分類體系和編排[2]。在 digest 中，American digest system 指「美國判例摘要彙編檢索體系」[3]，收錄了全美所有終審法院（包括聯邦和各州）的判例，按編年史的順序依照不同的法律主體進行編排，共分 7 大類，再分亞類及細目（topics），總共有 400 個細目，每個細目涉及一法律概念（legal concept），該體系包括一部《世紀判例摘要》（Century Digest，1897－1905），8 部《十年判例摘要》（Decennial Digest），《第九部十年案例摘要》（the Ninth Necennial Digest，分 Part 1 和 Part 2）以及《判例摘要大全》（General Digest）。英國的判例檢索體系則主要包括《英格蘭和帝國判例摘要》、《英格蘭判例法判例摘要》等。

注

① "A collection of summaries of reported cases, arranged by subject and subdivided by jurisdiction and court." Cf. Bryan A. Garner, *Black's Law Dictionary*, 7th Edition, West Group (1999), at P. 467.

② "As a legal term, digest is to be distinguished from abridgement. The latter is a summary or epitome of the contents of a single work, in which, as a rule, the original order or sequence of parts is preserved, and in which the principal labor of the compiler is in the matter of consolidation. A digest is wider in its scope; is made up of quotations or paraphrased passages, and has its own system of classification and arrangement." Cf. The Publisher's Editorial Staff, *Black's Law Dictionary*, Abridged 6th Edition, West Publishing Co. (1991), at P. 313.

③ "The American digest system covers the decisions of all American courts of last resort, state and federal." Cf. Bryan A. Garner, *Black's Law Dictionary*, 7th Edition, West Group (1999), at P. 467.

Diligence

diligence的含義是注意和謹慎，它與 negligence（過失）的意思相反，因「過失」剛好是指不謹慎或不注意所導致的失誤。在有關

diligence 的規定上，大陸法系和英美系有些相同。大陸法系將其分為三個級別：一般級別（ordinary）、特別級別（extraordinary）和怠慢級別（slight）。英美系也有三個級別，分別是：普通或一般級別（common or ordinary）、高級或大級別（high or great）以及低或怠慢級別（low or slight）的注意。

注

Cf. The Publisher's Editorial Staff, *Black's Law Dictionary*, Abridged 6th Edition, West Publishing Co. (1991), at P. 314.

Diplomatic personnel

該術語為「外交人員」，指一國派駐他國辦理外交事務的人員，包括⑴使館館長（head of diplomatic mission），其通常分為大使（ambassador），其是派遣國向駐在國派遣的最高級的代表，其為大使館館長；其次是公使（envoy），其是第二級外交代表，其為公使館館長；然後是代辦（charge d'affaires），其是最低級的外交代表，為代辦處的館長，如其缺位或因故不能履行職務，則由臨時代辦（charge d'affaires ad interim）主持使館工作，除級別和禮儀事項之外，各使館館長不應有任何差別。⑵其他外交代表，除使館館長外，使館中有外交級位的人員還有：參贊（counselor），在未設有公使或「公使銜參贊」（counselor with the rank of minister 或 minister counselor）的使館中，counselor 的位置僅次於館長；秘書（secretary），其位於參贊之後，可分為一等秘書（first secretary）、二等秘書（second secretary）和三等秘書（third secretary）共三個等級；武官（military *attache*），指軍事部門派遣的外交代表，有的國家按軍種可分為陸軍武官（military *attache*）、海軍武官（naval *attache*）和空軍武官（air *attache*）；隨

169

員（*attache*），其是位於秘書之後最低級外交官，可分爲外交隨員和辦理專門事項的專員，如文化專員（cultural *attache*）、商務專員（commercial *attache*）、新聞專員（news *attache*）等。此外，有時爲執行特殊外交使命，一國還可專門派遣特使（special envoy），特使多在使命完成即返回派遣國。

Direct investment ▸ Portfolio investment

兩片語均有證券投資的含義。兩者的主要區別在於 direct investment（DI）爲「直接投資」，多用在海外，其所指的投資量大，所占產權一般應在企業的 10% 以上，由此投資者對企業具有一定的控制權①。而 portfolio investment（證券投資）則指數量較少的投資，投資者主要關心的是收益，因其投資所占的企業產權比例較少，故投資者多對企業無控制權，其只能被動地接受企業的盈利或虧損事實②。

注

① "Investment by US business firms or individuals in overseas business operations over which the investor has a considerable measure of control." Cf. Douglas Greenwald & Associates, *The Concise McGraw-Hill Dictionary of Modern Economics*, 3rd Edition, McGrew-Hill Book Company (1984), at P. 101.

② "Direct investment differs somewhat from portfolio investment, which includes holdings intended primarily for their income yields." *Id.* at P. 101.

Direct liability ▸ Indirect liability

二者在證券或銀行業務中均有負債的含義。前者爲「直接負債」，指貸款的債務人或票據的發票人所付的義務。而後者爲「間接負債」，指因對票據或債務的背書或擔保而應承擔的或有責任或第二性責任，其只有在主要債務人不能履約時才成爲絕對債務。

Cf. 倪克勤，《證券交易與銀行業務術語詞典》，四川人民出版社（1992），第 138、203 頁。

Directors

該單詞在法律英語中作爲複數形式出現時，其翻譯應引起高度重視，因在法律英語翻譯中，有些名詞複數含義會發生變化，即這些名詞的複數形式常用作表示由其所組成的機構。故 directors 常用作表示董事會，如：Subject to these Regulations, any member may transfer all or any of his shares by instrument in writing in any usual or common form or in any other form which the directors may approve[1]，該句子意思是：根據本條例之規定，任何股東均可經通常或一般或由董事會另行同意的其他形式的書面文據轉讓其全部或部分股份。在此句話中，directors 便應翻譯爲「董事會」。如翻譯成「董事們」，該句子的含義便會有不少疑義。同理，在一些法律文件中，auditors 可用於表示審計委員會；shareholders表示股東大會；supervisors 表示監事會[2]。

[1] Cf. *Regulations for Management of a Company Limited by Shares*,

s. 20, Singapore.

② Cf. 宋雷，《文化差異對法律及經貿英語翻譯的影響》，西南政法大學學報（1999、1），第46頁。

Disbarment ▸ Sticking off the solicitor's roll

英國律師嚴格分為「巴律師」（barrister）和「沙律師」（solicitor）兩種。其取得資格的方法不同，取消資格的方式也不同，巴律師的資格由四大律師學院（four Inns of Court）授予，如嚴重違紀，也由其取消資格（disbar）；相比較，沙律師資格由沙律師協會（Law Society）授予，如嚴重違紀，則由一根據議會立法專門成立的紀律委員會（Disciplinary Committee）予以除名（to stick sb.off the solicitors roll）。美國律師如嚴重違紀，則由法院提起「取消律師資格之訴」（disbarment 或 debarment），其為法院內部任命的行政事務之訴訟，故既不屬於民事範疇，也不屬於刑事訴訟領域，其一般採用簡易程序處理。

注

請參見本書 lawyer 條目。

Discovery ▸ Disclosure

二者在訴訟法中均有讓對方知曉證據的含義。discovery（證據開示，等同 documentary discovery）主要適用於民事訴訟程序，具有強制性，由法院主持進行，主要形式包括：interrogatories（書面詢問對方當事人）、depositions（書面詰問證人）、requests for admissions（事實確認請求）以及 requests for production（出示證據請求）①。disclosure（證據披露）過去多用於刑事案件，由控方向被告方展示某些情況，特定情況下被告方也會向控方披露情況，此種披露多不帶強制性，但如控方所占有的證據能幫助被告人進行辯護，根據正當程序規則，該證據必須向被告方披露。在當今的民事程序改革浪潮中，英國大法官（Lord Woolf）在其「司法審判參與權」（Access to Justice）報告中建議在民事訴訟程序中用 disclosure 替換 discovery，以避免無限制地要求證據開示而導致訴訟的拖延。總體說來，民事訴訟中的 disclosure 應比其在刑事訴訟中的原含義更具強制性，披露的事項由法律規定而不是像證據開示那樣由當事人隨意要求②。

注

① "The compulsory disclosure, at a party's request, of information that relates to the litigation." Cf. Bryan A. Garner, *Black's Law Dictionary*, 7th Edition, West Group (1999), at P. 468.

② "In some jurisdictions discovery is usually referred to as disclosure, which is just the same thing from the point of view of the giver of the information rather than the receiver." Cf. James E. Clapp, *Random House Webster's Dictionary of the Law*, Random House (2000), at P. 140.

Dismissal

在法律英語中該單詞可用於指法院作出的撤銷案件而不作進一步考慮的裁定，其可在訴訟的任何階段作出，其應被翻譯為「駁回（訴訟或訴訟請求）」①。駁回訴訟的理由有多種，如因案件的法律根據不足，原告不在期限內遞交索賠陳述，或不披露證據，或不到庭受審等。讀者必須注意的是法院將已受理的訴訟或訴訟請求「駁回」與法院對案件「不予受理」（法院不予受理案件可譯為

The court refused to accept the case）之間的差別很大。遺憾的是不少英漢（法律）詞典卻將兩者混爲一談②。與 dismissal 相關的術語還有 dismissal with prejudice（不利於原告的駁回）和 dismissal without prejudice（有利於原告的駁回）。它們之間的主要差異在於 dismissal with prejudice 是指法庭根據案件實體作出的最終裁決，故當事人不得以同一訴訟理由重新提起任何訴訟③。而 dismissal without prejudice 則是指法院作出駁回裁定時未考慮訴訟案件的實體部分，故當事人可以以同一訴因再次向法院起訴④。

注

① "An order or judgment finally disposing of an action, suit, motion, etc., without trial on the issue involved. Such may be either voluntary or involuntary." Cf. The Publisher's Editorial Staff, *Black's Law Dictionary*, Abridged 6th Edition, West Publishing Co. (1991), at P. 324.

② Cf.《英漢法律詞典》，Revised Edition，法律出版社（1999），第244—245頁；「dismiss：（律）駁回，不受理」，陸谷孫，《英漢大詞典》，上海譯文出版社（1995），第 898 頁。

③ "Term meaning an adjudication on the merits, and final disposition, barring the right to bring or maintain an action on the same claim or cause." Cf. The Publisher's Editorial Staff, *Black's Law Dictionary*, Abridged 6th Edition, West Publishing Co. (1991), at P. 325.

④ "A dismissal that does not bar the plaintiff from refilling the lawsuit within the applicable limitations period." Cf. Bryan A. Garner, *Black's Law Dictionary*, 7th Edition, West Group (1999), at P. 482.

Dissolution (of marriage) ▸ Annulment ▸ Divorce

三者均與婚姻關係有關，divorce（離婚）和annulment（宣布婚姻無效）的區別在於 divorce 指的是終止一種合法的婚姻地位[1]，而 annulment 則是確認此種合法地位從未存在過[2]。dissolution（解除婚姻關係），多被認為是 divorce 的一種委婉說法，也是指終止一種合法的婚姻地位，包括因配偶死亡而使婚姻關係解除。須注意的是，*Black's Law Dictionary*第 6 版說其不包括 annulment[3]，但 *A Dictionary of Modern Legal Usage* 卻認為其包括 annulment[4]。在涉及離婚時，人們一般用 divorce，而不用 dissolution of marriage，但在美國，無過錯離婚或除「感情破裂而無法重修舊好」外的不列舉具體離婚原因之「離婚」，卻通常不稱 divorce 而稱 dissolution of marriage。

注

[1] "the dissolution of a valid marriage granted esp. on specified statutory grounds (as adultery) arising after the marriage", Cf. Linda Picard Wood, J.D., *Merriam Webster's Dictionary of Law*, Merriam-Webster, Incorporated (1996), at P. 148.

[2] "Unlike a divorce，an annulment establishes that marital status never existed in law." Cf. Bryan A. Garner, *Black's Law Dictionary*, 7th Edition, West Group (1999), at P. 89.

[3] Cf. The Publisher's Editorial Staff, *Black's Law Dictionary*, Abridged 6th Edition, West Publishing Co. (1991), at P. 328.

[4] Cf. Bryan A. Garner, *A Dictionary of Modern Legal Usage*, 2nd Edition, Oxford University Press (1995), at P. 549.

Division bell ▸ Division lobby

　　二者均是英國議會之下議院進行分組表決時的術語。其中，division bell 為「分組表決鈴」，指下議院中提醒議員分組表決即將開始之鈴聲[1]。division lobby為「分組表決走廊」，指下議院議會分組表決所經過之走廊[2]，其分為兩個，一為「贊成過廳」（the Ayes lobby），一為「反對過廳」（the Noes lobby）。英國下議院進行「分組表決」（to call a division）時，先由「議長」（Speaker）提名 4 位議員為「點票人」（teller），待分組表決鈴聲（division bell）響後，議員分兩組各自透過贊成過廳或反對過廳，經過廳門時經點數然後回到會議廳（chamber），最後，點票員報告贊成及反對票數，由議長宣布贊成者獲勝（the Ayes have it）或反對者獲勝（the Noes have it）。

注

① "bell which is ring to warn MPs that a vote is going to be taken", Cf. P. H. Collin, *Dictionary of Law*, Peter Collin Publishing (1993), at P. 180.

② "one of the two corridors beside the House of Commons where MPs pass to vote (the Ayes lobby and the Noes lobby)", *Id.* at P. 180.

Divorce

　　該單詞可用於指完全意義的離婚（也稱為 absolute divorce）[1]，也可指中止婚姻關係的效力（即部分離婚或有條件限制的離婚），至少是中止雙方當事人的同居[2]。在英國，離婚的依據只有一個，即婚姻無法挽回的破裂（irretrievable breakdown[3]），其可以五種情況予以證明：通姦（adultery）、無理行為（unreasonable conduct）、遺棄長達 2 年（desertion for two years）、分居 2 年且雙方同意離婚（separation for two years and the parties agree to a divorce）、分居 5 年（separation for five years）。離婚訴訟多由郡法院或倫敦的離婚法院（divorce registry[④]）受理，除少數因爭議抗辯之案件（defended cases）須移送高等法院外，大部分案件均按一種特別程序（a special procedure）不經完全審理即可離婚。美國的離婚屬制定法調整，由於其國情較開放，離婚依據也較多，且各州的規定不一，其分為過錯離婚（fault divorce[⑤]）和無過錯離婚（non fault divorce[⑥]）兩種。過錯離婚之依據總體說來有以下幾種：通姦（adultery）、重婚（bigamy）、虐待（cruelty）、違反自然的性行為或反常性行為（crimes against nature or sexual perversions）、遺棄（desertion）、酗酒或吸毒（drunkenness）、犯重罪或被監禁（felony or imprisonment）、詐欺或暴力脅迫（fraud or force）、性無能（incapacity or impotency）、精神病（insanity）、近親結婚（marriage to a relative）等，其他還包括如信奉禁止結婚之宗教（membership in a religious cult that opposes marriage）、企圖謀殺對方（attempted murder of a spouse）、妻子賣淫（wife's prostitution）、對方為逃犯（a spouse is a fugitive from justice）等。無過錯離婚的依據有：雙方同意離婚（mutual consent）、分居長達一定期限（separation for a certain time）、感情不和（incompatibility）、婚姻關係無法挽回的破裂（irretrievable breakdown of a marriage）。應注意的是過去無過錯離婚僅在幾個州內施行，其他許多州均需要有輔助的過錯依據，而現在許多州正趨向無過錯離婚以減少其敵對性質。美國的過錯離婚一般由州最高法院（state supreme court）受理，其程序基本如下：確定離婚所需的制定法依據，由無過錯方起訴，向過錯方送達傳票，參加聽證會（在此之前可能會由一調解委員會 "conciliation board" 進行調解以挽救婚姻），達成審前協定離婚，如協定不果則由法官判決離婚。

對於無過錯離婚的程序，如雙方無子女，且對財產分割達成協定，則較過失離婚簡單一些，有些州還規定有簡易離婚程序（summary dissolution procedure⑦），但仍須由州最高法院處理。

注

① "the termination of a valid marriage other than by death. In the United States this can be accomplished only by obtaining a judgment from a court in accordance with state law", Cf. James E. Clapp, *Random House Webster's Dictionary of the Law*, Random House (2000), at P. 143.

② "In older usage, the legal termination of cohabitation of a husband and wife without termination the marriage, corresponding in modern law to a court-ordered legal separation." *Id.* at P. 143.

③ "situation where the two spouses can no longer live together, where the marriage cannot be saved and therefore divorce proceedings can be started: Under English law, the only basis of divorce is irretrievable breakdown of marriage." Cf. P. H. Collin, *Dictionary of Law*, 2nd Edition, Peter Collin Publishing Ltd. (1993), at Ps. 293, 180.

④ "court which deals with divorce cases in London." *Id.* at P. 180.

⑤ "A fault divorce is granted on the premise that one party is at fault." Cf. Gail J. Koff, *Practical Guide to Everyday Law*, Simon & Schuster, Inc. New York (1985), at P. 209; "Traditionally, divorce was permitted only if one party proved wrongdoing by the other, such as adultery, cruelty, or desertion." Cf. James E. Clapp, *Random House Webster's Dictionary of the Law*, Random House (2000), at P. 144.

⑥ "A divorce in which the parties are not required to prove fault or grounds beyond a showing of the irretrievable breakdown of the marriage or irreconcilable differences. The system of no fault divorce was adopted throughout the United States during the late 1960s and the 1970s." Cf. Bryan A. Garner, *Black's Law Dictionary*, 7th Edition, West Group (1999), at P. 495.

⑦ Cf. Gail J. Koff, *Practical Guide to Everyday Law*, at P. 209.

Doctor of Law ▸ Doctor of Laws
▸ Doctor of Juridical Science ▸ Doctor of Jurisprudence
▸ Juris Doctor ▸ Master of Laws ▸ Bachelor of Law

以上片語均爲美國（或英國、加拿大等國）的法學學位。其中 Juris Doctor（法律博士，縮略爲 J.D.）爲最低的一種學位，其於 1969 年取代了 Bachelor of Laws（法學學士，在英國其仍被保留），由取得其他學科學士學位者在法學院學習 3 年後取得，有些類似中國的「大法學」碩士學位，多數州要求開業律師應取得此學位。Doctor of Law（法律博士，縮略爲 D&L）等同 J.D.。Master of Laws 爲法學碩士，是在 J.D. 之基礎上再研究學習且完成論文後授予，其常縮略爲 LL.M.。Doctor of Juridical Science（常縮略爲 D.J.S. 或 S.J.D.）與 Doctor of the Science of Law（常縮略爲 D.S.L.）相同，爲法學博士，是在 LL.M. 之基礎上經學習研究並完成學術論文答辯後授予。Doctor of Jurisprudence（縮略爲 D&J）有兩個含義，一爲 J.D.，二爲 D.S.L，故既可譯爲「法律博士」，又可譯爲「法學博士」。Doctor of Laws 爲榮譽學位（縮略爲 LL.D），故譯爲「法律榮譽博士」。

注

請參閱有關 J.D. 條目的說明。

Domestic company ▶ Domestic corporation

二者的含義基本相同，均有本國公司、當地公司、本州公司的意思。主要區別是有些國家，如加拿大，其公司的名稱多按公司註冊登記所在的省（或州）之具體規定命名，即有的省（或州）規定，必須用 company 命名在該省（或州）建立的公司，而有的地方則規定凡在本地建立的公司只能用 Corporation 命名。如在加拿大紐芬蘭省組建的公司便稱爲 domestic company，而在新斯科舍省組建的公司則稱爲 domestic corporation。

Cf. Daphne Dukelow, *The Dictionary of Canadian Law*, Thomson Professional Publishing Canada (1991), at P. 299.

Domicile ▶ Residence

二者均是國際法中常用的術語。domicile 爲「住所」，被視爲永久生活地，戶籍所在地，其與國籍和實際居住國不同①。任何人只能有一個住所。一個人的住所部分取決於事實推定，即他親自居住這一事實，部分取決於本人明示意圖，即他旨在將此地作爲其住所。法律認爲每個人均有一原始住所（domicile of origin），除非他移居別處且取得了選擇住所（domicile of choice）。受撫養者或無行爲能力者，如兒童，按制定法規定應以其監護人（多爲其父親）的住所而定。就公司而言，從納稅角度看，是指公司註冊登記地。自然人或法人的 domicile 多爲其相關訴訟的法定管轄地或審判地，某自然人住所地之法院對其有人身管轄權。residence 爲居所，其與住所不同，但它是確定住所的一個相關要素，居所的確定在於事實推定，即一個人在某地的實際生活居住②。居所常與法院管轄權的確定、納稅、投票選舉等事項有關。與一個人只能有一住所相對，人們可有多處居所③，如一處在城市，一處在鄉村。居所種類多種，最常見的是實際居所（actual residence）和通常居所（ordinary residence）。就公司而言，residence 則是指公司進行業務經營或被許可經營業務之地④。

注

① "A person's legal home. That place where a man has his true, fixed, and permanent home and principal establishment, and to which whenever he is absent he has the intention of returning." Cf. The Publisher's Editorial Staff, *Black's Law Dictionary*, Abridged 6th Edition, West Publishing Co. (1996), at P. 337.

② "The place where one actually lives, as distinguished from a domicile. Residence usually just means bodily presence as an inhabitant in a given place; domicile usu.requires bodily presence plus an intention to make the place one's home." Cf. Bryan A.Garner, *Black's Law Dictionary*, 7th Edition, West Group (1999), at Ps. 206, 516.

③ "One can have many residences, but only one domicile." Cf. James E.Clapp, *Random House Webster's Dictionary of the Law*, Random House (2000), at P. 146.

④ "a place in which a corporation does business or is licensed to do business", Cf. Linda Picard Wood, J.D., *Merriam Webster's Dictionary of Law*, Merriam-Webster, Incorporated (1996), at P. 428.

Dominant tenement ▶ Servient tenement

二者均是物權法上的術語，與土地的地役權（easement）相關。dominant tenement 為「承役地」或「需役地」，指得到其他地產給予的地役權的土地①。servient tenement 為「供役地」，指給予其他地產地役權之土地②。一般說來，dominant tenement 為英式英語③，在美國，其常被稱為 dominant estate、upper estate 或 dominant property。servient tenement 也被人稱為 servient estate、lower estate 或 servient property。

注

① "An estate that benefits from an easement." Cf. Bryan A.Garner, *Black's Law Dictionary*, 7ᵗʰ Edition, West Group (1999), at P. 567.

② "An estate burdened by an easement." *Id.* at P. 569.

③ Cf. P. H. Collin, *Dictionary of Law*, 2ⁿᵈ Edition, Peter Collin Publishing Ltd. (1993), at P. 182.

Dower ▸ Dowry

二者均與婚姻財產有關。dower 是指普通法上規定的丈夫去世後妻子繼承丈夫生前擁有或占有的 1/3 的永佃地享有權利（life estate in fee）以維持其生計的權利，且其子女可繼承此份產業，其為「亡夫遺產繼承權」①。dowry 則為「嫁妝」，指妻子的陪嫁②。儘管有個別詞典及詩歌等將兩詞混用③，但目前多數英語原文法律詞典均對兩詞作有明顯區分④。

注

① "the life estate in a man's real property to which his wife is entitled upon his death under common law and some state statutes", Cf. Linda Picard Wood, J.D., *Merriam Webster's Dictionary of Law*, Merriam-Webster, Incorporated (1996), at P. 151.

② "Marriage goods which a wife brings to the marriage." Cf. Daphne Dukelow, *The Dictionary of Canadian Law*, Thomson Professional Publishing Canada (1991), at P. 304.

③ Cf. James E. Clapp, *Random House Webster's Dictionary of the Law*, Random House (2000), at P. 144.

④ Cf. Bryan A. Garner, *A Dictionary of Modern Legal Usage*, 2nd Edition, Oxford University Press (1995), at P. 296.

Draft ▸ Bill of exchange

二者均有匯票的含義。在英國，前者為付款指令，包括匯票和支票等；後者才專指匯票。而在美國，根據《統一商法典》（UCC）之規定，draft 和 bill of exchange 含義完全相同，均指匯票，差別在於 draft 比 bill of exchange 通用，且前者一般用於國內，而後者則常用在國際交易（international transaction）之中。

注

Cf. Philip Babcock Gove, Ph.D., *Webster's Third New Dictionary of the English Language*, G&C Merriam Company (1971).

Due care ▸ Due diligence

二者均有應有的或適當的注意或小心的含義，且常互換使用①。其區別主要在於 due care（應有的注意，也稱為一般注意 ordinary care 或合理的注意 reasonable care）多適用於一般的侵權之訴；而 due diligence（應有的謹慎，也稱為合理的謹慎 reasonable diligence）則常用於與某專門職業，如律師、醫生等以及與信託義務相關之事項②。在海商法上，due diligence 常被翻譯為「恪盡職守」。

注

① Cf. Bryan A. Garner, *Black's Law Dictionary*, 7th Edition, West Group (1999), at Ps. 206, 516.

② "Due diligence is used most often in connection with the performance of a professional or fiduciary duty, or with regard to proceeding with a court action. Due care is used more often in connection with general tort action." Cf. Linda Picard Wood, J.D., *Merriam Webster's Dictionary of Law*, Merriam-Webster, Incorporated (1996), at P. 152.

Duplicate ▶ Copy ▶ Duplicate orisinal ▶ Original

二者之間的差別在於 duplicate（複本）指複製的或重新製作的具有與正本同等法律效力的文件（a reproduction of an original document having the same particulars and effect as the original or a new original, made to replace an instrument that is lost or destroyed①）。而 copy（副本）則無此種效力，儘管其也可作爲證據被法院採信。original 和 duplicate original（也稱爲 duplicate）則均有正本的含義，從法律角度上看，其具有同等效力②。original 爲眞正的「正本」，是當事人眞正完成的第一份文件；而 duplicate original 則爲正本遺失或毀損情況下製作的一份複製本，爲「複製正本」，即替代正本之複本。我們經常所說的「契約一式三份，均具有同等效力」，按西方人的習慣可譯爲 "one original contract and two duplicates are made and all are of the same effect"，如果譯爲 "three contracts are made" 或 "one original contract and two copies are made" 等則似有不妥。

注

① Cf. Bryan A. Garner, *Black's Law Dictionary*, 7th Edition, West Group

(1999), at P. 517.

② *Id.* at P. 517.

E

Edict ▸ Public proclamation

　　二者均有法律告示或公告的含義，其區別在於 edict 是對新的制定法的頒布，隨著頒布該法律即產生法律效力，故其應為「法律頒布告示」。而 public proclamation 則多指在法律尚未頒布（enact）之前的一種公示。

"An *Edict* differs from a *public proclamation*, in that it enacts a new statute, and carries with it the authority of law, whereas the latter is, at most, a declaration of a law before enacted." Cf. The Publisher's Editorial Staff, *Black's Law Dictionary*, Abridged 6th Edition, West Publishing Co. (1991), at P. 355.

Ejectment ▸ Ouster ▸ Eviction

　　三者均有將某人驅逐出不動產的含義。ejectment 為「驅逐非法占有人之訴」，主要指普通法所規定的一訴訟，原告目的是驅逐土地或建築物的不法占有人且主張得到損害賠償金，即將不法占有人驅逐而恢復自己的合法權益。現在，ejectment 已經逐漸演變成純粹的就不動產產權進行爭議的訴訟[①]。ouster 則剛好相反，多指非法將某人從其合法占有的不動產中驅逐出去而達到非法占有的目的，故其為「非法驅逐他人而強占財產」，為一過錯行為（wrong）[②]。eviction 多指對房客或佃戶的驅逐，其可為合法驅逐，特別是依法向法院提起訴訟；其也可指非法驅逐，如非法入侵者驅逐合法所有人，或房東或地主違法將租戶或佃戶驅逐[3]。

注

① "an action at common law that is to determine the right to possession of property and for the recovery of damages and that is brought by a plaintiff who claims to hold superior title", Cf. Linda Picard Wood, J.D., *Merriam Webster's Dictionary of Law*, Merriam-Webster, Incorporated (1996), at P. 157.

② "The wrongful dispossession or exclusion of someone (esp. a cotenant) from property (esp. real property)." Cf. Bryan A.Garner, *Black's Law Dictionary*, 7th Edition, West Group (1999), at P. 1128.

③ "the dispossession of a tenant of leased property by force or esp. by legal process", Cf. Linda Picard Wood, J.D., *Merriam Webster's Dictionary of Law*, Merriam-Webster, Incorporated (1996), at P. 171.

Elegit ▸ Writ of fieri facias

　　二者均指以往法院根據有關債務訴訟或損害賠償之訴的判決等所簽發的一種執行令狀，原告可自行選擇申請其中之一。elegit 為「動產取得令」，其本意為 "he has chosen"，指債權人可根據此令狀取得債務人的所有動產（牛和用作畜力的牲畜除外）以清償債務，如此種取得仍不足以使債務得以清償，債權人還可占有債務人一半的租有地並獲得土地的收益直至債務清償為止（該令狀現已被廢除）[1]。而 writ of fieri facias（或 fieri facias）則為「動產扣押令」，其本意為 "you cause it to be done"，指由法院司法執行官對債務人的動產予以扣押和拍賣以清償債權人債務之令狀，基本等同現在的 writ of execution[2]。由此可知，elegit 和 writ of fieri facias 之間的主要差異在於前者是授權由債權人「自行」取得或占有債務人的財產，而後者則是授權由「他人」，即法院的執行官員對債務人的財產進行的扣押。

注

① "By it the defendant's goods and chattels were appraised and all of them (except oxen and beasts of the plow) were delivered to the plaintiff, at such reasonable appraisement and price, in part satisfaction of his debt. If the goods were not sufficient, then the moiety of his freehold lands, which he had at the time of the judgment given, were also to be delivered to the plaintiff, to hold till out of the rents and profits thereof the debt be levied, or till the defendant's interest be expired." Cf. Joseph R. Nolan, *Black's Law Dictionary*, 5th Edition, St. Paul Minn. West Publishing Co. (1979), at P. 467.

② "Judicial writ directing sheriff to satisfy a judgment from the debtor's property. In its original form, the writ directed the seizure and sale of goods and chattels only, but eventually was enlarged to permit levy on real property, too. Largely synonymously with modern writ of execution." Cf. The Publisher's Editorial Staff, *Black's Law Dictionary*, Abridged 6th Edition, West Publishing Co. (1991), at P. 433.

Embryo ▶ Fetus

　　二者均指小孩未出生在子宮內時的情況，有的詞典將它們都當作「胎兒」講解①。實際上，embryo 是指卵子受孕後頭 3 個月時的胚狀體，應譯為「胚」或「胚胎」②。fetus 則指受精卵在子宮內後 2/3 期間的胎狀體，應譯為「胎」或「胎兒」。「胚胎」和「胎兒」決不應該混為一談。在國外，兩術語在病理證據學以及墮胎法規中

均有較嚴格區分，如反對墮胎者一般都主張小孩到達胎兒階段便應
具有公民權，此時墮胎即應被視爲犯殺人罪[3]。

注

① Cf. 《英漢法律詞典》，法律出版社（1999），第 267、308 頁；
陸谷孫，《英漢大詞典》，上海譯文出版社（1995），第 1031、
1174 頁。

② "The child developing in the uterus during the first three months of
pregnancy." Cf. F. A. Jaffe, *A Guide to Pathological Evidence*, 2nd
Edition, Toronto, Carswell (1983), at P. 175.

③ "A child developing in the uterus during the last two thirds of
pregnancy." *Id.* at P. 176.

Eminent domain ▸ Condemnation ▸ Expropriation

三者均與財產的徵用相關。eminent domain 爲「國家徵用權」，
在美國，多指州、市政府或經授權行使公職的個人或法人擁有的徵
用私人財產（尤指土地）的權力[1]，徵用之財產應用於公共目的，
對徵用財產應作合理補償。condemnation 和 expropriation 都爲「徵
用」，是指對 eminent domain 這種權利的實施程序，但在路易斯安
那州，expropriation 的含義則等同 eminent domain [2]。

注

① "A government's right to take private property for public purposes,
a doctrine which is American in origin." Cf. Daphne Dukelow, *The
Dictionary of Canadian Law*, Thomson Professional Publishing
Canada (1991), at P. 329.

② "A taking, as of privately owned property, by government under eminent domain. This term is also used in the context of a foreign government taking an American industry located in the foreign country. In Louisiana, the word has the same general meaning as eminent domain." Cf. The Publisher's Editorial Staff, *Black's Law Dictionary*, Abridged 6th Edition, West Publishing Co. (1991), at P. 403.

Employ ▸ Retain

二者均有聘請和僱傭的含義。但聘請律師則多用後者,而不用前者,如:to retain a solicitor。同樣,與它們相對應的 retainer 用於指聘請律師的行為[1],而其他一些諸如雇主與雇員之間的聘用行為則可用 employment 來表示[2]。

注

① "the act of contracting for someone's service—especially a lawyer's—or the fact of being so retained", Cf. James E. Clapp, *Random House Webster's Dictionary of the Law*, Random House (2000), at P. 375.

② "contractual relationship between an employer and his employee", Cf. P. H.Collin, *Dictionary of Law*, 2nd Edition, Peter Collin Publishing Ltd. (1993), at P. 195.

Enabling act/legislation/statute ▸ Delegated laws/legislation

上述詞語之間的區別很大。enabling act/legislation/statute 指賦予某人或某機構或部門權力以制定法規之法律,其為「授」(enabling 表示主動)權,故其應當譯為「授權法」、「授權立法」、「授權法令」，其爲母法（parent law）或本位立法（primary legislation）之範疇①。而 delegated laws/legislation 則是因接受授權法、授權立法、授權法令所授予的權力後所制定的法規或立法，其爲「受」（delegated 表示被動）權，故後者（也稱爲 regulation、agency regulation 或 subordinate legislation）應譯爲「受權法規」、「受權立法」，其屬次位法規（secondary law）範疇②。現在幾乎所有的法律詞典把兩者都不加區別地列爲「授權立法」或「授權性法規」等，肯定是錯誤的③。一字之差，謬之千里，此種謬誤，對中國法學界影響較大，希望讀者注意。

注

① "Term applied to any statute enabling persons or corporation, or administrative agencies to do what before they could not. It is applied to statutes which confer new powers." Cf. The Publisher's Editorial Staff, *Black's Law Dictionary*, Abridged 6th Edition, West Publishing Co. (1991), at P. 364.

② Cf. Li Rong-fu/Sung Lei, *A Course Book of Legal English*, *Sources of English Law*, Law Press, China (1999), at P. 17.

③ Cf. 《英漢法律詞典》，Revised Edition，法律出版社（1999），第 225 頁；陳慶柏翻譯，《英漢雙解法律詞典》，世界圖書出版公司（1998），第 169 頁；李盛平等翻譯，《牛津法律大詞典》，光明日報出版社（1983），第 250 頁。

Engross ▶ Enroll

二者均與文件的製作謄寫有關。engross 是指在議案或決議最終透過之前，準備一種正式的書寫或印刷文本以備表決透過等，故譯爲「製作文件清樣本」，因文件還須透過最終一次審核①。而 enroll

則是指就已經正式透過的文件而製作一副本以作存檔之用，故譯爲「製作備案文本」[2]。同樣，engrossed bill 應譯爲「議案清樣文本」，而 enrolled bill 則爲就已經正式透過且簽署的文件所製作的留存爲見證的一種副本，故譯爲「議案備存副本」。

注

① "to prepare the usu.final handwritten or printed text of (as a bill or resolution) esp. for final passage or approval. A bill or resolution is engrossed in the Congress and some state legislatures before its third reading and final passage by one of the legislative houses." Cf. Linda Picard Wood, J.D., *Merriam Webster's Dictionary of Law*, Merriam-Webster, Incorporated (1996), at P. 161.

② "to prepare a final copy of (a bill passed by a legislature) in written or printed form", *Id.* at P. 162.

Enlist ▶ Induct

二者均有從軍入伍的含義。它們之間的區別在於，enlist 是指自願參軍服役，而 induct 則指應徵入伍[1]。同樣，與它們相對應的 enlistee 則爲「自願入伍者」，其爲自願兵，enlistment 爲「自願參軍」[2]，而 inductee 則爲「應徵入伍者」，其爲義務兵。

注

① "To enroll for military service." Cf. Bryan A. Garner, *Black's Law Dictionary*, 7th Edition, West Group (1999), at P. 779.

② "Voluntary entry into a branch of the armed services." *Id.* at P. 551.

Enrollment ▶ Registry

二者均可用於指登記或註冊，但在某些領域其有較明顯的差異。如在美國的船舶註冊登記事項方面，enrollment 多指對國內航線和沿海岸航行的船舶的註冊登記，而 registry 則指對從事國際貿易運輸的船舶的註冊登記。故 enrollment of vessels 實際上等於「非遠洋船隻的船舶註冊登記」，而 registration of vessels 則爲「遠洋船舶註冊登記」。

E

注

"Generally speaking, terms registered and enrolled are used to distinguish certificates granted to two classes of vessels; registry is for purpose of declaring nationality of vessels engaged in foreign trade, and enrollment evidences national character of a vessel engaged in coasting trade or home traffic." Cf. The Publisher's Editorial Staff, *Black's Law Dictionary*, Abridged 6th Edition, West Publishing Co. (1991), at P. 366.

Enumerated power ▶ Reserved power

二者均與《美國聯邦憲法》（US Constitution）對聯邦政府和州政府的授權事宜相關。enumerated power（明確授予權力，也稱爲 express power）是指由《美國聯邦憲法》逐條羅列的具體授予聯邦政府的權力以及具體禁止州政府行使的權力，故爲「明確規定的權力」[1]。reserved power（保留權力）則是指那些既未明確授予聯邦政府又未明文禁止州政府行使的權力，即爲「保留之權力」[2]，根據法無明文不爲過原則，州政府或人民便可以行使這些保留權力。

① "A political power specifically delegated to a government branch by a constitution." Cf. Bryan A. Garner, *Black's Law Dictionary*, 7ᵗʰ Edition, West Group (1999), at P. 1189.

② "A political power that is not enumerated or prohibited by a constitution, but instead is reserved by the constitution for a specified political authority, such as a state government." *Id.* at P. 1190.

Equal Employment Opportunity Commission
▶ Equal Opportunities Commission

　　二者均是政府旨在消除就業時因種族、膚色、宗教、性別等方面產生歧視而成立的一種機構。其中，Equal Employment Opportunity Commission（就業機會均等委員會）為美國官方機構的名稱；而 Equal Opportunities Commission（機會均等委員會）則多指英國之機構[①]。而與此相關的實施方案在英國被稱為 equal opportunities program（機會均等方案），而在美國則被稱為 affirmative action program（優惠性差別待遇）[②]。

① "The US equivalent is Equal Employment Opportunity Commission." Cf. P. H. Collin, *Dictionary of Law*, 2ⁿᵈ Edition, Peter Collin Publishing Ltd. (1993), at P. 200.

② *Id.* at P. 200.

Equitable action ▶ Legal action

　　二者的分類儘管是依據在有關制定法頒布之時，此類案件究竟屬於何範疇予以決定的，即此時屬於衡平法範疇的今後便屬 equitable action（衡平法上的訴訟），否則便屬於 legal action（普通法上的訴訟）。但其主要區別卻在於 equitable action 的訴訟請求一般不與金錢相關，因而凡是要求實際履行契約、恢復原狀、頒發禁令等的訴訟，均屬衡平法上的訴訟。而 legal action 之目的則主要是要求金錢賠償（damages），如要求得到違約賠償金或因侵權而要求得到損害賠償金等訴訟都屬於其範疇[1]。在英國，衡平法訴訟和普通法訴訟多為不同的法院（庭）管轄，其主要的衡平法法院是 Court of Chancery[2]。而在美國，衡平法法院和普通法法院多合二為一，因此，凡法院受理民事案件後，首先便決定其性質，即看它是屬於 equitable 或屬於 legal，然後才進行其他處理[3]。

注

[1] "Action in equity is an action that seeks equitable relief, such as an injunction or specific performance, as opposed to damages." Cf. Bryan A. Garner, *Black's Law Dictionary*, 7th Edition, West Group (1999), at P. 29.

[2] "The main English court in which the part of law known as equity was enforced." Cf. Daphne Dukelow, *The Dictionary of Canadian Law*, Thomson Professional Publishing Canada (1991), at P. 229.

[3] "Rule 1 of the Federal Rules of Civil Procedure abolishes the distinction between law and equity, and therefore there are no longer courts of equity in the federal system." Cf. Gall J. Koff, *Practical Guide to Everyday Law*, Simon & Schuster, Inc. (1985), at P. 17.

E

Equitable title ▸ Legal title

二者代表英、美等國對物權的一種分類。其中，equitable title
（衡平法上的產權）代表的是物權中的實際利益權利，諸如占有、
監護、收益、享用等權利（possession、custody等）[①]；而 legal title
（普通法上的產權）則多指的是名義上的所有權（ownership）[②]。
按英、美物權法，一財產的普通法上的產權可為一當事人享有，
而其衡平法上的產權，又可為另一當事人享有。同理，equitable
interest（衡平法上的權益[③]）和 legal interest（普通法上的權益）以
及 equitable estate（衡平法上的不動產權益）和 legal estate（普通
法上的不動產權益）也具有此種區別。如香港的《合夥經營條例》
規定，合夥企業的不動產，不論是參股用的或而後購置的，其所有
權益（equitable estates and interests）應為企業所有，而該不動產的
普通法上的權益（legal estates and interests），則應經信託轉移他
人（或機構）[④]。又如不動產按揭（mortgage），凡採用產權轉移
論（title theory[⑤]）的州（在美國，僅有部分州適用該理論，其稱為
title state、title theory state 或 title jurisdiction），均規定 mortgagor
具有衡平法上的權益，而 mortgagee 則具有普通法上的權益，直至
mortgagor 支付所有按揭貸款或按揭財產因按揭人未付款而被拍賣為
止（until the mortgage has been satisfied or foreclosed）。

注

① "A title that indicates a beneficial interest in property and that gives
the holder the right to acquire formal legal title." Cf. Bryan A. Garner,
Black's Law Dictionary, 7th Edition, West Group (1999), at P. 1493.

② "title that is determined or recognized as constituting formal or valid
ownership (as by virtue of instrument) even if not accompanied by
possession or use", Cf. Linda Picard Wood, J.D., *Merriam Webster's*

Dictionary of Law, Merriam-Webster, Incorporated (1996), at P. 496.

③ "An interest held by virtue of an equitable title or claimed on equitable grounds, such as the interest held by a trust beneficiary." Cf. Bryan A. Garner, *Black's Law Dictionary*, 7th Edition, West Group (1999), at P. 816.

④ "Provided that the legal estate or interest in any land which belongs to the partnership shall devolve according to the nature and tenure thereof and the general rules of law applicable thereto, but in trust, so far as necessary, for the persons beneficially interested in the land under this section." Cf. *Partnership Ordinance* (Chapter 38)(Hong Kong), s. 22(1).

⑤ "The idea that a mortgage transfers legal title of the property to the mortgagee, who retains it until the mortgage has been satisfied or foreclosed. Only a few American states have adopted this theory." Cf. Bryan A. Garner, *Black's Law Dictionary*, 7th Edition, West Group (1999), at P. 1495.

Escape ▶ Prison breach

　　二者均指罪犯或被拘押人員非法從 prison 或 jail 等合法拘押場所或矯正設施逃走之行為。區別在於 escape（脫逃）是指罪犯不使用暴力從監獄逃走（unlawful departure from legal custody without the use of force）①，由此，escape from prison 只能是從監獄脫逃的行為，故應翻譯為罪犯的「脫逃」。同理，escape artist 也應被譯為是「善於（從監獄）脫逃者」，而非有些詞典上的「善於越獄的罪犯」②。相比之下，prison breach（也稱為 prison breaking）則是指罪犯使用暴力從關押場所脫逃（forcible breaking and departure from a place of lawful confinement）③，此才是真正意義上的越獄逃跑，故應譯為

「越獄」。但需注意的是在美國一些州，上述兩個術語之間的這種傳統區別目前正在逐漸消失。

注

① Cf. Bryan A. Garner, *A Dictionary of Modern Legal Usage*, 2nd Edition, Oxford University Press (1995), at P. 325.

② Cf. 《英漢法律詞典》，法律出版社（1999），第 276 頁；陸谷孫，《英漢大詞典》，上海譯文出版社（1995），第 1075 頁。

③ Cf. Bryan A. Garner, *Black's Law Dictionary*, 7th Edition, West Group (1999), at P. 1213.

Eatablishment Clause ► Free Exercise Clause

二者均是指《美國聯邦憲法》第一修正案（the First Amendment to US Constitution）中與宗教信仰有關的條款。其中，Establishment Clause 為「禁止建立國教條款」，主要目的是禁止政府出面建立具有壟斷性質的宗教①。而 Free Exercise Clause 則為「自由信奉宗教條款」，規定國會不得制定任何法律以禁止自由信奉宗教。但如果政府證明因國家利益緊迫需要，由此條款衍生的宗教自由（freedom of religion）可受到限制，某些宗教陋習，如吸毒或重婚便由此被禁止②。

注

① "The first Amendment provision that prohibits the government from creating or favoring a particular religion." Cf. Bryan A. Garner, *Black's Law Dictionary*, 7th Edition, West Group (1999), at P. 566.

② "the clause in the First Amendment to the U.S. Constitution prohibiting Congress from making any law prohibiting the free exercise of religion", Cf. Linda Picard Wood, J.D., *Merriam Webster's Dictionary of Law*, Merriam-Webster, Incorporated (1996), at P. 177.

Estate by entirety ▶ Joint tenancy ▶ Tenancy in common

三者均與永佃地權益或土地永佃權有關。estate by entirety（也稱爲 tenancy by the entireties、tenancy by the entirety、estate by the entireties）和 joint tenancy 的意義比較接近，前者主要指夫妻之間對永佃地權益之共有，後者內涵較廣，不一定特指夫妻之間的共有關係。其共同點在於兩者所指的關係中，如發生一公同共有人死亡的情況，生存者可獲得死者的權益。不同之處在於，在 estate by entirety 所確定的關係中，夫妻被視爲一人而擁有土地權益，當一方死亡，只有生存的配偶才有享有死者財產權益的權利，即當一方配偶死亡，其名下的財產權益便自動由其配偶受領，而其他人，包括死者的其他繼承人均不能享受，故 estate by entirety 應譯爲「夫妻公同共有不動產權益」[1]，在此點上，其與中國婚姻法中的「夫妻共同財產制」有較大的差異。在 joint tenancy 所確定的關係中，如一方死亡，其財產可由其他任何數量的生存的公同共有者分享，直至最後一個 survivor。因 joint tenancy 涉及兩人以上的公同共有關係，故譯爲「公同共有權益」[2]。tenancy in common（也稱爲 estate in common 或 common tenancy）則爲「按份共有權益」，指兩人或多人共有一份土地，如其中一人死亡，其權利應由其繼承人享有，而不是由其他共同所有人享有，在此點上其與 joint tenancy 有明顯差異[3]。

注

[1] "A common-law estate, based on the doctrine that husband and wife are one, and that a conveyance of real property to husband and wife creates but one estate. An estate held by husband and wife together so

long as both live, and, after the death of either, by the survivor." Cf. The Publisher's Editorial Staff, *Black's Law Dictionary*, Abridged 6th Edition, West Publishing Co. (1991), at P. 380.

② "a tenancy in which two or more parties hold equal and simultaneously created interest in the same property and in which title to the entire property is to remain to the survivors upon the death of one of them (as a spouse) and so on to the last survivor", Cf. Linda Picard Wood, J.D., *Merriam Webster's Dictionary of Law*, Merriam-Webster, Incorporated (1996), at P. 491.

③ "A tenancy by two or more persons, in equal or unequal undivided shares, each person having an equal right to possess the whole property but no right of survivorship." Cf. Bryan A. Garner, *Black's Law Dictionary*, 7th Edition, West Group (1999), at P. 1478.

Estate on conditional limitation
► Estate subject to a conditional limitation

　　二者之間的差別在於 estate on conditional limitation（也稱為 contingent estate）是指當某種緊急事件發生時才允許對財產權益轉讓予以限制，即財產權益將從原受讓人手中轉為授予其他人，但如緊急情況不發生，則不會出現對財產權益的轉讓進行限制的情況，故為「受意外條件限制的權益」①。相比之下，estate subject to a conditional limitation 則主要指一種時間上的限制，即即使不發生緊急情況，到時也會對財產權益轉讓予以限制，故為「受時間限制的權益」②。

注

① "An estate conveyed to one person so that, upon occurrence or failure of occurrence of some contingent event, whether conditional or limitative, the estate shall depart from original grantee and pass to another." Cf. The Publisher's Editorial Staff, *Black's Law Dictionary*, Abridged 6th Edition, West Publishing Co. (1991), at Ps. 381—382.

② "The distinction between an estate upon condition subsequent and an estate subject to a conditional limitation is that in former words creating condition do not originally limit term, but merely permit its termination upon happening of contingency, while in latter words creating it limit continuation of estate to time preceding happening of contingency." *Id*. at P. 382.

Evidence

　在美國，evidence（證據）之類型（types of evidence）基本可分爲兩種，即直接（direct evidence）和間接證據（indirect evidence），間接證據也稱爲環境證據（circumstantial evidence）。證據又可分爲三種基本形式（forms of evidence），即言詞證據（testimonial evidence）、實物證據（tangible evidence）和司法認知（judicial notice）。其中，實物證據即案件中的展示物品（physical exhibit），其包括實在證據（real evidence）和示意證據（demonstrative evidence）。實在證據指案件中如兇器等「實實在在的東西」，而示意證據則指能表明案件某些情況的視聽材料，如現場模型和圖示等。司法認知是指無須專門證明即可由法官確認的事實。此外，證據一般有三大規則：即相關性（relevant）、有證據能力（competent 或 admissible）和實質性（material），與之相對則爲無相關性（irrelevant），不具證據能力（incompetent）和非實質性（immaterial）。

注

Cf. Bryan A. Garner, *Black's Law Dictionary*, 7th Edition, West Group (1999).

Evidentiary fact ▸ Ultimate fact

　　二者之間的區別在於 evidentiary fact（證據證明事實）是指確認證據成立之事實[1]，其也稱為間接事實（mediate fact）或依據事實（predicate fact）或證據確認事實（evidential fact），而 ultimate fact（最終訴爭事實）則是指法律或事實和法律的一種結論，其是在 evidentiary fact 的基礎上所確立的，即 evidentiary fact 是 ultimate fact 成立的前提[2]，ultimate fact 也可稱為訴爭事實（issuable fact、elemental fact、principal fact），其是決定原告訴權或被告辯護最終是否成立的事實，故譯為「最終訴爭事實」。

注

① "A fact that is necessary for or leads to the determination of an ultimate fact. A fact that furnishes evidence of the existence of some other fact." Cf. Bryan A. Garner, *Black's Law Dictionary*, 7th Edition, West Group (1999), at P. 611.
② "A fact essential to the claim or the defense." *Id*. at P. 612.

Excise ▸ Franchise ▸ Royalty

　　乍看上去，以上三者似乎均與特權稅相關。從廣義上講，excise 可譯為「特許權稅」，指就幾乎任何特權的授予所徵收之稅，如與繼承權相關的繼承稅（inheritance tax）也屬該範疇，只有所得稅例外；而從狹義上講，excise 則是就特定的某些商品的製造、銷售、消費等權利徵收之稅，鑒於其主要體現在銷售環節上，故譯爲「特種商品銷售稅」[1]。相比之下，franchise 爲特權或特許，其所涉及的是一種特許的經營權，如政府特許公司、個人或其他實體等經營某項業務或公司准許他人用自己的商標等經營某種產業等，因而 franchise tax 則僅爲「特許經營稅」，其所涵蓋的範疇比 excise 小得多[2]。royalty 多指知識產權的使用費，如專利權使用費、版稅等[3]，其與眞正的稅收無關，故不宜像有些詞典那樣將其列爲使用稅、特權稅或專利權稅。

注

[1] "1) a tax levied on the manufacture, sale, or consumption of a commodity; 2) any of various taxes on privileges assessed in the form of a license or other fee", Cf. Linda Picard Wood, J.D., *Merriam Webster's Dictionary of Law*, Merriam-Webster, Incorporated (1996), at P. 177.

[2] "a tax imposed upon a corporation for the privilege of doing business in a state", Cf. James E. Clapp, *Random House Webster's Dictionary of the Law*, Random House (2000), at P. 193.

[3] "A finicial consideration paid for the right to use a copyright or patent or to exercise a similar incorporeal right; payment made from production from a property which the grantor still owns." Cf. H. G. Fox, *The Canadian Law of Trade Marks and Unfair Competition*, 3rd Edition, Toronto, Carswell (1972), at P. 696.

Excise ▶ Sales tax

二者均指與商品的製造、銷售以及提供某些服務相關的稅收，有些詞典曾將它們都譯為「營業稅」，但按中國新稅法之規定，營業稅只對勞務收入徵收，對動產買賣所得徵收的是增值稅和消費稅，故筆者認為營業稅的譯法欠妥，故建議考慮使用銷售稅對它們進行翻譯。這兩種銷售稅的區別在於 sales tax 是就幾乎所有商品銷售徵收之稅，故其屬於廣義的銷售稅，應被譯為銷售稅[①]。相比之下，excise（也稱為 excise tax、excise duty）卻限於特定的、一般不屬於生活必需品範疇的商品的銷售製造，最常見的為香煙、酒精和汽油等的銷售，故其應被譯為「特種商品銷售稅」。sales tax 可在銷售每個環節徵收，如在法國，商品每次易手均應交納一次稅費，而在美國則只使用一次，通常在商品零售環節徵收。美國聯邦政府不徵收 sales tax，其歸各州和地方政府徵收。如果買賣雙方不在同一個州，商品在一州購買而在另一州使用或儲存，且購買該商品時沒交或少交 sales tax，買方則可能被徵收「商品使用稅」（use tax）。使用稅的目的是為平衡不同州所課處的銷售稅的差異，因此，使用稅則可根據兩州就同一商品徵收銷售稅的差異進行調整。美國的 excise tax 則歸屬聯邦政府和州政府稅收體系雙重管轄，美國聯邦政府就 60 多種商品徵收 excise tax，此稅的徵收有利於調節消費。對於特種商品的銷售，英國等也專門成立有關稅和特種商品銷售稅總署（Customs and Excise Department）以管理相關稅收事務。excise tax 還有另外一種含義，即「特種商品銷售特許稅」[②]。

注

① "A flat percentage levy on the selling of an item.Sales taxes differ from excise taxes in that they are assessed on all, or almost all, commodities. They can be levied at any level of distribution." Cf. Douglas Greenwald & Associates, *The Concise McGraw-Hill Dictionary of Modern Economics*, McGraw-Hill Book Company (1984), at P. 307.

② "Excise tax has two quite distinct meanings: 1) a tax imposed on specific commodities that are produced, sold, or transported within a country, for example, liquor and tobacco; or 2) a tax imposed on a license to pursue a specified trade or occupation." Cf. Bryan A. Garner, *A Dictionary of Modern Legal Usage*, 2nd Edition, Oxford University Press (1995), at P. 336.

Exclusion ▸ Deportation

　　二者均可指對外國人的一種處罰。exclusion（拒絕入境令）的含義是拒絕尚未入境者進入國境，如在美國，指美國移民局所作出的拒絕某人進入美國之命令①。deportation（驅逐出境）則爲另一種刑罰，主要指將已經入境的違法犯罪之外國人逐出國境，其有時也包含 exclusion，即在邊境地區因拒絕某人入境而將其遞解出邊境的情況②。因此，移民局所作的 deportation and exclusion orders 則應含有驅逐和禁止入境雙重含義，其中 deportation order 是指將罪犯驅逐出境，而 exclusion order 則是指禁止其進入該國國（邊）境。在此情況下如像有些詞典將 exclusion order 譯爲「驅逐令」恐有不準確之嫌。

注

① "denial of permission for an alien to enter the country", Cf. James E. Clapp, *Random House Webster's Dictionary of the Law*, Random House (2000), at P. 169.

② "The removal under this Act of a person from any place in Canada to the place whence he came to Canada or to the country of his nationality or citizenship or to the country of his birth or to such country as may be approved by the Minister under this Act, as the case may be." Cf. *Immigration Act*, R.S.C. 1972, c.1－2, s. 2.

Executive agreement ▶ Treaty

　　二者均是指美國政府和其他政府之間締結的協定。executive agreement 爲「行政協定」，指由總統就其職權範圍的事項與外國政府簽訂的，毋需經國會批准的協定①。treaty 爲「條約」，指由正式授權的代表與兩個或更多的主權國家等簽署的書面協定，通常由國家立法機關批准②。executive agreement 的權力通常不如 treaty，且其只能取代州法而非聯邦立法，但 treaty 則能取代聯邦立法。

注

① "An international agreement entered into by the President, without the need for approval by the Senate, and usu. involving routine diplomatic matters." Cf. Bryan A. Garner, *Black's Law Dictionary*, 7th Edition, West Group (1999), at P. 47.

② "An agreement, league, or contract between two or more nations or sovereigns, with a view to the public welfare, formally signed by commissioners properly authorized and solemnly ratified by the several sovereigns or the supreme power of each state." Cf. The Publisher's Editorial Staff, *Black's Law Dictionary*, Abridged 6th Edition, West Publishing Co. (1991), at P. 1044.

Executor ▶ Administrator

　　二者均指具有對遺產進行清理和管理、變賣以及分配遺產等的職責的人。區別在於 executor 爲「遺囑執行人」，是指遺囑上寫明的由立遺囑人指定的負責執行該遺囑者①。而 administrator 則爲「遺產管理人」，是指因遺囑上沒有指定或在無遺囑繼承情況下由法院指定的屬於法定繼承中的管理死者遺產者[2]。與這兩個單詞相關的術語都應根據它們的基本含義進行翻譯。如有詞典將 administrator with the will annexed 譯為「依遺囑（而由法院認可的）指定的遺產管理人」[3]，此種譯法顯然跟 administrator 的基本含義相悖。實際上該術語的真正意思是「因遺囑未指定執行人或指定的執行人不作為或無能力作為或死亡，而由法院指定的遺產管理人」[4]。

E

注

① "a person named by a testator to execute or carry out the instructions in a will", Cf. Linda Picard Wood, J.D., *Merriam Webster's Dictionary of Law*, Merriam-Webster, Incorporated (1996), at P. 177.

② "a person appointed by a court to administer all or part of a decedent's estate in the absence of an executor, as when the decedent left no will, or the will failed to designate an executor or failed to dispose of the entire estate, or the designated executor is unwilling or unable to serve", Cf. James E. Clapp, *Random House Webster's Dictionary of the Law*, Random House (2000), at Ps. 15—16.

③ Cf. 《英漢法律詞典》，Reversed Edition，法律出版社（1999），第26頁。

④ "An administrator appointed by the court to carry out the provision of a will when the testator has named no executor, or the executors named refuse, are incompetent to act, or have died before performing their duties." Cf. Bryan A. Garner, *Black's Law Dictionary*, 7th Edition, West Group (1999), at P. 47.

Expiration ▶ Maturity ▶ Expiry

　　二者均有「到期」的含義。區別在於 expiration 多指到期無效或期滿結束，如 on expiration of the lease，其表示租賃期限已滿，租賃自此後將不再生效①。而 maturity 則剛好相反，其多指到期或期滿開始生效，如 maturity of bill，其為匯票到期，指自此即可到銀行予以兌現②。與它們相對應的動詞 expire 和 mature 也有此種區別。expiry 的含義則等同 expiration。但對於票據或證券而言，片語 expiration date 則與 maturity date 等同，均指到期應予以支付的日期。

注

① "Cessation; termination from mere lapse of time, as the expiration date of a lease, insurance policy, statute, and the like. Coming to close; termination or end." Cf. The Publisher's Editorial Staff, *Black's Law Dictionary*, Abridged 6th Edition, West Publishing Co. (1991), at P. 401.

② "The date on which a note, loan or obligation becomes due." Cf. Daphne Dukelow, *The Dictionary of Canadian Law*, Thomson Professional Publishing Canada (1991), at P. 621.

Exposure of child ▶ Deserted child

二者之間的差別較大。exposure of child 指有意不履行看護孩子之責任而使其接觸有害或危險物質或場景從而受到傷害，或使其得不到應有的監護和庇護，其並非與小孩的撫養有關，即並非屬於法定的故意不履行撫養責任之遺棄範疇，故不能像有的詞典那樣將其譯為「遺棄嬰兒」，而應譯為「置兒童於危險境地（罪）」①。與 exposure 相對應的 expose、exposing、exposition 等也不應像有些詞典那樣譯為「遺棄兒童」或「遺棄嬰兒」②，而應為「故意置人於危險境地」。deserted 則多指放棄或不履行對小孩的法定監護權與撫養義務，屬於法律上規定的遺棄範疇，故 deserted child 應為「被遺棄兒童」。

注

① "Placing child in such a place or position as to leave it unprotected against danger to its health or life or subject it to the peril of severe suffering or serious bodily harm." Cf. The Publisher's Editorial Staff, *Black's Law Dictionary*, Abridged 6th Edition, West Publishing Co. (1991), at P. 402.

② Cf. 《英漢法律詞典》，Revised Edition，法律出版社（1999），第 292 頁。

Extraordinary resolution ▸ Ordinary resolution ▸ Special resolution

三者都可用來指公司股東大會等的不同的決議，外國公司法在這方面規定之細微值得讀者注意。總體說來，ordinary resolution 為「一般決議」，多指以簡單多數，即過半數透過的決議，如以郵寄等方式寄送表決票進行表決，其是指以 3/4 或 75% 的壓倒多數透過的決議，由於此種表決結果按規定仍等同過半數親自出席或代理出席大會的股東之表決結果，故其仍然稱為「一般決議」①。special resolution 為「特別決議」，公司法中多指親自或代理出席大會的股東以 2/3 或 75% 的多數表決透過的決議，且該大會必須提前 21 天予以通知；如以郵寄等方式寄送表決票進行表決，其是指有表決權的全體股東全票透過的決議；在破產法中，其指 3/4 壓倒多數的債權人透過的決議②。extraordinary resolution 為「臨時決議」，指由親自出席大會之股東以 2/3 多數透過的決議；如章程允許代理出席，則指由親自和代理出席的股東以 3/4 壓倒多數透過的決議③。表決 extraordinary resolution 的大會須提前通知，但法律並無明確的提前時間之規定。就決議有關的事項而言，ordinary resolution 有關的事項為一般性；extraordinary resolution 相關的事項較重要，如有關公司自願解散等；special resolution 相關的事項最重要，涉及修改公司章程、變更公司名稱或更改公司經營目的等。

注

① "A resolution passed by the member of a company in general meeting by a simple majority of the votes cast in person or by proxy; or a resolution that has been submitted to the members of a company who would have been entitled to vote on it in person or by proxy at a general meeting of the company and that has been consented to in writing by such members of the company holding shares carrying not less than 3/4 of the votes entitling to be cast on it, and a resolution so consented to shall be deemed to be an ordinary resolution passed at a general meeting of the company." Cf. *Canada Company Act*, R.S.B.C. 1979, c. 59, s. 1.3.(a).

② "A resolution passed by a majority of not less than 2/3 of the votes cast by the shareholders who voted in respect of that resolution or signed by all the shareholders entitled to vote on that resolution. A resolution decided by a majority in number and 3/4 in value of the creditors with proven claims present, personally or by proxy, at a meeting of creditors and voting on the resolution. A resolution passed A) at a general meeting of which not less than 21 days notice specifying the intention to propose the resolution has been duly given; and B) by a majority of not less than 75% of the votes of those members who, if entitled to do so, vote in person or by proxy. A resolution proposed and passed as a special resolution at a general meeting of which less than 21 days notice has been given, if all members entitled to attend and vote at that general meeting so agree; or a resolution consented to in writing by all the members who would have been entitled at general meeting to vote on the resolution in person or, if proxies are permitted, by proxy." Cf. *Bankruptcy Act* (Canada), R.S.C. 1985, c. B-3, s. 2.3.

③ "A resolution passed by a majority of not less than three fourths of the members of the company for the time being entitled to vote present in person or by proxy (in cases where by the act, charter, or instrument of incorporation, or the resolutions of the company, proxies are allowed) at any general meeting of which notice specifying the intention to propose such resolution has been duly given; a resolution passed by 2/3 of the members entitled to vote who are present in person at a general meeting of which notice specifying the intention to propose the resolution as an extraordinary resolution has been given." Cf. Daphne Dukelow, *The Dictionary of Canadian Law*, Thomson Professional Publishing Canada (1991), at P. 363.

Extrinsic fraud ▶ Intrinsic fraud

　　二者均用於指與訴訟案件相關的詐欺行為。extrinsic fraud 為「訴外詐欺」，其所指的行為與訴訟本身無直接關係，屬於一種外在性的詐欺行為，如對當事人提出假和解協議以誘惑其不訴諸法院或使其不參加聽審等，其同時還指就提交法院的非實質性問題進行詐欺以阻止法院進行全面公正聽證的行為①，其也被稱為 collateral fraud（間接詐欺）。intrinsic fraud 則為「訴內詐欺」，指在法庭上使用假的或偽造的文件、假權利主張或偽造證據以欺騙事實審之裁決者，且導致得出對詐欺者有利的判決，此種詐欺行為會對訴訟本身產生直接影響②。

① "Deception that is collateral to the issues being considered in the case; intentional misrepresentation or deceptive behavior outside the transaction itself (whether a contract or a lawsuit), depriving one party of informed consent or full participation." Cf. Bryan A. Garner, *Black's Law Dictionary*, 7th Edition, West Group (1999), at P. 671.

② "Deception that pertains to an issue involved in an original action." *Id.* at P. 671.

F

Factor ▸ Broker

二者均可指經紀人，差別在於 factor（也稱爲 commission merchant）經受託有權占有、管理和控制貨物，此種情況使其對商品獲得一種特殊的產權。而 broker 只發揮中間人的作用，對財產無占有或控制權。此外，factor 可以像委託人一樣，以自己的名義進行買賣，而 broker 一般不得以自己的名義進行買賣。

注

"A factor differs from a broker because the factor possesses or controls the property." Cf. Bryan A. Garner, *Black's Law Dictionary*, 7th Edition, West Group (1999), at P. 613.

False arrest ▸ False imprisonment

二者均有非法限制他人自由的含義。false arrest 爲「非法拘捕」，其等同unlawful arrest，指用非法手段不經他人同意限制其人身自由，其多屬於侵權行爲，除可處以補償性（compensatory）或名義（nominal）賠償金外，還可處以懲罰性賠償金（punitive damages）。如被拘捕者被關押（be taken into custody），不論其時間長短即構成非法拘禁（false imprisonment），故有時 false arrest 也被認爲是非法拘禁的一種形式（a species of false imprisonment）[1]。false imprisonment 是指故意或過失地限制他人人身自由，其可屬普通法上民事侵權行爲，也可屬於一種犯罪，如綁架罪即爲非法拘禁的一種形式[2]。

注

① "A species of false imprisonment, consisting of the detention of a person without his or her consent and without lawful authority. Such arrest consists in unlawful restraint of an individual's personal liberty or freedom of locomotion. An arrest without proper legal authority is a false arrest and because an arrest restrains the liberty of a person it is also false imprisonment. The gist of the tort is protection of the personal interest in freedom from restraint of movement. Neither ill will nor malice are elements of the tort, but if these elements are shown, punitive damages may be awarded in addition to compensatory or nominal damages." Cf. The Publisher's Editorial Staff, *Black's Law Dictionary*, Abridged 6ᵗʰ Edition, West Publishing Co. (1991), at P. 416.

② "the tort and crime of restricting a person to a particular area without legal justification, whether by means of physical restraints (as in a prison, a locked room, or a speeding automobile) or through force or threat of immediate harm to one's person or valuable property", Cf. James E. Clapp, *Random House Webster's Dictionary of the Law*, Random House (2000), at P. 177.

False swearing ▸ Perjury ▸ False oath

　　三者均有作虛假陳述的含義。其中，false swearing（僞誓）是指在發誓或聲明情況下作不實陳述或認定以前所作的虛假陳述，僞誓多發生在訴訟之外，如與訴訟實質性事項相關，則可構成輕罪（misdemeanor）① 。perjury（僞證）指在刑事訴訟中在發誓或負有義務的情況下作虛假陳述或認定他人的虛假陳述② ，其屬於

misdemeanor 中情節嚴重的罪行。其與偽誓的差異在於 false swearing 多在庭外所作，而 perjury 多在庭上所作，且前者所包括的範疇一般比後者廣，情節也比後者輕[3]。false oath（假誓）構成普通法上的偽證的所有要件，其常用於如破產等訴訟程序中[4]。

注

① "the making of false statement under oath or affirmation in a sitting other than a judicial proceeding", Cf. Linda Picard Wood, J.D., *Merriam Webster's Dictionary of Law*, Merriam-Webster, Incorporated (1996), at P. 177.

② "With intent to mislead, making before a person who is authorized by law to permit it to be made before him a false statement under oath or solemn affirmation, by affidavit, solemn declaration or deposition or orally, knowing that the statement is false." Cf. *Criminal Code*, R.S.C. 1985, c. C-46, s. 131(1).

③ "False swearing is a broader and less serious offense than perjury." Cf. James E. Clapp, *Random House Webster's Dictionary of the Law*, Random House (2000), at P. 178.

④ "To defeat discharge in bankruptcy false oath must contain all the elements involved in perjury at common law, namely, an intentional untruth in matter material to a material issue. It must have been knowingly and fraudulently made." Cf. The Publisher's Editorial Staff, *Black's Law Dictionary*, Abridged 6th Edition, West Publishing Co. (1991), at P. 417.

Farm produce ▶ Farm product

二者均有「農產品」的含義，差別在於按有些國家（如加拿大）的法律規定，farm produce 只指大豆、玉米、穀物、草種和植物油種子等純農業原始產品以及相關的加工產品[①]。而 farm product 所涵蓋的範圍則較廣，其包括所有農業、園藝、養殖和林業原始產品及其相關的加工產品，諸如肉、禽、蛋、羊毛、乳製品、穀物、水果、蔬菜、蜂蜜、煙草、木材、釀酒、食物加工產品等。換句話說，如果說農業這個總體術語本包括農、林、牧、副、漁五個方面，而 farm produce 所指便僅是狹義涵蓋「農」或「副」的「農產品」，而 farm product 則指涵蓋所有五個方面的「農產品」[②]。

注

① "Beans, corn, grain, grass seeds and oil seeds and all kinds thereof produced in Ontairo." Cf. *Grain Elevator Storage Act*, Canada, 1983, c. 40, s. 1.

② "Those plants and animals useful to mankind and includes, but not limited to, forages and sod crops, grains and field crops; poultry and poultry products; livestock and livestock products; fruits, vegetables, mushrooms, tobacco, nuts, flower and floral products, nursery products, apiaries and furbearing animal products..." Cf. *Farm Products Marketing Act*, (Canada) R.S.O. 1980, c. 158, s. 1.

Fatal error ► Harmless error

二者用於指審判中出現的兩種不同性質的錯誤。其中，fatal error（也稱為 reversible error、harmful error、prejudicial error）為侵犯當事人實質性權利或影響案件結果的「嚴重錯誤」（也稱為「可撤銷判決的錯誤」、「有害錯誤」、「可更改的錯誤」），此種錯誤可使得當事人有權以此為由要求法院重新審理[①]。而 harmless error（也稱為 technical error、error in vacuo）為「無害錯誤」，指審判中

出現的未損害當事人實質性權利或未影響案件結果的輕微錯誤，上
訴法院一般不得以此爲由推翻原判而命令重新審理[2]。

注

① "An error that affects a party's substantive rights or the case's
outcome, and thus is grounds for reversal if the party properly
objected." Cf. Bryan A. Garner, *Black's Law Dictionary*, 7th Edition,
West Group (1999), at P. 563.
② "An error that does not affect a party's substantive rights or the case's
outcome. It is not grounds for reversal." *Id.* at P. 563.

Fault ▸ Negligence

　　二者所指的是侵權法中最常見的責任原因。fault 常用作指一種
故意違法行爲或一種故意不作爲[1]，而 negligence（也稱爲 actionable
negligence、simple negligence、ordinary negligence，過失）是指沒
有盡到應有的小心或注意[2]。但需關注的是 fault 有時也可被視爲包
括 negligence 或等同 negligence，故此時其應爲「過失」；有時 fault
又不同於 negligence，此時其便應爲「過錯」[3]，此時其可能觸犯刑
法。

注

① "a usu. intentional act forbidden by law; also a usu.intentional
omission to do something (as to exercise due care) required by law",
Cf. Linda Picard Wood, J.D., *Merriam Webster's Dictionary of Law*,
Merriam-Webster, Incorporated (1996), at P. 188.
② "The failure to exercise the standard of care that a reasonably prudent
person would have exercised in a similar situation." Cf. Bryan A.

Garner, *Black's Law Dictionary*, 7th Edition, West Group (1999), at P. 1056.

③ "Sometimes when fault is used in legal contexts it includes negligence, sometimes it is considered synonymous with negligence, and sometimes it is distinguished from negligence." Cf. Linda Picard Wood, J.D., *Merriam Webster's Dictionary of Law*, Merriam-Webster, Incorporated (1996), at P. 188.

Federation ▸ Confederation

二者用於指不同的兩種政府體制。Federation 為「聯邦制」，在聯邦制度下，同時存在一個聯邦或中央政府（立法機關和行政機關）以及若干州或省等的地方立法機關和政府①。confederation 為「邦聯制」，在邦聯制度下，多由幾個主權國家或幾個相對獨立的州等為共同目的而建立具有共同機構的聯盟或同盟②。federation 和 confederation 之間的差別主要在於後者強調的是各國或各州的獨立主權，而前者則強調中央政府的最高地位和權力③。目前世界上有不少聯邦制國家，如美國、加拿大、澳大利亞、德國等，儘管它們之中有的國名上並無聯邦兩字。

注

① "A composite of state whose constitution distributes certain functions to a central authority and others to member states." Cf. Daphne Dukelow, *The Dictionary of Canadian Law*, Thomson Professional Publishing Canada (1991), at P. 380.

② "A league or compact for mutual support, particularly of nations, or states. Such was the colonial government during the Revolution." Cf. The Publisher's Editorial Staff, *Black's Law Dictionary*, Abridged 6th

Edition, West Publishing Co. (1991), at P. 205.

③ Cf. David M. Walker, *The Oxford Companion To Law*, Oxford University Press, New York (1980), at P. 195; "A confederation (as in Switzerland) is a less centralized form of government than a federation (such as Germany)." Cf. The Publisher's Editorial Staff, *Black's Law Dictionary*, Abridged 6th Edition, West Publishing Co. (1991), at P. 116.

Feigned action ▸ False action

二者均用於指不實之訴訟。它們之間的區別在於 feigned action 爲「虛構訴訟」，指當事人呈送的訴狀中的陳詞尚爲事實，只是原告所主張的權利不屬實（pretended right），故原告並無眞正訴因，其是原告爲達某種非法目的而提起的訴訟，現此種訴訟已經被廢除。相比之下，false action 爲「僞造訴訟」，所指的情況更糟，其連訴狀中所稱的事實均是僞造的。

注

"An action, now obsolete, brought on a pretended right, when the plaintiff has no true cause of action, for some illegal purpose. In a feigned action, the words of the writ are true. It differs from false action, in which case the words of the writ are false." Cf. The Publisher's Editorial Staff, *Black's Law Dictionary*, Abridged 6th Edition, West Publishing Co. (1991), at P. 428.

Filiate ▸ Legitimate ▸ Acknowledge

三者均與確任父親身分事項相關。Acknowledge 爲「認領」，指父親認領自己的（非婚生）子女，承認其親子關係，即：
admission that the child is one's own[1]。legitimate 爲「確立婚生地
位」，是指確認（非婚生子女）婚生子女的法律地位，由此將該子
（女）立爲嫡嗣[2]。而 filiate 則爲「確定親子關係」，指宣布某人
爲孩子的父（母）親（特別指父親），即法律上認可父（母）子
（女）關係，除含對私生子的認領外，還包括收養關係的成立，
如 adopted children are filiated by the adoption proceeding（養子女與
其父母的關係經收養程序予以確立）[3]。由上可知，legitimate 和
acknowledge 各指一種認領或承認非婚生子女的行爲，而 filiate則強
調從法律角度確定父（母）子（女）之關係：both legitimation and
acknowledgement filiate an illegitimate child（確立婚生地位和認領均
可使非婚生子女其與生父的關係得以確認）。

注

① Cf. The Publisher's Editorial Staff, *Black's Law Dictionary*, Abridged 6th Edition, West Publishing Co. (1991), at P. 16.

② "to confer the status of legitimacy upon a child born out of wedlock, as by subsequent marriage of the parents or acknowledgement of paternity by the father", Cf. James E. Clapp, *Random House Webster's Dictionary of the Law*, Random House (2000), at P. 269.

③ Cf. Linda Picard Wood, J.D., *Merriam Webster's Dictionary of Law*, Merriam-Webster, Incorporated (1996), at P. 194.

Final judgment

該片語常被誤認爲是「終審判決」，目前幾乎所有流行的英漢
（法律）詞典或相關工具書都難逃此錯①。依定義，「終審判決」
即法院對訴訟案件進行最後一級審判時所作的判決，終審判決一經

宣布，即爲發生法律效力的判決，不能再行上訴②。從此意義上講，final judgment（最終判決）決非終審判決，因爲 final judgment 本身的含義剛好與此相反，其是指初審法院對案件實體（merits）審理後作出的可上訴的判決（故它也稱爲 final appealable judgment、final appealable order 等），其與法院的審級完全無關③。final judgment rule 對此作有專門規定：a party may appeal only from a district court's final judgment that ends the litigation on the merits④。而我們所說的不能再行上訴的終審判決應是 judgment of court of last resort 或 judgment of last resort 才對⑤。

F

注

① Cf. 《英漢法律詞典》，法律出版社（1999），第 311 頁；陳慶柏等（翻譯），《英漢雙解法律詞典》，世界圖書出版公司（1998），第 221 頁；薛波，《漢英法律詞典》，外文出版社（1995），第 912 頁：《漢英法律詞典》，中國商業出版社（1995），第 997 頁。

② Cf. 周振想，《法學詞典》，上海辭書出版社（1980），第484 頁。

③ "A court's last action that settles the rights of the parties and disposes of all issues in controversy, except for the award of costs and enforcement of the judgment. Also termed final appealable judgment; final decision; final decree; definitive judgment; determinative judgment; final appealable order." Cf. Bryan A. Garner, *Black's Law Dictionary*, 7th Edition, West Group (1999), at P. 847.

④ *Id.* at P. 644.

⑤ Cf. Philip R. Bilancia, *Dictionary of Chinese Law and Government*, Stanford University Press (1981), at P. 121.

Final judgment ▸ Interlocutory judgment

二者之間的差異在於 final judgment（最終判決）是指法院就任何案件（any judicial proceedings）的實體（merits）進行正式審理（trial）後，作出的有關當事人的實質性權利（substantive right）的判決，只有就此判決才可進行上訴。而 interlocutory judgment（訴訟中期裁定）則是在訴訟中期，就動議（motion）等所提出的程序問題進行聽審（hearing）後所作出的裁定，由於其未對案件的實體進行審判，故多不得提起上訴。

注

參見以上有關 final judgment 的說明。

Finance ministry ▸ The treasury ▸ The department of treasury

三者均指財政部。finance ministry 為多數國家財政部的名稱，用以指其處理財政事務的政府部門，其也可稱為 ministry of finance 或 department of finance，這些國家的財政部長也就被稱為 finance minister。而在美國和英國，財政部卻是用 treasury 來表示，在英國稱為 the treasury，在美國，稱為 the department of treasury。同理，英國的財政大臣被稱為 the Chancellor of the Exchequer，而美國的財政部長則被稱為 the Treasury Secretary。

注

Cf. P. H. Collin, *Dictionary of Law*, 2nd Edition, Peter Collin Publishing Ltd. (1993), at P. 225.

Financial statement ▸ Financing statement

二者均與財政有關。financial statement（也稱爲 financial report）爲「財政報告」，指個人或組織在某日或某期間財政或收入情況的報告，其包括資產負債表、收入報告以及經濟地位變更報告等[1]。financing statement 則是一種債務擔保文件，說明有擔保的當事人對抵押品或擔保品（動產）的物權擔保或擔保利益情況，用以通知其他買方或借方有關此財產已有可強制執行的擔保利益等，故其應爲「籌資擔保情況說明」，其只有證明物權擔保成立的作用，本身並非擔保協議，按《統一商法典》的規定，此說明一經被擔保人提交州擔保署或類同機構予以存檔，則可推定已經通知所有潛在的借方或第三方當事人[2]。

注

[1] "Any report summarizing the financing condition or financial results of a person or organization on any date or for any period. Financial statements include the balance sheet and the income statement and sometimes the statement of changes in financial position." Cf. The Publisher's Editorial Staff, *Black's Law Dictionary*, Abridged 6th Edition, West Publishing Co. (1991), at P. 436.

[2] "A document filed in the public records to notify third parties, usu. prospective buyers and lenders, of a secured party's security interest in goods." Cf. Bryan A. Garner, *Black's Law Dictionary*, 7th Edition, West Group (1999), at P. 646.

Floor trader ▸ Floor broker ▸ Account executive

三者均是指證券或期貨交易所的經紀人。它們之間的區別在

於 account executive（也稱爲 stockbroker、account representative）
爲「業務經紀人」，其位於交易所之外，主要負責與客戶打交道，
接受客戶的買賣指令且將此種指令傳達到交易所。而 floor trader 或
floor broker 則爲「場內經紀人」，指位於交易所交易廳現場，負責
具體執行該客戶的買賣命令的另一類經紀人。由此，一樁證券或期
貨交易通常須經此兩種經紀人通力合作才予以完成。

注

"There are two different kinds of brokers. An account executive for a
brokerage firm is often called a broker. The account executive could be
located in any town or city and the account executive deals with his or
her customers, conveying their orders to the exchange. A second type
of broker is a floor broker, a broker on the floor of the exchange who
executes orders for other customers." Cf. Li Rong-fu/Sung Lei, *A Course
Book of Legal English*, Law Press (1999), at P. 369.

Force majeure ▸ *Force majesture* ▸ Act of God ▸ *Vis major* ▸ Superior force

以上片語均有不可預見和無法抵禦的事件或後果的含義，均
可作爲契約免責理由。其中，源於法文的 *force majeure* 爲「不可
抗力」，其包括人爲和自然的使得契約無法履行的行爲事件（an
unforeseeable natural or human event beyond the control of the parties to
a contract, rendering performance of a contract impossible[①]），其也稱
爲 superior force、*vis major*、*force majesture*。只是 superior force 和
vis major 還有另外一個含義，即「天災直接損失」[②]，此時其也稱
爲 *vis divina*）。act of God 爲人類活動之外的「自然災害」或「天
災」，包括雷擊、地震、洪澇等[③]。制定法將其內容擴大到任何不

可預見和抵禦的自然事件情況，有些可作爲契約或侵權責任免責理由，但其內涵肯定比 *force majeure* 窄，不包括人爲因素，故不宜像有些詞典那樣將其譯爲「不可抗力」[④]。

注

① Cf. James E. Clapp, *Random House Webster's Dictionary of the Law*, Random House (2000), at P. 189.

② "A loss that results immediately from a natural cause without the intervention of man, and could not have been prevented by the exercise of prudence, diligence, and care." Cf. The Publisher's Editorial Staff, *Black's Law Dictionary*, Abridged 6th Edition, West Publishing Co. (1991), at P. 1086.

③ "an extraordinary natural event (as a flood or earthquake) that cannot be reasonably foreseen or prevented." Cf. Linda Picard Wood, J.D., *Merriam Webster's Dictionary of Law*, Merriam-Webster, Incorporated (1996), at P. 177.

④ Cf. 《英漢法律詞典》，Revised Edition，法律出版社（1999），第13頁。

Forced labor ► Reform through labor

這是兩個很容易被混淆的術語。事實上，它們所適用的法律領域各不相同。forced labor 爲國際法上的用語，其爲「強迫勞動」，指非自願提供的在處罰威脅下進行的勞動，爲違反人權和政治權利的行爲，應受國際法的處罰[①]。按聯合國公約，即 UN Convention on Civil and Political Rights 第 8 條之規定，forced labor 不包括法庭對罪犯科處的刑罰、義務兵役、搶險行爲、公民義務以及公共服務等（penalties imposed by a court, compulsory military service, action taken

in an emergency, normal civil service, and minor communal services），
其也被稱為 compulsory labor。同理，forced labor farm 也不應是刑法
意義上的勞改農場（目前不少法律詞典上均有此種錯誤[2]），而只能
是強制勞動場所（如第二次世界大戰中的勞動集中營或上世紀 60 年
代中國「文化革命」中出現的非法迫使所謂的「牛鬼蛇神」勞動的
場所等）。而 reform through labor（或 labor reform）才是刑法意義
上適用於罪犯改造的「勞改」[3]。同理，「勞改農場」也應為 labor
reform farm 而非 forced labor farm。譯者在翻譯勞改農場時如不注意
此種差異，便很容易誤使外國人認為中國違反人權和踐踏國際法。

注

① "Work exacted from a person under threat or penalty; work for which
a person has not offered himself or herself voluntarily." Cf. Bryan
A.Garner, *Black's Law Dictionary*, 7th Edition, West Group (1999), at
P. 657.

② Cf. 《英漢法律詞典》，法律出版社（1999），第 319 頁；薛
波，《漢英法律詞典》，外文出版社（1995），第 457 頁。

③ Cf. Philip R. Bilancia, *Dictionary of Chinese Law and Government*
(Chinese-English), Stanford University Press (1981), at P. 406.

Forcible detainer ▶ Forcible entry

　　二者均有普通法上所指的非法進入他人住宅或占有他人土地且
不願歸還的含義。不同之處在於 forcible detainer 可指和平方式進
入他人住宅或領地，用恐嚇或暴力阻礙他人合法進入，從而達到占
有住宅或土地的目的，其也可以用作指拒絕歸還他人的動產，故為
「強行侵占」（他人土地、住宅或財產等）[1]。而 forcible entry 則是
指以暴力方式進入他人住宅或土地以期達到占有的目的，故為「搶

占」（他人土地或住宅），搶占過去曾爲一種犯罪②。

注

① "Exists where one originally in rightful possession of realty refuses to surrender it at termination of his possession of right. Forcible detainer may ensure upon a peaceable entry, as well as upon a forcible entry; but it is most commonly spoken of it in the phrase forcible entry and detainer." Cf. The Publisher's Editorial Staff, *Black's Law Dictionary*, Abridged 6th Edition, West Publishing Co. (1991), at P. 445.

② "At common law, the act or an instance of violently and unlawfully taking possession of lands and tenements against the will of those entitled to possession." Cf. Bryan A. Garner, *Black's Law Dictionary*, 7th Edition, West Group (1999), at P. 657.

Foreign ministry

該片語用於指多數國家處理對外關係事務的政府部門，即「外交部」。與之相對，這些國家的外交部長也被稱爲 foreign minister。但在英國，外交部卻被稱爲 foreign office，外交大臣則爲 foreign secretary。美國的外交部門也屬例外，其被稱爲「國務院」（the state department），它的外交部長則被稱爲「國務卿」（secretary of state）。

Former adjudication ▶ Collateral estoppel ▶ *Res judicata*

Former adjudication 爲「既判效力原則」，是訴訟法上的一個原則，指禁止當事人就已經作出判決的相同問題或主張重新進行訴訟。其包括兩個類型：collateral estoppel（為「一事不二訴原則」，也稱為 estoppel by judgment、issue preclusion）和 *res judicata*（「一主張不二提原則」，也稱為 *res adjudicata*、claim preclusion）[1]。collateral estoppel 和 *res judicata* 的區別在於前者指禁止當事人就某項已經裁決的具體事項再提起訴訟；而後者則是指禁止再提出某一訴訟主張或訴因。[2]

注

[1] "Collateral estoppel and *res judicata* are the two types of former adjudication." Cf. Bryan A. Garner, *Black's Law Dictionary*, 7th Edition, West Group (1999), at P. 663.

[2] "Collateral estoppel is distinguished from *res judicata* in that the former bars relitigation of a specific issue in a case whereas the latter bars reassertion of an entire claim or cause of action." Cf. James E. Clapp, *Random House Webster's Dictionary of the Law*, Random House (2000), at 164.

Fornication ▶ Adultery ▶ Spouse-breach

三者均用於指男女雙方之間自願發生的非法性行為。其中，fornication 為「私通」，adultery 為「通姦」。它們之間的區別主要在於前者是指未婚男女之間發生非法性行為[1]，而後者則指已婚男女之間發生的非法性行為[2]。按一般規定，如兩個性行為者中一方未婚而另一方已婚，已婚者構成 adultery，未婚者則構成 fornication[3]。但在美國，各州的法律就此還有一些不同規定。有些州適用羅馬法或猶太法的規定，如果女方已婚，則雙方均可定性為犯有 adultery，如果女方未婚，不論男方已婚否，雙方均不得定性為 adultery；而在有些州，只要其中一方已婚，兩人苟合即構成 adultery[4]。就通姦而言，有的州還規定有「雙重通姦罪」（double adultery）和「單一通姦罪」（single adultery），前者是指兩個已婚男女之間發生非法性行爲，後者指其中一方是已婚而另一方是未婚的情況⑤。此外，儘管過去 fornication 和 adultery 均可被視爲一種成文法而非不成文法犯罪，但 fornication 卻較輕，爲一種輕罪（misdemeanor）⑥，且一般均未眞正執行。現在在多數司法管轄區，fornication和adultery已經不再被視爲犯罪，但與在「有權同意性行爲年齡」（age of consent，多數州規定爲 16 歲）以下的女方私通或通姦者則除外⑦。spouse-breach 等同 adultery，只是比 adultery 更爲正式一些。

F

注

① "fornication: the crime of engaging in sexual intercourse while unmarried", Cf. James E. Clapp, *Random House Webster's Dictionary of the Law*, Random House (2000), at P. 191.

② "voluntary sexual intercourse by a married person with someone other than that person's spouse.In a strict sense, only a married person can commit adultery", *Id*.at Ps. 17—18.

③ "Further, if one of the persons be married and the other not, it is fornication on the part of the latter, though adultery for the former." Cf. The Publisher's Editorial Staff, *Black's Law Dictionary*, Abridged 6ᵗʰ Edition, West Publishing Co. (1991), at P. 451.

④ "In some states, sexual intercourse between two married persons, who are not married to each, constitutes adultery on the part of both; sexual intercourse between a married person and an unmarried person likewise constitutes adultery on the part of both. In other states, adultery can be committed only by a married person. Thus sexual intercourse between two married persons, who are not married to each other, constitutes adultery on the part of both; but if only one party to the sexual intercourse is married, the intercourse constitutes adultery on the part of the married person and fornication on the part of the unmarried person.In other states, sexual intercourse constitutes adultery only where the woman is the married party. Thus, sexual intercourse between a married woman and a married man other than her spouse or sexual intercourse between a married woman and an unmarried man constitutes adultery on the part of both; but if the woman is unmarried, neither party is guilty of adultery even if the man is married." Cf. Charles E. Torcia, *Wharton's Criminal Law*, 15th Edition, s. 211 (1994), at P. 531.

⑤ Cf. Bryan A. Garner, *Black's Law Dictionary*, 7th Edition, West Group (1999), at P. 52.

⑥ "Where still considered a crime, fornication is classified as a misdemeanor." Cf. Linda Picard Wood, J.D., *Merriam Webster's Dictionary of Law*, Merriam-Webster, Incorporated (1996), at P. 201.

⑦ "fornication: This crime has been abolished in more than half the states", Cf. James E. Clapp, *Random House Webster's Dictionary of the Law*, Random House (2000), at P. 191; "adultery: Many states have abolished the crime and eliminated the requirement of an accusation of wrongdoing in order to obtain a divorce", *Id.* at P. 18.

Forswear ▶ Abjure ▶ Disavow ▶ Disclaim ▶ Disown

這些單詞均有拋棄和否認的含義。其中，forswear 指發誓拋棄或公開承認某種行為有罪或有過錯，強烈表示希望完全放棄此種行為，故該單詞具有一種悔罪或懺悔的內涵①。abjure 常指憤怒地否認或拒絕，該詞曾具有的發誓拋棄的含義，而今已不常用②。disavow 和 disclaim 常用於對牽連關係或責任的斷然否認，因而正好與

forswear 的認罪內涵相反。disavow 曾經指正式發誓否認，現在則常指拒絕承認某事有效或否認與他人的關係，如否認代理人未經授權的行為，或否認某授權的效力等③。儘管 disclaim 也可用於對責任的否認（如to disclaim all complicity in the assassination），但它卻更常用於指放棄原可屬於自己的權利或資格④。disown 可指拋棄任何事物，此外，其還用於指否認並脫離與他人，尤其是與親人的關係，如：The father disowned his son and wrote him out of his will（父親斷絕了與兒子的關係，將他從自己的遺囑中除名）⑤。

注

① "to reject, renounce, or deny under oath", Cf. Linda Picard Wood, J.D., *Merriam Webster's Dictionary of Law*, Merriam-Webster, Incorporated (1996), at P. 201.

② "Abjure is more forceful in sometimes implying an angry rejection; it also referred once to renunciation under oath, but less often applied in this way now." Cf. The Editors of The Reader's Digest, *Use the Right Word*, The Reader's Digest Association Proprietary Ltd. (1971), at P. 229.

③ "To repudiate the unauthorized act of an agent; to deny the authority by which he assumed to act." Cf. The Publisher's Editorial Staff, *Black's Law Dictionary*, Abridged 6th Edition, West Publishing Co. (1991), at P. 299.

④ "to renounce or disavow a right, interest, benefit, or claim", Cf. James E. Clapp, *Random House Webster's Dictionary of the Law*, Random House (2000), at P. 139.

⑤ "Disown at its most general can suggest any sort of abandonment. The word is often used in a special way, however, referring to the total rejection of a disliked person, often a near relative." Cf. The Editors of The Reader's Digest, *Use the Right Word*, The Reader's Digest Association Proprietary Ltd. (1971), at P. 229.

Forward contract ▶ Futures contract

　　二者常被一些詞典混爲一談，實際上，它們之間的差異極大[①]。事實上，futures contract 應爲「期貨契約」，forward contract 卻爲「遠期契約」。兩者之間的差異在於：⑴期貨契約是在有組織的交易所中交易，而遠期契約則沒有此種交易場所；⑵期貨契約具有標準的契約條款，而遠期契約則無此規定；⑶期貨交易所有相關的票據交換所以確保期貨契約義務的履行，遠期交易無此保障；⑷期貨交易規定有保證金制和每日結算制，契約遠期交易則無此種體制；⑸期貨頭寸交割迅速；⑹期貨市場（futures market）有專門的機構予以調整管理，而遠期市場（forward market）則爲自我調節[②]。

注

① Cf. 陸谷孫，《英漢大詞典》，《上海譯文出版社》（1995），第1252頁；陳伯初，《英漢商業大詞典》，中國商業出版社（1994），第683頁。

② "Forward contracts and futures contracts can be distinguished by several important features of futures markets: the existence of an organized futures exchange, the trading of standarized contracts, the role of clearinghouse, the system of margins and daily settlement, the ability to close contracts easily, and the regulatory structure of the markets." Cf. Li Rong-fu/Song Lei, *A Course Book of Legal English*, Law Press, China (1999), at Ps. 367—368.

Foster ▸ Adopt

二者均指對與自己無血緣關係的兒童進行如父（母）般的養育或撫養的行為。差別在於 foster（非親撫養）一般是指在無正式的法律收養關係時對兒童的養育或撫養[1]，其有些類似中國舊的婚姻法所規定的事實收養或由政府等指定的撫養，如兒童村裡假定的母親與她們負責養育的兒童之間的關係。由此，與 foster 相關聯的一些術語，如 foster father 或 foster mother 也應譯為「非親撫養養父」或「非親撫養養母」，表示受撫養者與撫養者之間無任何父母親情關係，不論是血親或由法律認定的收養關係，而不能像目前幾乎所有的詞典那樣將其等同於 adopt 而把它們譯為「養父」或「養母」[2]。相比之下，adopt（收養）則是指收養人和被收養人之間已經履行且具有正式的收養法律關係[3]。故 adopted father 或 adopted mother 才是真正意義上的養父或養母。

注

[1] "affording, receiving, or sharing nature or parental care though not related by blood or legal relationships", Cf. Linda Picard Wood, J.D., *Merriam Webster's Dictionary of Law*, Merriam-Webster, Incorporated (1996), at P. 201; "foster parent: one who acts as a parent in place of a natural parent, but without legal relationship", Cf. A. S. Hornby, *Oxford Advanced Learner's Dictionary of Current English*, Oxford University Press, London (1974), at P. 346.

[2] Cf. 陸谷孫，《英漢大詞典》，上海譯文出版社（1995），第 1252 頁；張芳傑等翻譯，《牛津現代高級英漢雙解詞典》，牛津大學出版社（1985），第 465 頁；薛波，《漢英法律詞典》，外文出版社（1995），第 799 頁。

[3] "An act which creates a familial relationship in which the adopted

child is in law and fact, treated as the adoptive family's natural child."
Cf. McLeod, *The Conflict of Laws*, Calgary, Carswell (1983), at
P. 310.

Fraud in the *factum* ▸ Fraud in the inducement

二者之間的差異在於 fraud in the *factum*（契據簽署詐欺，也稱為 fraud in the execution、fraud in the making）是指因詐欺而導致他人誤解自己正在從事的交易的性質，特別是誤解了如契約或票據（如本票等）之內容，如騙盲人在契約上簽字，但卻告訴他簽署的是一封普通信件[①]。而 fraud in the inducement（誘因詐欺）則指被詐欺者知道自己所進行的交易的性質，然而因某種誘因之誘惑而仍然上當之情況[②]。

注

① "Fraud occurring when a legal instrument as actually executed differs from the one intended for execution by the person who executes it, or when the instrument may have had no legal existence." Cf. Bryan A. Garner, *Black's Law Dictionary*, 7th Edition, West Group (1999), at P. 671.

② "Fraud occurring when a misrepresentation leads another to enter into a transaction with a false impression of the risks, duties, or obligations involved; an intentional misrepresentation of a material risk or duty reasonably relied on, thereby injuring the other party without vitiating the contract itself, esp. about a fact relating to value." *Id.* at P. 671.

Frisk ▸ Search

二者均有搜尋或搜查的含義。區別在於 frisk（也稱為 pat down）為「搜身」，其目的僅限於尋找疑犯身上所藏匿的武器以保證作偵破工作的警察等的人身安全，其搜尋範圍只限於武器而不是為發現其他證據[1]。search 為「搜索」，其搜尋範圍大於 frisk，其目的主要是尋找違法犯罪活動的證據，搜查一般需要合理理由或搜索狀[2]。

注

[1] "Contact of the outer clothing of a person to detect by the sense of touch whether a concealed weapon is being carried. The scope of a frisk is limited by the courts to be less than a full scale search." Cf. The Publisher's Editorial Staff, *Black's Law Dictionary*, Abridged 6th Edition, West Publishing Co. (1991), at P. 299.

[2] "inspection by law enforcement officials of a person's body, home, or any area that the person would reasonably be expected to regard as private, for weapons, contraband, or evidence of criminal activity. Under the 4th Amendment, a search ordinarily may not be conducted without probable cause." Cf. James E. Clapp, *Rando House Webster's Dictionary of the Law*, Random House (2000), at P. 387.

Frivolous answer ▸ Sham answer

二者都指被告針對原告的指控進行的事實不充分的答辯（insufficient defense）。主要區別在於 frivolous answer 為「形式要件不足的答辯」，指形式要件不充分，在表面上沒有作充足的辯護，儘管事實上可能是真實的[1]；而 sham answer 則為「虛偽答

辯」，指形式要件完備，但列舉的事實不眞實，不是眞誠善意地進
行辯護②。

注

① "A frivolous answer, on the other hand, is one which on its face sets
up no defense, although it may be true in fact." Cf. The Publisher's
Editorial Staff, *Black's Law Dictionary*, Abridged 6ᵗʰ Edition, West
Publishing Co. (1991), at P. 60.

② "One sufficient on its face but so clearly that it presents no real issue
to be tried. One good in form, but false in fact and not pleaded in good
faith." *Id*. at P. 60.

Fruit of the poisonous tree ▸ Cat out of the bag

　　二者均爲證據法則中的術語，都與刑事案件中證據的證據能力
相關。fruit of the poisonous tree 爲「毒樹之果」，主要是指以非法程
序手段所獲證據不得被法院所採納，而根據此一非法取得之證據而
找到的其他證據也一樣不具證據能力①。cat out of the bag 爲「無意
洩露之秘密」（或直譯爲「出袋之貓」），其與「毒樹之果」密切
相關，主要指被告在非法程序手段下，如刑訊逼供之下招供後，又
安排被告在合法的取證程序中進行供述，此次供述儘管程序合法，
但因此次供述可能會受「毒樹」的影響（因被告可能認爲秘密已經
無意洩露或貓已經跑了，再次重複供述也無關緊要，故再次予以供
述），因而此次供述所得證據也不具證據能力②。

注

① "Evidence which is spawned by or directly derived from an illegal
search or illegal interrogation is generally inadmissible against the

defendant because of its original taint, though knowledge of facts gained independently of the original and tainted search is admissible." Cf. *Wong Sun v. U.S.*, 371 U.S. 471, 83 S.Ct. 407, 9 L.Ed.2d 441.

② Cf. Peter Mirfield, Jesus College, Oxford, *Successive Confession and the Poisonous Tree*, Criminal Law Review (1996), at P. 551.

Full court ▶ Court in bank ▶ Panel (of judges)

三者均用於指法院審理案件時的一種法庭組成形式。其中，full court（也稱爲 full bench）爲「全席法庭」，指由法院所有法官所組成的一種法庭，通常目的是爲聽審以訴求不充分爲由的抗辯（arguments on demurrers）、重新審判的動議（motion for new trial）等①。court in bank（也稱爲 court *en banc*）爲「全席聽審」，是指由法院所有法官或法定數額（quorum）的法官出席所組成的法庭聽證會，受理的事項較少，事實上，court in bank 或 court *en banc* 在多數情況均等同 full court②。panel（of judges）則爲數個法官所組成的合議庭，尤指上訴審法庭③。如上訴法院共有 9 名法官，9 名法官共同組成一個法庭審理訴訟則爲 full court，其也可分爲 3 組，即組成三個法庭各自審理案件，此時的法庭則爲「合議庭」（panel）。

注

① "A court session that is attended by all the court's judges; an *en banc* court." Cf. Bryan A. Garner, *Black's Law Dictionary*, 7th Edition, West Group (1999), at P. 358.

② "A meeting of all the judges of a court, usually for the purposes of hearing arguments on demurrers, motions, for new trial, etc, as distinguished from sessions of the same court presided over by a single judge or panel of judges." Cf. The Publisher's Editorial Staff,

Black's Law Dictionary, Abridged 6th Edition, West Publishing Co. (1991), at P. 245.

③ "A set of judges selected from a complete court to decide a specific case; esp. a group of three judges designated to sit for an appellate court." Cf. Bryan A. Garner, *Black's Law Dictionary*, 7th Edition, West Group (1999), at P. 1135.

G

Gambling ▶ Betting ▶ Gaming ▶ Lottery ▶ Wagering

以上單詞均有賭博的含義，英國法律對它們有較明確的界定。其中，gambling 爲「賭博」，其是一般用語，指作爲遊戲、比賽或其他行爲方式，以金錢或其他有價值的東西作賭注的一種冒險，可含合法或違法成分。總體說來，賭博（gambling）包括：betting（打賭）、gaming（博彩）、lottery（彩票）和 wagering（對賭）幾種。betting 是指用錢或物對未確定的事情的結局進行冒險，可經常進行，涉及兩方以上，這是其與「對賭」之間的區別。gaming 也稱「遊戲賭」，是指靠機遇或技巧贏取參與者所下賭注的冒險，如跑馬、賽犬、打麻將、老虎機等。lottery 是指以抽籤中獎的方式憑運氣進行的獎金分配，如主要是靠技巧獲勝的競獎則不屬於彩票賭範疇。wagering 實際是打賭的一種形式，只限於兩人之間進行，指雙方對未來某一事件的結果相互持相反預測觀點，然後根據事件結果按預先約定的條件付給對方錢或物[1]。在美國，上述單詞有時則沒有明顯的區別，如美國人將 gambling 也稱爲 gaming，而將 gambling policy 也稱爲 wager device[2]。

注

[1] Cf. David M. Walker, *The Oxford Companion To Law*, *Gambling*, Oxford University Press (1980), at P. 366.

[2] Cf. Bryan A. Garner, *Black's Law Dictionary*, 7th Edition, West Group (1999), at P. 687.

Gaol ▸ Jail

兩個單詞同義，均爲「監獄」或「看守所」，指縣（或郡）或市設立的關押未決犯或輕罪犯之場所[1]（其與其他監獄場所的差異請另參見條目 prison），也稱爲 holding cell、lockup 以及 jailhouse。其中，gaol 爲英國人通用，而 jail 則爲美式英語[2]。

注

[1] "an institution, usually run by a county or municipality, for locking up offenders serving short sentences and accused people awaiting trial", Cf. James E. Clapp, *Random House Webster's Dictionary of the Law*, Random House (2000), at P. 250.

[2] Cf. Bryan A. Garner, *Black's Law Dictionary*, 7th Edition, West Group (1999), at P. 838.

Gender ▸ Sex

二者均有「性別」的含義。其區別，尤其在諸如刑法學中解釋兩性犯罪和受害者性別時（male and female offending and victimization）之區別在於 sex（male/female）主要是指按生殖器官特徵之不同而在生物學上（biological classification indicated primarily by genital characteristics）的一種分類，其更多地強調性或性別分類。而gender（masculine/feminine）則主要是一種複雜的社會、歷史、文化產物，其與人們生理上的特徵，即性器官或生殖器功能有關（it is related to biological sex difference and reproductive capacities），但非完全衍生於此（but not simply derived from them），其還與服飾、舉態、語言、職業等（dress, gestures, language, occupation, and so on）有關，其更多的是強調綜合意義上的一種性別，尤指性別差異。

"The sum of the peculiarities of structure and function that distinguish a male from a female organism." Cf. Bryan A. Garner, *Black's Law Dictionary*, 7th Edition, West Group (1999), at P. 1379.

General appearance ▶ Special appearance

G

　　二者之間的差異在於 general appearance（一般性出庭）是指出庭當事人承認法院的司法管轄權，對管轄權並不爭執，但提出其他事項的答辯①。與此剛好相反，special appearance（特別出庭）則是指當事人出庭的唯一目的只是爲弄清法院是否對自己有屬人管轄權②。根據美國《聯邦民事訴訟規則》以及凡是採用了該規則之州的規定，special appearance 和 general appearance 已經被廢除，故凡聯邦法院和有關州的法院均不再使用這兩種出庭方式，當事人有關管轄許可權問題的異議可在訴辯狀或審判前的動議中提出③。

注

① "a court appearance by which a party submits to the jurisdiction of the court esp. by asking for any relief other than a ruling that the court has no jurisdiction over the appearing party", Cf. Linda Picard Wood, J.D., *Merriam Webster's Dictionary of Law*, Merriam-Webster, Incorporated (1996), at P. 211.

② "an appearance by a party in court for the sole purpose of challenging the court's assertion of personal jurisdiction over the party", *Id.* at P. 461.

③ "Under the Federal Rules of Civil Procedure and the rules of states that have adopted it, the use of a special appearance to challenge jurisdiction has been abolished, and jurisdiction may be challenged in the pleadings or in a pretrial motion." *Id.* at P. 461.

General demurrer ▸ Special demurrer ▸ Speaking demurrer

三者用於指被告所作出的三種不同類型的抗辯。其區別在於 general demurrer（也稱爲 general exception）爲「一般抗辯」，指就指控事實不充足，即不能構成充足訴因而進行的抗辯[1]。special demurrer 爲「特殊抗辯」，是就訴狀的格式或結構不當而提起的抗辯，一般需指出訴狀中具體的不當部分[2]。speaking demurrer 則爲「以講述新事實而進行的抗辯」，是以講述訴辯狀中未有的且法院也不瞭解的事實的方式進行的一種抗辯[3]。

注

[1] "An objection pointing out a substantive defect in an opponent's pleading, such as the insufficiency of the claim or the court's lack of subject matter jurisdiction; an objection to a pleading for want of substance." Cf. Bryan A. Garner, *Black's Law Dictionary*, 7th Edition, West Group (1999), at P. 583.

[2] "An objection that questions the form of the pleading and states specially the nature of the objection, such as that the pleading violates the rules of pleading or practice." *Id.* at P. 445.

[3] "A speaking demurrer is one which, in order to sustain itself, requires the aid of a fact not appearing on the face of the pleading objected to, or, in other words, which alleges or assumes the existence of a fact not already pleaded, and which constitutes the ground of objection and is condemned both by the common law and the code system of pleading;

A speaking demurrer is one which alleges some new matter, not disclosed by the pleading against which the demurrer is aimed and not judicially known or legally presumed to be true." Cf. The Publisher's Editorial Staff, *Black's Law Dictionary*, Abridged 6th Edition, West Publishing Co. (1991), at P. 299.

Government

廣義的 government（政府）一般由三大部門（branch）所組成，即(1) legislature（立法機關），其為一個國家的最高權力機關，具有透過立法活動制定和修改法律的職能；(2) executive（行政機關），其職責是負責政策的執行以及法律的適用；(3) judiciary（司法機關），其職責是負責解釋法律和依法斷案。如更廣義，在美國，其還指聯邦政府和各州，以及地方政府等[1]。狹義的 government 則僅指行政機關，即 executive branch[2]。

注

[1] "In the United States, government consists of the executive, legislative, and judicial branches in addition to administrative agencies. In a broader sense, includes the federal government and all its agencies and bureaus, state and county governments, and city and township governments." Cf. The Publisher's Editorial Staff, *Black's Law Dictionary*, Abridged 6th Edition, West Publishing Co. (1991), at P. 479.

[2] "The executive branch of the U.S. government." Cf. Bryan A. Garner, *Black's Law Dictionary*, 7th Edition, West Group (1999), at P. 703.

Graft ▸ Corruption

二者均可用於指官員的貪污。其區別在於 graft 沒有 corruption 正式，即 corruption 是法律上正式所指的 improper and usually unlawful conduct intended to secure a benefit for oneself or another，其為一正式法律用語，除指貪污之外，同時還指受賄等[①]。相比之下，graft 則指利用職位非法謀取錢財，尤指官員貪污公款（public official's fraudulently acquisition of public funds）[②]，指受賄時，其為一非正式用語，即 informally indicates corruption of officials[③]。

注

① "granting of favors inconsistent with official duties", Cf. Daphne Dukelow, *The Dictionary of Canadian Law*, Thomson professional Publishing Canada (1991), at P. 222.

② Cf. Bryan A. Garner, *Black's Law Dictionary*, 7th Edition, West Group (1999), at P. 706; "The popular meaning is the fraudulent obtaining of public money unlawfully by the corruption of public officers." Cf. The publisher's Editorial Staff, *Black's Law Dictionary*, Abridged 6th Edition, West Publishing Co. (1991), at P. 482.

③ "(informal) corruption of officials", Cf. P. H. Collin, *Dictionary of Law*, 2nd Edition, Peter Collin Publishing Ltd. (1993), at P. 246.

Grass ▸ Informant ▸ Informer

三個單詞均有向警方告密以提供他人犯罪事實的人的含義。區別在於 grass 是指本身是罪犯而向警方提供其他罪犯情況者，故其具有「污點證人」的含義[①]。告發許多其他罪犯的 grass 則被稱為 supergrass。而 informant 或 informer（為同義詞）則多指為獲得一筆酬金而向警方提供有關罪犯情況的人，其為「線人」，此種人可能但並非一定是罪犯②。

注

① "criminal who gives information to the police about other criminals", Cf. P. H. Collin, *Dictionary of Law*, 2nd Edition, Peter Collin Publishing Ltd. (1993), at P. 247.

② "one who informs against another; specific: one who makes a practice esp. for money of informing police of other's criminal activities", Cf. Linda Picard Wood, J.D., *Merriam Webster's Dictionary of Law*, Merriam-Webster, Incorporated (1996), at P. 244.

Gross earnings ▸ Gross income ▸ Gross salary ▸ Gross profit ▸ Gross receipts ▸ Gross revenue

以上這些片語的意思十分近似，且經常相互競合。其中，gross earnings 為「毛收入」，指個人或企業在去除稅收扣減和開支前的總收入①。gross income 有兩種含義，就個人而言，其為「總收入」，所指範圍極廣，包括法律規定除外的一切在扣減之前的來源收入。按美國《國內稅收法典》規定，其共有 15 類：(1)服務報酬，包括附加福利收入和傭金（compensation for services, including fringe benefits and commissions）；(2)營業總收入（gross income derived from business）；(3)財產交易收入（gains derived from dealings in property）；(4)利息（interest）；(5)租金（rents）；(6)特權稅（royalties）；(7)紅利（dividends）；(8)贍養費和分居扶養費（alimony and separate maintenance payments）；(9)年金（annuities）；(10)人壽保險養老保險金（income from life insurance and contracts for endowment insurance）；(11)退休金（pensions）；(12)

債務收入（income from discharge of a debt）；(13)合夥總收入中分配所得（distributive share of partnership gross income）；(14)遺產繼承所得（income received (as by an estate or heir) by reasons of a person's death）；(15)遺產利益或信託收入（income from an interest in an estate or trust）。就企業而言，gross income 為「毛利潤」，此時其等同 gross profit[2]。gross salary 則多指個人的總薪資收入。gross profit 為「毛利潤」，指完稅和去除支出之前企業銷售收入與產品成本之間的差額，即在完稅和除去其他開支前所有的銷售或總收入（gross receipts）與成本的差額[3]。gross receipts 為「總收入」或「總收益」，指某納稅人在特定的期間進行商品銷售或提供服務所獲得的所有金錢收入或其他報償[4]。gross revenue 為「毛收益」，指企業在稅收扣減前的所得，法律規定減免的除外[5]。

注

① "Total income and receipts of a person or business before deductions and expenses." Cf. The Publisher's Editorial Staff, *Black's Law Dictionary*, Abridged 6th Edition, West Publishing Co. (1991), at P. 484.

② *Id.* at P. 485.

③ "Total sales revenue less the cost of the goods sold, no adjustment being made for additional expenses and taxes." Cf. Bryan A. Garner, *Black's Law Dictionary*, 7th Edition, West Group (1999), at P. 1227.

④ "the total amount of value in money or other consideration received by a taxpayer in a given period for goods sold or services performed", Cf. Linda Picard Wood, J.D., *Merriam Webster's Dictionary of Law*, Merriam-Webster, Incorporated (1996), at P. 218.

⑤ "Receipts of a business before deductions for any purpose except those items specifically exempted." Cf. The Publisher's Editorial

Staff, *Black's Law Dictionary*, Abridged 6th Edition, West Publishing Co. (1991), at P. 486.

Guaranty ▸ Suretyship ▸ Warranty

三個單詞均有擔保或保證的含義，且有時還可以交替使用，但它們之間仍有不少差異。其區別主要在於，在指契約時，guaranty 所指的是對他人（another）所作的一種附屬性質的保證，必須作成書面形式。在契約中，guaranty 所作的保證，僅應被視爲是原契約的一種附屬契約，對保證人不構成任何主要責任，他（她）僅應對其他人的違約或過失負賠償責任而已。且 guaranty 所指的也常是對某些瑕疵或事故的一種有條件的附屬保證，故其等同一般擔保或賠償責任保證，債權人只有在對主債務人窮盡一切救濟方法後方可要求 guarantor 進行債務賠償[1]。suretyship 雖然也是指對他人（a second party）的行爲、債務等的一種保證，但在契約中，其屬於獨立和單獨性質的一種保證，在 contract of suretyship 中，保證人和被保證人的責任同時發生，即擔保人（surety）在此成爲了主要責任人〔即也負主要責任（principal liability）〕之一，故其等同連帶擔保或連帶責任保證，債權人不等窮盡對主債務人的救濟方法即可要求 surety 進行賠償[2]。相比之下，warranty 則是對自己本身的行爲、產品等物（thing）的一種擔保，可不經書面文件，其對擔保人構成主要責任，是一種絕對的嚴格法律責任意義上的擔保，故其爲「單方承諾保證」。在商事交易等中，warranty 經常用作指對產品瑕疵、質量、數量的絕對擔保，如中國的「三包卡」之類所作的保證。對於契約而言，warranty 指一種十分嚴格的責任擔保，即除非擔保人嚴格按字面意義執行契約，否則契約便應視爲無效[3]。

注

① "A collateral agreement for performance of another's undertaking. An agreement in which the guarantor agrees to satisfy the debt of another (the debtor), only if and when the debtor fails to repay (secondarily liable). An undertaking or promise that is collateral to primary or principal obligation and that binds guarantor to performance in event of nonperformance by the principal obligor." Cf. The Publisher's Editorial Staff, *Black's Law Dictionary*, Abridged 6th Edition, West Publishing Co. (1991), at P. 486.

② "The relationship among three parties whereby one person (the surety) guarantees payment of a debtor's debt owed to a creditor or acts as a co debtor." *Id.* at P. 1006.

③ "An express or implied promise that something in furtherance of the contract is guaranteed by one of the contracting parties; esp., a seller's promise that the thing being sold is as represented or promised." Bryan A. Garner, *Black's Law Dictionary*, 7th Edition, West Group (1999), at P. 1581.

H

Habitation ▶ Usufruct

二者均與使用他人不動產的權利相關。區別在於 habitation（居住權）是指大陸法中所規定的在無損於他人財產的前提下居住的權利，使用人只能將不動產用於自己或其家庭成員的居住，故其應被譯為「居住權」[1]。而 usufruct（用益權）的範圍則較 habitation 廣，指在一定期限，在不損害財產的前提下使用他人財產之權利，除用作居住之外，其還包括其他諸如收穫土地上的莊稼或產物等權利[2]。

注

[1] "A right to dwell in the property of another." Bryan A. Garner, *Black's Law Dictionary*, 7th Edition, West Group (1999), at P. 716.

[2] "In the civil law, a real right of limited duration on the property of another. The features of the right vary with the nature of the things subject to it as consumables or non consumables." Cf. The Publisher's Editorial Staff, *Black's Law Dictionary*, Abridged 6th Edition, West Publishing Co. (1991), at P. 1073.

Hashish ▶ Marijuana

二者均是指由印度大麻所製成的毒品。區別在於 hashish（大麻製劑）指的是以大麻的花頭（cannabis）所提煉製作的一種液體製劑[1]。而 marijuana（大麻煙）則是包括由切碎的大麻葉、莖及花等製作的煙草[2]。

注

① "A resinous juice found in the upper leaves and the flowering tops of the plant Cannabis sativa." Cf. F. A. Jaffe, *A Guide to Pathological Evidence*, 2nd Edition, Toronto, Carswell (1983), at P. 177.

② "Marijuana means all parts of the plant Cannabis sativa." Cf. *Uniform Controlled Substances Act*, 21 USCA, Art. 802.

Hawker ▸ Pedlar

兩個單詞均可用於指領取執照前往他人住宅、居所挨戶推銷或沿街叫賣貨物和商品者。以往，hawker 和 pedlar（也拼寫為 pedler、peddler）之間的區別在於前者指使用畜力或推車等來運載自己的貨物進行叫賣者，而後者則僅靠人力攜帶商品，現在此種區別已基本消失，二者幾乎可通用。須注意的是，hawker 和 pedlar 推銷的均是他人生產的產品。如 hawker 和 pedlar 的銷售規模很小，屬 petty hawker 或 petty pedlar，則稱為 huckster（走街小販）。

注

"A hawker was a peddler who used beast of burden to carry ware and who cried out merits of wares in street." Cf. The Publisher's Editorial Staff, *Black's Law Dictionary*, Abridged 6th Edition, West Publishing Co. (1991), at P. 495.

Hearing ▸ Trial

二者常用於指對案件的審理。主要差別在於 hearing 多指在訴訟中期就程序事項和動議等進行的審理，相對說來，其形式沒有 trial

正式，其經常由一名法官主持，且無陪審團參加，主要目的是向訴爭各方提供爭辯機會，有時有證人參與，故將其譯為「聽審」①（在行政法中 hearing 為「聽證」，指相關者聚會向行政決策人提供意見和見解②）。而 trial 則是指訴訟的最後開庭正式審理（絕大多數民事案件在到達此階段前已經透過其他途徑結案），其是就案件事實，即就 merits of the case 進行的正式審理，trial 比 hearing 正式，其多採用合議庭審理形式，且可適用陪審團。一般說來，就 hearing 的裁定不能進行上訴（final order 等除外），而只有就案件的實體進行審理的裁判，即對 trial 所作的判決不服方可提起上訴，其為正式審判③。

注

① "A proceeding of relative formality (though generally less formal than a trial), generally public, with definite issues of fact or of law to be tried, in which witnesses are heard and evidence presented. It is a proceeding where evidence is taken to determine issue of fact and to render decision on basis of that evidence." Cf. The Publisher's Editorial Staff, *Black's Law Dictionary*, Abridged 6th Edition, West Publishing Co. (1991), at P. 498.

② "Administrative law. Any setting in which an affected person presents arguments to an agency decision maker." Cf. Bryan A. Garner, *Black's Law Dictionary*, 7th Edition, West Group (1999), at P. 725.

③ "a formal judicial examination of evidence and determination of legal claims in an adversary proceeding", *Id.* at P. 1510.

Heir

　按其接受遺產的方式，繼承人（heir）可分為兩類，即：heir

beneficiary（也稱為 beneficiary heir，限定繼承人）和 unconditional heir（無條件繼承人）。在美國，heir beneficiary 是實施大陸法系的路易斯安那州的術語，指根據繼承人只承擔正式遺產清單所列財產範圍內的債務之權利規定（benefit of inventory）而接受遺產者[1]。unconditional heir 也是大陸法系上的術語，其所指的繼承人則無任何保留權利，或沒有制定任何遺產清單[2]。如一個繼承人擔心其繼承債務會大於繼承財產價值，他可選擇作為 heir beneficiary，從而按繼承人只承擔正式遺產清單所列財產範圍內的債務之權利的方式接受遺產，由此可免除多餘的債務負擔。

注

① "an heir who exercises the benefit of inventory which limits the amount of his or her liability for the decedent's debts", Cf. Linda Picard Wood, J.D., *Merriam Webster's Dictionary of Law*, Merriam-Webster, Incorporated (1996), at P. 225.

② "A person who chooses—expressly or tacitly—to inherit without any reservation or without making an inventory." Cf. Bryan A. Garner, *Black's Law Dictionary*, 7th Edition, West Group (1999), at P. 728.

Heirloom ▸ Heirship moveables

二者均是蘇格蘭法律中有關遺產的術語。它們均是指按特定習慣不能用遺囑處分，而只能在所有人死亡時傳給其繼承人，而不是先移交遺囑執行人，然後由遺囑執行人處理的動產。heirship moveables（繼承動產）是早期術語，其在 1868 年已被廢止[1]。而 heirloom（祖傳動產，如物權證明、契據、擔保等）則是在 1964 年採用的概念，其所指的動產只能傳給家族的某成員，而不能由無遺囑死亡者的生存配偶所繼承[2]。

① Cf. 《牛津法律大詞典》（根據David M. Walker, *The Oxford Companion to Law* 翻譯），光明日報出版社（1989），第 402 頁。

② "Popularly, a valued possession of great sentimental value passed down through generations within a family." Cf. Bryan A. Garner, *Black's Law Dictionary*, 7th Edition, West Group (1999), at P. 729.

Herein ▸ Therein ▸ Wherein

在法律英語中，這類由 here、there 以及 where 加上其他介詞構成的類似單詞很多，除上述三個之外，還包括：hereinafter、hereafter、hereby、hereof、hereto、heretofore、hereunder、hereunto、thereafter、thereby、therefor、therefrom、therein、thereinafter、thereinbefore、thereinunder、thereof、thereto、theretofore、therewith 以及 whereby、wherein、whereof、whereon 等。這些詞乍看上去非常複雜，實際上，只要弄清楚它們的結構，翻譯或理解便十分簡單了。一般說來，讀者可將 here、there 和 where 都視爲是單詞 "which"，然後將其後面所跟的介詞放到其前面，這樣一來，herein 便可被視爲 in which，hereof 則爲 of which，而 therefrom 則爲 from which，whereby 也成爲 by which 等。它們之間的主要區別在於 here、there 和 where 的指代有所不同。首先，here 指代「本」文件、文書、契約、協議等，即是指法律文件載體本身。如 herein 出現在一個契約（contract）中，我們前面所說的 in which 中的 which 則指代的是 contract，而 herein 也就成爲 in this contract，而該契約中的 the parties hereof 也就成爲 the parties of this contract。同樣，如 herein 出現在《公司法》（Companies Act）中，我們便可

把該 herein 視爲「in this Companies Act」理解①。而當 herewith 出現在信函中時，如：please find the check enclosed herewith，其等同於 with this letter，該句子則可譯爲「請查收隨函所附的支票」。相比之下，there 和 where 則均可視爲是指代文件、文書、契約等前面所出現的單詞、片語、事物等，如在 if a member fails to pay any call or installment of a call on the day appointed for the payment thereof 裡，當我們把 thereof② 視爲 of which 時，此時的 which 所指代的則是其前面所出現的 call（催繳股款）或 installment of a call（催繳的分期支付股款），該句子意思則是「如果股東沒有按規定繳款的日期繳納任何所催繳的股款或催繳的分期支付股款」。同樣，a deed whereby 中的 whereby 當被視爲「by which」時，此時的 which 也是指代其前面的 deed。there 和 where 之間的區別在於 there 常指代其緊跟的前面的單詞或片語等，而 where 加介詞所構成的單詞更常指代前面所說的整個句子、事物等，產生一種類似非限制性形容子句的作用。

注

① "herein: In this thing (such as a document, section, or matter)", Cf. Bryan A. Garner, *Black's Law Dictionary*, 7th Edition, West Group (1999), at P. 731.
② "thereof: Of that, it, or them", *Id.* at P. 1488.

Heritable ► Moveable

這兩個形容詞均可用於修飾遺產。heritable（世襲的）主要用於蘇格蘭和大陸法系①，修飾不動產，特別是土地以及土地上或與之相關的權益（現分爲世襲的有體和無體財產兩大類），在發生無遺囑死亡時應不加任何分割而直接轉移給法定繼承人，其與動產相對。而屬於 moveable（動產性質的）部分，則先轉移給指定的遺囑執行人，由其在近親屬中進行分配[2]。

注

① "Heritable is infrequent enough today to be classed a needless variant for most purpose, although it persists in Scotland and in civil-law jurisdiction." Cf. Bryan A. Garner, *A Dictionary of Modern Legal Usage*, 2nd Edition, Oxford University Press (1995), at P. 446.
② Cf. David M. Walker, *The Oxford Companion To Law*, Oxford University Press (1980).

High crime ▶ Felony

　　在以往二者均被一些詞典當作「重罪」處理[1]，讓人覺得它們似乎是完全相同的法律術語，但實際上它們的內涵有很大差異。high crime 主要是指因違反公共道德而導致聲名狼籍的犯罪，從技術角度上講它不構成重罪（felony），其尤其指美國參議院視爲的可以此爲理由而對總統、副總統以及任何其他公職官員進行彈劾的犯罪[2]，在《美國聯邦憲法》中，片語 high crimes and misdemeanors 則用於表示可導致聯邦官員被彈劾的犯罪[3]，high crime 在此也並非一定等於重罪，故將它譯爲「嚴重違反公德罪」，以與眞正意義上的felony（重罪）相區分。而「重罪」（felony）則是最初英國刑法中所規定的四種犯罪之一，指最高刑可處以死刑並處沒收其財產的犯法行爲，與另外的叛國罪（treason）、輕罪（misdemeanor）、簡易審判程序審理的犯罪（summary offense）等三種罪行相對（summary offense 實際屬於 misdemeanor，故其也爲三種分類，參照 treason）。

注

① Cf.《英漢法律詞典》，法律出版社（1999），第 307 頁、第 361 頁。

② "a crime of infamous nature contrary to public morality but not technically constituting a felony; specifically, an offense that the US Senate deems to constitute an adequate ground for removal of the president, vice president, or any civil officer as a person unfit to hold public office and deserving of impeachment", Cf. Linda Picard Wood, J.D., *Merriam Webster's Dictionary of Law*, Merriam-Webster, Incorporated (1996), at P. 226.

③ Cf. James E. Clapp, *Random House Webster's Dictionary of the Law*, Random House (2000), at P. 216.

Hire-purchase ▶ Installment plan

　　二者的含義幾乎完全相同，均是指分期付款購買體制。區別在於 hire-purchase 是英式英語，而 installment plan 則為美式英語。

注

Cf. P. H. Collin, *Dictionary of Law*, 2nd Edition, Peter Collin Publishing Ltd. (1993), at P. 259.

Historic ▶ Historical

　　它們之間的差異在於 historic 所指的事物通常具有重要意義或在歷史上是著名的①。而 historical 所指的事物則主要是與歷史相關的，曾在過去某時間發生過的等，其並非一定具有重要意義或著名[2]。

注

① "important, famous, or decisive in history", Cf. Philip Babcock Gove, Ph.D. and the Merriam-Webster Editorial Staff, *Webster's Third New International Dictionary*, G &C Merriam Co. (1976), at P. 1079.

② "of, relating to, or having the character of history esp. as distinguished from myth or legend", *Id.* at P. 1073.

Hold-up ▸ Robbery

二者均有「搶劫」的含義，指透過對受害人人身實施暴力或威脅所完成的一種掠奪動產的犯罪。其區別在於 robbery 爲通用詞，而 hold-up 則指使用武力，尤其是用槍械企圖實施或已逐的搶劫犯罪。

注

"hold-up: an attempted or completed robbery carried out with the use of force and esp. at gunpoint", Cf. Linda Picard Wood, J.D., *Merriam Webster's Dictionary of Law*, Merriam-Webster, Incorporated (1996), at P. 228.

Home Office ▸ Interior Department

二者很容易被混淆。Home Office 爲「內政部」，是英國政府的一個機構，處理國內事務，包括法律、秩序、員警、監獄等事項[1]。而 Interior Department（也稱爲 Department of the Interior）爲「內務部」，是美國聯邦政府的一個機構，也是處理其國內的事務，包括印第安人、採礦、捕魚、野生動物、地質勘探、土地管理、自然公園、紀念碑、領土、防洪、水土保持、公共事務等相關領域事項，但卻不包括有關法律、秩序、警察、監獄等司法事項[2]。故我們可以說英國的「內政部」和美國的「內務部」的職能事實上相差較大。同樣可知，英國的 Home Secretary（內政大臣）和美國的 Minister of Interior Department（內務部長）的職責也就差異較大。

注

① "British government ministry dealing with internal affairs, including the police and prisons." Cf. P. H. Collin, *Dictionary of Law*, 2nd Edition, Peter Collin Publishing Ltd. (1993), at P. 261.

② "A federal department responsible for managing federally owned land and natural resources, and for overseeing American Indian reservations." Cf. Bryan A. Garner, *Black's Law Dictionary*, 7th Edition, West Group (1999), at P. 448.

Homicide ▸ Killing ▸ Manslaughter ▸ Murder

以上這些單詞均有殺人的含義。killing 爲通用詞，其並非嚴格意義上的法律術語，其可用於指一切殺人行爲，即包括 homicide（他殺，即 to kill someone），與 suicide（自殺，即 to kill oneself）兩種。homicide 爲一正式法律術語，指一個人的作爲或不作爲導致或促使他人的死亡，其爲中性詞，並非就道德或法律判定該行爲一定爲犯罪或有過錯。[1]在刑法上，他殺可分爲無罪殺人及有罪殺人兩種。無罪殺人（lawful homicide）包括正當殺人（justifiable homicide），即指合法將人致死的行爲，行爲人應被推定無罪，其常發生在處決死刑罪犯或罪犯拒捕、警方驅散暴民等場合[2]；可寬恕的殺人（excusable homicide），指意外事故致人死亡或自衛過程中的殺人，殺人者的行爲合法，且盡了應有的注意，其不應受到法律的懲處。值得注意的是，justifiable homicide 有時也用於指 excusable homicide。有罪殺人（felonious homicide），也稱爲 criminal homicide 或 culpable homicide，指無正當法律理由殺人而觸犯刑律之情況。普通法上的有罪殺人（felonious 或 criminal homicide）又包括 murder（謀殺）和 manslaughter（非預謀殺人罪）兩種。murder 常可按其情節分爲一級和二級等多種等級（參照 murder），而非預謀殺人罪則分可爲 involuntary manslaughter（無故意非預謀殺人罪，如過失殺人，指在履行合法行爲或有過錯但非犯罪行爲中因未盡到應有的注意或疏忽或因缺乏規定的技術等原因導致他人死亡）和 voluntary manslaughter〔非預謀但故意殺人罪，如義憤殺人（heat of passion）或行爲能力減退情況（diminished capacity）下殺人，指一時衝動而故意殺人，也稱爲 intentional manslaughter〕。以往不少英漢法律詞典都將 manslaughter 翻譯爲「過失殺人」（注：過失殺人應爲：negligent homicide 或 criminally negligent homicide），此種譯法當然不全面，一是 manslaughter 與謀殺相對，主要指是否有預謀（malice），是否有作案的預備過程，而非特指是否具有過失（neglect）；二是其有義憤殺人的含義，有殺人故意，故此時將其譯爲過失殺人肯定不妥。此外，有的法律詞典還將 manslaughter in self-defense 譯爲「自衛殺人」，這也爲一錯誤[③]，因爲 manslaughter 本身是一種犯罪，故其只能譯爲「防衛過當致人死亡罪」。

注

① "an act or omission resulting in the death of another person", Cf. James E. Clapp, *Random House Webster's Dictionary of the Law*, Random House (2000), at P. 218; "Homicide is not necessarily a crime. It is a necessary ingredient of the crimes of murder and manslaughter, but there are other cases in which homicide may be committed without criminal intent and without criminal consequences, as, where it is done in the lawful execution of a judicial sentence, in self-defense, or as the only possible means of arresting an escaping felon. The term homicide is neutral; while it describes the act, it pronounces no judgment on its moral or legal quality." Cf. The Publisher's Editorial Staff, *Black's Law Dictionary*, Abridged 6th Edition, West Publishing Co. (1991), at P. 506.

② "A killing mandated or permitted by the law, such as execution for a capital crime or killing to prevent a crime or a criminal's escape." Cf. Bryan A. Garner, *Black's Law Dictionary*, 7th Edition, West Group (1999), at P. 739.

③ Cf.《英漢法律詞典》，Revised Edition，法律出版社（1999），第 485 頁。

House counsel ▶ Outside counsel

　　二者均可用於指公司等的法律顧問。區別在於 house counsel（也稱為 in house counsel）是作為內聘的公司雇員，且領取工資的律師，故為公司的內部法律顧問①。outside counsel 則指公司的外聘法律顧問②。

注

① "a lawyer employed by a business to work in-house on its legal matters", Cf. Linda Picard Wood, J.D., *Merriam Webster's Dictionary of Law*, Merriam-Webster, Incorporated (1996), at P. 230.

② "any counsel performing services for a company other than in-house counsel", Cf. James E. Clapp, *Random House Webster's Dictionary of the Law*, Random House (2000), at P. 112.

House property ▶ Building property

二者均有「房產」的含義，但鑒於在此術語中，house 的含義只含住宅，而非其他建築物，故 house property 便只指私人住宅而非用作商店、辦公室、工廠等用途的房產[*]。與此相對，building property 的含義則廣得多，可用於指各種目的的房屋財產。此外，籠統含義的房產也可用 real property 來表示。

注

[*] "private houses, not shops, offices or factories", Cf. P. H. Collin, *Dictionary of Law*, 2nd Edition, Peter Collin Publishing Ltd. (1993), at P. 264.

Immediate cause ▸ Proximate cause

二者之間的差異在於 immediate cause（也稱為 effective cause）是指在一系列原因中最後一個直接導致結果產生或事件發生之原因[1]，而 proximate cause（也稱為 direct cause、direct and proximate cause、efficient proximate cause、efficient cause、efficient adequate cause、legal cause、primary cause、jural cause，近因）也與結果有直接關聯，但它則不一定是直接原因[2]。如一酒醉者不小心墜入池塘淹死，酒醉（intoxication）則是該人死亡的近因（proximate cause），而溺水則是致其死亡的直接原因（immediate cause）。

注

① "The last event in a chain of events, though not necessarily the proximate cause of what follows." Cf. Bryan A. Garner, *Black's Law Dictionary*, 7th Edition, West Group (1999), at P. 212.

② "a cause that such in motion a sequence of events uninterrupted by any superseding causes and that results in a usu. foreseeable effect (as an injury) which would not otherwise have occurred", Cf. Linda Picard Wood, J.D., *Merriam Webster's Dictionary of Law*, Merriam-Webster, Incorporated (1996), at P. 69.

Imminent danger ▸ Imminent peril ▸ Immediate danger

上述片語均有即將來臨的危險的含義。其中，imminent danger（緊急危險）在刑法中主要適用於對阻卻違法的辯護中，指被告感到對自己的人身傷害危險即將發生而無法求助他人或獲得法律保護，只能馬上予以自衛①。imminent peril（緊迫危險）主要用於人道主義原則（humanitarian doctrine）中，指在交通事故中，如果原告，即受害的步行者能證明在事故發生前其正處於急迫危險（immediate danger）中，而被告，即機動車駕駛員本應該能在最後時刻避免事故發生，原告則可免於任何混合過失之原則②。immediate danger 除主要用於交通事故中外，也可用在刑法上的自衛中，指即將發生的危險（此時其等同 imminent danger）③。

注

① "In relation to homicide in self-defense, this term means immediate danger, such as must be instantly met, such as cannot be guarded against by calling for the assistance of others or the protection of the law. Or, as otherwise defined, such as an appearance of threatened and impending injury as would put a reasonable and prudent man to his instant defense." Cf. The Publisher's Editorial Staff, *Black's Law Dictionary*, Abridged 6th Edition, West Publishing Co. (1991), at P. 515.

② "That position of danger to the plaintiff in which, if the existing circumstances remain unchanged, injury to him is reasonably certain." *Id.* at P. 515.

③ "A definition that contemplates that there be some inexorable circumstance, situation or agency bearing down on plaintiff with reasonable probability of danger prior to negligence act of defendant." *Id.* at P. 514.

Impossibility ▶ Impracticability ▶ Frustration

　　上述單詞均可用作違約之訴的辯護理由。它們的區別在於 impossibility（也稱爲 impossibility of performance）爲契約的給付不能，是契約法中一原則，指因無法抗拒的情況發生，如契約必要的執行人死亡、契約變爲非法等[①]。impracticability 爲「履約的不實際性」（也稱爲 commercial impracticability、impracticability of performance），它所指的範圍比 impossibility of performance 廣，包括因某種無法預見的意外事故的發生，導致履約極端困難、危險或費用太高，從而可以免除履約責任的情況[②]，如在銷售契約中，因無法預見的情況導致契約所規定的貨物不存在等均屬於 impracticability 的範疇。frustration 爲「契約受挫原則」（也稱爲 frustration of contract、frustration of purpose、frustration of the venture），其是普通法一原則，指契約雙方當事人均認爲或契約條款規定，某物的存在爲履行允諾的必要條件，在履約時如果該物因意外事故或不屬於雙方當事人的過失而不復存在，允諾方可免除履行允諾的義務[③]。

注

① "A fact or circumstance that excuses performance because 1) the subject or means of performance has deteriorated, has been destroyed, or is no longer available; 2) the method of delivery or payment has failed; 3) a law now prevents performance; or 4) death or illness prevents performance." Cf. Bryan A. Garner, *Black's Law Dictionary*, 7th Edition, West Group (1999), at P. 759.

② "relief from obligation under a contract may be granted when performance has been rendered excessively difficult, expensive, or harmful by an unforeseen contingency", Cf. Linda Picard Wood, J.D., *Merriam Webster's Dictionary of Law*, Merriam-Webster, Incorporated

(1996), at P. 238.

③ "This doctrine provides, generally, that where existence of a specific thing is, either by terms of contract or in contemplation of parties, necessary for performance of a promise in the contract, duty to perform promise is discharged if thing is no longer in existence at time for performance." Cf. The Publisher's Editorial Staff, *Black's Law Dictionary*, Abridged 6th Edition, West Publishing Co. (1991), at P. 462.

In chamber ▸ Open court

二者用於指不同的審理方式。前者指在法官工作室裏秘密審議，如 the judge sits in chamber，其相對應的拉丁文是 *in camera*[①]。後者則指公開開庭審理，如 the judge sits in an open court[②]。

注

① "(of judicial business or proceedings) in private, not in open court. Usually referring to something that takes place in CHAMBERS, in the ROBING ROOM, or in a court room form which spectators have been excluded", Cf. James E. Clapp, *Random House Webster's Dictionary of the Law*, Random House (2000), at P. 226.

② "a session of a court that is open to the public", Cf. Linda Picard Wood, J.D., *Merriam Webster's Dictionary of Law*, Merriam-Webster, Incorporated (1996), at P. 340.

Inchoate offences

該片語（也稱為 inchoate crime、anticipatory offense、preliminary

crime）爲「初始罪」，是英美法系刑法中犯罪的一種分類，意思是 incipient crime，指可導致其他犯罪行爲發生，而其本身也屬犯罪之行爲，其外延大於犯罪預備①。以 assault 而言，因爲其用意是企圖致使毆打罪（battery）發生，故可被視爲初始毆打罪（inchoate battery），而 assault 本身又是一種犯罪行爲（暴力脅迫罪）。一般說來，初始罪包括煽動罪（incitement）、預備罪（attempt，也稱爲 criminal attempt）、密謀犯罪罪（conspiracy）、教唆罪（solicitation）等（後三種是美國《示範刑法典》所規定的初始罪），它只要求有初始犯罪行爲，而不論是否有實質性犯罪結果。大陸法系中一般無初始罪之分。如中國刑法中雖有殺人未遂（unaccomplished murder，指未遂之殺人罪），卻無殺人未遂罪（inchoate murder），故只能將殺人未遂歸於殺人罪範疇處理，即根據其某些犯罪階段未完全實施而酌情予以從輕處罰。在英美法系中，attempted murder 本身便是單獨的犯罪，爲 criminal attempt，屬於 inchoate offences 的範疇，應譯爲「預備謀殺罪」或「謀殺預備罪」，其定義爲 a notifiable offence of trying to murder someone②，將其譯爲「謀殺未遂」則有悖於其本意。需要注意的是我們最好不要片面理解 inchoate offences 的含義，而按以往有些人的作法將其譯爲「犯罪未遂」或「未完成之罪」③（未完成之罪應爲 unaccomplished offences），事實上，該術語中的 inchoate 除有「未完成」（unaccomplished）的含義外，還有「前期或初始」（incipient）的意思。以「預備犯罪罪」（而非「未遂」）爲例，attempt: the crime of having the intent to commit and taking action in an effort to commit a crime that fails or is prevented, called also criminal attempt④，我們便知道，只要犯罪人有企圖並有前期準備行爲，單就 inchoate offences 這個初始犯罪行爲而言，其應當已經實施並完成了該罪名所規定的行爲，如果說是未完成，則應指罪犯企圖並準備實施的初始罪之外的另一樁犯罪，即上文中的 "a crime" 而非 "the crime"。

注

① "An incipient crime which generally leads to another crime. An assault has been referred to as an inchoate battery, though the assault is a crime in and of itself. The Model Penal Code classified attempts, solicitation, and conspiracy as such." Cf. The Publisher's Editorial Staff, *Black's Law Dictionary*, 6th Edition, West Publishing Co. (1991), at P. 523.

② Cf. P. H. Collin, *Dictionary of Law*, 2nd Edition, Peter Collin Publishing Ltd. (1993), at P. 38.

③ Cf. 陳慶柏等譯，《英漢雙解法律詞典》，世界圖書出版公司（1998），第273頁；《英漢法律詞典》，Revised Edition，法律出版社（1999），第383頁。

④ Cf. Linda Picard Wood, J.D., *Merriam Webster's Dictionary of Law*, Merriam-Webster, Incorporated (1996), at P. 38.

Incidental beneficiary ▶ Direct beneficiary

　　二者均指契約的第三方受益人，差異在於 incidental beneficiary（附帶受益人）是契約的締約雙方在締約時並不旨在讓其受益的第三人，其無權要求強制執行契約[①]。而 direct beneficiary（直接受益人，也稱為 intended beneficiary）則是締約雙方當事人均旨在使其受益的第三人，其有權要求對契約進行強制執行[②]。

注

① "a third-party beneficiary to a contract whom the parties to the contract did not intend to benefit", Cf. Linda Picard Wood, J.D., *Merriam Webster's Dictionary of Law*, Merriam-Webster, Incorporated

(1996), at P. 48.

② "A third-party beneficiary who is intended to benefit from a contract and thus acquires rights under the contract as well as the ability to enforce the contract once those rights have vested." Cf. Bryan A. Garner, *Black's Law Dictionary*, 7ᵗʰ Edition, West Group (1999), at P. 149.

Inculpatory statement ▸ Confession

二者的區別在於 inculpatory statement（也稱為 incriminating statement）指被告承認事實、情節或關係之陳述，其可用作確立或推定被告有罪，故譯為「顯示犯罪的供述」①。而 confession 則指罪犯直接承認犯罪（admit commission of a crime），有對犯罪供認不諱的含義，故譯為「自白」②。

注

① "A statement which tends to establish guilt of the accused or from which, with other facts, his guilt may be inferred, or which tends to disprove some defense." Cf. The Publisher's Editorial Staff, *Black's Law Dictionary*, 6ᵗʰ Edition, West Publishing Co. (1991), at P. 528.

② Cf. James E. Clapp, *Random House Webster's Dictionary of the Law*, Random House (2000), at P. 97.

Indecent assault ▸ Sexual assault

二者均與性犯罪相關，它們之間的差異在於 indecent assault 為「猥褻罪」，故 indecent assault on women 是指不經受害人同意猥褻婦女，且可與其發生性器官接觸，但其行為卻未達到性交或生殖器插入的程度的犯罪，原因是罪犯沒有強姦的故意（without the intent to commit a rape[①]）。故從這點而言，該術語便沒有某些英漢法律詞典上的強姦未遂之含義[②]。相比較，sexual assault 則為「性侵害罪」，其有雙重含義，一是等同 indecent assault，指除性交之外的其他猥褻行為，但它同時也指未經受害人同意（或受害人無行為能力，或騙得受害人同意，如醫生欺騙病人）即與其發生性行為，其罪行程度包括從嚴重的一級性侵犯罪（first degree sexual assault），即不經受害人同意便發生生殖器插入情況，到情節較輕微的制定法上的強姦罪（statutory rape）[③]。目前，美國有些州的刑法已經用性侵害罪取代了強姦罪。

注

① Cf. Linda Picard Wood, J.D., *Merriam Webster's Dictionary of Law*, Merriam-Webster, Incorporated (1996), at P. 34.

② Cf. 《英漢法律詞典》，Revised Edition，法律出版社（1999），第386頁。

③ "1) Sexual intercourse with another person without that person's consent. 2) Offensive sexual contact with another person, exclusive of rape. Also termed in sense 2) indecent assault." Cf. Bryan A. Garner, *Black's Law Dictionary*, 7th Edition, West Group (1999), at P. 110.

Indemnify ▶ Hold harmless

在契約或協議中，人們常見 indemnify 和 hold harmless（也稱為 save harmless）兩術語連用的情況，如：We will indemnify and hold you harmless from any loss which may be incurred[①]。有關這兩個術語的解釋和認識，不少法律詞典或著述有一定差異，如 Bryan A. Garner 在其主編的著名的 *Black's Law Dictionary*（7th Edition）以

及 *A Dictionary of Modern Legal Usage* 中，認爲這兩個術語完全無任何實質性的差異，應爲同源異形詞（doublets），同時一起使用只是因法律人的習慣，爲一種同義詞連用習慣（synonym strings）[②]。而其他詞典，如 *Merriam Webster's Dictionary of Law* 等則認爲 indemnify 主要指擔保不受到損失或損害或即便受到損失也同意予以補償，而 hold harmless 則主要是指自己承擔責任而免去對方的責任[③]。在 *Practical Guide to Everyday Law* 一書中，作者更明確指出 indemnify 是指擔保某人不受任何損失或損害；而 hold harmless 則是保護某人不得因承擔責任而受到法律訴訟指控[④]。就上述種種見解而言，筆者更傾向於 Webster 與 Gail 的觀點，擬將 indemnify 譯爲「擔保免受損害」，而將 hold harmless 譯爲「免責」。以此類推，hold harmless agreement 則爲「免責協議」，hold harmless clause 即「免責條款」。

注

① Cf. Henson and Davenport, *Uniform Commercial Code Forms and Materials*, West Publishing Co. (1985), at P. 356.

② Cf. Bryan A Garner, *Black's Law Dictionary*, 7th Edition, West Group (1999), at Ps.772, 737; Cf. Bryan A Garner, *A Dictionary of Modern Legal Usage*, 2nd Edition, Oxford University Press Ltd. (1995), at P. 436.

③ "hold harmless: to release from liability or responsibility for loss or damage; to abandon any claim that one might have against someone", Cf. James E. Clapp, *Random House Webster's Dictionary of the Law*, Random House (2000), at P. 212; "indemnify: 1. to secure against hurt, loss, or damage; 2. to compensate or reimburse for incurred hurt, loss, or damage", Cf. Linda Picard Wood, J.D., *Merriam Webster's Dictionary of Law*, Merriam-Webster, Incorporated (1996), at P. 240.

④ "Indemnify means to secure you against loss or damage. Hold harmless means to protect you against legal action." Cf. Gail J. Koff, *Practical Guide to Every Law*, Simon & Schuster, Inc., New York (1985), at P. 208.

Indispensable party ▸ Necessary party

二者均指與訴訟緊密相關的當事人。區別在於 indispensable party（必不可少的當事人）指由於其權利與訴訟主張緊密相關，故任何判決都勢必影響到他（她）的利益，如果沒有其作為共同訴訟人的參與，必將導致訴訟被駁回（dismissal of the action）①。相比之下，necessary party（必要當事人）與訴訟的關聯沒有 indispensable party 緊密，儘管他（她）的參與會對妥善解決訟爭起作用，但如果其有合法的理由而不作為共同訴訟人參與，不會導致訴訟被駁回②。

注

① "A party who, having interests that would inevitably be affected by a court's judgment, must be included in the case. If such a party is not included, the case must be dismissed." Cf. Bryan A. Garner, *Black's Law Dictionary*, 7th Edition, West Group (1999), at P. 1144.

② "a person or entity whose rights are sufficiently involved in an action to require joinder as a party if that is possible; but if it is not possible, the action will be allowed to proceed without that additional party", Cf. James E. Clapp, *Random House Webster's Dictionary of the Law*, Random House (2000), at P. 97.

Inferior court ▸ Trial court ▸ Appellate court

　　三者均可用作指法院的一種級別分類。其中，trial court 為「審判級法院」，多為案件提起之法院，故常被當作初審法院（court of first instance）理解。美國聯邦法院體系的 trial court 為聯邦地區法院（United States district courts）。各州的審判級法院的名稱各異，如地方法院（district court）、高級法院（superior court）、縣法院（county court）、巡迴法院（circuit court）等，但其職能卻幾乎相同。appellant court 為「上訴法院」，職能是復審審判級法院（或低級上訴法院）移送的上訴案件，對原審法院的判決作出諸如維持（affirm）、撤銷（reverse）或發回重審（remand）等裁決。美國聯邦法院體系的上訴法院為聯邦上訴法院（United States courts of appeal）和聯邦最高法院（US Supreme Court）；州法院體系則有州中級上訴法院（intermediate appellate courts）和州高級法院（state high courts，不少州稱為 supreme court）。inferior court 為「低級法院」，其等級在 trial court 之下，一般不屬於記錄法院（court of record），州法院體系的低級法院有市鎮法院（municipal court）、違警法院（police court）、治安法院（justices of the peace）等，其上訴首先移送審判級法院復審。聯邦體系的低級法院則有聯邦破產法院（United States bankruptcy courts）等，不服此種法院判決之上訴多先由聯邦審判級法院，即聯邦地方法院（US district court）受理。

注

Cf. Li Rong-fu/Song Lei, *A Course Book of Legal English, The Structure of the Court System of the United States*, Law Press, China (1999), at Ps. 66—69.

Infringement of trade mark

該術語爲「侵犯商標權」。就此被侵權人（infringee）可向侵權人（infringer）提起訴訟。一般說來，侵犯商標權之訴多爲反假冒（仿冒）商標之訴（passing-off action[①]，也稱爲 palming off action）、商標申請異議之訴（trade-mark opposition[②]）以及要求撤銷不當註冊商標之訴（expungement action/proceeding 或 expunction action/proceeding[③]）三種。商標權利人可據此保護自己的合法權益。

注

① "Passing off is actionable in tort under the law of unfair competition." Cf. Bryan A. Garner, *Black's Law Dictionary*, 7th Edition, West Group (1999), at P. 1146.

② Cf. Li Rong-fu/Song Lei, *A Course Book of Legal English, Protection Foreign Trade-Mark Rights in Canada*, Law Press, China (1999), at Ps. 428—435.

③ "The decision in *Orkin* stands for the principle that a foreign trade-mark owner can prevent the use of its mark in Canada. The *Orkin* case has been considered in passing-off actions, trade-mark oppositions and expungement proceeding, with widely varying results." *Id.* at P. 432.

Inhabitant ▶ Resident

二者均有居民的含義，區別在於 inhabitant 所指的居住狀態比 resident 更穩定和長久，由此 inhabitant 所擁有的權利和義務比 resident 要多，故相對說來，inhabitant 的界定也嚴格一些，如一個法人（corporation）只能在其註冊登記州（state of its incorporation）才能成爲 inhabitant。

"But the terms resident and inhabitant have also been held not synonymous, the latter implying a more fixed and permanent abode than the former, and importing privileges and duties to which a mere resident would not be subject. A corporation can be an inhabitant only in the state of its incorporation." Cf. The Publisher's Editorial Staff, *Black's Law Dictionary*, Abridged 6th Edition, West Publishing Co. (1991), at P. 538.

Injunction ▸ Cesae and desist order ▸ Mandamus

　　三者均有強制性命令的含義。其區別在於 injunction 爲「強制令」，指法庭作出的強迫一方當事人實施或不予實施某特定行爲的命令。其包括禁止和強迫實施雙重含義①，故不宜像有些詞典那樣將其譯爲狹義的「禁令」或「禁制令」②，而應爲廣義的強制令。其是衡平法上的一種救濟，主要是預防未來傷害行爲的發生而非對已經發生的損害進行補償，違反強制令者將以藐視法庭（is subject to penalty of contempt）論處。cease and desist order 指的是由法院或準司法裁判庭所作出的制止繼續進行某個具體的活動或行爲之命令，故應譯爲「制止令」③。mandamus（也稱爲 writ of mandamus）則與 cease and desist order 正好相反，它是指主管法院對下級法庭、官員、行政機構、法人、個人發出的迫使其履行法定責任範圍內的職責的特別令狀（extraordinary writ），故應譯爲「執行令」④，其主要針對行政行爲的履行而言，而非其他法院根據其自由裁量權而對被告施加的其他行爲。

① "a court order directing a person to do or refrain from doing some act", Cf. James E. Clapp, *Random House Webster's Dictionary of the Law*, Random House (2000), at P. 237.

② Cf.《英漢法律詞典》，Revised Edition，法律出版社（1999），第 394 頁；陸谷孫，《英漢大詞典》，上海譯文出版社（1995），第 1666 頁；《新英漢詞典》，增補本，上海譯文出版社（1979），第 652 頁。

③ "A court's or agency's order prohibiting a person from continuing a particular course of conduct." Cf. Bryan A. Garner, *Black's Law Dictionary*, 7th Edition, West Group (1999), at P. 215.

④ "A writ issuing from a court of competent jurisdiction, commanding an inferior tribunal, board, corporation, or person, to perform a purely ministerial duty imposed by law." Cf. The Publisher's Editorial Staff, *Black's Law Dictionary*, Abridged 6th Edition, West Publishing Co. (1991), at P. 663.

Injury ▸ Damage

二者均可指對人身或財產造成的損失或傷害，且經常互換使用，但現在它們之間開始出現一定的區別，主要在於前者多指人身傷害或實際所受的損失或傷害，而後者則多指財產損失或出於賠償目的對實際傷害或損害進行的測定估算。

注

"There is a modern tendency to refer to damage to property, but injury to the person. It is not an established distinction." Cf. Bryan A. Garner, *A Dictionary of Modern Legal Usage*, 2nd Edition, Oxford University Press (1995), at P. 243.

(the) Inland Revenue ▸ Internal Revenue Service

二者均爲國內稅收機構。其中，the Inland Revenue 應爲「國內稅收總局」，指英國的稅收機構，其主要負責英國境內所得稅和資本稅等的徵收①。Internal Revenue Service 爲「國內稅收署」，指美國同類型的處理其境內所得稅事務之稅收機構②。在美國，國內稅收爲 internal revenue，而在英國、加拿大等國，則稱爲 inland revenue。

注

① "British government department dealing with income tax", Cf. P. H. Collin, *Dictionary of Law*, 2nd Edition, Peter Collin Publishing Ltd. (1994), at P. 279.

② "The branch of the US Treasury Department responsible for administering the Internal Revenue Code and providing taxpayer education." Cf. Bryan A. Garner, *Black's Law Dictionary*, 7th Edition, West Group (1999), at P. 821.

Inquisitorial system ▸ Accusatorial procedure sysetm ▸ Adversary system

三者均用於指不同的訴訟形式。其中，inquisitorial system 爲「糾問制」，指大陸法國家所實行的一種審判制度，奉行職權主義，即由法官代表國家利益進行審判，其可訊問當事人，可依職權自己調查事實並直接提取證據①。accusatorial procedure system 爲「控訴式訴訟」，與糾問式訴訟相對，主要特徵爲控訴和審判職能分離，司法機關不主動追究犯罪，雙方當事人在訴訟中居主導地位，審判機關居消極仲裁地位，雙方當事人享有平等的訴訟地位，各自對訴訟主張分擔舉證責任，審判實行公開原則、言辭辯論原則和陪審原則，該種訴訟形式多流行於羅馬共和時期和英國的封建時代，與 adversary system 相同，差異在於前者只用於刑事案件，而後者則可用於刑事及民事訴訟②。adversary system 為「對抗制」，是指目前英美法系國家實行的一種審判制度，奉行當事人主義，即當事人在訴訟中居主導地位，允許糾紛中對立各方，一般由律師代理，向陪審團提出證據和主張，多數情況下，法官只主持訴訟活動而非進行實際的事實調查③。

注

① "Proceedings in which the judge, not the parties, adduces evidence in contrast to the adversarial system." Cf. Daphne Dukelow, *The Dictionary of Canadian Law*, Thomson Professional Publishing Canada (1991), at P. 519.

② "The Anglo American system of criminal prosecution, in which the government, having accused the defendant, must prove its allegations by the adversary process, with the judge acting only as a neutral referee. Same as adversary system, except that the latter term applies to both civil and criminal cases." Cf. James E. Clapp, *Random House Webster's Dictionary of the Law*, Random House (2000), at P. 10.

③ "The jurisprudential network of laws, rules and procedures characterized by opposing parties who contend against each other for a result favorable to themselves. In such system, the judges acts as an independent magistrate rather than prosecutor; distinguished from inquisitorial system." Cf. The Publisher's Editorial Staff, *Black's Law Dictionary*, Abridged 6th Edition, West Publishing Co. (1991), at P. 34.

Instruction to the jury ▸ Summing-up

　　二者均爲「法官給陪審團的指示」，都是指在陪審團審理（jury trial）結束時由法官對陪審團所作的例行講話。講話一般要回顧所有有關的證據、法庭的辯論，同時向陪審團提示了在作事實裁決時應當注意的與案件相關的主要法律問題。兩者的差別只在於 instruction to the jury 爲美式英語，而 summing-up 則爲英式英語。

注

"Instruction to the jury: speech by a judge at the end of a trial where he reviews all the evidence and arguments and notes important points of law for the benefit of the jury. Note: GB English is summing-up." Cf. P. H. Collin, *Dictionary of Law*, 2nd Edition, Peter Collin Publishing Ltd. (1993), at P. 283.

Instrument ▸ Document

　　二者有時可相互交替使用。instrument 雖然可等同 document，指法律文據，如契約、文書等，但更主要的是指票據，即一種表示金錢所有權關係的文據（instrument is a document of title to money）[1]。在西方，票據分爲兩大類：匯票（bill of exchange 或者 bill）和支票（cheque，cheque 爲英式英語，相應的美式英語則是 check）。中國票據法規定的基本類別則爲：匯票、支票和本票（promissory note，也作 note）。票據也可按其流通性質分爲流通票據（negotiable instruments）和不流通票據（non-negotiable instruments）兩種。前者如：promissory notes（本票）、checks（支票）、bill of exchanges（匯票）、bank notes（銀行券）、treasury bills（短期國庫券）、bearer-bond（不記名有擔保債券）、bearer debentures（不記名無擔保債券）、share warrants（認股證書）、bearer scrip certificate（持有人憑證）、negotiable certificates of deposit（流通存款單）、dividend warrants（紅利支付單）、interest warrants（利息支付單）、banker's drafts（銀行匯票）、circular notes（定額流通旅行券）；後者如：letters of allot（認股分配書）、postal orders（郵政匯票）、money orders（匯款單）、pension warrants（年金支付單）、child benefit orders（兒童津貼付款單）等。有些票據，如旅行支票（travelers check），則有可流通旅行支票和不可流通旅行支票兩種[2]。相比較，儘管 document 的含義較廣，可指任何記錄資訊或證明事實的文據，包括契據、協議、文件、信函、單據等以及與法律無關的其他文據[3]，但並不常專門用於表示票據。

注

① Cf. The Publisher's Editorial Staff, *Black's Law Dictionary*, Abridged 6th Edition, West Publishing Co. (1991), at P. 550.

② Cf. Li Rong-fu/Song Lei, *A Course Book of Legal English*, *Instruments*, Law Press, China (1999), at P. 184.

③ "Document and instrument are similar in meaning, but document is slightly broader. Document refers to anything written, whereas instrument usually refers to a legal document with a specific legal import." Cf. Bryan A. Garner, *A Dictionary of Modern Legal Usage*, 2nd Edition, Oxford University Press (1995), at P. 289.

Insurance agent ▶ Insurance broker

二者均是指替保險公司推銷保險者。它們之間的區別在於 insurance agent 多指附屬於某保險公司的固定的推銷人，其為「保險代理人」[1]。如在州或更大範圍開展工作，可稱為 general agent；如只在當地行使職務,則稱爲 local agent。相比之下,insurance broker 則不固定附屬於某具體的保險公司,爲表示區別,筆者建議將其譯爲「保險經紀人」②。

注

① "An agent employed by an insurance company to solicit insurance business." Cf. The Publisher's Editorial Staff, *Black's Law Dictionary*, Abridged 6th Edition, West Publishing Co. (1991), at P. 557.

② "An insurance agent is tied to his company, whereas an insurance broker is an independent middleman not tied to a particular company." *Id*. at P. 557.

Intent ▸ Intention

二者均有故意和企圖的含義,區別在於 intent 比 intention 更具有嚴格的法律含義,常用於指犯罪或侵權領域的故意和企圖等。

注

"*Intent* is more commonly used than *intention* when speaking technically esp.about the criminal and tort concepts of intent." Cf. Linda Picard Wood, J.D., *Merriam Webster's Dictionary of Law*, Merriam-Webster, Incorporated (1996), at P. 253.

Interest arbitration ▸ Grievance arbitration

二者均與工會與雇主的集體談判協議(collective bargaining agreement)有關。區別在於 interest arbitration 爲「勞資權益關係仲裁」,指的是雙方就即將締結之協議中的權益問題的爭執進行的仲裁[①]。而 grievance arbitration（也稱爲 right arbitration）爲「勞資爭議仲裁」，是指勞資雙方就已經締結生效的集體談判協議中的爭議提請的仲裁[②]。

注

① "Arbitration that involves settling the terms of a contract being negotiated between the parties; esp., in labor law, arbitration of a dispute concerning what provisions will be included in a new collective-bargaining agreement." Cf. Bryan A. Garner, *Black's Law Dictionary*, 7th Edition, West Group (1999), at P. 101.

② "arbitration of a dispute over something in an existing collective bargaining agreement", Cf. Linda Picard Wood, J.D., *Merriam Webster's Dictionary of Law*, Merriam-Webster, Incorporated (1996), at P. 31.

Interim injunction ▸ Interlocutory injunction

二者均指在正式審判（trial）之前，由法院作出的強制令，有的法律，如美國的《貿易慣例法》（Trade Practice Act）規定它們可互換使用，具有相同含義。而 G. H. L. Fridman 在其所著的《加拿大契約法》（*The Law of Contract in Canada*）中則認爲 interim injunction 是在當事人向法院申請 interlocutory injunction 之前所適用的時間很短的一種命令，屬於 interlocutory injunction 的一種（a species of interlocutory injunction granted for a very brief period until application for an interlocutory injunction is made），由此 interim injunction 除可被譯爲「訴訟中間強制令」之外，還可指「臨時強制令」。而 interlocutory injunction 則只有「訴訟中間強制令」的含義。

Cf. Daphne Dukelow, *The Dictionary of Canadian Law*, Thomson professional Publishing Canada (1991), at P. 531.

Invasion ▸ Aggression

　　讀者應注意二者在外交和法律領域中的區別，儘管現在絕大多數詞典都將它們統統譯爲「侵略」①。實際上，在國際法中二者的差別極大。invasion 等同 incursion，指一國的軍隊爲征服或掠奪等目的而入侵他國領土（the incursion of an army for conquest or plunder② or the act or an instance of invading or entering as an enemy, especially by an army③），但其並無政治意義上侵犯國家主權和獨立的侵略之含義，故只能譯爲「入侵」或「侵入」。如小布希下令美國出兵攻占伊拉克，美國政府及新聞界都自稱爲是對伊拉克的 invasion 或 incursion，而絕非是 aggression。aggression 則指一個國家用武力侵犯他國主權和領土完整的行徑，其是國際公法所不容許的行爲，其才是眞正意義上的侵略（The use of armed force by a state against the sovereignty, territorial integrity, or political independence of another state, or in any other manner inconsistent with the Charter of the United Nations④）。invader 也應譯爲「入侵者」或「侵入者」，而 aggressor 則是「侵略者」。

注

① Cf. 陸谷孫，《英漢法律大詞典》（上卷），上海譯文出版社（1991），第 1074、1075 頁；《英漢法律詞典》，法律出版社（1999），第 412 頁；《新英漢詞典》（1985），上海譯文出版社，第 668 頁；吳光華，《漢英大辭典》（下卷），上海交通大

學出版社（1995），第 203 頁；薛波，《漢英法律詞典》，外文出版社（1995），第 564 頁；危東亞，《漢英詞典》，外語教學與研究出版社（1995），第 801 頁。

② Cf. Bryan A. Garner, *Black's Law Dictionary*, 7th Edition, West Group (1999), at P. 378.

③ Cf. Jess Stein, *The Random House College Dictionary*, Revised Edition, Random House, New York (1966), at P. 701.

④ Cf. James E. Clapp, *Random House Webster's Dictionary of the Law*, Random House, New York (2000), at P. 22.

Invitee ▸ Guest

二者的區別在於 invitee（被邀請人）是指經明示或默示邀請而到他人住處者，其前往他人住處之目的與邀請人的商事事務直接或間接相關，該地方的占有人（occupier）必須對被邀請人的安全保護負責①。guest（客人）則指付費在旅店等住宿者，或在某人家中受款待者，或免費搭乘汽車者②。從法律的角度講，a guest 是一位 licensee（被特許人）而非 invitee③。如僅到旅店（inn）就餐者而不住宿者便只能算作顧客（customer），顧客可以算作 invitee，但卻非 guest（請參閱條目 social guest）。

注

① "a person who is present in a place by the express or implied invitation of the occupier in control of the place under circumstances that impose a duty on the occupier to use reasonable care to protect the safety of the invited person", Cf. Linda Picard Wood, J.D., *Merriam Webster's Dictionary of Law*, Merriam-Webster, Incorporated (1996), at P. 262.

② "A person receiving lodging for pay at an inn, motel, or hotel on general undertaking of keeper thereof. A person who is received and entertained at one's home, club, etc., and who is not a regular member. A guest in an automobile is one who takes ride in automobile driven by another person, merely for his own pleasure or on his own business, and without making any return or conferring any benefit on automobile driver." Cf. The Publisher's Editorial Staff, *Black's Law Dictionary*, Abridged 6th Edition, West Publishing Co. (1991), at P. 489.

③ "In law, a guest is a licensee, not an invitee." Cf. Daphne Dukelow, *The Dictionary of Canadian Law*, Thomson professional Publishing Canada (1991), at P. 542.

Irrelevant ▸ Immaterial ▸ Incompetent

證據的irrelevant（無相關性）、immaterial（無實質性）和 incompetent（不具證據能力）〔有時也稱爲 inadmissible（不可採性）〕是證據法上的三個概念，律師們常用它們反駁對方的證據。連在一起，它們常被人稱爲 "three I's"（「三無」規則）。

Irretrievable breakdown of the marriage ▸ Irreconcilable difference

二者均可用作無過錯離婚（no-fault divorce）之理由，區別在於 irretrievable breakdown of marriage（也稱爲 irretrievable breakdown of the marriage relationship、irremediable breakdown of marriage、irretrievable breakdown）爲「不可挽回的婚姻破裂」，指夫妻矛盾發展，表明關係無法挽回，在許多州這是唯一無過錯離婚理由①。irreconcilable difference 則爲「難以和解的分歧」，指夫妻之間存

在實質性矛盾及不和，內容廣泛，在有些州可替代 irretrievable breakdown of the marriage，用作無過錯離婚訴訟理由[2]。

注

① "A ground for divorce that is based on incompatibility between marriage partners and that is used in many states as the sole ground of no-fault divorce." Cf. Bryan A. Garner, *Black's Law Dictionary*, 7th Edition, West Group (1999), at P. 835.

② "substantial incompatibility between marriage partners that is a broad ground for esp. no-fault divorce", Cf. Linda Picard Wood, J.D., *Merriam Webster's Dictionary of Law*, Merriam-Webster, Incorporated (1996), at P. 262.

J

J.D. ▸ LL.M ▸ S.J.D.

　　以上三者均為美國法學院所設置的主要學位名稱的縮寫。J.D.（Juris Doctor，也稱為 Doctor of Jurisprudence、Doctor of Law）為「法律博士」，該學位始於 20 世紀 60 年代，用於取代 LL.B[1]，所招收的學生必須是已經獲得其他專業，如政治學、經濟學、社會學或新聞學等學士學位者，其學制一般為 3 年，開設的課程則是法學院的基本教育課程，等同中國法學專業本科的課程，故從某種程度上，J.D. 學位有些類似中國的雙學位或目前的「法律碩士」。此學位十分重要，按規定，凡想在美國取得律師資格，一般必須擁有該學位（極少數州例外）。LL.M（Master of Law）為「法學碩士」，所招收的學生則是已經獲得 J.D. 學位或在其他國家獲得法學學士學位（LL.B）者，其學制一般為 1 至 2 年，學習方式以修課為主，法學院多允許學生以增修一定學分的方式以替代畢業論文[2]。S.J.D.（Doctor of Juridical Science 或 Doctor of the Science of Law，也稱為 J.S.D.）源於拉丁文 *Scientiae Juridicae Doctor*，為「法學博士」，所招收的學生則一般是已經獲得 LL.M 學位或 J.D. 學位者，其學制一般為 3 至 5 年，其學習內容主要為撰寫學位論文，但法學院也可要求學生選修一定課程或從事一定研究工作。一般說來，獲得此學位的人很少，即使在法學院也不多見[3]。此外，LL.B（Bachelor of Laws，法學學士）也曾是美國 Law School 的一種學位，但自從美國法學院實行研究生教育之後，該學位被取消。但英國的法學院現在仍然保留有此種學位[4]。LL.D（Doctor of Laws）為「法律博士」，一般為一種榮譽頭銜[5]。

注

① "This is now the basic law degree, replacing the LL.B in the late 1960's." Cf. The Publisher's Editorial Staff, *Black's Law Dictionary*, Abridged 6th Edition, West Publishing Co. (1991), at P. 580.

② "A law degree conferred on those completing graduate-level study, beyond the J.D. degree." Cf. Bryan A. Garner, *Black's Law Dictionary*, 7th Edition, West Group (1999), at P. 990.

③ "The S.J.D. is a Ph.D.-level degree held by very few lawyers; it is sought primarily by individuals who plan a career of legal scholarship and teaching, and even on law school faculties it is relatively rare. Requirements for the degree generally include a minimum of one year's study beyond the LL.M, or its equivalent, completion of a dissertation, and an oral examination on the topic of the dissertation. At some law schools the degree is called J.S.D." Cf. James E. Clapp, *Random House Webster's Dictionary of the Law*, Random House (2000), at P. 403.

④ "This was formerly the law degree ordinarily conferred by American law schools. It is still the normal degree in British law schools." Cf. Bryan A. Garner, *Black's Law Dictionary*, 7th Edition, West Group (1999), at P. 946.

⑤ "commonly an honorary law degree", *Id.* at P. 946.

Job action ▸ Strike

二者都是在勞動法（labor law）中指工人為抗議和達某種要求而進行的一種鬥爭行為。其中，job action 指工人臨時性的抗議行為，如怠工等，故為「怠工行為」而非「罷工行為」①。而 strike 則多指工人有組織的罷工行動，聲勢、規模和期限遠比 job action 大或長[2]。

 注

① "A concerted, temporary action by employees (such as sickout or work slowdown), intended to pressure management to concede to the employees demand without resorting to a strike." Cf. Bryan A. Garner, *Black's Law Dictionary*, 7th Edition, West Group (1999), at P. 840.

② "a concerted work stoppage, interruption, or slowdown by a body of workers to enforce compliance with demands made on an employer", Cf. Linda Picard Wood, J.D., *Merriam Webster's Dictionary of Law*, Merriam-Webster, Incorporated (1996), at P. 474.

Joint custody ▸ Joint legal custody ▸ Joint physical custody

三者均與對未成年人的監護有關。其中，joint custody（共同監護權，也稱爲 shared custody）是指離婚或分居時法院判決或經協議夫妻雙方均對子女擁有的監護權[1]，其理由是婚姻雖然破滅，但父母關係卻是永恆的。實踐中，joint custody 又分爲法定共同監護權（joint legal custody）和實際共同監護（joint physical custody）兩種。前者僅要求對於有關子女的重大決策須由父母雙方共同商議決定；而後者則包括一種法定居住地的安排，即須安排子女輪流在一段時間內住宿在離婚父母各自的家中[2]。

 注

① "Custody of children shared by both divorced or separated parents under an order or agreement." Cf. Daphne Dukelow, *The Dictionary*

of Canadian Law, Thomson professional Publishing Canada (1991), at P. 549.

② "it may involve joint legal custody and joint physical custody. Such includes physical sharing of child in additional to both parents participating in decisions affecting child's life, e.g., education, medical problems, recreations, etc.", Cf. The Publisher's Editorial Staff, *Black's Law Dictionary*, Abridged 6ᵗʰ Edition, West Publishing Co. (1991), at P. 267.

Joint liability ▶ Joint and several liability

　　二者的區別在於 joint liability 為「共同負債」或「共同責任」，指兩個或兩個以上者共同對第三人的負債，或在侵權案件中兩個或兩個以上侵權人對被侵權人應負的責任，債務人或責任人在訴訟中有權要求其共同債務人或共同責任人作為本訴的共同被告，且要求他們共同償還債務或賠償損失①。joint and several liability 則為「連帶債務」，指債權人可就兩個以上債務人所欠的債務同時對所有債務人提起訴訟，也可單獨就其中某一債務人提起而要求他（她）歸還所有其他人所欠債務，一旦歸還，其他債務人也就免去自己的債務。此種情況經常出現在夫妻的共同債務中，如夫妻雙方申明對債務負連帶債務責任，債權人只對丈夫或妻子一方起訴要求歸還夫妻所欠的全部債務即可。同樣，在侵權責任中，joint and several liability 指「連帶責任」，即准許被侵權人只要求共同侵權人之一賠償其全部損失②。

注

① "Liability that is owed to a third party by two or more other parties together. One wherein joint obligor has right to insist that co-obligor be joined as a codefendant with him, that is, that they be sued jointly." Cf. The Publisher's Editorial Staff, *Black's Law Dictionary*, Abridged 6th Edition, West Publishing Co. (1991), at P. 583.

② "liability for damages caused by the combined action of two or more persons, or for an obligation undertaken by two or more persons, under circumstances in which the law permits the plaintiff to proceed either against the whole group or against member individually." Cf. James E. Clapp, *Random House Webster's Dictionary of the Law*, Random House (2000), at P. 271.

Joint resolution ▸ Concurrent resolution

二者均指議會兩院所透過的決議。其區別在於 joint resolution（聯合決議）一經總統簽署或否決了行政機關所提出的反對意見後即產生法律效力①。而 concurrent resolution（共同決議）所指的決議則不具備法律效力②。

注

① "Bill passed by both House and Senate, sent to the President for signature to become law." Cf. P. H. Collin, *Dictionary of Law*, 2nd Edition, Peter Collin Publishing Ltd. (1993), at P. 479.

② "a resolution passed by both houses of a legislative body that lacks the force of law", Cf. Linda Picard Wood, J.D., *Merriam Webster's Dictionary of Law*, Merriam-Webster, Incorporated (1996), at P. 93.

Joint venture ▸ Joint adventure

二者均爲「聯合投資」，指一種大型的合夥企業經營形式。在美國，這兩個術語的含義幾乎相同[1]；在英國，人們一般只使用 joint venture，認為 joint adventure 為美式英語[2]。聯合投資是外國直接投資（foreign direct investment）的一種形式，常分為合作經營和合資經營兩種，即契約式合作企業（contractual joint venture）和股權式合營企業（equity joint venture），在前者中，合作雙方一般各自保持自己原有的獨立法人資格；後者則多透過共同投資，建立一個具有法人資格的獨立經營實體[3]。

注

[1] Cf. Bryan A. Garner, *Black's Law Dictionary*, 7th Edition, West Group (1999), at P. 843.

[2] Cf. P. H. Collin, *Dictionary of Law*, 2nd Edition, Peter Collin Publishing Ltd. (1993), at P. 296.

[3] Cf. Li Rong-fu/Song Lei, *A Course Book of Legal English*, *Foreign Direct Investment*, Law Press, China (1999), at P. 306.

Judge ▸ Court ▸ Justice

三者均有「法官」的含義，且常作同義詞交互使用，但它們仍有一些區別，主要在於 justice 多指較高等級法院的法官，如美國的州最高法院（state supreme court）、（聯邦）巡迴法院（circuit court）、聯邦最高法院（US Supreme Court）以及英國的王座法院（King's Bench or Queen's Bench）、上訴法院（Court of Appeals）的法官[1]。值得注意的是在美國，除最高級法院的法官外，最低級法院（inferior court）的法官也稱為 justice，如 justice of the peace court 以及 justice of police court。judge 則為一般級別法院，如審判級或中級上訴法院的法官[2]。當文章涉及案例分析以及案件的上訴，且上下文中出現交替使用 judge 和 justice 的時候，讀者則應注意 judge 多指 trial judge，即一審法官或初審法官，且其多是獨任審理案件，而 justice 則常指 appellant court justice，即上訴法院法官，且其多為合議庭審案。而 court 則既可用於替代 judge，又可用於替換 justice[3]。

 注

① "Justice: judge, esp. a judge of an appellate court or court of last resort (as a supreme court)." Cf. Linda Picard Wood, J.D., *Merriam Webster's Dictionary of Law*, Merriam-Webster, Incorporated (1996), at P. 277.

② "Trial judges and appellate judges on intermediate levels are called judges, not justice." Cf. Bryan A. Garner, *A Dictionary of Modern Legal Usage*, 2nd Edition, Oxford University Press (1995), at P. 480.

③ "Judge, justice and court are often used synonymously or interchangeably." Cf. The Publisher's Editorial Staff, *Black's Law Dictionary*, Abridged 6th Edition, West Publishing Co. (1991), at P. 585.

Judgment ▸ Decree

二者都有司法「判決」的含義。在普通法和衡平法未合併之前，凡普通法案件的判決稱為 judgment，而衡平法上的判決則稱為 decree。現在，儘管在美國此種區分已逐漸取消，judgment 已經成為最通用單詞，但 decree 仍常用作 judgment 的同義詞，且常用於以往按傳統為衡平法領域的一些場合，如 bankruptcy decree、divorce decree。

注

"Before the merger of law and equity, the final order disposing of a case was called a *judgment* at law but a *decree* in equity. Now judgment is the usual term for most cases, but *decree* is often used as a synonym and is the usual term in certain contexts.", Cf. James E. Clapp, *Random House Webster's Dictionary of the Law*, Random House, New York (2000), at Ps. 127—128; "Traditionally, judicial decisions are termed *decrees* in courts of equity, admiralty, divorce, and probate; they are termed *judgments* in courts of law." Cf. Bryan A. Garner, *A Dictionary of Modern Legal Usage*, 2nd Edition, Oxford University Press Ltd. (1996), at P. 253.

Judicial aid ▸ Legal aid

二者的差異在於 judicial aid（司法救助）是審判機關的行為，指法院對於民事、行政案件中有充分理由證明自己合法權益受到侵害，但經濟確有困難的當事人實行緩交、減交和免交訴訟費用的法律制度。而 legal aid（法律援助）則爲司法行政部門的法律援助，指律師等法律援助工作人員接受經濟困難的人的申請爲其提供免費訴訟代理，或是受法院指派爲特殊案件的當事人免費提供法律幫助、提供辯護的一種法律制度。

注

"Legal Aid: Country-wide system administered locally by which legal services are rendered to those in financial need and who cannot afford private counsel." Cf. The Publisher's Editorial Staff, *Black's Law Dictionary*, Abridged 6th Edition, West Publishing Co. (1991), at P. 619.

Judicial officers

英國法院體系中，除正式審理案件的法官外，還有許多司法

官員（judicial officers），其在 Rules of the Supreme Court 中被統稱
爲 the court，負責處理各種訴訟中間事項（interlocutory matters）。
高等法院（High Court）的司法官員包括：Queen's Bench masters
（女王座法院主事官）、Chancery masters（大法官法院主事官）、
District registrars（地方法院登記官）、judges in chambers（內庭法
官）和 Taxing masters（訴訟費評定官）。Queen's Bench masters 從
從業至少 10 年的沙律師或巴律師中任命，主要負責行政事務工作，
包括受理單方面申請（ex part application）以及簽發雙方當事人認
可的判決書（consent order）等，不服其裁定向 judges in chamber 上
訴。Chancery masters 也必須是具有 10 年以上資歷的沙律師或巴
律師，其更多負責審判後的事務工作，如進行賬簿活動、變賣資
產、調查和詢問受益人或近親屬、對財產清算人或受託人等作指示
或監督等。同樣，不服其裁定也上訴至 judge in chamber。District
registrars 必須具有 7 年的沙律師資歷，他們同時也在該地區的郡
法院擔任 registrars，職責等同 London 高等法院的 master 的職責。
judges in chambers 負責受理不服 master 裁決的上訴以及一些不屬於
master 管轄權範疇的訴訟中期事項。Taxing masters 由至少具有 10 年
資歷的沙律師或巴律師擔任，主要負責訴訟費評定工作[1]。郡法院的
judicial officers 主要有 circuit judges（巡迴法官）和 registrars（司法
常務官）兩種[2]。

注

[1] Cf. John O'Hare & Robert N. Hill, *Civil Litigation*, Longman Group
   UK Ltd. (1990), at Ps. 4—6.
[2] 請參見本書的 County Court 條目。

Junior division ► Primary division

二者均用於指國外的階段教育。差別在於 primary division 為「基本教育階段」，其含「初級幼稚園階段」（junior kindergarten）、「幼稚園階段」（kindergarten）和緊接之後的 3 年小學教育階段[1]。junior division 為「初級教育階段」，指緊接 primary division 之後的又一個 3 年小學教育階段[2]。

注

[1] "The division of the organization of an elementary school comprising junior kindergarten, kindergarten and the first 3 years of the program of studies immediately following kindergarten." Cf. *Education Act*, R.S.O. 1980, c. 129, s. 1.

[2] "The division of the organization of an elementary school comprising the first three years of the program of studies immediately following the primary division." Cf. *Education Act*, R.S.O. 1980, c. 129, s. 2.

Jurisdiction ► Power ► Competence

三者經常在國際民事訴訟法中指對訴訟管轄或處理的一種能力。jurisdiction 多指法院廣義的受理及審判案件的能力，決定法院或準司法機構，如行政法庭審判案件的範圍，如法院的受案範圍便為 subject matter jurisdiction，故 jurisdiction 應譯為「司法管轄權」或「審判管轄權」[1]。power 具有特定授權及 privilege 的含義[2]，常指特定類型的法院處理特種類型的案件的能力，如法國的商事法庭便沒有權力（power）處理婚姻訴訟，其上訴法院也無權力受理一審案件。competence 有時也指法院對案件的管轄權，如：the case falls within the competence of the court[3]。此時其多指在地域觀念上的一種許可權或權力，如域內管轄權、屬地管轄權、內國地域管轄權等。此外，在區分屬於國家權力的管轄權和屬於法院權力的管轄權時，jurisdiction 多指國家對審判事務的權力，而 competence 則多指法院對審判事務的權力。

注

① "Jurisdiction determines which court system should properly adjudicate a case. Questions of jurisdiction also arise regarding quasi judicial bodies (as administrative agencies) in their decision making capacities." Cf. Linda Picard Wood, J.D., *Merriam Webster's Dictionary of Law*, Merriam-Webster, Incorporated (1996), at P. 271.

② "A right or privilege." Cf. Daphne Dukelow, *The Dictionary of Canadian Law*, Thomson Professional Publishing Canada (1991), at P. 794.

③ Cf. P. H. Collin, *Dictionary of Law*, 2nd Edition, Peter Collin Publishing Ltd. (1993), at P. 110.

Juvenile ► Minor

在法律上二者均可指未成年人。主要區別在於它們各自所適用的場合，juvenile 多用於指具有部分行為能力的青少年，即未成年人的違法或犯罪①。而minor 則主要指未成年人的法律資格、地位、權利、義務等，與未成年人的犯罪及刑事責任無關②。

注

① "a youth, a minor, especially, a person not yet old enough to be treated as an adult by the criminal justice system", Cf. James E. Clapp, *Random House Webster's Dictionary of the Law*, Random House

(2000), at P. 260.

② "A term derived from the civil law, which described a person under certain age as less than so many years." Cf. The Publisher's Editorial Staff, *Black's Law Dictionary*, Abridged 6th Edition, West Publishing Co. (1991), at P. 689.

J

K

Kickback ► Bribery ► Payoff

三者均指向他人非法支付之行為。kickback 為「回扣」，多指按百分比返回部分收益以表示酬勞的一種支付，與合法的折扣（discount）不同，kickback 為非法[1]。在美國，其為聯邦和州法律所禁止的犯罪[2]，故最好不將其譯為「傭金」或「酬金」等[3]，以免導致讀者誤解和誤用。payoff 與 kickback 同義（但 *Merriam Webster's Dictionary of Law* 則說其與 bribery 同義），也為「回扣」[4]，它們與 bribery（賄賂）的區別主要在於 kickback 或 payoff 主要是因得到或即將得到一筆收入（income）而向控制該收入淵源或幫助獲得該收入者（尤指政府官員）的一種回報。而 bribery 所包括的內容及範圍則遠不限於此，kickback 只是屬於 bribery 所包括的一種行為[5]。

注

① "illegal commission paid to someone (especially a government official) who helps in a business deal", Cf. P. H. Collin, *Dictionary of Law*, 2nd Edition, Peter Collin Publishing Ltd. (1993), at P. 302.

② "Under federal statute kickbacks are a criminal offense in connection with a contract for construction or repair of a public building or a building financed by loans from the government. Such acts are also generally prohibited by state commercial bribery states." Cf. 18 U.S.C.A. s.874.

③ Cf.《英漢法律詞典》，Revised Edition，法律出版社（1999），第 435 頁；陸谷孫，《英漢大詞典》，上海譯文出版社（1995），第 1785 頁。

④ Cf. Bryan A. Garner, *Black's Law Dictionary*, 7th Edition, West Group (1999), at P. 1151.

⑤ "kickback: a form of bribery in which a company that is awarded a contract, or from which a purchase is made, turns over a portion of the money received to an official or employee of the other party to the tran saction, as a reward for helping to bring about the transaction or as an incentive to exercise such influence in the future." Cf. James E. Clapp, *Random House Webster's Dictionary of the Law*, Random House (2000), at P. 261.

L

Lagan ▶ Jetsam ▶ Flotsam

三者都可在海商法中用於指海上的漂流物。其中，lagan（也稱為 lagend、lagon、ligan、ligen、logan，繫標投棄物）和 jetsam（投棄物）都是指船舶遇到風暴或其他危險時為減輕船載而故意投向大海的貨物（goods deliberately thrown over to lighten ship），區別在於 lagan 是指貨主為今後尋找到它們，故在貨物上繫有浮標（goods cast into the sea tied to a buoy so that they may be found again by the owner）的投棄物①。jetsman 則屬於完全放棄情況下未繫標誌的投棄貨物。在英國，jetsman 如被重新發現，除原所有人有權請求償還外，應屬於國王所有②。flotsam（海上漂流物，也稱為floatage、flotage）除包括為減輕船載而有意投棄的貨物外，還包括失事船舶中漂出的物品（goods which float upon the sea when cast overboard for the safety of the ship or when a ship is sunk）③，若在 1 年零 1 天內貨物所有人不予認領，該貨物即歸王室所有。

① Cf. Daphne Dukelow, *The Dictionary of Canadian Law*, Thomson Professional Publishing Canada (1991), at P. 561.

② "Various legal authorities at various times have attempted to distinguish jetsam from flotsam and lagan by restricting the use of this term either to jettisoned material that floated ashore or to jettisoned material that sank and was not attached to a buoy." Cf. James E. Clapp, *Random House Webster's Dictionary of the Law*, Random House (2000), at P. 251.

③ Cf. The Publisher's Editorial Staff, *Black's Law Dictionary*, Abridged 6th Edition, West Publishing Co. (1991), at P. 443.

Landed estate ▶ Real estate

二者均有不動產，即地產權益的含義，區別在於 landed estate （也稱為 landed property）為「地產」，用於指郊區或農村的不動產或地產（suburban or rural land）。而 real estate 為「不動產」，泛指包括landed estate以及城市裡的不動產（real estate situated in a city）。

注

"Landed estate is an interest in real property, esp. suburban or rural land, as distinguished from real estate situated in a city." Cf. Bryan A. Garner, *Black's Law Dictionary*, 7th Edition, West Group (1999), at P. 568.

Landowner ▶ Landlord

二者在各種英漢詞典中均有「地主」的定義[①]。地主，顧名思義，即「占有土地，自己不勞動，依靠出租土地剝削農民為主要生活來源的人」[②]。其實，這兩個術語是有一定差異的。就土地而言（指耕地而非宅基地 residential premises），landowner 僅為土地所有人，指擁有土地者（person who owns land）[③]，究竟是否用於出租尚不得而知，故其不能譯為「地主」或至少與「地主」的含義相去甚遠。而 landlord 則是土地出租人，指擁有土地且將其出租給他人，以獲得部分莊稼或莊稼的收益者（person who rents land to another person for a share of the crop or of the proceeds of the crop produced on such land）[④]，故它似乎才可以被譯為「地主」（含義當然也不盡完全相等）。

注

① Cf. 《英漢法律詞典》，Revised Edition，法律出版社（1999），第 440 頁；陸谷孫，《英漢大詞典》，上海譯文出版社（1995），第 1829 頁；梁實秋，《遠東英漢大辭典》，遠東圖書公司（1977），第 1154 頁；《新英漢詞典》，增補本，上海譯文出版社（1979），第 710 頁。

② Cf. 《現代漢語詞典》，商務印書館（1988），第 239 頁。

③ Cf. Bryan A. Garner, *Black's Law Dictionary*, 7th Edition, West Group (1999), at P. 883.

④ Cf. The Publisher's Editorial Staff, *Black's Law Dictionary*, Abridged 6th Edition, West Publishing Co. (1991), at P. 607.

Larceny ▸ Theft

　　二者均有「竊盜罪」的含義。其中，larceny（也稱為 larceny by trick）指竊盜他人動產，原屬於普通法上的犯罪，多為重罪（felony）①，與它相近似的犯罪還有 obtaining money under false pretense（詐騙錢財罪②，也稱為 false pretense、obtaining property by false pretense、fraudulent pretense，其與 larceny 的差異在於 larceny 指罪犯只占有實物而非產權，而 obtaining money under false pretence 則指罪犯以非法手段，如欺騙等取得了財產的產權，即 title③）以及 embezzlement（侵吞信託財產罪④，其也稱為 peculation，與 larceny 和 false pretense 不同的是 embezzlement 是在先取得占有權的情況下的犯罪⑤）。目前，這三種普通法上的犯罪（也有人認為 embezzlement 不屬於普通法上的犯罪⑥）已被制定法上的 theft（竊盜罪）所取代⑦。總體說來，theft 的含義較廣，其指未經同意而竊走他人財產或服務的犯罪（a crime taking of the property or services of another without consent），包括原先普通法上被視爲不同犯罪的多種偷竊罪（theft commonly encompass by statute a variety of forms of stealing formerly treated as distinct crimes），即貪污（embezzlement）、詐騙他人財產（obtaining another's property by false pretense）以及竊盜（larceny）。在美國，凡適用《模範刑法典》的各州，larceny 均被視爲theft 的一種（under the Model Penal Code and in states that follow it，larceny is a type of theft），其指非法竊走他人動產，旨在永久性剝奪所有人的權利（unlawful taking and carrying away of personal property with the intent to deprive the rightful owner of it permanently）。但在有些州，larceny 卻被單獨定爲一種犯罪，此時它已包括了以往按普通法規定而與它有區別的其他兩種犯罪，即詐騙錢財罪（obtaining money under false pretense）和侵吞信託財產罪（embezzlement）⑧。

注

① "Felonious stealing, taking and carrying, leading, riding, or driving away another's personal property, with intent to convert it or deprive owner thereof." Cf. The Publisher's Editorial Staff, *Black's Law Dictionary*, Abridged 6th Edition, West Publishing Co. (1991), at P. 609.

② "the crime of obtaining title to another's property by false pretense", Cf. Linda Picard Wood, J.D., *Merriam Webster's Dictionary of Law*, Merriam-Webster, Incorporated (1996), at P. 187.

③ "Under tradition classification schemes, if only possession, rather than title, is obtained by trick, then the crime is not false pretenses by larceny." Cf. James E. Clapp, *Random House Webster's Dictionary of the Law*, Random House (2000), at P. 178.

④ "The fraudulent taking of personal property with which one has been entrusted, esp. as a fiduciary." Cf. Bryan A. Garner, *Black's Law Dictionary*, 7th edition, West Group (1999) at P. 540.

⑤ "The criminal intent for embezzlemen—unlike larceny and false pretense—arises after taking possession (not before or during the taking)." *Id.* at P. 540.

⑥ "Embezzlement is not a common law crime.It is the result of legislative efforts to make provision for an unreasonable gap which appeared in the law of larceny as it developed." Cf. Rollin M. Perkins & Ronald N. Boyce, *Criminal Law*, 3rd Edition (1982), at P. 351.

⑦ "To avoid this difficulty some states have employed another word to designate a statutory offense made up of a combination of larceny, embezzlement, and false pretense." Cf. Bryan A. Garner, *Black's Law Dictionary*, 7th Edition, West Group (1999), at P. 1487.

⑧ "Common law distinctions between obtaining money under false pretense, embezzlement, and larceny no longer exist in many states, all such crimes being embranced within general definition of larceny." Cf. The Publisher's Editorial Staff, *Black's Law Dictionary*, Abridged 6th Edition, West Publishing Co. (1991), at P. 609.

Law ▸ Equity

　　law 與 equity（衡平法）相對時應當譯爲「普通法」，此時其爲 common law 的縮略形式①。這正如 legal 與 equitable（衡平法上的）相對時應譯爲「普通法上的」一樣道理②。由此我們便得到 legal charge（普通法上的擔保）與 equitable charge（衡平法上的擔保）等，但翻譯實踐中，不少人都忽略了此種區別，一味只將 legal 譯爲「法定」，或「合法」，這種作法當然不妥③。同樣，court of law 在一般情況下譯為「法院」即可，但其在與 court of equity（衡平法法院）放置一起時，則應譯為「普通法法院」[4]。

注

① "Abbr. L. common law, e.g. Law but not equity", Cf. Bryan A.Garner, *Black's Law Dictionary*, 7th edition, West Group (1999), at P. 889.
② "legal: Of or relating to law as opposed to equity." *Id*. at P. 902.
③ Cf.《牛津法律大詞典》，光明日報出版社（1989），第533頁。
④ "a court that hears cases and decides them on the basis of statute and common law—compare *court of equity*", Cf. Linda Picard Wood, J.D., *Merriam Webster's Dictionary of Law*, Merriam-Webster, Incorporated (1996), at P. 112.

Law merchant ▸ Commercial law

二者的區別在於 law merchant 為「商業法則」（此時的 merchant 不是名詞而是形容詞），指的是按中世紀英國普通法所發展而成的商事規則，包括有關調整商人關係的習慣和規則，商事方面的慣例、規章、原則等，其對現代的 commercial law 有較大影響，在美國《統一商法典》和各州法典中，其被當作補充性規則（supplementing rules）[1]。commercial law 則為「商法」，所指範圍極廣，包括與商業有關的各種法律，如契約、代理、買賣、流通票證、產權文據、破產等[2]。但在美國，commercial law 所擴展的領域並未為人們認可，故在美國，其與 law merchant 的區別沒有在其他歐洲國家那樣大[3]，它們經常被人當作同義詞相互替換使用[4]。

注

① "The commercial rules developed under English common law

that influenced modern commercial law and that are referred to as supplementing rules set down in the Uniform Commercial Code and in state codes." Cf. Linda Picard Wood, J.D., *Merriam Webster's Dictionary of Law*, Merriam-Webster, Incorporated (1996), at P. 282.

② "A phrase used to designate the whole body of substantive jurisprudence applicable to the rights, intercourse, and relations of persons engaged in commerce, trade, or mercantile pursuit." Cf. The Publisher's Editorial Staff, *Black's Law Dictionary*, Abridged 6th Edition, West Publishing Co. (1991), at P. 185.

③ "Today the term commercial law has assumed a new meaning, a meaning that is new at least to Europe, but not so to the United States or to Louisiana. I refer, of course, to the meaning in which the term is used to describe a certain area of expertise in legal practice or learning, or that branch of law... of special interest to business people." Cf. Max Rheinstein, *Problems and Obligations*, in *Essays on the Civil Law of Obligations*, Joseph Dainow ed. (1969), at Ps. 10—11.

④ Cf. Bryan A. Garner, *Black's Law Dictionary*, 7th Edition, West Group (1999), at P. 893.

Law of obligation ▸ Law of property ▸ Law of status

　　三者均代表英美法系民法中三大分類或三大組成部分之一（其與中國的民法分類有差異）。其中，law of obligation 主要是規定特定個人之財產關係的法律（the category of law dealing with proprietary rights in personam），其中的 proprietary 意思是「有關財產的」（of, relating to, or holding as property），所以其為「債權法」，也譯為「債法」。law of property 主要是規定物的地位以及公眾與物的產權關係之法律（the category of law dealing with proprietary rights in rem），故其爲「產權法」或「物權法」，它與債權法一起構成民法上的兩大財產權法。law of status 則是指規定人身屬性的或非財產性質的權利，特定個人或大眾不論（the category of law dealing with personal or nonproprietary rights，whether in personam or in rem），故其爲「身分法」。

注

"Law of obligation is one of the three departments into which civil law is divided. Cf. Law of Property; Law of Status." Cf. Bryan A. Garner, *Black's Law Dictionary*, 7th Edition, West Group (1999), at P. 893.

L

Lawyer ▸ Attorney ▸ Attorney-at-law ▸ Barrister ▸ Solicitor ▸ Counsel ▸ Counselor ▸ Conveyancer ▸ Law agent ▸ Advocate ▸ Proctor

　　這些單詞或片語均有律師的含義。其中，lawyer 爲最通用詞，除指律師外，可泛指取得法律專業資格有權從事法律工作者。在英國，其可包括法官、開業律師、法學教師等。在美國，其可指參與法庭訴辯或提供法律諮詢的任何人，該單詞有時也用於專指開業律師。現有人將其譯爲「法律人」〔與「非法律人」（layman）相對〕[①]。在英國，attorney 最初是指在普通法法院執業的律師（與其相對，solicitor 在衡平法法院，proctor 在宗教法法院[②]），即指由當事人指定，以委託人名義行使職責，代寫訴訟文書、財產轉讓書等的法律代理人，後被 solicitor 取代，現在英國 attorney 已鮮用。在美國，attorney 廣泛用來指行使英格蘭的巴律師、沙律師和代理人等全部職能的律師，其比 lawyer 正式，範圍窄，多僅限於法律事務代理律師。attorney-at-law 爲美國用語，通常在名片上使用。barrister 和 solicitor 多用於英國或一些英聯邦國家或地區，這與美國和加拿大等國的律師不分類別的情況不同。這兩個單詞的譯法很多，前者有出庭律師、高級律師、專門律師、大律師等，後者有訴狀律師、初級律師等，這些譯法均不太準確，易誤導讀者③。事實上，這兩種律師的職能各有差異，根本不能簡單用高級和低級區分。此外，solicitor 也常常在高等法院之外的其他法庭上出庭辯護，故也不能用出庭律師或不出庭律師加以區別，至於專門、大小、訴狀等詞也不適當。鑒於 barrister 和 solicitor 的培養、職責和區別等決非能用一兩個字準確表達，筆者推崇上海陳忠誠教授的音譯法，即將前者譯爲「巴律師」，後者譯爲「沙律師」，然後加上適當的注釋，如：沙律師：透過律師事務所實踐（practice）培養，與代理人直接交往，負責接案和收取訴訟費，只可在 high court 以外的初級法庭出庭辯護，遇到在 high court 的案件，得懇請巴律師替其出庭辯護（solicit the services of a barrister to plead his case，solicitor 也因此而得名）；巴律師：學院派律師（由四大律師學院培養），不與當事人直接交往，從沙律師處分得訴訟費，應沙律師請求負責案件相關法律問題和出庭辯護④。counsel 爲「顧問律師」，在英國多指爲沙律師提供意見或建議的巴律師，有時也指成爲王室法律顧問的巴律師，即 Queen's（或 King's）Counsel。在美國，其多指爲公司或政府擔當法律顧問的律師，如 in house counsel。counselor 在英國已經被廢棄，其在愛爾蘭和美國等地有時仍在使用，基本等同 counsel，但比 counsel 正式。主要是指提供法律諮詢，處理各種法律事務，出庭進行訴、辯等的法律代理人，也應譯爲「顧問律師」⑤。conveyancer 主要指從事不動產轉讓事務的專門律師，故爲「不動產轉讓律師」。在英國，巴律師和沙律師均可從事（a lawyer who specializes in real estate transactions⑥）。advocate 爲「出庭律師」（a lawyer who works and argues in support of another's cause, esp. in court⑦）。此外，蘇格蘭的巴律師也被稱爲 advocate，而沙律師則被稱爲 law agent⑧。proctor 現指宗教法院的教堂的辯護律師或宗教事務律師

（an advocate of a religious house, one who represents a religious society in its legal affairs），其也稱爲 procurator[9]。

注

① "One who is licensed to practice law." Cf. Bryan A. Garner, *Black's Law Dictionary*, 7th edition, West Group (1999), at P. 895; "one whose profession is to advise clients as to legal rights and obligations and to represent clients in legal proceedings", Cf. Linda Picard Wood, J.D., *Merriam Webster's Dictionary of Law*, Merriam-Webster, Incorporated (1996), at P. 283; "person who has studied law and can act for people on legal business", Cf. P. H. Collin, Dictionary of Law, Peter Collin Publishing (1995), at P. 310.

② "Originally, attorney denoted a practitioner in common-law courts, solicitor one in equity courts, and proctor one in ecclesiastical courts." Cf. Bryan A. Garner, *A Dictionary of Modern Legal Usage*, Oxford University Press Ltd. (1995), at P. 90.

③ Cf. 姚棟華等，《香港法律辭彙》，商務印書館（1995），第 25、163 頁；《英漢法律詞典》，Revised Edition，法律出版社（1999），第 76、747 頁；陸谷孫，《英漢大詞典》，上海譯文出版社（1995），第 244、3281 頁。

④ Cf. Li Rong-fu/Song Lei, *A Course Book of Legal English*, Law Press, China (1999), at Ps. 42—44.

⑤ "In American English, *counsel* and *counselor* are both, in one sense, general terms meaning '*One who gives legal advise*'; the latter being the more formal term." Cf. Bryan A. Garner, *A Dictionary of Modern Legal Usage*, Oxford University Press Ltd. (1995), at P. 90.

⑥ Cf. Bryan A. Garner, *Black's Law Dictionary*, 7th edition, West Group (1999), at P. 335.

⑦ Cf. Linda Picard Wood, J.D., *Merriam Webster's Dictionary of Law*, Merriam-Webster, Incorporated (1996), at P. 16.

⑧ Cf. Li Rong-fu/Song Lei, *A Course Book of Legal English*, Law Press, China (1999), at P. 44.

⑨ Cf. Bryan A. Garner, *Black's Law Dictionary*, 7ᵗʰ edition, West Group (1999), at P. 1224.

Leasehold

　該術語（也稱爲 leasehold estate、leasehold interest）爲「不動產租賃權益」，指佃戶或房客占有土地或房屋的權益①。其被定義爲 chattle real（土地附屬動產，指從土地或房屋等所派生出的非永佃或自由保有土地權益，如土地租賃權或租借土地保有權等）而非 real property②。總體說來，leasehold可分爲四大類：⑴ tenancy for years（定期租賃權），指固定期限的租賃，值得注意的是其期限並非按其字面含義一定得一年，如確定租期爲一週，其也稱爲 tenancy for years）；⑵ periodic tenancy（自動展期的定期租賃），可一月一月地或一年一年地自動展期，直至經通知終止爲止，也稱爲 tenancy from period to period、periodic estate、estate from period to period、month to month tenancy/estate、year to year tenancy/estate；⑶ tenancy at will（任意性租賃），指一種非協議的默許土地占有，對租賃期限或租金等條件均未作明確規定，任意一方只要願意均可以通知形式隨時終止此種租賃，也稱爲 at-will tenancy、estate at will；⑷ tenancy at sufferance（默許租賃），指合法租賃期滿後經默許而非協議繼續占有財產，也稱爲hold over tenancy、estate at sufferance。

① "a right to temporary possession of real property by agreement with the owner of the freehold or of a superior leasehold on the same property", Cf. James E. Clapp, *Random House Webster's Dictionary of the Law*, Random House (2000), at P. 267.

② "Historically it is classified as a chattle real, a species of personalty." Cf. The Publisher's Editorial Staff, *Black's Law Dictionary*, Abridged 6th Edition, West Publishing Co. (1991), at P. 616.

Legacy ▶ Bequest ▶ Devise

三者均有遺贈物的含義。一般說來，legacy 等同 bequest①，爲「動產遺贈」，都是指屬人財產或動產（personal property）的贈與，legacy 更常指遺贈的金錢②。而 devise 則爲「不動產遺贈」，指不動產（real property，尤指 land）的贈與③。但以上三個術語的明顯區別正在逐漸消失。如法律規定如立遺囑人在遺囑中明確表示，則 legacy 和 bequest 也用於指不動產遺贈④。現在按美國《統一遺囑檢驗法典》之規定，devise 也可用於指任何形式的財產的遺贈⑤。

注

① "legacy: same as bequest", Cf. James E. Clapp, *Random House Webster's Dictionary of the Law*, Random House, New York (2000), at P. 267.

② "A gift by will, esp. of personal property and often of money." Cf. Bryan A. Garner, *Black's Law Dictionary*, 7th Edition, West Group (1999), at P. 901.

③ "giving freehold land to someone in a will. Giving of other types of property is a bequest", Cf. P. H. Collin, *Dictionary of Law*, 2nd Edition, Peter Collin Publishing Ltd. (1993), at P. 169.

④ "In a technical sense and strictly construes, *legacy* is a gift or *bequest* by will of personal property, whereas a *devise* is a testamentary disposition of real estate, but such distinction will not be permitted to defeat the intent of a testator, and such terms may be construed interchangeably or applied indifferently to either personalty or real estate if the context of the will shows that such was the intention of the testator." Cf. The Publisher's Editorial Staff, *Black's Law Dictionary*, Abridged 6th Edition, West Publishing Co. (1991), at P. 617.

⑤ "Formerly *devise* was used to refer only to gifts of real property, and *legacy* and *bequest* were used only to refer to gifts of personal property. These distinctions are no longer closely followed. The Uniform Probate Code uses devise to refer to any gifts made in a will." Cf. Linda Picard Wood, J.D., *Merriam Webster's Dictionary of Law*, Merriam-Webster, Incorporated (1996), at P. 137.

Legal adviser ▸ Counsel(l)or

二者均有「法律顧問」的含義。相比之下，counsellor（也稱爲counsel）顯得正式；而 legal adviser 則較爲通用，且常指有關個人事務的法律顧問。

參見 advice。

Legal aid

在英國，legal aid（法律援助）過去僅指向貧窮的當事人提供法律援助證書或命令（order or certificate of legal aid），現在已經成爲一總體概念，一種體制方案①。其包括三種內容，一是法律諮詢

（advice），即向當事人提供有關法律和程序步驟的口頭或書面諮詢服務[2]。此種服務主要為綠色表格服務（green form help），當有資格獲得法律援助的當事人填寫了綠色表格後，律師便可向他提供免費或有補貼的諮詢服務。二是代理服務（representation），指協助當事人提起訴訟或達成和解或進行刑事辯護，包括協助當事人獲得緊急證書或民事法律援助證書等[3]。三是司法協助（assistance），指具體履行法律援助方案計畫，協助當事人完成訴訟或和解或刑事案件辯護等各種步驟，其包括綠皮文書格式規定的協助（green form help）和代理方式的協助（assistance by way of representation）兩種形式規定的各個步驟[4]。

注

① "Under the old scheme the term legal aid referred to a certificate or order of legal aid. Now the term legal aid refers to the whole scheme." Cf. John O'Hare & Robert N. Hill, *Civil Litigation*, 5th Edition, Longman Group UK Ltd. (1990), at P. 50.

② "Advice means oral or written help on any question of English law, and advice as to what steps the client might take in the circumstances." *Id.* at P. 50.

③ "Assistance means taking steps to help a person in connection with a question of English law, including helping them to go to court, or making certain court applications for them." *Id.* at P. 51.

④ "Representation means taking all steps necessary to bring the matter to court or to arrive at a compromise with or without proceedings, or conducting a criminal defense." *Id.* at P. 51.

Legal Aid Board ▸ Law Society

Legal Aid Board 為英國的法律援助委員會，其接替了原先 Law Society 履行的職責，負責對窮人提供法律援助的事務。其由一名主席和 11 至 17 名成員組成，下設常務主任（Chief Executive），其下再設集團或地區經理（Group/Area Managers），再下設地區委員會（Area Committee），最基層為地方分支機構（Area Office），其負責對申請法律援助人員資格的審查。

注

Cf. Robert N. Hill, *Civil litigation*, 5th Edition, Longman Group UK Ltd. (1990), at Ps. 49—50.

Legal doctrine ▸ Legal principle ▸ Legal rule

三者都是指法律規範（legal norm）的種類，但各自表述的範圍以及普遍性程度具有差異。legal doctrine（法律原理）的概括性最強，常表示實質性的法律規範，包括具共同主題的、系統的一套處理特殊情況、典型事例和法律秩序的原則、規則和準則，它們在邏輯上相互關聯，結合為有機的統一體，可從其基礎和邏輯前提進行法律推理，如英美法系中的契約對價原理以及公共政策原理等。legal principle（法律原則）多指對較具體的簡單陳述、法律適用進行論證、統一和解釋，並作為更進一步的法律推理的權威前提的普遍性規範。legal rule（法律規則）則多指比較專門和具體的規範，用以規定某種法律事實的特定法律後果，如必須有兩人或兩人以上者證明遺囑方能生效規則等。

注

Cf. Lewis Mayers, *The Machinery of Justice—An Introduction to Legal Structure and Process*, Prentice Hall, Inc., London (1962).

Legal estate ▸ Equitable estate ▸ Legal mortgage ▸ Equitable mortgage ▸ Common-law mortgage

國外的房地產權益一般有普通法上的權益（legal estate）和衡平法上的權益（equitable estate）之分，按照傳統的法律規定，如 legal 權益受到侵害，則可提起普通法上的訴訟以要求索賠，而屬 equitable 權益受到侵害時多只能提起衡平法上的訴訟以得到衡平法上的救濟。此時的 legal 等同 of common law，其與 equitable 相對[1]。需注意的是，在美國路易斯安那州的房地產抵押中還設立有 legal mortgage（也稱爲 tacit mortgage），指由法律實施而不是由雙方當事人約定而成立的一種按揭。由於該術語是大陸法系而非英美法系之術語，此時便不能再適用上述的「legal 在與 equitable 相對時等同 of common-law」之一般規則，因而，legal mortgage 只能譯爲「法定按揭」[2]。實際上，與英美法系中的 equitable mortgage（衡平法上的按揭，指有意思表示但無形式要件的按揭抵押，衡平法法院可經推定視其爲按揭）相對的普通法上的按揭應爲 common-law mortgage[3]。

注

[1] 參見本書中的條目 Law 和 Equity。

[2] "a mortgage that secures an obligation which is created by a law and which does not have to be stipulated to by the parties", Cf. Linda Picard Wood, J.D., *Merriam Webster's Dictionary of Law*, Merriam-Webster, Incorporated (1996), at P. 318.

③ Cf. The Publisher's Editorial Staff, *Black's Law Dictionary*, Abridged 6th Edition, West Publishing Co. (1991), at P. 699.

Legal person ▶ Corporation

在法律詞典中，legal person 和 corporation 均被稱爲法人，它們之間實際存在一定差異，legal person（也稱爲 artificial person、fictitious person、juristic person、moral person）爲一通用語，指民事權利主體之一，其與自然人（natural person）相對，指按照法定程序設立，有一定的組織機構和獨立的（或獨立支配的）財產，並能以自己的名義享有民事權利，承擔民事義務的社會組織①。其可指企業、事業、社團等各種性質的法人機構。相比之下，corporation（也稱爲 corporation aggregate、aggregate corporation、body corporate、corporate body）則是專門用語，即我們所說的企業公司法人，其屬於 legal person 所包含的範疇②。

注

① Cf. 張友漁，《中國大百科全書》法學卷，中國大百科全書出版社（1984），第 105 頁。

② "An entity (usu. a business) having authority under law to act as a single person distinct from the shareholders who own it and having rights to issue stock and exist independently." Cf. Bryan A. Garner, *Black's Law Dictionary*, 7th Edition, West Group (1999), at P. 341.

Legal representative

該片語曾被人誤當作企事業單位及公司的法定代表人或法人代表，在多種契約範本以及法律詞典中出現過①。實際上，它的含義與公司的法定代表人的含義相去甚遠。在多數情況下，legal representative 都等同 legal personal representative，指遺產繼承中的遺產管理人（administrator）、遺囑執行人（executor）、法院指定的遺產受託人（judicial trustee of the estate）以及未成年人的財產或（和）人身監護人（guardian of the person or estate, or both, of a minor）。此外，其可在專利法（或版權法）中指專利權人（或版權人）的代理人或律師（包括專利權或著作權人的繼承人、遺囑執行人、保佐人、遺產管理人、受遺贈人、受讓人等）。此外，它也可指企業、團體等的按授權委託書指定的法律事務的代理人（an agent having legal status, especially, one acting under a power of attorney）。一句話，legal representative 的基本含義應為「法定代理人」，即法律事務代理人，其根本不是中國公司等企業或事業實體中的法定代表人[2]。此外一些別的表達方式，如 authorized agent of corporation 或 corporate agent 等，也與法定代表人差異較大。筆者最近在翻譯《美國加州公司法示範性章程》有關的公司組織大綱（Articles of Incorporation）等文件中發現其中有 initial agent for service of process 一術語，指註冊登記時指明的公司負責收受法院司法文件以及負責承擔公司法律責任等的代表人，其含義基本等同中國公司的法定代表人[3]，故建議是否可套用 initial agent for service of process 作為法定代表人的對等翻譯，這與該章程將公司的法定地址譯為 address for service of process（意思是接收法律文件包括傳票等的位址）同出一個道理。由此我們可得出：公司法定代表人：corporation's initial agent for service of process；企業法定代表人：business's initial agent for service of process；大學的法定代表人：university's agent for service of process等。

注

① Cf.《英漢法律詞典》，法律出版社（1999），第 454 頁；陳伯

初，《英漢商業大詞典》，中國商業出版社（1994），第934頁。

② "one who represents or stands in the place of another under authority recognized by law esp. with respect to the other's property or interests: as a) personal representative: b) an agent having legal status, esp. one acting under a power of attorney", Cf. Linda Picard Wood, J.D., *Merriam Webster's Dictionary of Law*, Merriam-Webster, Incorporated (1996), at P. 286: "one who represents another by operation of law, most often as a guardian, but may be an executor, an administrator, a trustee, a receiver, etc." Cf. Philip R. Bilancia, *Dictionary of Chinese Law and Government*, Stanford University Press (1981), at P. 197.

③ "Article Three: The name and address in this state of the corporation's initial agent for service of process is:…" Cf. Attorney Anthony Mancuso, *How to Form Your Own California Corporation*, Nolo Press (1994).

Legislative appointment ▸ Executive appointment

二者均可指美國任命法院法官的方式。legislative appointment（立法任命）是一些州所採用的方法，其包括立法機關自身對法官候選人的提名，如提名者得到立法機關一個院或兩個院的多數贊成票，他（她）即可獲得任命。在 1776 至 1830 年期間，多數州均採用該方式任命法官，後受民主思想的影響，在有些州，此方式逐漸被民主選舉所取代。executive appointment（行政任命）則是指《美國聯邦憲法》第 2 條第 2 款所規定的由總統提名，經參議院批准以任命最高法院的法官和其他官員的規定，以及州長提名或由其臨時任命法官填補空缺等程序規定。

注

Cf. Lewis Mayers, *The Machinery of Justice—An Introduction to Legal Structure and Process*, Prentice-Hall, Inc., London (1962).

Legislator ▸ Law-maker

二者均有「立法者」的含義。區別在於 legislator 與 legislature 相關，故其多指屬於立法機關成員者（member of a legislature）[1]。而 law maker 則範圍較廣，除包括 legislator 之外，透過判例制定法律的法官，甚至締結契約的雙方當事人，在某種意義上都可以稱為 law maker[2]。

注

[1] "a person who makes laws, esp. a member of a legislative body", Cf. Linda Picard Wood, J.D., *Merriam Webster's Dictionary of Law*, Merriam-Webster, Incorporated (1996), at P. 287.

[2] "Although historically lawmaker was thought to be equivalent to legislator, the advent of legal realism made it apply just as fully to a judge as to a legislator. Thus Pound's use of the phrase legislative lawmaker is not a careless redundancy." Cf. Bryan A. Garner, *A Dictionary of Modern Legal Usage*, 2nd Edition, Oxford University Press Ltd. (1995), at P. 506.

Lie detector ▸ Polygraph

二者均有測謊器的含義。其區別在於 polygraph 原義為「多波掃描器」，指一種測量人體生理機能脈衝波動的醫療器械，此種器械因可用作檢查伴隨扯謊而出現的緊張脈衝波動而被警方作爲一種測謊器使用,因此,lie detector 實際是 polygraph 的一種特殊用途時的稱呼。

注

"Polygraph: an instrument that records physiological pulsations; esp. lie detector." Cf. Linda Picard Wood, J.D., *Merriam Webster's Dictionary of Law*, Merriam-Webster, Incorporated (1996), at P. 368.

Lineup ▸ Show-up

　　二者均用於指對疑犯進行的一種指認行爲。區別在於 lineup (也稱爲 line-up identification) 爲「列隊辨認」,是讓犯罪嫌疑人與其他人一起列隊後一個挨一個地讓證人(或受害人)進行辨認 (a line of persons assembled by police for possible identification of a suspect by a witness to a crime) [①]。而 show-up 爲「當面指認」,它沒有 lineup 正式,是當情況不容許列隊辨認時所採取的一種替代方式,一般讓犯罪嫌疑人單獨與證人(或受害人)進行面對面的辨認 (one-to-one confrontation between suspect and witness to crime 或 a presentation of a criminal defendant or a arrestee individually to a witness for identification) [②],要想此種方式辨認所得的證據爲法院所採信,該程序必須遵守正當法律程序(due process)才行。

注

① Cf. Linda Picard Wood, J.D., *Merriam Webster's Dictionary of Law*, Merriam-Webster, Incorporated (1996), at P. 297.
② Cf. The Publisher's Editorial Staff, *Black's Law Dictionary*, Abridged 6th Edition, West Publishing Co. (1991), at P. 962.

Liquidator ► Receiver

二者均與破產事項相關。區別在於 liquidator 多指由法庭或公司指定的處理公司事務，負責託收並變賣公司資產，償付公司債務，根據債權人權利的先後向債權人分配資產餘額者，為「清算人」，主要用於公司的破產[1]。而 receiver 則指由法院所指定的債務人財產的管理人，負責管理、保護、恢復或清算破產公司資產以保護或救濟債權人者，故為「破產財產管理人」，既用於公司，也用於個人的破產[2]。

注

[1] "A person appointed to carry out the winding up of a company. In England and Canada, a receiver who liquidates a corporation on dissolution." Cf. The Publisher's Editorial Staff, *Black's Law Dictionary*, Abridged 6th Edition, West Publishing Co. (1991), at P. 643; "The person appointed to wind up a company." Cf. Daphne Dukelow, *The Dictionary of Canadian Law*, Thomson Professional Publishing Canada (1991), at P. 585.

[2] "a person appointed by a court, or by a corporation or other person, for the protection or collection of property. Usually the receiver administers the property of a bankrupt, or property that is subject of litigation, pending the outcome of a lawsuit", Cf. Bryan A. Garner, *A Dictionary of Modern Legal Usage*, 2nd Edition, Oxford University Press Ltd (1995), at P. 739.

Loan for consumption ▸ Loan for exchange ▸ Loan for use

三者均指物品借用協議或契約。區別在於 loan for consumption 為「消費物品借用協議」，指在借用一定數量的物品用作消費後，借用人必須歸還同種類且數量類似財產給出借人，其主要用於美國路易斯安那州屬於大陸法系的民法（civil law of Louisiana）中[1]。loan for exchange 為「調換借用契約」，指借用動產給他人，而借用人同意今後歸還其他類似動產給出借人，不管所借物品使用與否[2]。loan for use 則為「使用性借出協定」，指借出動產，使用後歸還原物，其也主要用於美國的 civil law of Louisiana[3]。

注

① "a loan in which the borrower is obliged to return property of the same kind as that borrowed and consumed", Cf. Linda Picard Wood, J.D., *Merriam Webster's Dictionary of Law*, Merriam-Webster, Incorporated (1996), at P. 298.

② "A contract by which a lender delivers personal property to a borrower who agrees to return similar property, usu. without compensation for its use." Cf. Bryan A. Garner, *Black's Law Dictionary*, 7th Edition, West Group (1999), at P. 948.

③ "A agreement by which a lender delivers an asset to a borrower who must use it according to its normal function or according to the agreement, and who must return it when finished using it." *Id*. at P. 948.

Ltd. ▸ Plc.

二者都是有限公司的縮寫形式。區別在於 Ltd.（或 Limited）代表的是 Private Limited Company〔閉鎖型責任有限公司或不上市責任有限公司（whose shares are not traded on the Stock Exchange）〕的縮寫，而 Plc.（或 PLC、plc）代表的卻是 Public Limited Company〔公開發行有限公司或股票上市有限公司（whose shares can be bought on the Stock Exchange）〕的縮寫。

Lunatic ▸ In sane person

二者均有精神病患者的含義，且兩術語可交替使用。區別僅在於 lunatic 爲以前的術語（used especially formerly），而insane person 爲現在的用語。

注

Cf. Linda Picard Wood, J.D., *Merriam Webster's Dictionary of Law*, Merriam-Webster, Incorporated (1996), at P. 310.

M

Magistrate's court

　　magistrate's court（治安法院，也稱爲 court of petty sessions、court of summary jurisdiction）通常負責受理輕微的刑事案件以及有關收養、親子鑒定、撫養和家庭暴力等民事案件之預審（preliminary examination）或簡易程序審判，並有決定是否將疑犯送交刑事法院（Crown Court）作進一步審理的權力。在英國的治安法院中，支薪治安官（stipendiary magistrate）由具有律師（lawyer）資格者擔任，其可獨任審案。非支薪的兼職治安法官（lay magistrate）則多任參審員，擔任由 3 人組成的合議庭的成員；不支薪的治安法官也被稱爲 justice of peace。在美國，magistrate's court 是對輕微犯罪（minor criminal offenses）擁有管轄權的法院，其也稱爲 police court。在聯邦體系，magistrate 指「限權法官」，指在聯邦地區法院協助法官處理法官事務的權力有限的司法官員（稱爲 US magistrate、federal magistrate 或 US magistrate judge），多主持犯罪案件預審等（此時稱爲 committing magistrate），一般爲城市（city）的機構設置；在鄉村（rural area），其職責則爲治安法官（justice of peace）所行使。

注

Cf. John O'Hare & Robert N. Hill, *Civil Litigation*, 5th Edition, Longman Group UK Ltd. (1990).

Maiming ▶ Mayhem

　　二者均有使人肢體致殘而喪失戰鬥力的含義，區別在於 maiming

現已經逐漸演變為專指使肢體致殘的傷害行為（或對動物的殘害）[1]。而 mayhem 則指致殘罪行，即有意地致人永久性殘廢或毀容之犯罪（offence），此外，mayhem 的內涵比 maim 廣泛，按美國 Model Penal Code 以及適用該模範法典的各州的刑法典之規定，mayhem 現除包括 maiming 所指的傷害行為外，還包括暴力脅迫（assault）和加重情節的暴力脅迫（aggravated assault）行為等[2]。

注

① "Inflicting upon a person any injury which deprives him of the use of any limb or member of the body, or renders him lame or defective in bodily vigor." Cf. Bryan A. Garner, *Black's Law Dictionary*, 7th Edition, West Group (1999), at P. 657.

② "Under the Modern Penal Code and the codes of the states that follow it, mayhem is encompassed by assault and aggravated assault." Cf. Linda Picard Wood, J.D., *Merriam Webster's Dictionary of Law*, Merriam Webster, Incorporated (1996), at P. 309.

Maintenance ▸ Barratry ▸ Champerty

三者均有助（唆）訟的含義。差別在於 maintenance 是過去普通法上的一種犯罪行為，指與案件無利害關係者慫恿他人訴訟之行為，其範圍廣泛，可指任何目的的助訟或唆訟行為，包括給予錢財支援等[1]。barratry（也稱為 common barratry）指無端挑起或鼓動訴訟事端，為普通法上一犯罪，現在在有些州的制定法上仍為罪名存在。主要為美語，英國少用[2]。而 champerty 則指局外人與訴訟當事人達成協定以幫助訴訟當事人進行訴訟，目的是為得到一定的利益，如得到一定報償或分得部分損害賠償金等，因此 champerty 實際為一種以獲利為目的的助訟行為，也有法律詞典將它歸類為一種

maintenance[3]。

① "the common law crime of giving financial or other support to assist a litigant in pursuing a case in which one has no legal, family, or other legitimate interest", Cf. James E. Clapp, *Random House Webster's Dictionary of the Law*, Random House (2000), at P. 278.

② "US offense of starting lawsuit with no grounds for doing so", Cf. P. H. Collin, *Dictionary of Law*, 2nd Edition, Peter Collin Publishing Ltd. (1993), at P. 48.

③ "An agreement under which a third party is to share in the proceeds of a litigated claim; a form of maintenance." Cf. Daphne Dukelow, *The Dictionary of Canadian Law*, Thomson Professional Publishing Canada (1991), at P. 149.

Major dispute ▶ Minor dispute

二者都是與美國《鐵路勞動法》（Railway Labor Act）相關的術語，均指鐵路工會與雇主之間的爭議。其中，major dispute（也稱爲 new contract dispute）爲「重大爭議」，指涉及勞資集體協議（collective bargaining agreement）的制定或修改而非解釋的爭議，按法律規定，必須經調解或仲裁解決[1]。而 minor dispute 則爲「次要爭議」，指僅涉及有關勞資集體協議解釋的非重大的爭議[2]。

注

① "Under the Railway Labor Act, a disagreement about basic working conditions, often resulting in a new collective-bargaining agreement or a change in the existing agreement." Cf. Bryan A. Garner, *Black's*

Law Dictionary, 7th Edition, West Group (1999), at P. 485.

② "a dispute between an employer and a union that under the Railway Labor Act can be resolved through interpretation of the existing collective bargaining agreement", Cf. Linda Picard Wood, J.D., *Merriam Webster's Dictionary of Law*, Merriam-Webster, Incorporated (1996), at P. 313.

Malicious prosecution ▸ Abuse of process

　　二者在英美法中均屬侵權行為。其中，abuse of process 為「濫用訴訟程序」，僅指所提起的民事或刑事訴訟程序與旨在提起的訴訟目的有差異，情節輕微，無明顯惡意①。而 malicious prosecution 則為「惡意訴訟」，其性質嚴重，帶有明顯無任何理由而提起刑事或民事指控之惡意②，惡意訴訟也稱為 malicious use of process，等同 malicious abuse of process。

注

① "the tort of bringing and following through with a civil or criminal action for a purpose known to be different from the purpose for which the action was designed", Cf. Linda Picard Wood, J.D., *Merriam Webster's Dictionary of Law*, Merriam-Webster, Incorporated (1996), at P. 5.

② "the tort of initiating or continuing a criminal prosecution or civil case without probable cause and for an improper purpose", Cf. James E. Clapp, *Random House Webster's Dictionary of the Law*, Random House (2000), at P. 279.

Mandatory injunction ▸ Prohibitiory injunction

二者均用作指法院對被告頒發的強制令，不同之處在於 mandatory injunction 爲「強制行爲令」，指強制被告實施某些主動行爲或活動而非保持原狀[1]，其也被稱爲 affirmative injunction。而 prohibitory injunction 則爲「禁止性強制令」，指禁止被告進行某項具體行爲，保持原狀直至爭議得以解決[2]。

注

[1] "An injunction that orders an affirmative act or mandates a specified course of conduct." Cf. Bryan A. Garner, *Black's Law Dictionary*, 7th Edition, West Group (1999), at P. 788.

[2] "An injunction that forbids or restrains an act." *Id.* at P. 788.

Mandatory presumption ▸ Permissive presumption

二者均指陪審團就法庭所列舉的事實進行的推定。mandatory presumption（也稱爲 absolute presumption、conclusive presumption、irrebuttable presumption、presumption *juris et de jure*）爲「必然性推定」，指法律規定陪審團必須就特定事實爲基礎的證據作出的推定（a presumption that a jury is required by law to make upon proof of a given fact）[1]。而 permissive presumption 則爲「隨意性推定」，指陪審團可以作出的但非法律所規定必須就某特定事實所作的推定，其也稱爲 permissive inference（隨意性推論）[2]。

注

[1] Cf. Linda Picard Wood, J.D., *Merriam Webster's Dictionary of Law*, Merriam Webster, Incorporated (1996), at P. 379.

② "A presumption that a trier of fact is free to accept or reject from a given set of facts." Cf. Bryan A. Garner, *Black's Law Dictionary*, 7th Edition, West Group (1999), at P. 1204.

Marine insurance

嚴格說來，marine insurance 應為「水運保險」，即「水險」，指為貨物水上運輸以及運輸工具，即船舶等設立的一種險種[1]。其又包含兩種類別，即 inland marine insurance（內陸水運險）[2]和 ocean marine insurance（海運保險）兩種[3]。但鑒於內陸水運量不大，多數情況下 marine insurance 實際是指 ocean marine insurance，故人們常將 marine insurance 也就當作海上保險。此外，按照商業慣例，水運保險可擴展適用於附屬於水運的陸路運輸及空運[4]，由此其便成了運輸保險。

注

① "Insurance against marine losses; that is to say, the losses incident to marine adventures." Cf. Daphne Dukelow, *The Dictionary of Canadian Law*, Thomson Professional Publishing Canada (1991), at P. 613.

② "An agreement to indemnify against losses arising from the transport of goods on domestic waters, i.e., rivers, canals, and lakes." Cf. Bryan A. Garner, *Black's Law Dictionary*, 7th Edition, West Group (1999), at P. 805.

③ "Insurance that covers risks arising from the transport of goods by sea." *Id.* at P. 806.

④ "insurance against losses by damage to or destruction of cargo or the means or instruments of its transportation whether on land, sea, or air", Cf. Linda Picard Wood, J.D., *Merriam Webster's Dictionary of Law*, Merriam Webster, Incorporated (1996), at P. 306.

Marque ▸ Reprisal

二者常作同義詞使用，但從詞源學的觀點看，reprisal（報復性反擊）原是指 taking in return（奪回），其衍義為報復，至於具體方法則未明確界定。而 marque（報復）則指 the passing the frontiers in order to such taking（越過邊境奪取），即 marque 原先具有穿越邊界進行報復性捕獲的含義[1]。如今，這兩個單詞的區別已經逐漸縮小，如 law of marque 指的就是 a sort of law of reprisal[2]。

注

[1] These words, marque and reprisal, are frequently used as synonymous, but, taken in their strict etymological sense, the latter signifies a *taking in return*, the former, *the passing the frontiers in order to such taking*." Cf. The Publisher's Editorial Staff, *Black's Law Dictionary*, Abridged 6th Edition, West Publishing Co. (1991), at P. 671.

[2] *Id.* at P. 671.

Marriage certificate ▸ Marriage license

二者均是有關結婚的文件證書的術語，現不少詞典都當作結婚證書或結婚登記證書[1]，但實際上它們與我們心目中的結婚證書差別較大。相比較，marriage certificate 是證明婚姻儀式已經舉行，雙方婚姻關係正式成立的一種文據（an instrument which certificates that a marriage has taken place，因國外的婚姻多注重婚禮儀式而非註冊登記），其含有婚禮舉行的時間、地點等，並由雙方當事人、證人（witnesses）、主持婚禮之牧師（officiant）等簽字，故其應為「婚禮證書」[2]。marriage license 則是由法定的政府官員（legally qualified government official）所簽發的准允特定的男女結婚的一種官方書面授權證書，多發給主持婚禮者，為合法舉行婚禮的先決條件，故其應為「婚禮許可證」[3]。鑒於中國婚姻法規定的結婚應適用登記制度，故從嚴格意義上講，中國人心目中的結婚證書肯定不宜翻譯為 marriage license，也不宜翻譯成嚴格意義上的 marriage certificate。筆者建議將其譯為 "marriage registration paper" 或 "marriage registration"，這樣才最能符合其結婚登記證書的真正內涵。

注

① Cf. 陸谷孫，《英漢大詞典》，上海譯文出版社（1995），第 2017 頁；《新英漢詞典》，增補本，上海譯文出版社（1993），第785頁；《英漢法律詞典》，Revised Edition，《法律出版社》（1999），第 489 頁；吳光華，《漢英大詞典》，上海交通大學出版社（1995），第 1336 頁；危東亞，《漢英詞典》，修訂版，外語教學與研究出版社（1995），第 497 頁。

② "a document which certifies that a marriage has taken place, which contains information (as time and place) about the ceremony, and which is signed by the parties, witness, and officiant", Cf. Linda Picard Wood, J.D., *Merriam Webster's Dictionary of Law*, Merriam Webster, Incorporated (1996), at P. 307.

③ "A license or permission granted by public authority to persons who intend to intermarry, usually addressed to the minister or magistrate who is to perform the ceremony, or, in general term, to any one authorized to solemnize marriages. By statute in most jurisdiction, it is made an essential prerequisite to the lawful solemnization of the marriage." Cf. The Publisher's Editorial Staff, *Black's Law Dictionary*, Abridged 6ᵗʰ Edition, West Publishing Co. (1991), at P. 672.

Martial law ▸ Military law

二者極易被人們當作同一術語「軍法」，事實上兩者之間差異較大。區別在於 martial law 是「軍事管制法」，指：⑴軍事當局在一占領領地所實施的法律；⑵非常時期，在文職政府執法機構無法維持秩序與安全時由軍隊所實施的一種緊急管制法，其適用的對象爲整個國家或國民①。而 military law 則是指由軍隊實施的法律，按規定，其適用對象應爲軍人以及軍隊中相關的文職雇員，故應譯爲「軍法」②，其也被稱爲 military justice，在不嚴謹情況下有時可被當作 martial law，但 martial law 卻不能當作 military law 使用③。

注

① "The law by which during wartime the army, instead of civil authority, governs the country because of a perceived need for military security or public safety. The military assumes control purportedly until civil authority can be restored." Cf. Bryan A. Garner, *Black's Law Dictionary*, 7ᵗʰ Edition, West Group (1999), at P. 989.

② "law enforced by military rather than civil authority, specifically law prescribed by statute for the government of the armed forces and accompanying civilian employees", Cf. Linda Picard Wood, J.D., *Merriam Webster's Dictionary of Law*, Merriam-Webster, Incorporated (1996), at P. 313.

③ "The branch of public law governing military discipline and other rules regarding service in the armed forces. Sometimes loosely termed martial law." Cf. Bryan A. Garner, *Black's Law Dictionary*, 7ᵗʰ Edition,

West Group (1999), at P. 1007.

Mayor ▸ Provost

二者均有「市長」（爲城市、市鎭等的主要行政官員）的含義[1]，不同的是前者爲通用詞，後者僅限於蘇格蘭用語[2]。

注

[1] "An official who is elected or appointed as the chief exccutive of a city, town, or other municipality." Cf. Bryan A. Garner, *Black's Law Dictionary*, 7th Edition, West Group (1999), at P. 994.

[2] "official in a Scottish town, with a position similar to that of a mayor in England", Cf. P. H. Collin, *Dictionary of Law*, 2nd Edition, Peter Collin Publishing Ltd. (1994), at P. 441.

Mediation ▸ Conciliation ▸ Reconciliation ▸ Settlement ▸ Compromise

上述單詞均有「調解」或「調停」以解決爭議的含義。其中，mediation 多指第三方參與進行調解的程序和過程（a process），其目的是透過該程序以促進爭議得以 reconciliation、settlement 或 compromise[1]，如 the case was settled through mediation（該案經調解得以協議解決）。conciliation 常指法庭審判前或勞資爭議仲裁前讓當事人透過友好的非對抗方式協定談判解決爭議，不強調第三人之作用，其也多表示一種過程，有時等於 mediation[2]。而 reconciliation 則指調停爭端，使雙方重新恢復原有的協調關係[3]，尤指夫妻雙方自願恢復夫妻共同生活關系，故爲「重修舊好」。settlement 指當事人透過談判達成協議（agreement）以了結法律訴訟，其常指一種

mediation 的結果，多為庭外進行，故為「（庭外）協議調解」④。
compromise 指雙方當事人為解決爭議，均作出適當的妥協讓步的協
議，故為「妥協性和解協議」⑤。

注

① "Private, informal dispute resolution process in which a neutral third
person, the mediator, helps disputing parties to reach an agreement."
Cf. The Publisher's Editorial Staff, *Black's Law Dictionary*, Abridged
6th Edition, West Publishing Co. (1991), at P. 678.

② "The process by which a third party attempts to assist an employer
and a trade union to achieve a collective agreement." Cf. Daphne
Dukelow, *The Dictionary of Canadian Law*, Thomson Professional
Publishing Canada (1991), at P. 192.

③ "settlement of a quarrel, etc.", Cf. Della Thompson, *The Concise
Oxford Dictionary*, 9th Edition, Oxford University Press (1995), at
P. 1146.

④ "an agreement reducing or resolving differences, esp. an agreement
between litigants that concludes the litigations", Cf. Linda Picard
Wood, J.D., *Merriam Webster's Dictionary of Law*, Merriam-Webster,
Incorporated (1996), at P. 453.

⑤ "An agreement between two or more persons to settle matters in
dispute between them." Cf. Bryan A. Garner, *Black's Law Dictionary*,
7th Edition, West Group (1999), at P. 281.

Mental disease ▶ Mental illness

　　總體說來，二者基本同義，但在用法上有一定的差異。mental
disease（也稱為 emotional distress、emotional harm、mental anguish、

mental suffering，精神病）多限於法律事務中，現已發展成爲專指刑法上導致反覆的刑事犯罪或反社會行爲的一種非正常精神病狀。而 mental illness（精神疾患）則更多指醫學界所認知的精神上的疾病或病症，其也被稱爲 mental disorder。

注

"Mental disease and mental illness are in general use synonymous, but mental disease has developed a settled meaning in criminal law while mental illness is often explained or defined by reference to the medical community's understanding of the term." Cf. Linda Picard Wood, J.D., *Merriam Webster's Dictionary of Law*, Merriam-Webster, Incorporated (1996), at P. 311.

Migrant ▸ Emigrant ▸ Immigrant

三者均有「移民」的含義。其中，emigrant 指移居國外的人[1]，如因戰爭、政治迫害等而被迫離開，則稱爲 *émigré*（流亡者）[2]。而 immigrant 剛好相反，指從他國移居本國永久居住者[3]。migrant 則無方向性區分，既可指移居外國，也可指從國外移居國內。同樣，與他們相對應的 migration、emigration 和 immigration 也有此種區別[4]。

注

[1] "a person who leaves one's own country to settle in another", Cf. Della Thompson, *The Concise Oxford Dictionary*, 9th Edition, Oxford University Press (1995), at P. 441.

[2] "if forced to do so, by war, political oppression, or other circumstances, he may be called an emigre", Cf. Laurence Urdang, *The Dictionary of Confusable Words*, Laurence Urdang Inc. (1988), at

P. 129.

③ "a person who enters a country intending to reside there permanently", James E. Clapp, *Random House Webster's Dictionary of the Law*, Random House, New York (2000), at P. 223.

④ "a person moves from one place of abode to another, esp. in a different country", Cf. Laurence Urdang, *The Dictionary of Confusable Words*, Laurence Urdang Inc. (1988), at P. 862.

Military court ▸ Court-martial

　　二者均有軍事法庭（院）的含義。區別在於 military court 爲通用詞，泛指軍事法院，在美國，其主要對三軍軍事人員具有管轄權，並執行 Code of Justice 的規定，故其爲「軍事法院（庭）」①，可包括 court martial、court of military review、military court of inquiry 以及 court of military appeals 等②。相比之下，court-martial 只是 military court 中的一種（儘管諸多詞典都將其混同 military court 而譯爲「軍事法院」或「軍事法庭」③），指軍事當局爲懲罰違反軍事法令（如在美國，指違反 Uniform Code of Military Justice 規定）之人員，尤指軍隊成員而臨時設立的一種軍事法庭（an *ad hoc* military court），故其應爲「臨時軍事法庭」④。court-martial 一般分爲三級，其中最高級別爲 general court-martial，由 5 人或以上成員組成合議庭，有權審理所有違法軍事人員；中間爲 special court-martial，由 3 人或以上成員組成，審理最高刑爲死刑以下的犯罪；最低級別爲 summary court-martial，由一名官員獨任審理案件，管轄權有限⑤。

注

① "A court that has jurisdiction over members of the armed forces and that enforces the Code of Military Justice." Cf. Bryan A. Garner,

Black's Law Dictionary, 7th Edition, West Group (1999), at P. 1007.

② "Courts convened subject to the Code of Military Justice; e.g. Courts-martial, Court of Military Review, Military Court of Inquiry, Court of Military Appeals." Cf. The Publisher's Editorial Staff, *Black's Law Dictionary*, Abridged 6th Edition, West Publishing Co. (1991), at P. 685.

③ Cf. 陸谷孫，《英漢大詞典》，上海譯文出版社（1995 印刷），第 721 頁；張芳傑，《牛津現代英漢雙解辭典》，牛津大學出版社（1985），第 271 頁。

④ "An *ad hoc* military court, convened under military authority, to try and punish those who violate the Uniform Code of Military Justice, particularly members of the armed forces." Cf. Bryan A. Garner, *Black's Law Dictionary*, 7th Edition, West Group (1999), at P. 362. 此外，儘管 ad hoc 有「特別」之含義，但 court martial 也不宜翻譯爲「特別軍事法庭」，關鍵是 court-martial 本身可分爲三級，其中便有特別臨時軍事法庭（special court-martial）（參見下文）。

⑤ "The type (e.g. summary, special, or general) and composition of court martial varies according to the gravity of offenses." Cf. The Publisher's Editorial Staff, *Black's Law Dictionary*, Abridged 6th Edition, West Publishing Co. (1991), at P. 249; Cf. Bryan A. Garner, *Black's Law Dictionary*, 7th Edition, West Group (1999), at P. 362.

Ministry ▶ Department

　　二者均可譯爲「部」，表示政府的一個部門。差別在於 department 所表示的部門多爲重要的部門，如英國的貿易工業部（department of trade and industry）等。在美國，ministry of justice 爲「司法部」，其在美國政府的地位便沒有 defence department 重要。

英國沒有設立司法部，國家的執法監督責任由大法官事務部（Lord Chancellor's Office）和內務部（Home Office）予以履行。

"In Britain and the USA, important ministries are called departments: the Department of Trade and Industry; the Commerce Department." Cf. P. H. Collin, *Dictionary of Law*, 2nd Edition, Peter Collin Publishing Ltd. (1993), at P. 348.

Minor ▸ Infant ▸ Baby ▸ Child

　　以上單詞均有「未成年人」的含義。infant 是過去用語，儘管目前仍有人使用，如在英國的《最高法院民事訴訟規則》（RSC）中，但其使用率已經不高[1]。baby 和 child 也基本屬於同一情況，如 child 儘管仍在術語「delinquent child」等中使用，但其使用率也不高。而 minor 則為常用的很正式的用語，在法典及其他法律文件中頻繁出現。至於上述 4 個單詞所指的具體的年齡，不同的司法管轄區或不同的法律法規各有不同的規定。如英國有的法律規定 18 歲以下者為 minor，其是否結婚不論。在加拿大，按不同情況或法規，infant 的具體年齡可為 18、19 或 21 歲[2]。而在美國，則多為 21 歲，且即便未達到法定年齡，一旦結婚，也有可能被視為成年人。

注

① "Infant is an old term, now replaced by minor." Cf. P. H. Collin, *English-Chinese Bilingual Law Dictionary*, 2nd Edition, Peter Collin Publishing, 世界圖書出版社 (雙解版本)(1998), at. P.276; "The more usual, and less confusing term is minor." Cf. Bryan A. Garner, *A Dictionary of Modern Legal Usage*, 2nd Edition, Oxford University

Press (1995), at P. 442.

② Cf. Daphne Dukelow, *The Dictionary of Canadian Law*, Thomson Professional Publishing Canada (1991), at P. 511.

Misfeasance ▸ Nonfeasance ▸ Malfeasance

三者均有類似瀆職的含義，但嚴格說來，三個術語的區別很大，這種區別在判定代理人對第三人的責任時尤爲重要①。misfeasance 應爲「作爲不當」，指不當履行某人本應合法行使的行爲（the improper performance of some act which one may lawfully do），如在履行契約時犯有過失，其有主動不當行爲導致他人損害的含義（active misconduct working positive injury to others）②。而 nonfeasance 爲「不履行義務」，指對某人本應履行的職責採取不作爲的態度（the omission of an act which one ought to do），爲消極不作爲或未採取對他人的保護（passive inaction or a failure to take steps to protect others from harm）③。相比之下，malfeasance 則爲「不當作爲」，指行使了某人本完全不應當行使的行爲（the doing of an act which one ought not to do at all）④。

注

① "There is a distinction between nonfeasance and misfeasance or malfeasance; and this distinction is often of great importance in determining an agent's liability to third persons." Cf. The Publisher's Editorial Staff, *Black's Law Dictionary*, Abridged 6th Edition, West Publishing Co. (1991), at P. 729.

② *Id.* at P. 691.

③ Cf. Daphne Dukelow, *The Dictionary of Canadian Law*, Thomson Professional Publishing Canada (1991), at P. 688.

④ Cf. The Publisher's Editorial Staff, *Black's Law Dictionary*, Abridged 6th Edition, West Publishing Co. (1991), at P. 729.

Mistake of fact ▸ Mistake of law

二者均可用在契約法或刑法中作爲免責或免罪的一種辯護理由。相比之下，以 mistake of fact（事實錯誤）爲理由基礎的辯護的力度遠比以 mistake of law（法律錯誤）爲理由基礎強。

注

"In both contract and criminal law a mistake of law is a weaker ground for relief or acquittal than a mistake of fact." Cf. Linda Picard Wood, J.D., *Merriam Webster's Dictionary of Law*, Merriam-Webster, Incorporated (1996), at P. 315.

Motive ▸ Intent ▸ *Mens rea*

三者在刑法中的含義各不相同。motive 爲「動機」，指導致一個人行爲的需要或願望（need or desire）的情感原因或意圖①，其不是構成犯罪的要素（element），但有關犯罪動機證據的採信可有助於確認犯罪故意，即 intent 的存在。因此我們知道，intent（也稱爲 criminal intent）便是刑法中所指的犯罪故意，其含義是 the design or purpose to commit a wrongful or criminal act②，是構成犯罪的要素之一。*mens rea* 則爲「犯意」或「犯罪意圖」，指一種犯罪的精神狀態（a culpable mental state），特指犯罪故意（intent）或對犯罪的知情（knowledge），其也是構成犯罪的要素之一③。

注

① "The emotion which prompted an act or the intention with which one does an intentional act." Cf. P. K. McWilliams, *Canadian Criminal Evidence*, 3rd Edition, Aurora, Canadian Law Book (1988), at P. 18.

② Cf. Linda Picard Wood, J.D., *Merriam Webster's Dictionary of Law*, Merriam-Webster, Incorporated (1996), at P. 253.

③ "The state of mind that makes the performance of a particular act a crime, or a crime of a particular degree; the element of fault that makes an otherwise innocent act or omission punishable." Cf. James E. Clapp, *Random House Webster's Dictionary of the Law*, Random House (2000), at P. 286.

Multinational corporation ▶ International corporation

二者的含義相近，且經常可交替使用，但從嚴格意義上講，multinational corporation 指一個在許多國家都設有經營中心（centers of operation），而無一絕對的本部基地之公司，故其為「跨國公司」。而 international corporation 則指雖在許多國家開展業務活動，但卻只在一個國家設有本部基地之公司，現將其翻譯為「國際公司」，以便與 multinational corporation 相區別。

N

Needy ▸ Necessitous

二者均有非常貧困的含義。相比之下，needy 所指的貧困期限更長久，但其窘迫情況卻不如 necessitous。故 needy 應譯爲「貧窮的」，而 necessitous 則應譯爲「赤貧的」。

注

"Needy implies a more permanent and less urgent condition than necessitous." Cf. Bryan A. Garner, *Black's Law Dictionary*, 7th Edition, West Group (1999), at P. 1054.

Negative act ▸ Forbearance ▸ Omission

三者均有「不作爲」的含義。其中，negative act（也稱爲 act of omission）爲總稱，指不履行法定義務等，爲「不作爲」[1]。嚴格說來，negative act 包括兩種情況，即 forbearance 和 omission[2]。forbearance 指有意不作爲，爲一種 intentional negative act[3]。而 omission（古時稱爲 omittance）則多指一種非故意的不作爲行爲（an unintentional negative act）[4]。

注

1. "the failure to do something that one has a legal duty to do", Cf. Linda Picard Wood, J.D., *Merriam Webster's Dictionary of Law*, Merriam-Webster, Incorporated (1996), at P. 10.
2. "Negative Act takes the forms of either a forbearance or an omission."

Cf. Bryan A. Garner, *Black's Law Dictionary*, 7th Edition, West Group (1999), at P. 25.

③ Cf. David M. Walker, *The Oxford Companion To Law*, Oxford University Press, New York (1980).

④ "An omission is an unintentional negative act, whereas a forbearance is an intentional negative act. Unfortunately, some legal writers use omission when they means forbearance—a habit contributing to sloppy analysis." Cf. Bryan A. Garner, *A Dictionary of Modern Legal Usage*, 2nd Edition, Oxford University Press (1995), at P. 617.

Negotiability ▸ Assignability

二者均有「轉讓」的含義。區別在於 negotiability 主要用於指商業票據議付形成的轉讓，而 assignability 則主要用於指契約的轉讓。negotiability 所指的轉讓為一種完全轉讓，受讓人（transferee）得到票據所附的一切產權和權利，不必通知債務人，也不受票據前手（transferor）瑕疵之影響。就 assignability 而言，如果不通知債務人（debtor），則不能視為一種完全轉讓（not complete）。

注

"Negotiability (which pertains to commercial paper) differs from assignability (which pertains to contracts in general) because an assignee traditionally takes title subject to all equities, and an assignment is not complete without notice to the debtor, whereas an endorsee takes free of all equities and without any notice to the debtor." Cf. Bryan A. Garner, *Black's Law Dictionary*, 7th Edition, West Group (1999), at P. 1158.

Next friend ▸ Guardian *ad litem* ▸ Official solicitor

三者均有未成年人或精神病患者的輔佐人的含義。在英國，如未成年人或其他無行爲能力者作爲原告，充當其輔佐人者稱爲 next friend，法院多指定未成年人或無行爲能力者的親屬，如父或母充任此職；如未成年人或無行爲能力者爲被告，其辯護人則稱爲 guardian *ad litem*（A minor sues by his "next friend" and defends by his "guardian *ad litem*"[1]）。如在王座法院或郡法院的傳票上便如此寫明[2]：

CIVIL LITIGATION（民事訴訟）

BETWEEN NIGEL MICK（minor）

  by IVAN MICK（his father and next friend）

     Plaintiff（原告）

  AND

PETER POLL（minor）

  by RICHARD POLL（his guardian *ad litem*）

     Defendant（被告）

但在美國一些司法管轄區，這兩個術語有時卻沒有上述實質性的差異，只是 next friend 不是無行爲能力者的監護人（guardian），而 guardian *ad litem* 則指定爲無行爲能力者的監護人的律師（其也稱爲 special guardian）[3]。official solicitor 則指最高法院的一名官員，經法院任命，既可充任 next friend，又可充任 guardian ad litem[4]。

注

① Cf. John O'Hare & Robert N. Hill, *Civil litigation, Longman Law*, Tax and Finance, Longman Group UK Ltd. (1990), at P. 111.

② *Id.* at P. 112.

③ "*guardian ad litem*: A guardian, usu. a lawyer, appointed by the court to appear in a lawsuit on behalf of an incompetent or minor party, also termed special guardian", Cf. Bryan A. Garner, *Black's Law Dictionary*, 7th Edition, West Group (1999), at P. 713; "next friend: a person appearing in or appointed by a court to act on behalf of a person (as a child) lacking legal capacity", Cf. Linda Picard Wood, J.D., *Merriam Webster's Dictionary of Law*, Merriam-Webster, Incorporated (1996), at P. 326.

④ Cf. P. H. Collin, *English-Chinese Bilingual Law Dictionary*, 2nd Edition, Peter Collin Publishing, 世界圖書出版社 (1998), at P. 375.

Non-arrestable offence ▶ Arrestable offence

二者均爲英國刑法所規定的犯罪分類術語。其中 non-arrestable offence 爲「不得無證拘捕之犯罪」，指一種較輕的犯罪，處刑通常在 5 年以下，此種罪犯只能在簽發拘捕令之後進行拘捕[1]。值得注意的是該術語被不少法律詞典錯誤地譯爲「不受逮捕的罪行」或「不構成逮捕的罪行」，估計這種譯法是由於譯者望文生義所造成的[2]。相比較，arrestable offense 則爲「可無證拘捕之犯罪」（該術語也不得像有些法律詞典那樣譯爲「應受逮捕的罪行」或「構成逮捕的罪行」[3]），指較爲嚴重的犯罪，其處刑多在 5 年以上[4]，該術語體現了傳統的 "In pursuit of felony, as the phrase has it, no warrant for arrest is necessary"（追捕重罪犯，如習語所說，無需拘捕令）英國刑法精神[5]。事實上，此兩種法定犯罪分類也正是英國於 1967 年爲取代原有的犯罪分類 felony（重罪）和 misdemeanor（輕罪）而新創立之罪名，non-arrestable offence 用於替代 misdemeanor，而 arrestable offence 則用於替代 felony。同理，arrestable offender 也就應爲「可無證拘捕之罪犯」，指原先所劃分的「重罪犯」[6]。

注

① "crime for which a person cannot be arrested without a warrant. Non-arrestable offenses are usually crimes which carry a sentence of less than five years imprisonment", Cf. P. H. Collin, *English-Chinese Bilingual Law Dictionary*, 2nd Edition, Peter Collin Publishing, 世界圖書出版社 (1998), at P. 364.

② Cf. 《英漢法律詞典》，法律出版社（1999），第 533 頁。

③ *Id.* at P. 58

④ "crime for which someone can be arrested without a warrant (usually an offense which carries a penalty of at least five years-imprisonment)", *Id.* at P. 32.

⑤ Cf. Li Rong-fu/Song Lei, *A Course Book of Legal English*, Law Press, China (1999), at P. 10.

⑥ Cf. David M. Walker, *The Oxford Companion to Law*, (felony), Oxford University Press (1980), at P. 332.

O

Objective theory of contract
▸ Subjective theory of

二者均是有關契約構成的學說（doctrine），差別在於 objective theory of contract（契約客觀原理）認爲契約並非是主觀合意之產物，相反，契約是由外部一系列行爲所構成的客觀上類似協議的東西[1]，原理常簡稱爲 objective theory（客觀原理）。而 subjective theory of contract（契約主觀原理）則認爲契約是雙方當事人合意（meets of minds）協定之產物，該學說現已基本過時[2]。該原理也常簡稱爲 subjective theory（主觀原理）。

注

[1] "The doctrine that a contract is not an agreement in the sense of a subjective meeting of the minds but is instead a series of external acts giving the objective semblance of agreement." Cf. Bryan A. Garner, *Black's Law Dictionary*, 7th Edition, West Group (1999), at P. 1101.

[2] "The doctrine (now largely outmoded) that a contract is an agreement in which the parties have a subjective meeting of the minds." *Id.* at P. 1438.

Obrogate ▸ Abrogate

二者均有使法律作廢或無效的含義。obrogate（取代法律）是大陸法（civil law）上的術語，指以通過新法律的方式來取代（或修正）舊有的法律的全部或部分[1]。abrogate（廢除法律）則是指用正式的官方命令廢除法律或習慣或宣布其無效[2]。與它們相對應的名詞 obrogation 和 abrogation 也有相同之區別。

注

① "To modify or repeal a law in whole or in part by passing a new law." Cf. Bryan A. Garner, *Black's Law Dictionary*, 7th Edition, West Group (1999), at P. 1104.

② "to abolish by authoritative, official or formal action", Cf. Linda Picard Wood, J.D., *Merriam Webster's Dictionary of Law*, Merriam-Webster, Incorporated (1996), at P. 3.

Obsolescence ▶ Depreciation

　　二者均有固定資產貶值的含義。區別在於 obsolescence 指的是因替代產品的出現、產品換代、公眾口味變更等原因而導致財產不再具有競爭性或失去市場吸引力或不再具有實用性等，其並非指資產或設備等本身形體的磨損導致的貶值。而 depreciation 所指的範圍較廣，其既包括 obsolescence 所含原因引起的貶值，又包括因財產本身的磨損等導致的財產價值的降低。

注

"Obsolescence is the shortening of the life of a capital asset, such as a plant, machine, or piece of equipment, because of technological progress, such as an invention, improvement in processes, changed economic conditions, or legislation. Obsolescence differs from depreciation, which is the actual wearing out of plants and equipment because of use." Cf. Douglas Greenwald & Associate, *The Concise McGraw-Hill Dictionary of Modern Economics*, McGraw-Hill Book Company (1983), at P. 247.

Occurrence policy ► Claims made policy

二者均與保險理賠之時效有關。差別在於 occurrence policy（依發生之時為準之保險單）指只要事故發生在保險期內，不論是保險期之後再發現或提出理賠均可獲賠之險種保險單[1]。而 claims made policy（也稱為 discovery policy，依權利提出之時為準之保險單）則指規定只有在保險期內提出理賠主張方可獲得賠償之險種之保險單[2]。

注

[1] "This type policy provides for indemnity, regardless of when the claim is made or reported, if act giving rise to the claim occurred during policy period." Cf. The Publisher's Editorial Staff, *Black's Law Dictionary*, Abridged 6th Edition, West Publishing Co. (1991), at P. 558.

[2] "An agreement to indemnify against all claims made during a specified period, regardless of when the incidents that gave rise to the claims occurred." Cf. Bryan A. Garner, *Black's Law Dictionary*, 7th Edition, West Group (1999), at P. 807.

Offense against property ► Crime against property

二者均用於指侵犯他人財產的犯罪，由於形式相似，以往有不少人錯誤地將它們混淆為同一術語。實際在普通法中，它們有較明顯的差異。offense against property 應為「侵犯動產罪」，是一傳統術語，其基本上只限於指針對動產 "personal property" 之犯罪行為，罪名包括 larceny、embezzlement、cheating、cheating by false pretense、robbery、receiving stolen goods、malicious mischief、 forgery、uttering forged 和 instruments[①]等。相比之下，crime against property 則是較現代的用語，其範疇更廣，除動產之外，還包括了侵犯不動產（real property）的犯罪行爲，故譯爲「侵犯財產罪」，crime against property 可包括諸如 burglary、theft 和 arson 等犯罪[②]，儘管arson可能導致人身傷害或死亡，但其仍被稱爲「財產犯罪」（property crime）[③]。

注

① "A crime against another's personal property." Cf. Bryan A. Garner, *Black's Law Dictionary*, 7th Edition, West Group (1999), at P. 1109.

② "Although the term *crime against property*, a common term in modern usage, includes crimes against real property, the term *offense against property* is traditionally restricted to personal property." *Id*, at P. 1109.

③ "Examples includes burglary, theft, and arson (even though arson may result in injury or death)." *Id*. at P. 379.

Opinion ▸ Judgment ▸ Reason

三者均有對法官的判決以及對法律問題的「意見」或「解釋」（a court's explanation of how it reached a particular decision in a matter; its analysis and resolution of the legal issues involved in a motion or appeal[①]）的含義。其中，reason 不屬於正式或規範的法律語言，opinion 爲美國所通用的術語，而 judgment 則在英國及加拿大通用[②]。

注

① Cf. James E. Clapp, *Random House Webster's Dictionary of the Law*, Random House, New York (2000), at P. 310.

② Cf. Bryan A. Garner, *A Dictionary of Modern Legal Usage*, 2nd Edition, Oxford University Press (1995), at P. 621.

Ordinances ▸ Regulations

儘管在詞典中兩單詞均被譯爲「法規」，但兩者的區別卻較大。ordinances 多指由自治市或其他地方立法機關所頒布的一種地方性法規（of municipal and other local legislative bodies）①，其也稱爲 bylaw 或 municipal ordinance。而 regulations 則主要指由行政機構（executive agencies）所制定和頒布的規則，故其應爲「行政命令」②。

注

① "It is a legislative enactment, within its sphere, as much as an act of the state legislature." Cf. Judith O'Gallagher, *Municipal Ordinance* §1Ao1, at 3 (2d ed. 1998).

② "a directive adopted by an administrative agency, either for its own internal procedures or to govern public behavior in matters over which it has authority, and having the force of law", Cf. James E. Clapp, *Random House Webster's Dictionary of the Law*, Random House, New York (2000), at P. 368.

Originating process

在英國高等法院（the High Court）的民事訴訟（civil litigation）中，當事人可選擇適用不同訴狀（originating process）形式提起訴訟（其也可稱爲 originating document）。訴狀（Originating Process）爲通用語，其在高等法院有四種形式：writ（起訴令）、originating summons（起訴書）、originating notice of motion（起訴動議通知）

以及 petition（起訴狀），其可有與之相適應的程序（timetable）
等。其中，writ 用於 Queen's/King's Bench Division（女王座/王
座法院），其最為常見，多適用於爭議案件（contentious cases）
中，這些案件包括：(1)侵權之訴（非法入侵土地除外，tort cases
other than trespass to land）；(2)反詐欺之訴（actions in which
the claim is based on an allegation of fraud）；(3)涉及死亡、人身
傷害、財產損失之違約索賠之訴（actions in which the plaintiff
claims damages for breach of duty, whether contractual, statutory
or otherwise, where the damages claimed consists of or includes in
respect of death, personal injuries, or damage to property）；(4)專
利之訴（patent actions）；(5)其他由法律或法規規定由傳喚令提
起之訴訟，如無被告的海事訴訟或遺囑檢驗訴訟等（other actions
which are specifically required to be commenced by writ under any
statute or any other rule, e.g. admiralty actons in rem and probate
actions）。originating summons 用於大法官法院（Chancery
Court），其多適用於無爭議訴訟（non-contentious cases），
故其程序要比用 writ 提起的訴訟簡單，省略了所謂的訴訟武器
（weapon of litigation），即：訴辯狀、證據開示、口頭證據
（pleadings, automatic discovery, oral evidence）等程序。此類案
件多為：(1)有關法律或文據、契據、遺囑、契約或其他單據或法
律問題的解釋之案件（in which the sole or principal question is or
is likely to be one of the construction of an Act or of any instrument
made under an Act or of any deed, will, contract or other document
or some other question of law）；(2)無實質性事實爭議的案件（in
which there is unlikely to be any substantial dispute of fact）。根
據英國民事訴訟法之規定，只有選用 writ 和 originating summons
兩形式起訴者才能提起第三人之訴訟（third party proceedings）
[1]。originating notice of motion 及 petition，只在法律專門規定之

領域適用。如 originating notice of motion 可適用於某些無爭議的遺囑檢驗（certain non-contentious probate applications）或司法審查案件（application for what is known as judicial review）中。petition 則適用於諸如離婚、個人破產或公司破產之訴（Examples of petitions include divorces, and bankruptcy and winding up petitions）中，這些案件均有單獨的程序法典予以規定（如 Matrimonial Causes Rules 1977 和 Insolvency Rules 1986 等）②。與高等法院相對，英國郡法院（county court）的起訴書也分爲四種：即 summons、originating application、petition 以及 request for entry of appeal。其中，summons 基本等同高等法院的 writ；originating application 則適用於高等法院用 originating summons 起訴的案件；而 petition 和 request for entry of appeal 則等同 High Court 的另外兩種起訴書，只用在特定的訴訟中，其中，petition 多用於離婚及破產案件；request for entry of appeal 則多用於對行政命令的審查等訴訟中③。

注

① "Third party proceedings are possible only in cases commenced by writ or originating summons", Cf. John O'Hare & Robert N. Hill, *Civil Litigation*, 5th Edition, Longman Group UK Ltd (1990), at P. 348.

② *Id.* at Ps. 128—129.

③ "They are four types of originating process in the county court: the summons which is roughly equivalent to the High Court writ; the originating application which is used in cases which in the High Court might be started by an originating summons; petitions and requests for entry of appeals which, like High Court petitions and originating notice of motion, can only be used where an Act or rule so authorizes or requires and are usually in each case depends directly on the form of originating process used." Cf. *Housing Act* 1985, s. 269, set out in the *County Court Practice*, Part II.

P

Parliament ▸ Congress ▸ Diet ▸ Reichstag ▸ Bundestag ▸ Duma

上述單詞均有議會的含義。其中，Parliament 主要指英國、加拿大等國的議會，其包括君主、上議院和下議院（consisting of the monarch, the House of Lords, and the House of Commons）[①]。town council 則爲英格蘭或蘇格蘭等地的郡議會。Congress 是美國國會，包括參議院和眾議院（consisting of Senate and House of Representatives），但尤指眾議院[②]。而 General Assembly 是指美國的州議會[③]。Diet 指日本議會和丹麥議會等[④]。Reichstag 是指舊時德意志帝國國會或德國國民議會下議院[⑤]。德意志聯邦共和國議會（Federal Parliament）由 Bundestag（德意志聯邦共和國下議院）[⑥]和 Bundesrat 或 Bundesrath（聯邦德國上議院）[⑦]組成，各省的議會則稱爲 Landtage[⑧]。現在的法國議院則由一兩院制議會（bicameral Parliament）組成，包括參議院（Senate）和國民議會（National Assembly）[⑨]。中國的立法機關則是 National People's Congress（中國人民代表大會）。Duma 爲俄羅斯國的議會[⑩]。

注

① "The supreme legislative body of some nations, esp., in the United Kingdom, the national legislature consisting of the monarch, Commons." Cf. Bryan A. Garner, *Black's Law Dictionary*, 7th Edition, West Croup (1999), at P. 1139; "The Parliament of Canada." Cf. Daphne Dukelow, *The Dictionary of Canadian Law*, Thomson Professional Publishing Canada (1991), at P. 747.

② "the legislative branch of the United States government", Cf. Linda Picard Wood, J.D., *Merriam Webster's Dictionary of Law*, Merriam-Webster, Incorporated (1996), at P. 96.

③ "The name of the legislative body in many states." Cf. Bryan A. Garner, *Black's Law Dictionary*, 7th Edition, West Croup (1999), at P. 691.

④ "the legislative body of certain countries, as Japan", Cf. Jess Stein, *The Random House College Dictionary*, Revised Edition, Random House, Inc. (1973), at P. 370.

⑤ "the lower house of the German Parliament from 1871—1945", *Id.* at P. 1112.

⑥ "the lower house of the Federal Republic of Germany", *Id.* at P. 179.

⑦ "the upper house of the Federal Republic of Germany. Also Bundesrath", *Id.* at P. 179.

⑧ "Landtage, the state parliaments", Cf. Robert McHenry, *The New Encyclopaedia*, Vol. 4, Encyclopaedia Britannica Inc. (1993), at P. 59.

⑨ "Legislative responsibility rests with the bicameral Parliament, which consists of a Senate and a National Assembly." Cf. Robert McHenry, *The New Encyclopaedia*, Vol. 4, Encyclopaedia Britannica Inc. (1993), at P. 919.

⑩ "an elective council in Russia", Cf. Philip Babcock Grove, Ph.D., *Webster's Third New International Dictionary of the English Language Unabridged*, G&C Merriam Co. (1976), at P. 700.

Parricide ▸ Parenticide ▸ Patricide ▸ Matricide

這些單詞均可用於指殺害自己親人的行為。其中，parricide 指殺害自己的近親屬，特指殺害自己的親父或親母（the act of killing a close relative, esp. a parent）^①（值得注意的是在有些法律詞典上該單詞的定義只是殺父罪^②，*Black's Law Dictionary* 第 6 版上的定義也如此^③，只是在第 7 版時才做了修正）。parenticide 指謀殺自己的生父或生母的行爲（the act of murdering one's parent）^④。而 patricide 則僅指殺害自己的父親（act of killing one's own father）^⑤。matricide 則指殺害自己母親的犯罪行爲（act of killing one's own mother）^⑥。

注

① Cf. Bryan A. Garner, *Black's Law Dictionary*, 7th Edition, West Croup (1999), at P. 1141; "the act of murdering his or her mother or father", Cf. Linda Picard Wood, J.D., *Merriam Webster's Dictionary of Law*, Merriam-Webster, Incorporated (1996), at P. 96.

② "The murder of a father." Cf. Daphne Dukelow, *The Dictionary of Canadian Law*, Thomson Professional Publishing Canada (1991), at P. 747.

③ "The crime of killing one's father." Cf. The Publisher's Editorial Staff, *Black's Law Dictionary*, Abridged 6th Edition, West Publishing Co. (1991), at P. 771.

④ Cf. Bryan A. Garner, *Black's Law Dictionary*, 7th Edition, West Croup (1999), at P. 1138.

⑤ *Id.* at P. 1149.

⑥ *Id.* at P. 992.

Passive breach of contract ▸ Active breach of contract

以上是美國適用大陸法系的路易斯安那州的兩個術語。它們之間的差別在於 passive breach of contract 爲「消極違約」，指未履行契約規定的義務（failure to perform the contractual obligations），一般只會導致違約之訴（claims in contract）[1]。而 active of breach of contract 為「積極違約」，指在履行契約中的過失行為（negligence in performing a contract），此種行為除會導致違約之訴外，還可能導致侵權之訴[2]。

 注

① Cf. Bryan A. Garner, *Black's Law Dictionary*, 7th Edition, West Croup (1999), at P. 183.

② *Id.* at P. 182.

▌ Patient ► Mental patient

　　二者均有精神病人的含義，指因精神失常而無管理自己財產和事務的能力者。按照英國 Rules of the Supreme Court（1965）和 County Court Rules（1981）的相關規定，前者為高等法院中的用語，後者則用於各郡法院。

 注

"In High Court rules, patient means a person who, by reason of mental disorder within the meaning of the Mental Health Act 1983, is incapable of managing or administering his property and affairs (RSC Ord. 80, r 1). Hereafter, we shall use the county court designation which is metal patient (CCR Ord. 1, r 3)." Cf. John O'Hare & Robert N. Hill, *Civil Litigation*, 5th Edition, Longman Group UK Ltd. (1990), at P. 112.

Pension ▸ Annuity

二者在一定程度上可以通用。其中，annuity（年金）的涵蓋面較大，可指根據法令、契約或遺囑按年度或季度等獲得一定數額收入之權利，其也包括雇員按退休方案應獲得的退休金[1]。而 pension 多是指第三人如政府或雇主，基於雇員以前服務所提供的一種退休福利津貼或因雇員去世等給予其家屬的一種撫恤金[2]，故其可爲「退休金」、「撫恤金」，爲與 annuity 加以區別而不宜譯爲「年金」。在國外，pension 的種類較多，主要分爲 defined benefit 和 defined contribution benefit 兩種，前者爲按規定公式支付的退休金，即按《退休金法》規定的按工作年限、工資數量等爲基礎支付的退休金，此種退休金計畫或方案不需對雇主爲雇員所繳納之年金費情況作專門規定；而後者則爲按繳費情況確定支付的退休金，即根據雇主爲雇員（有時包括雇員爲自己）繳納退休基金之多少確定雇員退休後應領取的福利。

注

[1] "Includes an amount payable on a periodic basis, whether payable at intervals longer or shorter than a year and whether payable under a contract, will or trust or otherwise." Cf. Daphne Dukelow, *The Dictionary of Canadian Law*, Thomson Professional Publishing Canada (1991), at P. 48.

[2] "A fixed sum paid regularly to a person (or to a person's beneficiaries), esp. by an employer as retirement benefit." Cf. Bryan A. Garner, *Black's Law Dictionary*, 7th Edition, West Croup (1999), at P. 1155.

Perjury ▸ Forswearing

二者均有發誓作僞證之含義。其區別在於除其各自爲普通法上的單獨犯罪（apart from being separate offenses）外，forswearing 的範圍較 perjury 廣，其可泛指任何場合下發誓人明知不是事實而發誓確認之情況，故爲刑法規定之「僞誓罪」，等同 false swearing 或 false oath，其罪行較 perjury 輕[1]。而 perjury 爲「僞證罪」，是普通法上的輕罪（misdemeanor）中情節嚴重的犯罪，其爲一技術術語，專指在主管法院或官員面前發誓說假話，且所涉及問題均爲實質性問題，這兩點都是 forswearing 不必一定包含的因素[2]。perjury 還涉及有關道德等因素，這同樣也與 forswearing 無甚關係[3]。

注

[1] "the crime of making a false statement under oath or affirmation, other than in the belief that what is being said is true. A broader and less serious offense than perjury", Cf. James E. Clapp, *Random House Webster's Dictionary of the Law*, Random House, New York (2000), at P. 178.

[2] "*Forswearing* is wider in its scope than *perjury*, for the latter, as a technical term, includes the idea of the oath being taken before a competent court or officer, and relating to a material issue, which is not implied by the word forswearing." Cf. The Publisher's Editorial Staff, *Black's Law Dictionary*, Abridged 6th Edition, West Publishing Co. (1991), at P. 451.

[3] "The technical difference at common law between perjury and forswearing, apart from their being separate offenses, is that perjury connotes corruption and recalcitrance, whereas false swearing connotes mere falsehood without these additional moral judgment." Cf. Bryan A. Garner, *A Dictionary of Modern Legal Usage*, 2nd Edition, Oxford University Press (1995), at P. 652.

Physical disability ► Civil disability

二者均可用作指無行爲能力。不同的是 physical disability 與 physical 相關，指肉體或精神缺陷或疾病造成的生理上的無行爲能力[1]。而 civil disability 則與某人的民事地位（civil status）相關，該地位是由法律所決定的，故其是指法律上的無行爲能力，等同 legal disability[2]。

注

[1] "An incapacity caused by a physical defect or infirmity, or by bodily imperfection or mental weakness." Cf. Bryan A. Garner, *Black's Law Dictionary*, 7th Edition, West Croup (1999), at P. 474.

[2] "The condition of a person who has had a legal right or privilege revoked as a result of a criminal conviction, as when a person's driver's license is revoked after DWI conviction." *Id.* at P. 474.

P

Plaintiff ► Appellant ► Applicant ► Petitioner ► Demandant ► Pursuer ► Accuser ► Claimant ► Libel(l)ant

上述單詞均有訴訟之原告的含意。plaintiff 爲通用詞，常用於普通法法院的一般民事或刑事案件的初審中，與其相對的被告稱爲 defendant[1]。appellant 爲「上訴人」，可用於刑事或民事上訴案件中，與其相對的被上訴人稱爲 respondent[2]。applicant 用於申請某一特別命令的訴訟，也可譯爲「申訴人」，多用於國際訴訟中，與其相對的被申訴人或被告常被稱爲 respondent[3]。petitioner 多用於衡平法訴訟中，如衡平法院、大法官法院的訴訟以及家事法院的離婚案件、遺囑驗證法院的遺囑驗證案等，與之相對的被告常被稱爲 respondent[4]。demandant 爲古用語，常用於不動產訴訟，與之相對的被告被稱爲 tenant[5]。pursuer 則爲蘇格蘭法院用語，與之相對的被告爲 defender[6]。accuser 主要指提起刑事訴訟者，與之相對的被告爲 the accused[7]。claimant 常出現在英國民事訴訟中，與之相對的被告被稱爲 defendant[8]。libel(l)ant 則多指在海事或離婚案件中的原告，與其相對的被告則爲 libel(l)ee[9]。

注

① "The party who brings a civil suit in a court of law." Cf. Bryan A. Garner, *Black's Law Dictionary*, 7th Edition, West Croup (1999), at P. 1171; "The prosecution (i.e. State or United States) in a criminal case." Cf. The Publisher's Editorial Staff, *Black's Law Dictionary*, Abridged 6th Edition, West Publishing Co. (1991), at P. 796.

② "a person or party who appeals a court's judgment", Cf. Linda Picard Wood, J.D., *Merriam Webster's Dictionary of Law*, Merriam-Webster, Incorporated (1996), at P. 29.

③ "one who brings an application or petition." Cf. Daphne Dukelow, *The Dictionary of Canadian Law*, Thomson Professional Publishing Canada (1991), at P. 52.

④ "One who presents a petition to a court." Cf. The Publisher's Editorial Staff, *Black's Law Dictionary*, Abridged 6th Edition, West Publishing Co. (1991), at P. 793.

⑤ "The plaintiff in a real action." Cf. Bryan A. Garner, *Black's Law Dictionary*, 7th Edition, West Croup (1999), at P. 441.

⑥ "chiefly Scots and ecclesiastical law, plaintiff, prosecutor", Cf. Philip Babcock Grove, Ph.D., *Webster's Third New International Dictionary of the English Language Unabridged*, G&C Merriam Co. (1976), at P. 1848.

⑦ "A person who accuses another of a crime." Cf. Bryan A. Garner,

Black's Law Dictionary, 7ᵗʰ Edition, West Croup (1999), at P. 22.

⑧ "person who states a grievance in court", Cf. P. H. Collin, *Dictionary of Law*, Peter Collin Publishing Ltd. (1993), at P. 93.

⑨ "The plaintiff in a libel case was called libellant or libellant; the defendant was called libelee or libellee." Cf. James E. Clapp, *Random House Webster's Dictionary of the Law*, Random House, New York (2000), at P. 272.

Pleading ▸ Complaint ▸ Petition ▸ Clause ▸ Application ▸ Indictment ▸ Information ▸ Presentment ▸ Bill ▸ Statement of claim ▸ Particulars of claim ▸ Libel

以上單詞或片語均有「訴狀」的含義。其中，pleading 是指在民事訴訟訴辯程序中，當事雙方呈送法庭的各種訴辯狀，除包括訴狀（complaint）外，還指答辯狀（answer），原告對被告抗辯的再答辯狀（reply）等①。complaint 多指向普通法法院所提交的民事訴狀；或刑事自訴狀，此種自訴狀要提交給一位司法官員，並指控某人實施了犯罪，如有足夠的證據，則可簽發逮捕令，此時其也稱爲（criminal complaint）②。petition 是指向大法官法院或衡平法法院，以及在家事法院的離婚、子女撫養等案件中和遺囑檢驗法院有關遺囑檢驗的案件中所提交的訴狀（參見 originating process）③，如：a petitioner for equitable relief（一主張衡平法救濟的訴狀）④。clause 是指向宗教法院提交的訴狀。application 多指向國際法庭提交的要求得到法院某項專門命令的一種訴狀⑤。indictment、information 和 presentment 三個單詞都是指刑事訴狀。其中，indictment 多指對重罪犯提起公訴時提交的訴狀（在英格蘭是以國王的名義，在蘇格蘭是以檢察總長的名義，在美國是由大陪審團確認後向法院提交）⑥。在美國，information 與 indictment 的主要區別在於前者是以檢察官個

P

人名義，而不是經大陪審團作出決定後以大陪審團的名義提交⑦。在英國，如以 information 形式提起訴訟，檢舉人（informer）則可望得到一筆獎金，其有時也可用於民事訴訟的特權告發程序⑧。在加拿大，information 可由警官直接向治安法官提出，如果治安法官認定其事實充足，便可簽發傳票或逮捕令（如果被傳人不到庭）。presentment 與 indictment 的主要差別在於 indictment 是經一檢察官預先提出的指控請求，然後再由大陪審團作出裁定後提出（upon a prosecutor's previous indictment request），而 presentment 則指大陪審團（或其他團體）自己主動決定提交的控訴書（a formal written accusation returned by a grand jury on its own initiative, without a prosecutor's previous indictment request）⑨。bill 源於法文的通知（*libelle*），可用作衡平法之訴的訴狀（在美國，現已被 complaint 取代），所以也稱為 bill in equity⑩，在英格蘭，其指對犯罪行為的書面告發（經大陪審團認定，告發書即成為訴狀），還可指向國王、大法官或議院提交的申訴狀。statement of claim 和 particulars of claim 為英國或加拿大用於民事訴訟的文書，前者指向高等法院提交的訴狀，後者指向郡法院提交的訴狀，其作用有些等同美國的 complaint⑪。libel 所指的訴狀多用在海事和離婚案件（used especially in admiralty and divorce cases）⑫以及宗教法庭中⑬。

注

① "the formal document in which a party to a civil case sets out or responds to a claim or defense. Under modern rules, the principal pleadings are the *complaint*, the *answer*, and if the answer contains counterclaims, a *reply*." Cf. James E. Clapp, *Random House Webster's Dictionary of the Law*, Random House, New York (2000), at P. 330.

② "The initial pleading that starts a civil action and states the basis for the court's jurisdiction, the basis for the plaintiff's claim, and the demand for relief." Cf. Bryan A. Garner, *Black's Law Dictionary*, 7ᵗʰ Edition, West Croup (1999), at P. 279; "a document sworn to by a victim or police officer that sets forth a criminal violation and that serves as the charging instrument by which charges are filed and judicial proceedings commenced against a defendant in a magistrate's court", Cf. Linda Picard Wood, J.D., *Merriam Webster's Dictionary of Law*, Merriam-Webster, Incorporated (1996), at P. 90；賀衛方等翻譯，《美國法律詞典》，中國政法大學出版社（1998），第 148 頁。

③ "A formal written application to a court requesting judicial action on a certain matter… Formerly, in equity practice the original pleading was denominated a petition or bill." Cf. The Publisher's Editorial Staff, *Black's Law Dictionary*, Abridged 6ᵗʰ Edition, West Publishing Co. (1991), at P. 793.

④ Cf. Linda Picard Wood, J.D., *Merriam Webster's Dictionary of Law*, Merriam-Webster, Incorporated (1996), at P. 363.

⑤ "The commencement of proceedings before a court of tribunal", Cf. Daphne Dukelow, *The Dictionary of Canadian Law*, Thomson Professional Publishing Canada (1991), at P. 52.

⑥ "Any offense punishable by death, or for imprisonment for more than one year or by hard labor, must be prosecuted by indictment. An indictment is issuable only by a grand jury." Cf. Bryan A. Garner, *A Dictionary of Modern Legal Usage*, 2ⁿᵈ Edition, Oxford University Press Ltd. (1995), at P. 438.

⑦ "an instrument containing a formal accusation of a crime that is issued by a prosecuting officer and that serves the same function as an indictment. About half the states in the United States allow prosecutors to issue informations. The rest require indictment", Cf. Linda Picard Wood, J.D., *Merriam Webster's Dictionary of Law*, Merriam-Webster, Incorporated (1996), at P. 244.

⑧ Cf. David M. Walker, *The Oxford Companion To Law*, information, informer, Oxford University Press (1980), at P. 444.

⑨ Cf. Bryan A. Garner, *Black's Law Dictionary*, 7th Edition, West Croup (1999), at P. 1202.

⑩ "the pleading used to begin a suit in equity that sets forth the basis for one's claim against another", Cf. Linda Picard Wood, J.D., *Merriam Webster's Dictionary of Law*, Merriam-Webster, Incorporated (1996), at P. 50.

⑪ "English law: A plaintiff's initial pleading in a civil case." Cf. Bryan A. Garner, *Black's Law Dictionary*, 7th Edition, West Croup (1999), at P. 1417; Cf. John O'Hare & Robert N. Hill, Civil Litigation, 5th Edition, Longman Group UK Ltd. (1990), at Ps.19—49.

⑫ "complaint, used esp. in admiralty and divorce cases", Cf. Linda Picard Wood, J.D., *Merriam Webster's Dictionary of Law*, Merriam-Webster, Incorporated (1996), at P. 291.

⑬ "The complaint or initial pleading in an admiralty or ecclesiastical case." Cf. Bryan A. Garner, *Black's Law Dictionary*, 7th Edition, West Croup (1999), at P. 927.

Pleadings

pleadings 為「訴辯狀」，除指民事訴訟中的訴辯雙方當事人提出訴訟主張或進行辯護的正式文件之外①，同時也指民事訴訟開始後的第一個程序（即雙方當事人向法院呈送訴辯狀程序）②。在英國，原告首先向高等法院提交的 pleading 被稱為 statement of claim

（主張事實陳述狀）③，向郡法院提交的訴狀則稱爲 particulars of claim（主張事實陳述書）④，而被告針對原告主張的辯護狀則稱爲 defense⑤，如被告同時提出反訴，該 pleading 則稱爲 defense and counterclaim（辯護和反訴狀）⑥，而原告就反訴的辯護叫 defense to counterclaim（針對反訴之答覆）⑦，此外，原告就被告答辯中提出的問題的答覆稱爲 reply⑧，而被告的第二輪答辯則稱爲 rejoinder（二次抗辯狀）⑨，儘管這種情況鮮見。按美國的普通法規定，訴辯狀依其所呈送的順序，可分爲原告的申訴（declaration）、被告的抗辯（plea）、原告對被告抗辯的答辯（replication）、被告的第二次抗辯（rejoinder）、原告的第二次答辯（surrejoinder）、被告的第三次抗辯（rebutter）、原告的第三次答辯（surrebutter，此後的 pleading 則無專門的術語予以稱呼⑩）。按美國聯邦或州的訴訟法典或規則的規定，訴辯狀（pleadings）則包括訴狀（complaint）、被告的抗辯狀（answer）、原告對被告反訴的答辯（a reply to a counterclaim）、被告對共同當事人的主張的抗辯（an answer to a cross claim）、第三方訴訟的訴狀（a third party complaint）、第三方訴訟被告的抗辯（a third party answer）等⑪。

注

① "the formal document in which a party to a civil case sets out or responds to a claim or defense", Cf. James E. Clapp, *Random House Webster's Dictionary of the Law*, Random House, New York (2000), at P. 330.

② "a process or system through which the parties in al legal proceeding present their allegations", Cf. Linda Picard Wood, J.D., *Merriam Webster's Dictionary of Law*, Merriam-Webster, Incorporated (1996), at P. 366.

③ "A printed or written statement by the plaintiff in an action which

367

shows the facts relied upon to support any claim against the defendant and the remedy or relief sought." Cf. Daphne Dukelow, *The Dictionary of Canadian Law*, Thomson Professional Publishing Canada (1991), at P. 1024.

④ "County court pleading setting out the plaintiff's claims." Cf. P. H. Collin, *Dictionary of Law*, Peter Collin Publishing Ltd. (1993), at P. 391.

⑤ "A defendant's denial of a plaintiff's complaint." Cf. Daphne Dukelow, *The Dictionary of Canadian Law*, Thomson Professional Publishing Canada (1991), at P. 261.

⑥ "If the defendant also wishes to claim remedies against the plaintiff his pleading is called a *defense and counterclaim*." Cf. John O'Hare & Robert N. Hill, *Civil Litigation*, 5ᵗʰ Edition, Longman Group UK Ltd. (1990), at P. 164.

⑦ "Sometimes there are also subsequent pleadings: the plaintiff's defense to counterclaim." *Id.* at P. 165.

⑧ "written statement by a plaintiff in a civil case in answer to the defendant's defense", Cf. P. H. Collin, *Dictionary of Law*, Peter Collin Publishing Ltd. (1993), at P. 473.

⑨ "The defendant's answer to the plaintiff's reply." Cf. Daphne Dukelow, *The Dictionary of Canadian Law*, Thomson Professional Publishing Canada (1991), at P. 906.

⑩ "The individual allegations of the respective parties to an action at common law proceeded from them alternatively in the order and under the following distinctive names: the plaintiff's declaration, the defendant's plea, the plaintiff's replication, the defendant's rejoinder, the plaintiff's surrejoinder, the defendant's rebutter, the plaintiff's surrebutter; after which they have no distinctive names." Cf. The

Publisher's Editorial Staff, *Black's Law Dictionary*, Abridged 6th Edition, West Publishing Co. (1991), at P. 798.

⑪ "Under rules of civil procedure the pleadings consist of a complaint, an answer, a reply to a counterclaim, an answer to a cross-claim, a third party compliant, and a third party answer." Cf. *Federal Rules of Civil Proceedings*, 7(a).

Plurality ▸ Majority

二者雖均有多數的含義，但從嚴格的法律意義上講，它們仍有很大的差異。關鍵在於 plurality 只是指「相對多數」，而非構成過半數的多數，即：a large number or quantity that does not constitute a majority[①]。相比之下，majority 則指「過半數多數」，即 a number that is more than half of a total[②]。

注

① Cf. Bryan A. Garner, *Black's Law Dictionary*, 7th Edition, West Croup (1999), at P. 1177.

② Cf. Linda Picard Wood, J.D., *Merriam Webster's Dictionary of Law*, Merriam-Webster, Incorporated (1996), at P. 303.

Police officer ▸ Peace officer

二者均有治安警察的含義。相比之下，peace officer 的內涵更廣一些，其除指治安警察（police officer）之外，還可指 sheriff，有時甚至還包括審理刑事案件的法官（a judge who hears criminal cases）或其他法定的在有限範圍之內可維護治安的公共官員，如市長（a mayor）等，故其爲「治安官員」[①]，其也稱爲 officer of the peace 或

conservator of the peace。而 police officer 則指單純的治安警察②。

注

① "A civil officer (such as a sheriff or police officer) appointed to maintain public tranquility and order. This term may also include a judge who hears criminal cases or another public official (such as a mayor) who may be statutorily designated as a peace officer for limited purposes." Cf. Bryan A. Garner, *Black's Law Dictionary*, 7th Edition, West Croup (1999), at P. 1151.

② "A peace officer responsible for preserving public order, promoting public safety, and preventing and detecting crime." *Id.* at P. 1178.

Poll ▸ Vote ▸ Ballot

　　三者均有投票表決的含義。相比之下，vote 爲通用詞，含義最廣，包括表決的各種形式，如投票表決、舉手表決、鼓掌表決等①，因表決常用投票進行，故 vote 有時也就被人譯爲「投票」②，但其精確含義應爲「表決」，尤其是與 poll 用在一起時。而 poll 則多指表決的一種形式，即「投票表決」③。ballot 則又屬於投票表決中的一種形式，即不記名投票表決④。

注

① "The expression of one's preference or opinion by ballot, show of hands, or other type of communication." Cf. Bryan A. Garner, *Black's Law Dictionary*, 7th Edition, West Croup (1999), at P. 1571.

② Cf. 《英漢法律詞典》，法律出版社（1999），第 873 頁；薛波，《漢英法律詞典》，外文出版社（1995），第 697 頁。

③ "the giving of votes in writing at an election", Cf. Randolph Quirk,

Longman Dictionary of Contemporary English, Longman Group Ltd (1978), at P. 842.

④ "Process or means of voting, usually in secret, by writing or printed tickets or slips of paper, or voting machine. A means, or instrumentality, by which a voter secretly indicates his will or choice so that it may be recorded as being in favor of a certain candidate or for or against a certain proposition or measure." Cf. The Publisher's Editorial Staff, *Black's Law Dictionary*, Abridged 6th Edition, West Publishing Co. (1991), at P. 97.

Pornographic ▸ Obscene

在美國，這兩個單詞在法律上的含義有本質上的差異。 pornographic 爲「色情的」，與之相對應的 pornography 則是指諸如色情文學、色情圖畫等。按規定，色情文學等應受《美國聯邦憲法》第一修正案的保護，屬於合法範疇，並非貶義，除非其達到 obscene 的地步。而 obscene 則爲「淫穢的」，指諸如淫穢圖畫、文學等，其不在《美國聯邦憲法》第一修正案的保護範圍之內，屬於非法①。在上世紀 90 年代，美國社會曾對屬於憲政民主問題的 pornography 進行過激烈的爭辯，最終才導致了 pornographic 與 obscene 之間的區別劃分②。法律詞典對這兩術語的界定也反映了美國政治以及法律對色情資訊認識的演變。如在 1991 年， *Black's Law Dictionary* 第 6 版仍將 pornographic 定義爲 "That which is of or pertaining to obscene literature; obscene; licentious." ③，在此定義中，pornographic 仍然等同 obscene。而到 1999 年，該詞典第 7 版便將 pornography 重新定義爲： "material (such as writings, photographs, or movies) depicting sexual activity or erotic behavior in a way that is designated to arouse sexual excitement.Pornography is protected speech under the First Amendment unless it is determined to be legally obscene." 明確將 pornographic 與 obscene 區分開來④。嚴格說來，pornography（色情文學、色情圖畫）現可分為兩種，即 hard core pornography 和 soft pornography，其中前者為 obscene 的範圍，後者則屬於聯邦憲法保護的範圍。由此，廣義的 pornography 既含有合法的又含有非法的部分⑤。目前，聯邦或各州頒布的 anti-pornography law 實則變成有關禁止 obscenity 以及 child pornography 的法律，對未成年人而言，法院對此作有嚴格規定，即便所涉及內容不到法律規定的 obscene 或 nudity 的地步也應禁止⑥。鑒於以上問題的界定涉及敏感的憲法問題，目前美國的司法界在對待此問題時均十分謹慎，法院在判決書上很少只用 pornography 來指 obscene 部分的內容，而代替用 hard core 等術語⑦。總之一句話，目前的趨勢是非法文學、圖畫等為 obscene，而 pornographic 則被認為是或者起碼有部分應是得到憲法保護的。在中國，由於我們所說的「黃色」讀物或文學等都屬於狹義的非法而應受到打擊，在此意義上，「黃色」實際應等同 obscene 而非 pornographic 之部分。同理，pornography 和 obscenity 也有類似區別。因此，目前我們在作英譯漢時，最好將「黃書」或「黃畫」等譯為 obscene book 或 obscene picture 而非 pornographic book 或 pornographic picture。而「掃黃運動」也最好譯為 "obscenity campaign" 或 "obscenity sweeps"，而非 "pornography campaign" 或 "pornography sweeps"⑧。

注

① "material that depicts erotic behavior and is intended to cause sexual excitement. Pornographic material is protected expression unless it is determined to be obscene", Cf. Linda Picard Wood, J.D., *Merriam Webster's Dictionary of Law*, Merriam-Webster, Incorporated (1996), at P. 368.

② Cf. Laurence S. Rockefeller, *Book Review*: *Law, Democracy, and Moral Disagreement*, (1996), at P. 1388.

③ Cf. The Publisher's Editorial Staff, *Black's Law Dictionary*, Abridged 6th Edition, West Publishing Co. (1991), at P. 805.

④ Cf. Bryan A. Garner, *Black's Law Dictionary*, 7th Edition, West Croup (1999), at P. 1181.

⑤ "broadly, any sexually explicit material intended primarily to provide sexual entertainment and arousal to those who read or view it for that purpose, narrowly, sexual material satisfying the constitutional test for *obscenity*", Cf. James E. Clapp, *Random House Webster's Dictionary of the Law*, Random House, New York (2000), at P. 250.

⑥ *Id*. at P. 333.

⑦ "… a majority of this court has agreed on concrete guideline to isolate hard core pornography from expression protected by the First Amendment." Cf. *Miller v. California*, US Supreme Court, 413 U.S.15 (1973).

⑧ Cf. 陳忠誠，《法窗譯話》，法律出版社（1992），第 10 頁。

Prison ▸ Penitentiary ▸ Gaol (jail)

　　三者均有關押罪犯設施的含義。其中，gaol（英式英語，美式英語稱爲 jail）多指地方（縣、市等）的監獄設施，多關押未決犯或輕罪犯①，故應譯爲「看守所」或「地方監獄」。prison 和 penitentiary 詞義相近，指關押已決犯的聯邦或州監獄，被監禁者所犯罪行一般都較嚴重②，也稱爲 penal institution、adult correctional institution，而 penitentiary 則尤指關押重罪犯的場所③。

① "jail (gaol) is usually used to hold persons either convicted of misdemeanors (minor crimes) or persons awaiting trial or as luck-up for intoxicated and disorderly persons", Cf. the Publisher's Editorial Staff, *Black's Law Dictionary with Pronunciations*, Abridged 6th Edition, West Publishing Co. (1991), at P. 580; "an institution usually run by a county or municipality, for locking up offenders serving short sentences and accused people awaiting trial", Cf. James E. Clapp, *Random House Webster's Dictionary of the Law*, Random House, New York (2000), at P. 250; "a place of confinement for persons held in lawful custody; *specific*: such a place under the jurisdiction of a local government (as a county) for the confinement of persons awaiting trial or those convicted of minor crimes", Cf. Linda Picard Wood, J.D., *Merriam Webster's Dictionary of Law*, Merriam-Webster, Incorporated (1996), at P. 265.

② "a state or federal facility in which people convicted of serious crimes and given long sentences are incarcerated." Cf. James E. Clapp, *Random House Webster's Dictionary of the Law*, Random House, New York (2000), at P. 340; "an institution usu. under state control for confinement of persons serving sentences for serious crimes", Cf. Linda Picard Wood, J.D., *Merriam Webster's Dictionary of Law*, Merriam-Webster, Incorporated (1996), at P. 382; "A state or federal facility of confinement for convicted criminals, esp. felons.", Cf. Bryan A. Garner, *Black's Law Dictionary*, 7th Edition, West Croup (1999), at P. 1213.

③ "a state or federal prisons for the punishment and reformation of convicted felons", Cf. Linda Picard Wood, J.D., *Merriam Webster's*

Dictionary of Law, Merriam-Webster, Incorporated (1996), at P. 358.

Privy seal ▶ Great seal

　　二者均可指英國、加拿大等古時的印鑒。在翻譯和使用時，應當注意它們之間的一些差別。首先，privy seal 應爲「御印」（monarch's seal）而非「玉璽」〔玉璽之含義即：君主的玉印（imperial jade seal[①]），國外的印鑒是否像中國一樣用玉石（jade）製作尚不得而知，且從下文可知 privy seal 並非代表帝國政府的正式大印，這與「玉璽」的含義，即帝國之印（imperial seal）又有差別，故最好不翻譯爲玉璽〕；其次，儘管在英國，privy seal 是君主印鑒（British royal seal），但其僅是君主的私人引薦[②]，相比之下，其級別遠低於作爲王國政府正式引薦的 great seal〔在加拿大，privy seal 的級別更低，其僅用於指領地總督（Governor General）或行政長官（administrator）使用的公務印鑒，由此只應譯爲「官印」[③]〕。按規定，重要文件在蓋了 privy seal 之後才能獲准加蓋 great seal，而一些不甚重要的文件只需蓋上 privy seal 則可[④]，因而與作爲君主私人的「御璽」相比，great seal 應是代表王國政府的「國璽」[⑤]。

注

① Cf. *Contemporary Chinese Dictionary* (*Chinese-English Edition*), Foreign Language Teaching and Research Press (2002), at P. 2347；吳光華，《漢英大詞典》，上海交通大學出版社（1995），第3132頁。

② "a private seal, as a British royal seal used before 1885 to authorize use of the great seal (as on letters patent or pardons) or on documents not requiring the great seal (as discharges of debts)", Cf. Philip

Babcock Grove, Ph.D., *Webster's Third New International Dictionary of the English Language Unabridged*, G&C Merriam Co. (1976), at P. 1848.

③ "The seal adopted by the Governor General or the Administrator for the sealing of official documents that are to be signed by him, or with his authority by his deputy, and that do not require to be sealed with the Great Seal." Cf. Daphne Dukelow, *The Dictionary of Canadian Law*, Thomson Professional Publishing Canada (1991), at P. 818.

④ " (in the U.K.) a seal formerly affixed to documents that are afterwards to pass the Great Seal or that do not require it." Cf. Della Thompson, *The Concise Oxford Dictionary*, 9ᵗʰ Edition, Oxford University Press (1995), at P. 1089.

⑤ "The official seal of Great Britain, of which the Lord Chancellor is the custodian." Cf. Bryan A. Garner, *Black's Law Dictionary*, 7ᵗʰ Edition, West Group (1999), at P. 1350.

Process ▸ Subpoena ▸ Summons ▸ Writ of summons ▸ Writ of subpoena ▸ Citation

　　以上詞語均有訴訟出庭通知或傳票的含義。其中，process 等同一般術語（general term），概念較寬，可用作指法院簽發的有關訴訟的各種通知，如訴訟通知書、傳票、出庭通知等①。而 subpoena 則用於傳喚證人以在審判時提供證詞、書證等，而不是傳喚訴訟當事人出庭的文件，故其應為「出庭通知」②。summons 主要用於傳喚訴訟當事人，故其為「傳票」③（儘管有些美國法律詞典說其也可用於指傳喚證人出庭佐證的「出庭通知」④）。在加拿大和英國，人們常用 summons to witness 來替代 subpoena，指傳喚證人或證據的「出庭通知」⑤。writ of summons（傳票）和 writ of subpoena（出

庭通知）一般在加拿大和英國等地適用，writ（or writ of summons）
與 summons 的差別在於後者多用於較下級的法院，如小額索賠法院
（small claim court）、郡法院等，而前者則用於高等法院、最高法
院等⑥。citation 主要為蘇格蘭用語，指傳喚證人或證據，故為「出
庭通知」⑦。

① "a formal document through which a court obtains jurisdiction over a
person or property, compels a person to appear in court or participate
in a proceeding, or otherwise orders a person to do or not to do
something; e.g., a summons, a writ of attachment, or a subpoena",
Cf. James E. Clapp, *Random House Webster's Dictionary of the Law*,
Random House, New York (2000), at P. 343.

② "A subpoena is a document to appear at a certain time and place to
give testimony upon a certain matter. A subpoena duces tecum requires
production of books, papers and other things." Cf. The publisher's
Editorial Staff, *Black's Law Dictionary*, Abridged 6th Edition, West
Publishing Co. (1991), at P. 995.

③ "a process directing a defendant to appear in court to answer a civil
complaint or a criminal charge", Cf. James E. Clapp, *Random House
Webster's Dictionary of the Law*, Random House, New York (2000), at
P. 419; "official command from a court requiring someone to appear in
court to be tried for a criminal offense or to defend a civil action", Cf.
P. H. Collin, *Dictionary of Law*, 2nd Edition, Peter Collin Publishing
(1995), at P. 536.

④ "A notice requiring a person to appear in court as a juror or witness."
Cf. Bryan A. Garner, *Black's Law Dictionary*, 7th Edition, West Group
(1999), at P. 1450; "a notification to appear as a witness", Cf. Linda

Picard Wood, J.D., *Merriam Webster's Dictionary of Law*, Merriam-Webster, Incorporated, Springfield, Massachusetts (1996), at P. 482.

⑤ "Used instead of a subpoena, this document directs a witness to appear in court at a given time and place or to bring certain documents or things along." Cf. Daphne Dukelow, *The Dictionary of Canadian Law*, Thomson Professional Publishing Canada (1991), at P. 1046.

⑥ Cf. John O'Hare & Robert N. Hill, *Civil Litigation*, Longman Group UK Ltd (1990), at P. 164.

⑦ "Calling on a person who is not a party to a proceeding or an action to appear in court." Cf. Daphne Dukelow, *The Dictionary of Canadian Law*, Thomson Professional Publishing Canada (1991), at P. 161.

Promise ▶ Acceptance ▶ Offer

　　三者均為契約法中的常用詞。其中，promise 是要約人向被要約人所作要約，為一種主動的「允諾」或「許諾」①。而 acceptance 則為「承諾」，是被要約人（offeree）對要約（offer）的一種認可②。offer 則與 promise 意思相同，是主動對他人的「要約」③，但與 promise 不同的是 offer 可以撤銷（revocable），而promise作為「允諾」則不能撤銷④。

注

① "A party's undertaking about its future conduct." Cf. G. H. L. Fridman, *The Law of Contract in Canada*, 2nd Edition, Carswell (1986), at P. 1; "A declaration or manifestation, esp. in a contract, of an intention to act or refrain from acting in a specified way that gives the party to whom it is made a right to expect its fulfillment." Cf. Linda Picard Wood, J.D., *Merriam Webster's Dictionary of Law*, Merriam-

Webster, Incorporated, Springfield, Massachusetts (1996), at P. 389.

② "An agreement, either by express act or by implication from conduct, to the terms of an offer so that a binding contract is formed." Cf. Bryan A. Garner, *Black's Law Dictionary*, 7th Edition, West Group (1999), at P. 11.

③ "One person's indication to another that she or he is willing to enter into a contract with that person on certain terms." Cf. Daphne Dukelow, *The Dictionary of Canadian Law*, Thomson Professional Publishing Canada (1991), at P. 711.

④ "Therefore, an offer is revocable, a promise is not." Cf. William R. Arson, *Some Notes on Terminology in Contract*, 7 Law Q. Rev. (1891), at P. 337.

Proof of service ▸ Acknowledgment of service ▸ Affidavit of service ▸ Return of service ▸ Affidavit by process-server ▸ Notice of service

P

以上詞語均與法院傳票及其他文件等的送達有關。其中，proof of service 爲「送達證明」，其是通用術語，指將有關法院的傳票或其他文件或通知送達給當事人的證明書①，其包括 acknowledgment of service 與 affidavit of service。acknowledgment of service 爲傳票被送達人所出具的證明或認可，承認自己已經收到傳票，故爲「送達回執」②。affidavit of service（也稱爲 affirmation of service）則是指由傳票送達人所作的一種宣誓證明，證明傳票已經送達到有關當事人，故爲「送達宣誓證明」③。return of service 幾乎等同 affidavit of service，也是送達人而非被送達人出具的文件，與 affidavit of service 的差異在於它有時也用於傳票或文件未曾眞正送達給當事人的情況，在此時返還給法院的文書上便僅有一些如何努力企圖送達的說明而非是眞正送達的證明，故其應爲「送達情況說明」^④。affidavit by process-server 則是指傳票（包括其他法庭文件）的「送達人宣誓證明」，其也幾乎等同 affidavit of service，也是由送達人出具的一種證明，按美國聯邦法院以及英國高等法院或郡法院的慣例，如送達人不是司法行政官或其助手（marshal or his depute），則應由送達人在律師面前或在法庭宣誓以證明文件已經送達^⑤。notice of service 則是指傳票或其他文件、通知由法院負責送達時，由法院向原告簽發的一種通知，故爲「法院送達通知書」^⑥。

注

① "proof that a summons or other process or court paper has been served upon the person who was to receive it", Cf. James E. Clapp, *Random House Webster's Dictionary of the Law*, Random House, New York (2000), at P. 346.

② Cf. John O'Hare & Robert N. Hill, *Civil Litigation*, 5th Edition, Biddles of Guildford Ltd. Surrey (1990), at P. 221.

③ *Id.* at P. 231.

④ Cf. James E. Clapp, *Random House Webster's Dictionary of the Law*, Random House, New York (2000), at P. 377.

⑤ Cf. the Publisher's Editorial Staff, *Black's Law Dictionary*, Abridged 6th Edition, West Publishing Co. (1991), at P. 36.

⑥ Cf. John O'Hare & Robert N. Hill, *Civil Litigation*, 5th Edition, Biddles of Guildford Ltd. Surrey (1990), at P. 233.

Property

該詞有兩重含義，可指財產或物（thing or things capable of ownership），也可指產權，即 ownership of a thing。英國法財產有

多種分類，而土地作為最重要的一種財產，其分類又不同於其他財產。總體說來，property 可分為 real property（不動產）和 personal property（動產）兩大類。real property 是指不能移動或一經移動即會損害其經濟效益或價值的財產，如土地或建築物、樹木、橋樑等。personal property 則指能移動且不會損害其經濟效益或價值的財產。其中，personal property 又可分為 chattels real（土地附屬動產）和 chattels personal（屬人動產）兩種。chattels real（土地附屬動產，也稱為 real chattels）指從土地或房屋等派生出的非永佃或自由保有土地權益（a real property interest that is less than freehold or fee），如土地租賃權或租借土地保有權等。chattels personal（屬人動產，也稱為person chattels）則指有體財產和無體權利，如 patent 等，其又可分為 choses in possession（占有上的物）和 choses in action（訴訟上的物）兩類。choses in action（訴訟上的物或財產）指可透過法律程序請求或強制實施的屬人財產權利，如稅收或關稅，如尚未徵收，即為訴訟上的物，如已經繳納，則成為占有上的物，一般為無體財產；choses in possession（占有上的物或財產）指可以實際占有的財產權的有形客體。

注

Cf. Li Rong-fu/Song Lei, *A Course Book of Legal English*, *The Law of Property*, Law Press (1999), at P. 110.

Prosecutor ▸ Procurator ▸ Attorney

三者均有檢察官的含義。prosecutor 多為普通法系國家所用，這些國家的檢察人員一般由律師擔任[1]。procurator 則為大陸法系的有些國家，如法國所用，這些國家的檢察官員不必一定由律師充任[2]。因此，在翻譯中國的檢察員時，人們多採用 procurator。attorney 則常在普通法系國家中被用來稱呼具體的各種檢察官（因為這些國家規定檢察官必須由律師擔當），特別是在美國，如：地方檢察官（district attorney）、縣檢察官（county attorney）、州或地方檢察官（prosecuting attorney）、州檢察官（state's attorney）、聯邦檢察官（commonwealth attorney，用於 Virginia 與 Kentucky 州）、地方檢察長（district attorney general，用於 New Jersey 州）、助理檢察長（assistant attorney general，用於 Virgin Islands 州）等[3]。

注

① "A legal officer who represents the government in criminal proceeding." Cf. Bryan A. Garner, *Black's Law Dictionary*, 7th Edition, West Group (1999), at P. 1237.

② "public prosecutor", Cf. Philip B. Grove, *Webster Third New International Dictionary*, G&C Merriam Co. (1971), at P. 1806.

③ Cf. The Publisher's Editorial Staff, *Black's Law Dictionary*, Abridged 6th Edition, West Publishing Co. (1991), at Ps. 330, 849.

Proxy ▶ Power of attorney

二者均有授權委託書的含義。區別在於 power of attorney 指向具有律師資格者授權[1]，而 proxy（也稱為 the instrument appointing a proxy）則一般無此含義，即 proxy 指定的代理人不必一定是律師。此外，power of attorney 的用途較廣，而 proxy 則多指如公司法中授權替其他股東表決者[2]。

注

① "Authority for a donee or donees to do on behalf of a donor or principal anything which that donor can lawfully do through an attorney." Cf. G. H. L. Fridman, *The Law of Agency*, 5th Edition, London, Butterworth (1983), at P. 55.

② "A completed and executed form of proxy by means of which a security holder has nominated a person or company to attend and act on her or his behalf at a meeting of security holders." Cf. Daphne Dukelow, *The Dictionary of Canadian Law*, Thomson Professional Publishing Canada (1991), at P. 845.

Public corporation ► Private corporation

二者都有各自的含義。public corporation 可指由州政府爲政治目的而建立的公司，其作爲政府管理的代理機構，被授予一定權力，此時它爲「公營公司」，在此意義上，它又可稱爲「政治公司」（political corporation）或「官方公司」（government corporation）；其次，它可指股份對公眾進行銷售之公司，此時它爲「公開發行公司」，在此意義上，它又可稱爲 publicly held corporation，即「股份上市公司」①。而 private corporation 指由私人組建的非官方目的，多爲經營商事之公司，故爲「私公司」或「私人公司」。此外，它又指「股份不上市公司」，在此意義上，其又可稱爲「閉鎖公司」（close corporation、closed corporation、closely held corporation、privately held corporation）②。

注

① "a corporation established by legislative act to carry out special government purposes; a corporation owned by a diverse group of shareholders, with stock freely traded among members of the public", Cf. James E. Clapp, *Random House Webster's Dictionary of the Law*, Random House, New York (2000), at P. 110.

② "a corporation established for nongovernmental purposes; a corporation owned by a single shareholder or a small group of shareholders, who typically are all personally active in the business of the corporation or are related to each other, and ordinarily are not allowed to sell their shares to anyone else without approval of the group", *Id.* at P. 110.

R

Raider ▸ White knight

二者均與公司的接管有關，但其意思則剛好相反。其中，raider 指企圖以購買商事公司（business corporation）股票和置換公司管理層達到控制公司目的者或企業，多指一種敵意性的接管行為（hostile takeover）[1]，也稱為 corporate raider、hostile bidder 或 unfriendly suitor，故為「公司敵意接管人」。而 white knight 則是指一個人或公司為救援即將被敵意接管之目標公司，採取措施，尤指以收購目標公司的控制股權或以故意競標的方式阻止敵意接管人之接管，故為「公司接管救援者」[2]，也稱為 friendly suitor。

注

[1] "one that attempts a usu.hostile takeover of a business corporation", Cf. Linda Picard Wood, J.D., *Merriam Webster's Dictionary of Law*, Merriam-Webster, Incorporated, Springfield, Massachusetts (1996), at P. 404.

[2] "A person or corporation that rescues the target of an unfriendly corporate takeover, esp. by acquiring a controlling interest in the target corporation or by making a competing tender offer." Cf. Bryan A. Garner, *Black's Law Dictionary*, 7th Edition, West Group (1999), at P. 1591.

Real estate agent ▸ Real estate broker

二者均可用於指不動產交易中的中間人。差別在於 real estate

agent 是指代表買方或賣方或代表雙方當事人進行不動產買賣或租賃者，其可指 broker（其委託人為買方或賣方），也可指 salesperson（其委託人為 broker），故其為「不動產交易代理人」[1]。而 real estate broker 則指在不動產買賣雙方中間就買賣契約或按揭或租賃協定等進行談判等活動的中間人，其必須是在從事業務的州註冊登記的專門人員，故為「不動產經紀人」[2]。

注

[1] "An agent who represents a buyer or seller (or both, with proper disclosures) in the sale or lease of real property." Cf. Bryan A. Garner, *Black's Law Dictionary*, 7th Edition, West Group (1999), at P. 65.
[2] "A broker who negotiates contracts of sale and other agreements (such as mortgages or leases) between buyers and sellers of real property. Real-estate brokers must be licensed in the states where they conduct business." *Id.* at P. 188.

Recklessness ▶ Negligence ▶ Intentional wrong

三者均指行為人並非預謀損害他人但事實卻可能使他人遭受損失的一種違法行為。recklessness 是指雖然無故意，但行為人卻在可能預見危險的情況下有意不顧他人的安危而冒險，故其為「莽撞行為」[1]。negligence 則是指行為人未行使合理的或應有的注意或小心而給他人造成損害，但其行為常並非 willful 或 desired，故其為「過失」[2]。intentional wrong（也稱為 willful wrong）則為「有意過錯」[3]。三者相比，negligence 情節最輕，recklessness 的過錯情節雖較 negligence 嚴重[4]，但卻比 intentional wrongdoing 的過錯輕。

注

① "characterized by the creation of a substantial and unjustifiable risk to the lives, safety, or rights of others and by a conscious and sometimes wanton and willful disregard for or indifference to that risk that is a gross deviation from the standard of care a reasonable person would exercise in like circumstances", Cf. Linda Picard Wood, J.D., *Merriam Webster's Dictionary of Law*, Merriam-Webster, Incorporated, Springfield, Massachusetts (1996), at P. 409.

② "An independent tort which consists of breach of a legal duty to take care which results in damage, undesired by the defendant, to the plaintiff." Cf. John G. Fleming, *The Law of Torts*, 6th Edition, Sydney, The Law Book Co. (1983), at P. 101.

③ "A wrong in which the *mens rea* amounts to intention, purpose, or design." Cf. Bryan A. Garner, *Black's Law Dictionary*, 7th Edition, West Group (1999), at P. 1606.

④ "Sometimes the term recklessness is used as just another word for negligence, but usually it signifies a higher degree of culpability. To be negligence, it is enough that one fails to perceive a risk that a reasonably careful person would have perceived; to be reckless is to be aware of a significant risk to others and proceed anyway." Cf. James E. Clapp, *Random House Webster's Dictionary of the Law*, Random House, New York (2000), at P. 363.

R

Recording acts

該術語（也稱爲 recording statutes）是指有關財產，尤指不動產權益的登記，由此而確立決定某人對該財產權利主張的次序先後標準的法規，其應爲「不動產登記法」^①。此種立法的目的主要是保護善意買主對抗先前未登記的權益主張。在美國，此種法規主要分爲三種，即：notice statute、race statute 以及 race-notice statute。它們的區別在於：notice statute 爲「不知情購買人優先法」，指一種財產購置登記法規，規定凡購置之權益，尤指不動產權益，以最近購買財產權益且不知道原先有人曾購置過此財產，但未登記者具有對抗他人的優先權的法規，也稱爲 notice act 或 notice recording statute，在美國，約有一半的州實施該種法規^②。race statute 則爲「登記順序優先法」，指規定以登記先後決定優先順序的法規，而不管登記時當事人是否知悉先前有人曾購置過同一財產，這種法規類似中國的不動產登記法規，在美國也適用於適用大陸法的路易斯安那州等，其也被稱爲 race act^③。race-notice statute 爲「不知情登記優先法」，指不動產購置登記相關的法規，規定凡在不知道不動產已經被購置但卻未登記的情況下購置不動產且登記者具有對抗原先購置者的優先權，但預先知悉眞情者除外，也稱爲 notice race statute^④。

注

① "A law that establishes the requirements for recording a deed or other property interest and the standards for determining priorities between persons claiming interests in the same property (usu. real property)." Cf. Bryan A. Garner, *Black's Law Dictionary*, 7th Edition, West Group (1999), at P. 1279.

② "An unrecorded conveyance or other instrument is invalid as against a subsequent bona fide purchaser (creditor or mortgagee if the statute so provided) for value and without notice. Under this type of statute the subsequent bona fide purchaser prevails over the prior interest whether the subsequent purchaser records or not." Cf. The Publisher's Editorial Staff, *Black's Law Dictionary*, Abridged 6th Edition, West Publishing

Co. (1991), at P. 734.

③ "A recording act providing that the person who records first, regardless of notice, has priority. Only Louisiana and North Carolina have race statutes."

④ "In some jurisdiction, in recording of documents of title to real estate, the first grantee or mortgagee to record in the chain of title without actual notice of a prior unrecorded deed or mortgage prevails." Cf. The Publisher's Editorial Staff, *Black's Law Dictionary*, Abridged 6th Edition, West Publishing Co. (1991), at P. 734.

Redress ▸ Relief ▸ Remedy

三者均有司法救濟的含義。在美國，它們的區別在於 relief 主要是指衡平法上的救濟，如以 injunction（強制令）或 specific performance（契約或協議的強制履行）等而非損害賠償金（damages）所進行的救濟。Remedy 則主要指普通法上的救濟（*Relief* has historically been commonly used in the context of equity, and remedy in the context of law①）。如：the most common remedies are judgment that plaintiffs are entitled to collect *sums of money* from defendants（*sums of money* 為普通法上的救濟）and *orders* to defendants to refrain from their wrongful conduct or to undo its consequences（*orders* 為衡平法上的救濟）。而在加拿大，relief 則無此種限制："Relief: Includes every species of relief, whether by way of damages, payment of money, injunction, declaration, restitution of an incorporeal right, return of land or chattels or otherwise②"。相比之下，redress 既可指衡平法又可指普通法上的救濟，實際上，其可用於替代 remedy 和 relief。如 *Black's Law Dictionary* 對 redress 下的定義便是：remedy or relief③。又如：Money damages, as opposed to equitable relief, is the only redress available（金錢賠償，而非衡平法上的救濟，才是目前惟一可行的救濟手段），此時的 redress 指普通法上的救濟，等同 remedy。

注

① Cf. Bryan A. Garner, *A Dictionary of Modern Legal Usage*, 2nd Edition, Oxford University Press Ltd. (1995), at P. 752.
② Cf. Daphne A Dukelow, *The Dictionary of Canadian Law*, A Carswell Publication (1991), at P. 908.
③ Cf. Bryan A. Garner, *Black's Law Dictionary*, 7th Edition, West Group (1999), at P. 1263.

Registered mail ▸ Certified mail

二者是有關美國主要兩種為確保郵件送達的郵遞體制的術語。其中，registered mail 是指在郵寄以及在路途各站 US Postal Service 都要作登記以保證其安全送達的郵件，應譯為「登記郵件」或「掛號信件」①。certified mail 則是指交信人為確保信件或郵件的送達而要求被送達人須簽署回執的一種郵遞方式，也被稱為 return receipt requested，故其應被譯為「回執信」或「回執郵件」②。

注

① "Type of special mailing privilege given by the US Postal Service for an extra and which provides insurance of its delivery up to certain amount." Cf. The Publisher's Editorial Staff, *Black's Law Dictionary*, Abridged 6th Edition, West Publishing Co. (1991), at P. 888.
② "Mail for which the sender requests proof of delivery in the form of a receipt signed by the addressee." Cf. Bryan A. Garner, *Black's Law*

Dictionary, 7ᵗʰ Edition, West Group (1999), at P. 963.

Rejection ▸ Revocation

二者均指在商貿活動中買方可以適用的一種對付所交付的產品是瑕疵產品時之救濟方法，其均爲美國《統一商法典》（Uniform Commercial Code）所確認。區別在於 rejection 是指如發現交付的產品與契約規定不相符合，即可拒絕接受（acceptance），當然，此種行爲必須在合理期限內作出，並應向賣方送達通知，故其爲「拒收貨物」[①]。而 revocation 則是指交付的貨物已經爲買方接收之後（after acceptance of the goods），如發現貨物確實具有「實質性影響其價值之瑕疵」（a defect substantially impairing the goods value），買方則可要求退回交付之商品（refusing to keep goods），同樣，此種退回必須在買方發現或應當發現瑕疵後的合理期限內進行（within a reasonable period after the buyer has discovered or should have discovered the defect[②]），故其稱爲「退貨」。

注

① "Rejection and revocation are two remedies available to the buyer under the Uniform Commercial Code after the delivery of defective goods. Goods may be rejected if they do not conform to the contract. The rejection must be made within a reasonable period after delivery, before the goods have been accepted, and notice of the rejection must be given to the seller." Cf. Linda Picard Wood, J.D., *Merriam Webster's Dictionary of Law*, Merriam-Webster, Incorporated, Springfield, Massachusetts (1996), at P. 417.

② *Id*. at P. 417.

Relevance ▸ Relevancy

　　二者均為證據的相關性。區別在於 relevance 為目前的流行用詞，而 relevancy 在 19 世紀時曾在英、美流行，但現在除蘇格蘭之外，其已經逐漸不再為人們所使用（Relevance is preferred in both American and British English. Relevancy was the predominant form in American and British writings on evidence of the 19th century, but now relevance is more common except in Scotland）。

注

Cf. Bryan A. Garner, *A Dictionary of Modern Legal Usage*, 2nd Edition, Oxford University Press Ltd. (1995), at P. 750.

Remedial action ▸ Removal action

　　二者均可指根據美國聯邦法律 Comprehensive Environmental Response, Compensation, and Liability Act of 1980（CERCLA）所採取的減輕和消滅污染之行為。區別在於 remedial action 旨在恢復長期環境質量（to effect long-term restoration of environmental quality），永久性減輕或消除有毒物質的排放，減少對公共健康和環境的危害，故為「長期補救恢復行為」[①]。而 removal action 之目的則是臨時減輕或清除污染，如有毒物質等，其為一種短期性行為（short term abatement and clear-up of pollution[②]），故其應為污染物的「臨時清除行為」。

注

① "An action intended to bring about or restore long-term environmental quality; esp., under CERCLA, a measure intended to permanently alleviate pollution when a hazardous substance has been released or might be released into the environment, so as to prevent or minimize any further release of hazardous substances and thereby minimize the risk to public health or to the environment." Cf. Bryan A. Garner, *Black's Law Dictionary*, 7th Edition, West Group (1999), at P. 1296.

② "An action, esp. under CERCLA, intended to bring about the short-term abatement and cleanup of pollution (as by removing and disposing of toxic materials)." *Id*. at P. 1298.

Remittance

Remittance（匯付）是國際貿易中的一種常見支付方式，其與託收（collection）同屬於商業信用，指買方按契約約定的條件和時間，將貨款透過銀行主動彙寄給賣方，其可分為三種不同的方法：(1) mail transfer（M/T），即「郵匯」，指買方將款項交與進口地銀行（his local bank），由其開具付款委託書（trust deed for payment），透過郵遞交賣方所在地往來銀行（correspondent bank），委託其向賣方付款；(2) telegraphic transfer（T/T），即「電匯」（有時也稱為 cable transfer），指進口地銀行應買方之申請用電報向出口地往來行發出付款委託書，委託其向賣方付款（At the request of the buyer, the local bank sends a trust deed for payment by cable directly to a correspondent bank at the seller's end and entrusts him to pay money to the seller①）；(3) demand draft（D/D），即「票匯」，指買方從進口地銀行購買銀行匯票郵寄給賣方，由賣方或其指定人持票從出口地相關銀行取款（The buyer buys a bank draft from his local bank and sends it by mail to the seller. On the basis of the above bank draft，the seller or his appointed person takes the money from the relative bank in his place②），中國外貿實踐中的匯付多採用 mail

R

transfer 和 telegraphic transfer。

注

① Cf. 吳林康，*The Mode of Payment in International Trade*，外語與教學研究出版社（1993），第 11 頁。
② *Id.* at P. 10.

Rendition ▸ Extradition

　　二者均有引渡逃犯的含義，區別在於，在美國 rendition 是指州際間逃犯的引渡，等同 interstate extradition，故爲「州際間的引渡」[①]。而 extradition 則既可用於指州際也可指國家之間對罪犯的引渡[②]。同理，rendition warrant 和 extradition warrant 也有如此區別，前者主要用於州際間引渡罪犯，故爲「州際引渡令」，而 extradition warrant 則可用於州際或國際間的引渡。

注

① "extradition of a fugitive who has fled to another state", Cf. Linda Pacard Wood, J.D., *Merriam Webster's Dictionary of Law*, Merriam-Webster, Incorporated (1996), at P. 421.
② "The official surrender of an alleged criminal by one state or nation to another having jurisdiction over the crime charged." Cf. Bryan A. Garner, *Black's Law Dictionary*, 7th Edition, West Group (1999), at P. 605.

Renewal ▸ Extension

　　二者都可用作指契約期限的延續，意思雖然相近，但卻有較大差異。主要差別在於 renewal 是指重新創制一種法律關係或用一新契約取代舊契約，而非僅僅延展先前的關係或契約（The recreation of a legal relationship or the replacement of an old contract with a new contract, as opposed to the mere extension of a previous relationship of contract[①]），故其為契約的重訂或續訂而非舊契約的展期（先前不少英漢詞典不加區別地將 renewal of a contract 或 to renew a contract 譯為契約的展期顯然是錯誤的[②]）。而 extension 則指同一契約延續一定規定期間的效力（the continuation of the same contract for a specified period[③]），故其才真正是契約的展期。同理，與 renewal 和 extension 相對應的動詞 renew 及 extend 與契約或契約等連用時也應各自區別，分別譯為契約的續簽及契約的展期。

注

① Cf. Bryan A. Garner, *Black's Law Dictionary*, 7th Edition, West Group (1999), at P. 1299.
② Cf. 《英漢法律詞典》，法律出版社（1999），第678頁；陳慶柏等譯，《英漢雙解法律詞典》，世界圖書出版社（1998），第471頁；陳谷孫，《英漢大詞典》，上海譯文出版社（1995年印刷），第2863頁。
③ Cf. Bryan A. Garner, *Black's Law Dictionary*, 7th Edition, West Group (1999), at P. 604.

R

Reparation ▶ Satisfaction

二者是國際法上的兩個術語，均有國際補償或國際賠償的含義[①]。實際上，reparation 是一總概念，指一個國家因違反國際義務或責任而被要求終止違法行為，以及在某些情況下要求予以賠償（A state that has violated an international obligation is required to terminate

the wrong act and to appropriate cases to make reparation.[2]），其包括
兩種形式，即狹義的 reparation 和 satisfaction。狹義的 reparation 的
目的主要在於回復原狀或物質損害的賠償（The purpose of reparation
is simply to restore preexisting conditions or to compensate for material
injury[3]），其可以是純粹的回復原狀（restitution pure or simple）或
損害賠償（pure damages）的形式賠償，也可以是部分回復原狀及
部分損害賠償金的形式賠償（it may consist partly of restitution and
partly of damages）。相比之下，satisfaction 則主要指道義或非物
質的賠償，如以道歉或修復外交關係等方式進行。即便有時給予金
錢，也不是像 reparation 那樣是對物質損害的賠償，而只是作爲對
過錯行爲的一種額外的道歉（Satisfaction is a term primarily applied
to compensation for the moral or non-material consequences of an act
for which a state is internationally responsible. Some of the common
forms satisfaction may take include apology or amends of a diplomatic
character.In some cases a pecuniary compensation is paid not as reparation
for a material wrong, but as an additional apology for the wrongful act
committed[4]）。

注

① Cf. 《英漢法律詞典》，法律出版社（1999），第 679、711 頁。
② Cf. Hugh M. Kindred, *International Law Chiefly as Interpreted and
Applied in Canada*, Emond Montgomery Publications Limited (1987),
at P. 626.
③ *Id.* at P. 626.
④ *Id.* at P. 626.

Reprieve ▸ Probation

二者均與刑罰的執行有關，但二者的區別甚大，儘管在法律詞典中它們都被譯為「緩刑」[1]。reprieve 是指暫時延期對刑事判決的執行，尤指對死刑的執行（temporary postponement of the execution of a criminal sentence），其本身不能算作是法院課處的刑罰，即：a court imposed criminal sentence，而只能是對刑罰的一種緩期執行[2]。中國給緩刑的定義是：對判處一定刑罰的犯罪分子，在具備法定條件下，附條件地不執行原判刑罰的一種制度[3]。如被判處拘役、3 年以下有期徒刑的罪犯，根據其犯罪情節和悔罪表現，認為適用緩刑確實不致再危害社會的，可處以緩刑。從此意義上講，reprieve 更多地類似中國的現行緩刑制度，即「人犯受刑罰宣告後於一定期限內附條件地暫緩執行」[4]，只是緩刑後所宣判的刑罰是否執行的條件多取決於罪犯的表現。而在國外，在 reprieve 後所宣判的刑罰之是否執行取決於罪犯的上訴或申辯。相比之下，在英美法系國家，probation 本身便是一種處刑（criminal sentence），指按特定條件，允許已被定罪的罪犯（convicted person）在被監視的狀態下釋放回到社會而非送進監獄的刑事判決，其也可指中止全部或部分判決，將罪犯放歸社會，視其表現情況再決定是否對其進行判決[5]。從嚴格意義上講，其均不是對一定刑期以下剝奪自由的刑罰的緩期執行，故其在概念上與中國的緩刑有本質上的差異。〔編者按：作者此處似有誤解，probation 照其說明應該較近似我們所認知的緩刑制度。〕

注

① Cf. 《英漢法律詞典》，法律出版社（1999），第 681、627 頁；賀衛方，《美國法律詞典》，中國政法大學出版社（1998），第 187、199 頁。

② "the postponement of execution of a criminal sentence by executive order.The classical situation for a reprieve occurs when a person is about to be put to death for a capital crime; a reprieve does not necessarily mean that the prisoner will not be executed, but it does give her some extra time to make arguments", Cf. James E. Clapp, *Random House Webster's Dictionary of the Law*, Random House (2000)，at P. 372.

③ Cf. 肖揚，《中國新刑法學》，中國人民公安大學出版社（1997），第 262 頁。

④「採司法制的又有兩種情況，一種是緩宣布，在一定期間內，如果沒有新罪就不再作有罪的判決；另一種是緩執行，人犯受刑罰宣告後於一定期限內附條件地暫緩執行。中國就是採取這種制度。」Cf. 張友漁，《中國大百科全書》法學卷，緩刑，中國大百科全書出版社（1984），第 288 頁。

⑤ "probation as a sentence in itself; the suspension of all or part of a sentence and its replacement by freedom subject to specific conditions and the supervision of a probation officer", Cf. Linda Pacard Wood, J.D., *Merriam Webster's Dictionary of Law*, Merriam-Webster, Incorporated (1996), at P. 386.

Respondentia ▶ Bottomry

二者均與海商法中的抵押貸款有關，區別在於，respondnetia 是指以船上貨物而非船舶作抵押，須等船貨安全抵達目的地再付還的貸款，如貨物損失不能抵達目的地，借款即不償還，故其為「船貨抵押貸款」①。而 bottomry 則指船主或船長在危難情況下借貸修理或遣送船舶，並用船的龍骨或底部作象徵，將船舶抵押以償還貸款的一種契約，如船舶沉沒，借款人則喪失借款，如船舶平安歸來，借款人方可收回貸款和利息，且可提起對物訴訟以實現其權利請求，故其爲「船舶抵押貸款」[2]。

注

① "A loan secured by the cargo on one's ship rather than the ship itself", Cf. Bryan A. Garner, *Black's Law Dictionary*, 7th Edition, West Group (1999), at P. 1313; "The hypothecation of goods or cargo on a ship to secure repayment of a loan." Cf. Daphne Dukelow, *The Dictionary of Canadian Law*, Thomson Professional Publishing Canada Ltd. (1991), at P. 924.

② "a contract under which the owner of a ship pledged the ship as a collateral for a loan to finance a journey", Cf. Linda Pacard Wood, J.D., *Merriam Webster's Dictionary of Law*, Merriam-Webster, Incorporated (1996), at P. 58; "The hypothecation or mortgage of a ship in which her bottom or keel is pledged." Cf. Daphne Dukelow, *The Dictionary of Canadian Law*, Thomson Professional Publishing Canada Ltd. (1991), at P. 105.

R

Restriction ▸ Restraint

二者均可用作指軍隊中的一種懲罰。restriction 可作爲非司法性懲罰由軍官予以科處或由軍事法庭科處，其爲「限制自由」，且主要是指限制道德及法律方面的自由而非人身自由，被懲罰者仍可完全履行其軍事職責[1]。相比之下，restraint 的情況則要嚴重得多，被處罰者的人身自由均受到限制，故其爲「軍事禁閉」[2]。

注

① "A deprivation of liberty involving moral and legal, rather than physical, restraint. A military restriction is imposed as punishment either by a commanding officer's non-judicial punishment or by a summary, special, or general court-martial. Restriction is a lesser restraint because it permits the restricted person to perform full military duties." Cf. Bryan A. Garner, *Black's Law Dictionary*, 7th Edition, West Group (1999), at P. 1317.

② "restraint: confinement, abridgement or limitation, prohibition of action", Cf. The Publisher's Editorial Staff, *Black's Law Dictionary*, Abridged 6th Edition, West Publishing Co. (1991), at P. 911.

Retaining fee ▸ Attorney fee

二者均可用作指與律師相關的費用。區別在於 retaining fee 指為聘請律師為自己進行法律事務代理而支付的費用，等同一種 deposit，故譯為「律師聘用定金」，其也稱為 retainer①。而 attorney fee 則是當事人因律師的法律服務而向其支付的費用，包括按鐘點支付的費用（hourly fee）、固定費用或勝訴費用等，其為「律師費」或「律師代理費」，其也稱為 attorney's fee②。

注

① "an initial fee paid to a lawyer upon being retained by a new client or for a new matter, usually viewed as a deposit on fees to be incurred", Cf. James E. Clapp, *Random House Webster's Dictionary of the Law*, Random House (2000), at P. 374; "A deposit paid by a client which represents part of the fee a lawyer charges for services." Cf. Daphne Dukelow, *The Dictionary of Canadian Law*, Thomson Professional Publishing Canada (1991), at P. 930.

② "The charge to a client for services performed for the client, such as an hourly fee, a flat fee, or a contingency fee." Cf. Bryan A. Garner,

Black's Law Dictionary, 7th Edition, West Group (1999), at P. 124.

Retaliation ▶ Reprisal ▶ Retorsion

　　三者均爲國際法上的報復行爲。retaliation（報復）爲通用語，指對過錯或傷害行爲進行的報復（the act of striking back for an injury or wrong, return of like for like[①]）。reprisal 和retorsion 則爲具體的兩種報復行爲。其中，retorsion（也拼寫爲 retortion）爲「反報」，主要是指針對某國家不禮貌、不友好、不正當或不公正但不一定是非法的行爲，用相同或類似的行爲所進行的合法報復，如中斷外交關係、驅逐其國民、限制他們的旅遊權利（An act of lawful retaliation in kind for another's unfriendly or unfair act. Examples of retorsion include suspending diplomatic relations, expelling foreign nationals, and restricting travel rights[②]），以及設置貿易壁壘等。而 reprisal 所指的報復行爲或手段則比 retorsion 激烈，常包括諸如捕獲船舶或扣押貨物，轟炸或占領他國領土，或扣押人員等，但不包括戰爭（An act of retaliation, usually of one nation against another but short of war; The use of force, short of war, against another country to redress an injury caused by that country.[③]）。過去不少詞典和學者都將 reprisal 譯爲「報復」，這樣一來便與 retaliation 的譯法雷同。筆者認爲既然 reprisal 是 an act of retaliation，而且 retorsion 也是一種 an act of lawful retaliation，現 retaliation 已經是報復，再將 reprisal 簡單譯爲「報復」似乎不妥。鑒於人們已經習慣稱 retorsion 爲「反報」，建議將 reprisal 譯爲「反擊」（中國在上世紀六、七〇年代進行的中越、中印邊界自衛反擊戰不就是一種很好的例證），以消除 reprisal 與 retaliation 的混淆。

R

注

① Cf. Gerard M. Dalgish, Ph.D., *Random House Webster's Dictionary of American English*, Random House, New York (1997), at P. 1102.

② Cf. Bryan A. Garner, *Black's Law Dictionary*, 7th Edition, West Group (1999), at P. 1318.

③ Cf. Bryan A. Garner, *A Dictionary of Modern Legal Usage*, 2nd Edition, Oxford University Press Ltd. (1995), at P. 759; Bryan A. Garner, *Black's Law Dictionary*, 7th Edition, West Group (1999), at P. 1305.

Revendication ▸ Replevin

二者均指為收復被他人非法持有的財產及其權益的訴訟。區別在於 revendication（收復產權之訴）是大陸法系（civil law）中的用語，而 replevin（索還動產之訴）則為普通法（common law）上的術語，且 replevin 多指動產的收復。

注

"In civil-law, *revendication* is an action to recovery rights in any possession of the property that is wrongfully held by another. This is analogous to the common-law *replevin*." Cf. Bryan A. Garner, *Black's Law Dictionary*, 7th Edition, West Group (1999), at P. 1319.

Right of rescission ▸ Right of termination

二者均是英國法律賦予當事人的一種救濟，即撤銷已經簽訂之契約的權利。區別在於 right of rescission（也稱為 right to rescind）為

「解約權」，指一方當事人因違反了非契約所規定的，即與契約相獨立的其他義務時給予契約另一方當事人的一種救濟權利[1]。而 right of termination（也稱爲 right to terminate）則爲「終止契約權」，指當一方當事人違反了契約直接規定的責任或義務時，契約另一方當事人擁有的終止該契約的權利[2]。

注

[1] "The remedy accorded to a party to a contract when the other party breaches a duty that arises independently of the contract." Cf. Bryan A. Garner, *Black's Law Dictionary*, 7th Edition, West Group (1999), at P. 1327.

[2] "The right to rescind is contrasted with a right of termination, which arises when the other party breaches a duty that arises under the contract." *Id.* at P. 1327.

Rout ▸ Riot

二者均有三人或三人以上非法集會以滋事的含義。它們的區別在於 rout 源於 route，指非法集會者 on their way，故其不一定實際實施了其旨在的犯罪，且其行進的方式也並非是 tumultuous manner[1]，因而不宜像有些詞典那樣將其視爲 riot 而譯爲「聚眾鬧事罪」或「騷擾罪」[2]，實際上該單詞應爲「聚眾前往鬧事罪」。riot 則指三人或多人非法集會以暴力威脅或恐嚇公眾之方式破壞治安，故爲「聚眾騷亂罪」或「暴亂罪」，按普通法規定其爲輕罪（misdemeanor）[3]。根據 1714 年透過的制定法，即 Riot Act，凡 12 人以上不法集會擾亂治安，警告後仍聚集 1 小時以上者則可視爲重罪（felony），可處以終身監禁（在剛透過該法時，其是 capital offense）[4]。

① "The word *rout* comes from the same source as word route. It signifies that three or more who have gathered together in unlawful assembly are on their way. It is not necessary for guilt of this offense that the design be actually carried out, nor that the journey be made in a tumultuous manner." Cf. Rollin M. Perkins & Ronald N. Boyce, *Criminal Law*, 3rd Edition, (1982), at P. 483.

② Cf. 《英漢法律詞典》，修訂本，法律出版社（1999），第 703 頁；陸谷孫，《英漢大詞典》，上海譯文出版社（1995），第 2973 頁。

③ "An unlawful disturbance of the peace by an assembly of usu. three or more persons acting with a common purpose in a violent or tumultuous manner that threatens or terrorizes the public." Cf. Bryan A. Garner, *Black's Law Dictionary*, 7th Edition, West Group (1999), at P. 1327.

④ *Id.* at P. 1327.

S

Salary ▸ Wage

二者均指定期支付給雇員（employee）的工錢。差別在於，salary通常指定期支付給白領階層（white-collar workers）或管理層人士（executives in managerial positions）的工資，多以年薪總數爲基礎，再以週、半月或月進行計算支付，如 an executive salary starting at $10,000 a year。相比之下，wage 則是技工、體力勞動以及勤雜服務等崗位工種的工資（earnings of skilled workers and on down the scale to manual and menial positions），多以週或半月薪金爲基礎，再以日、小時等計算支付，如 the high wages paid for skilled labor、a minimum hourly wage of $1.5 等。

注

"Generally, professional and clerical workers are paid salaries; factory, occasional workers, and those in the trades—plumbers, electricians, etc.—are paid wages." Cf. Laurence Urdang, *The Dictionary of Confusable Words*, Laurnece Urdang Inc. (1988), at P. 277.

Satisfaction ▸ Performance

二者均有清償債務的含義（fulfillment of an obligation）。區別在於 satisfaction（也稱爲 satisfaction of debt）多指給予債權人以某種替換或同等事物（a substitute for or equivalent of something）以期解除存在的法律或道德上的債務。而 performance（也稱爲 full performance）則是給予債權人所允諾的同一事物而非替換物（the identical thing promised to be done）。

注

"Satisfaction differs from performance because it is always something given as a substitute for or equivalent of something else, while performance is the identical thing promised to be done." Cf. Bryan A. Garner, *Black's Law Dictionary*, 7th Edition, West Group (1999), at P. 1343.

Sea law ▸ Law of the sea

　　二者很容易讓人誤解爲同一術語，即「海洋法」[①]，其實它們是兩個差別極大的概念。其中，sea law 應爲「海商法」而非「海洋法」，其也稱爲 maritime law、admiralty law 或 admiralty，指調整海洋貿易、航行、交通運輸等事務的法律（governing commerce and navigation, the transportation at sea of persons and property, and marine affairs in general），其規則涉及契約、侵權以及因海上貿易而產生的勞工賠償等事項[②]。而 law of the sea 才是「海洋法」，是國際法中調整各國使用和控制海洋以及海洋資源（governing how nations use and control the sea and its resources）的一整套法律[③]。

注

① 「sea law：海洋法」，Cf.《英漢法律詞典》，法律出版社（1999），第 715 頁；「law of the sea：海洋法」，*Id.* 第 445 頁。
② "The body of law governing commerce and navigation, the transportation at sea of persons and property, and marine affairs in general; the rules governing contract, tort, and workers' compensation claims arising out of commerce on or over water. Also termed

maritime law, admiralty; admiralty law." Cf. Bryan A. Garner, *Black's Law Dictionary*, 7th Edition, West Group (1999), at P. 982.

③ "a body of international law promulgated by United Nations convention and covering a range of ocean matters including territorial zones, access to and transit on the sea, environmental preservation, and the resolution of international disputes", Linda Pacard Wood, J.D., *Merriam Webster's Dictionary of Law*, Merriam-Webster, Incorporated (1996), at P. 282.

Selling agent ▸ Listing agent

　　二者均可用於指房地產銷售（或出租）經紀行所作僱用的代理人（real estate broker's agent）。他們在房地產買賣（或出租）業務中各司其職，相得益彰。listing agent 為「代理銷售登記人」，專門與欲出售（或出租）房地產的所有人（owner）打交道，與其簽署不動產代理銷售（或出租）協定（listing agreement）。代理人將為賣方以某種價格尋找並確定買主（或租戶），作為回報，賣方則向其支付一定費用或傭金[①]。而 selling agent 則為「不動產銷售代理人」，即是在 listing agent 所簽署的協議基礎上，專門尋找合適的買主以銷售房地產者[②]。

注

① "The real-estate broker's representative who sells the property, as opposed to the agent who lists the property for sale." Cf. Bryan A. Garner, *Black's Law Dictionary*, 7th Edition, West Group (1999), at P. 1365.

② "The real-estate broker's representative who obtains a listing agreement with the owner." *Id*. at P. 943.

Separation of powers ► Division of powers

在法律語言中，這兩個片語為完全不同的兩種概念。separation of powers 為「權力分立」或「三權分立原則」，指為了相互制約，政府的立法、司法和行政權力的相互分立（the constitutional allocation of the legislative, executive, and judicial powers among the three branches of government; the doctrine under which the legislative, executive, and judicial branches of government are not to infringe upon each other's constitutionally vested powers[1]）。而 division of powers 則為「權力分配」，指一些國家，尤其像美國這樣的聯邦制國家，聯邦政府和州政府之間權力的分配（The allocation of powers between the national government and the states[2]），如美國《聯邦憲法》第10修正案（The Tenth Amendment to the Constitution of the United States of America）規定："Powers not delegated to the federal government are reserved to the states or to the people"。

注

① Cf. Linda Pacard Wood, J.D., *Merriam Webster's Dictionary of Law*, Merriam-Webster, Incorporated (1996), at P. 451.

② Cf. Bryan A. Garner, *Black's Law Dictionary*, 7th Edition, West Group (1999), at P. 494.

Serf ► Slave

二者均用於指奴隸，但仍有一些區別。主要在於 serf（農奴）是指囿於本鄉本土（bound to the native soil）為主人勞作者[1]。而 slave 則是完全屬於奴隸主的一種財產（absolute property of a master），其甚至可被當作商品出賣他方[2]。

注

① "In the feudal polity, a class of persons whose social condition was servile, and who were bound to labor and perform onerous duties at the will of their lords. They differed from slaves only in that they were bound to their native soil, instead of being the absolute property of a master." Cf. The Publisher's Editorial Staff, *Black's Law Dictionary*, Abridged 6th Edition, West Publishing Co. (1991), at P. 952.

② "a person who is the legal property of another or others and is bound to absolute obedience; a human chattel", Cf. Della Thompson, *The Concise Oxford Dictionary*, 9th Edition, Oxford University Press (1995), at P. 1305.

Series bonds ▶ Serial bond

　　二者均可用於指擔保發行的債券，但極容易被人混淆為是同一種債券。事實上，series bonds 為「系列債券」或「分批發行的債券」，指按同一契約所發行，屬同一債務，但在不同時間上市，到期時間和利息也不同的一批債券[①]。相比之下，serial bond 則為「分批償還的債券」或「序列債券」，指一種同時發行，但到期時間卻各自不同的債券（a bond issued concurrently with other bonds having different maturity dates）[②]。

S

注

① "A group of bonds issued under the authority of the same indenture, but offered publicly at different times and with different maturity dates and interest rates." Cf. Bryan A. Garner, *Black's Law Dictionary*, 7th Edition, West Group (1999), at P. 174.

② "Bond issue consisting of a number of bonds with different maturity dates. Bonds are issued at the same time as distinguished from series bonds which are issued at different times." Cf. The Publisher's Editorial Staff, *Black's Law Dictionary*, Abridged 6th Edition, West Publishing Co. (1991), at P. 124.

Servitude

該單詞主要指大陸法系而非英美法系民法上的一種物權（servitude is primarily a civil-law term, deriving from Latin servitus①），其定義為：an encumbrance consisting in a right to the limited use of a piece of land without the possession of it 或 a charge or burden of an estate for another's benefit②，即我們所說的他物權或限制物權〔其也稱為用益物權（usufruct）〕，其對物的非所有人來說是一種有限的支配權，對物的所有人來說對其所有權的行使也是一種限制。值得注意的是 servitude 雖然等同普通法系的 easement（servitude is equivalent to the term easement in common law），但並非完全是easement，故不宜將其翻譯為「地役權」。普通法中，servitude 一般分為三類，即：easement（地役權）、license（特許權）和 profit（收益權）（The three types of servitudes are easements, licenses, and profits③）。easement 指需役地（dominant estate）所有人使用供役地（servient estate）所有人土地的權利，如在供役地所有人土地上的通行權或在供役地上修建道路、通訊線路等設施的多種權利，其屬於一種財產權利（an easement is a property right④）。license 指一種可撤銷的允諾（license is a revocable permission to commit some act that would otherwise be unlawful⑤），如讓被特許人進入特許人的土地從事原本屬於非法的活動，如打獵等，特許的範疇尚未達到lease 或 profit 的程度。與 easement 相比，license 多為口

頭允諾創立，而 easement 為書面；license 期限較短，而 easement 的期限較長；easement 的所有權可隨需役地所有權的變更而變更，而 license 則純粹是人身屬性的權利，不得被轉讓或出售。profit 則指在他人所有的土地上放牧、採礦、伐木等取走某些有價值的產物的權利（a servitude that gives the right to pasture cattle, dig for minerals, or otherwise take away some part of the soil[6]），其也稱為 profit *a predre* 或 right of common。

注

① Cf. Bryan A. Garner, *A Dictionary of Modern Legal Usage*, 2nd Edition, Oxford University Press Ltd. (1995), at P. 797.

② Cf. Bryan A. Garner, *Black's Law Dictionary*, 7th Edition, West Group (1999), at P. 1372.

③ *Id.* at P. 1772.

④ Cf. Bryan A. Garner, *A Dictionary of Modern Legal Usage*, 2nd Edition, Oxford University Press Ltd. (1995), at P. 303.

⑤ *Id.* at P. 303.

⑥ Cf. Bryan A. Garner, *Black's Law Dictionary*, 7th Edition, West Group (1999), at P. 1372.

S

Share ▶ Stock

　　二者均可指公司的股份或股票，兩個單詞常交替使用，通常情況差別不大。在美國，只在某些情況二者稍微有些差異，share 常指所有公司，包括 company 和 corporation 的股份，而 stock 則指 corporation 中的股份（請參看 company 和 corporation 的差別）。如一個 company 的股東可稱為 shareholder 或 shareowner，而一個 corporation 的股東則稱為 shareholder 或 stockholder，即 stockholder

不用在 company 中。此外，如兩單詞用在一起，share 更多的指股份，而 stock 則指股票，即一種證券①。在遇到將 share 改變爲 stock 的時候，則是指將公司股份轉爲上市公司的股票②。

注

① "Stock: A security which represents equity or ownership in a corporation. Stocks are an instrument used to bring savers and investors together, which is crucial for economic expansion. The most important right that an individual stockholder has is sharing in the corporation's earnings when dividends are declared." Cf. Douglas Greenwald, *The Concise McGraw-Hill Dictionary of Modern Economics*, 3rd Edition, McGraw-Hill Book Company (1984), at P. 333.

② "The company may by ordinary resolution passed at a general meeting convert any paid-up shares into stock and reconvert any stock into paid-up shares." Cf. 宋雷，《國際經濟貿易標準法律文書範本》，第 2 版，中國民主法制出版社（2003），第 323 頁。

Single condition ▶ Copulative condition ▶ Disjunctive condition

三者均指法律文件（如契約、遺囑等）中所約定或規定的要求履行某些行爲的條件。區別在於 single condition 指要求只履行一種特定的行爲，故爲「履行一種行爲的條件要求」①。copulative condition 指要求履行多項行爲，故爲「履行多項行爲的條件要求」②。disjunctive condition 則爲「履行多項行爲中的一項的條件要求」③。

① "A condition requiring the performance of a specified thing." Cf. Bryan A. Garner, *Black's Law Dictionary*, 7th Edition, West Group (1999), at P. 290.

② "A condition requiring the performance of more than one act." *Id.* at P. 289.

③ "A condition requiring the performance of one of several acts." *Id.* at P. 289; "Conditions may be single, copulative, or disjunctive. Those of the first kind require the performance of one specified thing only; those of the second kind require the performance of divers acts or things; those of the third kind require the performance of one of several things." Cf. The Publisher's Editorial Staff, *Black's Law Dictionary*, Abridged 6th Edition, West Publishing Co. (1991), at P. 203.

Sleegping partner ▶ Silent partner

二者均指合夥企業（firm）中的合夥人，其強調的重心不一，故不能譯為同一術語①。其主要差別在於，sleeping partner 強調的是合夥人與企業的合夥關係對公眾隱瞞，為公眾所不知（a partner whose connection with the firm is concealed from the public②），故其為「秘密合夥人」，其也稱為 secret partner。而 silent partner 則主要指僅出資分利益而不參與積極經營管理，至於其與企業的關係，儘管常常但並非一定不為公眾所知（a partner who shares in the profits but who has no active voice in management of the firm and whose existence is often not publicly disclosed）③，故其為「隱名合夥人」，也稱為 dormant partner。

① 現不少法律詞典將其混同為同一術語，如：「sleeping partner
（dormant, silent, partnership）隱名合夥人，隱名股東（指不參與
實際業務的股東）」，參見《英漢法律詞典》（1999），此種譯
法肯定是不對的。

② Cf. Bryan A. Garner, *Black's Law Dictionary*, 7th Edition, West Group
(1999), at P. 1142.

③ *Id.* at P. 1142.

Social guest

在侵權法（tort law）中，social guest（社交客人）是指以社交性
質目的進入他人的房地產區域者①。其可分為兩類：licensee（被許
可人）和 invitee（被邀請人），二者的區別在於主人（指房地產的
occupier）對他們各自承擔的義務不同。就 invitee（也稱為 business
guest、licensee with an interest）而言，房地產所有人（property
owner）或占有人有行使適當的注意（due care）以防範或告誡被
邀請人免受四周環境潛在危險傷害的義務②。invitee 應比 licensee
受到更多的保護及關照（he is placed upon a higher footing than a
licensee），典型範例如商店的顧客（the customer in a store）。而
就 licensee 而言，其進入領地只是為自己的目的而非為房地產所
有人的利益③，在以往，就被特許人而言，所有人只承擔不得有
意或魯莽傷害或危害的責任（a duty only to refrain from willfully or
recklessly injuring or endangering the guest）。現在，在多數司法管轄
區（jurisdiction），房地產所有人也具有告知其自己知道但被特許人
不知道的有關房地產四周潛在危險的義務④。美國有些司法管轄區對
social guest 未作 licensee 和 invitee 的區分，按規定，這些地區所有

的 social guest 均應被視爲具有 invitee 的地位[5]。

注

① "For purpose of determining landowner's duty of care, social guest is a person who goes onto property of another for companionship, diversion and enjoyment of hospitality and is treated as licensee." Cf. The Publisher's Editorial Staff, *Black's Law Dictionary*, Abridged 6th Edition, West Publishing Co. (1991), at P. 968.

② "A person who has an express or implied invitation to enter or use another's premises, such as a business visitors or a member of the public to whom the premises are held open. The occupier has a duty to inspect the premises and warn the invitee of dangerous condition." Cf. Bryan A. Garner, *Black's Law Dictionary*, 7th Edition, West Group (1999), at P. 833.

③ "One who has permission to enter or use another's premises, but only for one's own purposes and not for the occupier's benefit." *Id.* at P. 932.

④ Cf. The Publisher's Editorial Staff, *Black's Law Dictionary*, Abridged 6th Edition, West Publishing Co. (1991), at P. 635.

⑤ "A social guest can be either a licensee or an invitee. Some jurisdictions make no distinction, in effect categorizing all social guests as invitees, which means that the property owner is required to exercise due care in guarding or warning any social guest against injury. In other jurisdictions a social guest may be categorized as a licensee, in which case the property owner has a duty only to refrain from willfully or recklessly injuring or endangering the guest." Cf. Linda Pacard Wood, J.D., *Merriam Webster's Dictionary of Law*, Merriam-Webster, Incorporated (1996), at P. 459.

Solidarity liability ▸ Joint and several liability

　　二者均為「連帶責任」，指數人共同負責同一債務，而對債權人各負清償全部債務的義務，債權人可對債務人中的一人或數人直至全體同時或先後請求全部清償，如一個債務人清償全部債務，其他債務人也對原債權人免除責任，此時負責償還全部債務者有向其他債務人請求償還應分擔部分的權利①。solidarity liability（也稱為 liability in solid）和 joint and several liability 的主要區別在於前者為大陸法系（civil law）之術語，而後者則是英美法系（common law）中所適用的術語。同樣，solidarity obligation（連帶債務）也是羅馬法或大陸法系之術語，而相對的英美法系的術語則是 joint and several obligation②。

注

① "Liability that may be apportioned either among two or more parties or to only one or a few select members of the group, at the adversary's discretion." Cf. Bryan A. Garner, *Black's Law Dictionary*, 7th Edition, West Group (1999), at P. 926.

② "solidarity liability. *Civil law*. This is equivalent to joint and several liability in the common law." *Id*. at P. 926; "in the civil law of Louisiana: liability that is shared by obligators and that makes any one obligator liable for the entire obligation to the obligee but also apportions the liability among the obligators so that contribution is allowed." Cf. Linda Pacard Wood, J.D., *Merriam Webster's Dictionary of Law*, Merriam-Webster, Incorporated (1996), at P. 291.

Special partner ▸ Partner in commendam

二者均有特別合夥人的含義，指僅從合夥企業中分利潤，但不參與企業業務管理，其責任只限於自己的投資數額的合夥人[1]。二者的區別在於 special partner〔也稱為「有限責任合夥人」（limited partner）〕為英美法系（common law）中的用語，而partner in commendam 則是大陸法系（civil law）的用語[2]。同理，「特別合夥」或「有限責任合夥」，即 special partnership 或 limited partnership 也是英美法系之術語，而 partnership in commendam 則為大陸法系術語[3]。

注

[1] "A partner who receives profits from the business but does not take part in managing the business and is not liable for any amount greater than his or her original investment." Cf. Bryan A. Garner, *Black's Law Dictionary*, 7th Edition, West Group (1999), at P. 1142; "a partner in a venture who has no management authority and whose liability is limited to the amount of his or her investment", Cf. Linda Pacard Wood, J.D., *Merriam Webster's Dictionary of Law*, Merriam-Webster, Incorporated (1996)，at P. 352.

[2] "in civil law, termed partner in commendam", Cf. Bryan A. Garner, *Black's Law Dictionary*, 7th Edition, West Group (1999), at P. 1142.

[3] *Id*. at P. 1143.

Spin-off ▸ Split-off ▸ Split-up

三者均指美國公司的 D 重組（D reorganization）方法，即根據 Internal Revenue Code 第 368 條第 1 項第 1 款規定的 7 種公司重組方法中的第 4 種方法①。其中，spin-off（也稱爲 spin-off method）是指公司透過部分資產轉讓或出售而使一子公司獨立，然後將所獲得的該獨立之新公司的股份分派給自己的股東，而股東則不用將原持有之股份交出之方法，故稱爲「派股式重組」②。split-off 是指公司透過部分資產轉讓或出售而使一子公司獨立，然後用所持的該獨立之新公司的股份向自己的股東調換回其所持有的原公司的部分股份的方法，故稱爲「易股式重組」③。split-up 則是指公司的全部資產轉移，原公司分爲兩個或兩個以上的新公司，然後用新公司的股份調換回原公司股東所持有的所有原公司股份，原公司由此清算（liquidated）停業（go out of business），故稱爲「易股式分立」④。

注

① Cf. Linda Pacard Wood, J.D., *Merriam Webster's Dictionary of Law*, Merriam-Webster, Incorporated (1996), at P. 464.

② "A corporate divestiture in which a division of a corporation becomes an independent company and stock of the new company is distributed to the corporation's shareholders." Cf. Bryan A. Garner, *Black's Law Dictionary*, 7th Edition, West Group (1999), at P. 1409.

③ "The creation of a new corporation by an existing corporation that gives its shareholders stock in the new corporation in return for their stock in the original corporation." *Id.* at P. 1409.

④ "The division of a corporation into two or more new corporations. The shareholders in the original corporation typically receive shares in the new corporations, and the original corporation goes out of business." *Id.* at P. 1409.

Statement of income ▸ Balance sheet

二者之間的差別在於 statement of income（也稱爲 income statement、profit and loss statement、earnings report）爲「收益報表」，指反映一企業在特定期間的一切收入、開支、利潤和損失（all revenues, expenses, gains and losses）的財務情況報表[1]，即反映企業營業情況的經營報表（operating statement），主要在於反映特定時間內收益及損失之間的差額（the difference being the income or loss for the period[2]）。而 balance sheet（也稱爲 statement of financial condition、statement of condition、statement of financial position）爲「資產負債表」，指反映一實體目前財務狀況（financial position）的報表，說明實體的資產價值、債務以及所有人的股份（value of the entity's assets, liabilities, and owners' equity）等情況[3]。

注

[1] "A summary statement of the revenues and expenses of an enterprise for a given period." Cf. Douglas Greenwald & Associates, *The Concise McGraw-Hill Dictionary of Modern Economics*, 3rd Edition, Mcgraw-Hill Book Company (1984), at P. 275.

[2] Cf. The Publisher's Editorial Staff, *Black's Law Dictionary*, Abridged 6th Edition, West Publishing Co. (1991), at P. 842.

[3] "A statement of a firm's financial position on a particular day of the year; as of that moment, it provides a complete picture of what the firm owns (its assets), what it owes (its liabilities), and its net worth. The balance sheet should not be confused with the income statement, which is a record of a year's operation." Cf. Douglas Greenwald & Associates, *The Concise McGraw-Hill Dictionary of Modern Economics*, 3rd Edition, Mcgraw-Hill Book Company (1984), at P. 20.

S

Statute of limitation ▸ Statute of repose

　　二者均與時效有關。儘管 statute of limitation（訴訟時效法）有時也可被稱為「statute of repose」（時效休眠法）[1]，但 statute of limitation 與所涉及的訴訟時效與傷害（after injury occurs）有關，按其規定，在傷害發生後一特定期間內如不起訴則會喪失訴權[2]。而 statute of repose 則與傷害無關，按其規定，不論是否有傷害發生（regardless of whether there has yet been an injury），只要超過某一特定時間，任何訴權便將終止[3]。

注

① "While statutes of limitation are sometimes called statutes of repose…" Cf. The Publisher's Editorial Staff, *Black's Law Dictionary*, Abridged 6th Edition, West Publishing Co. (1991), at P. 639.

② "The statute establishing a time limit for suing in a civil case, based on the date when the claim accrued (as when the injury occurred or was discovered)." Cf. Bryan A. Garner, *Black's Law Dictionary*, 7th Edition, West Group (1999), at P. 1122.

③ "Statute of limitation bars right of action unless it is filed within a specified period of time after injury occurs, while *statute of repose* terminates any right of action after a specific time has elapsed, regardless of whether there has as yet been an injury." Cf. The Publisher's Editorial Staff, *Black's Law Dictionary*, Abridged 6th Edition, West Publishing Co. (1991), at P. 639.

Stipulation ▸ Provision

　　二者均可譯為「規定」，區別主要在於 stipulation 的嚴格意義本應爲「約定」，指當事人經協商達成的約定性規定，故一般都用作指條約、協議或契約中的規定而非法律法規等中非約定性的規定（或約定）（A material condition or requirement in an agreement, esp., a factual representation that is incorporated into contract as a term[①]），如：breach of the stipulation of the contract（違反契約規定）。如將其用於法律中，如：the stipulations of the Environment Act，則應屬於一種錯誤用法。相比之下，provision 的適用範圍則較廣，其既可指契約中屬於約定性的條款規定，又可指法律或法規中屬於強制性的條款規定[②]。

注

① Cf. Bryan A. Garner, *Black's Law Dictionary*, 7th Edition, West Group (1999), at P. 1427.

② "provision: a stipulation (as a clause in a statute or contract) made beforehand", Cf. Linda Pacard Wood, J.D., *Merriam Webster's Dictionary of Law*, Merriam-Webster, Incorporated (1996), at P. 394: "In a legal document, a clause.", Cf. Daphne A. Dukelow, *The Dictionary of Canadian Law*, A Carswell Publication (1991), at P. 845.

Strict construction ▶ Strict interpretation

二者均指法律的解釋方法，其區別在於 strict construction 主要指法官在適用法律或其他法律文本時對這些文件嚴格按照字面或文字的含義，而非按其他淵源之解釋，故爲「嚴格解釋」[①]，其也稱爲 strict constructionism（嚴格解釋主義）、literal canon（字面解釋準則）、literal rule（字面解釋規則）或 textualism（文本主義）。而 strict interpretation 可指對法學著述等的解釋說明，其範疇更窄，局限於表明原作者的本意（which governs the ascertainment of the meaning of the maker of instrument），故爲「嚴格闡釋」或「狹義闡釋」[2]。

注

① "construction of a statute or constitutional provision that focuses on the specific words used and tends to reject application to circumstances not clearly within the ordinary meaning of those words", Cf. James E. Clapp, *Random House Webster's Dictionary of the Law*, Random House, Yew York (2000), at P. 102.

② Cf. The Publisher's Editorial Staff, *Black's Law Dictionary*, Abridged 6th Edition, West Publishing Co. (1991), at P. 265.

Structure of an act

該術語爲「法律結構」，指議會或立法機關制定的法律的形式結構。一般說來，按先後順序，一部法律的形式結構可包括 short title、long title、preamble、enacting formula、short title clause、extent clause、commencement clause、application section、definition section、arrangement of act generally、the main part，the general part、the miscellaneous part、schedule[1]等部分。其中，因 short title 被譯爲「簡稱」，並與 long title 相對，常使人誤認爲 long title 是正式名稱，而 short title 則是其省略稱呼，如誤認爲《聯邦民事訴訟法》（Federal Act of Civil procedure）是 long title，而其 short title 則應是民事訴訟法或訴訟法。實際上 short title 是立法的「簡短名稱」，指的是其正式名稱，而 long title 是對立法總體內容的簡要說明（It gives an idea of what the Act proposes to deal with in a nutshell.），如 the US Succession Act（《聯邦繼承法》）是該立

法的 short title，該法的 long title 是 "An Act to consolidate the law applicable to interstate and testamentary succession"。而 preamble 則與 long title 近似，上述《聯邦繼承法》的 Preamble 為："Whereas it is expedient to consolidate the law applicable to intestate and testamentary succession[②]"。在現在的立法中，long title 和 preamble 常被省略。

注

① Cf. S. N. Jain, *The Drafting of Laws*, N. M. Tripathi (P) Ltd. Institute (1981), at P. 40.
② *Id.* at P. 40.

(the) Supreme Court of England and Wales

其為「英格蘭和威爾士最高司法法院」。英格蘭和威爾士最高司法法院由高等法院（the High Court）、刑事法院（the Crown Court）以及上訴法院（the Court of Appeal）組成。其中，高等法院最複雜，其又由三個法院組成：大法官法院（the Chancery Division）、王（或女王）座法院（the King's/Queen's Bench Division）和家事法院（the Family Division）。而大法官法院又包括公司法庭（the Companies Court）和專利法庭（the Patents Court）；王座法院則包括海事法庭（the Admiralty Court）和商業法庭（the Commercial Court）。

注

"The High Court is one of tree constituent courts going to make up the Supreme Court of England and Wales (the other two courts are the Crown Court and the Court of Appeals). The High Court itself comprises three divisions: (i) the Chancery Division (which includes the Companies Court and the Patents Court); (ii) the Queen Bench Division (which includes the Admiralty Court and the Commercial Court); and (iii) the Family Division." Cf. John O'Hare & Robert N. Hill, *Civil Litigation*, 5th Edition, Longman Group UK Ltd (1990), at P. 3.

T

Tax avoidance ▶ Tax evasion ▶ Tax dodge

前兩者均用於指設法少交或不交賦稅，但從法律角度上看二者差異很大。tax avoidance 爲「避稅」，即「規避納稅」，指納稅人利用一切合法手段，如鑽稅法的漏洞，儘量減少應稅款額，以達到少繳或不繳稅的目的。總的說來，其屬於法律允許範圍內的活動（trying legally to minimize the amount of tax to be paid[①]）。而 tax evasion 則爲「偷稅」或「漏稅」，多指以隱瞞不報或少報收入等方式以達到少繳稅的目的，其也稱爲「納稅欺詐」（tax fraud[②]），爲非法行爲，爲民法和刑律所不容（The willful attempt to defeat or circumvent the tax law in order to illegally reduce one's tax liability. The tax evasion is punishable by both civil and criminal penalties[③]）。一句話，二者的差異在於 tax avoidance 是合法行爲，而 tax evasion 是非法行爲：「The difference between these phrases is the difference between what is legal (avoidance) and what is not (evasion)[④]」。至於 tax dodge（逃稅），其也屬於非法行爲，等同 tax evasion，但它一般不屬於很正式的法律用語。

注

① Cf. P. H. Collin, *Dictionary of Law*, Peter Collin Publishing (1993), at P. 542.

② "tax fraud: the crime of intentionally filling a false return or making other false statements under penalties of perjury to taxing authorities." Cf. James E. Clapp, *Random House Webster's Dictionary of the Law*, Random House, New York (2000), at P. 425.

③ Cf. Bryan A. Garner, *Black's Law Dictionary*, 7ᵗʰ Edition, West Group (1999), at P. 1474.

④ Cf. Bryan A. Garner, *A Dictionary of Modern Legal Usage*, 2ⁿᵈ Edition, Oxford University Press Ltd. (1995), at P. 868.

Tax credit ▸ Tax deduction ▸ Tax exemption

前兩者都有減少納稅金額的含義。區別在於 tax credit（稅額直接減讓）是指在計算出某人應付稅額之後，從其總額中扣除按規定應予減讓部分的款額，減 25 元則少 25 元稅費。而 tax deduction（稅額間接減讓）則是指在計算納稅稅額之前從某人的總收入（gross income）中減除某些款額，如在計算應稅所得時在總收入中減去業務支出、生產成本等，然後再根據由此計算出的應稅所得計算稅額，減 25 元則不會直接少 25 元稅費。由此，從某種意義上講，tax credit 的價值應高於 tax deduction 的價值①。tax exemption 則是「免稅」，其是按人頭（on a per capita basis）減免的稅收，與 tax credit 和 tax deduction 差異較大②。

注

① "A credit differs from a deduction in the following essential respect: It is subtracted after the total tax liability has been calculated, whereas a deduction is subtracted from the income subject to tax. Thus, a tax credit of a given amount is more valuable to a tax payer than a deduction of the same amount." Cf. Douglas Greenwald, *The Concise McGraw-Hill Dictionary of Modern Economics*, 3ʳᵈ Edition, McGraw-Hill, Inc. (1983), at P. 348; "tax credit: An amount subtracted directly from one's total liability, dollar for dollar, as opposed to a deduction from gross income", Cf. Bryan A. Garner, *Black's Law Dictionary*, 7ᵗʰ

Edition, West Group (1999), at P. 1473.

② Cf. Douglas Greenwald, *The Concise McGraw-Hill Dictionary of Modern Economics*, 3rd Edition, at P. 350.

Testament ▸ Will ▸ Devise

三者均有「遺囑」的含義。其中，will 是一般用語，指立遺囑人按照法律規定的方式處分遺產或其他事務並於其死亡時發生效力的行為，其所處分的遺產既可以是不動產也可以是動產[①]。testament作為「遺囑」時有兩種用法，一是為一般用語，此時其等於 will；二是和 devise 相對應，作為特別用語，此時它們的區別在於 testament 是作為「處分動產的遺囑」（a will disposing of personal property[②]），而 devise 則指「處分不動產的遺囑」（a will disposing real property[③]），或指「遺囑中處分不動產的條款」（a clause in a will disposing of property and esp. real property[④]）。

注

① "An instrument, executed with the formalities of state statutes, by which a person makes a disposition of his real and personal property, to take effect after his death, and which by its own nature is ambulatory and revocable during his life time", Cf. Publisher's Editorial Staff, *Black's Law Dictionary*, Abridged 6th Edition, West Publishing Co. (1991), at P. 1102.

② Cf. Bryan A. Garner, *Black's Law Dictionary*, 7th Edition, West Group (1999), at P. 1484.

③ *Id.* at P. 463.

④ Cf. Linda Pacard Wood, J.D., *Merriam Webster's Dictionary of Law*, Merriam-Webster, Incorporated (1996), at P. 138.

Theft ▸ Pilferage

二者均有偷竊的含義，區別在於 pilferage 多指「輕微偷竊行為」，所竊盜的錢財數額較少（stealing small sum of money or small items[①]）；而theft則指「竊盜罪」（crime of stealing），為重罪性質（felonious taking and removing of another's personal property with the intent of depriving the true owner of it[②]）。在海上保險領域中，包裝完善的貨物整件被偷為 theft，從整件包裝物中竊取部分貨物則稱為 pilferage[③]。

注

① Cf. P. H. Collin, *Dictionary of Law*, Peter Collin Publishing (1993), at P. 406.

② Cf. Bryan A. Garner, *Black's Law Dictionary*, 7th Edition, West Group (1999), at P. 1486.

③ Cf. 陳初柏，《英漢商業大辭典》, 條目 *theft and pilferage*，中國商業出版社（1994），第1513頁。

Third party ▸ Outside party ▸ Joint party ▸ Proper party ▸ Impleaded party ▸ third party defendant ▸ Intervenor

以上術語均有訴訟中的「第三人」的含義。其中，third party（也稱為 outside party）為「第三人」，泛指參與訴訟但不屬於主要當事人（principal party）的人[①]。按英、美程序法的規定，原告或被告均可按法定規則以 joinder（訴訟合併或訴訟主張合併）的形式，使一個原本不屬於本訴當事人的第三人成為本訴的共同原告或共同被告。此外，第三人也可自願以 joinder 的形式參與訴訟，即成為本訴的共同原告或被告[②]。一般說來，用 joinder 形式參與訴訟的第三人都可被稱爲 joint party（共同當事人）。其中，可以被原告以合併方式使其參與訴訟的第三人又被稱爲 proper party（適合參與訴訟的當事人）③。此外，被告爲保護自己的利益，可用 impleader 的方式，對原本不是本訴被告的第三人進行起訴，使之成爲本訴的共同被告。這種因被告指控而參與訴訟的第三人則被稱爲 impleaded party（被控參與訴訟的第三人）或 third party defendant（作爲被告的第三人）④。自願以 joinder 的形式參與訴訟的第三人稱爲 intervenor，其應當等同中國法律中的「具有獨立請求權的第三人」⑤。intervenor 參與訴訟的形式被稱爲 intervention。

注

① "Someone other than the principal parties, also termed outside party." Cf. Bryan A. Garner, *Black's Law Dictionary*, 7th Edition, West Group (1999), at P. 1489.

② "Various rules exist governing who may be joined by the plaintiff in a lawsuit, who may be added to the lawsuit by the defendant or who may enter a lawsuit of their own volition." Cf. Mary Kay Kane, *Civil procedure*, West Group (1999), at P. 114; "Joinder: A joining of parties as co-plaintiffs or codefendants in a suit." Cf. Linda Picard Wood, J.D., *Merriam Webster's Dictionary of Law*, Merriam-Webster,Incorporated (1996), at P. 266.

③ "The term property parties refers to those persons whom the plaintiff may join as parties to the action when it is commenced." Cf. Mary Kay Kane, *Civil procedure*, West Group (1999), at P. 114.

④ "In order to provide defending parties an opportunity to more fully protect themselves, most procedural systems provide some mechanism by which the defendant can bring in (implead) a third party defendant (impleaded party)." *Id.* at P. 116.

⑤ "An intervenor is a person who is not already a party to an ongoing action but who seeks to be made a party, typically because she shares some interest in the litigation and is concerned that in her absence that interest will not be adequately protected." *Id*. at P. 118.

Torment ▶ Torture

　　二者均有身體或精神上的「折磨」的含義。相比之下，torment 主要指長期和反覆的精神上的痛苦或煩惱（*Torment* suggests mental suffering. It hints at repeated or continuous instances of attacks[1]），如 the torments of an alcoholic husband（酗酒丈夫造成的長期的精神折磨）。而 torture 則指爲懲罰、逼供或獲得施虐快感而對他人身體或精神造成的痛苦（The infliction of intense pain to the body or mind to punish, to extract a confession or information, or to obtain sadistic pleasure[2]），且主要強調的是實施或導致折磨或痛苦的人或事（*Torture* puts great stress upon the agent which causes or inflicts it[3]），如 The Madman indulged in the torture of his victims before he killed them（該精神變態者喜歡在殺害受害人之前對他們進行折磨）。

注

① Cf. The Editors of the Reader's Digest, *Use the Right Word*, The Reader's Digest Association Proprietory Ltd. (1971), at P. 373.

② Cf. Bryan A. Garner, *Black's Law Dictionary*, 7th Edition, West Group (1999), at P. 1498.

③ Cf. The Editors of the Reader's Digest, *Use the Right Word*, The Reader's Digest Association Proprietory Ltd. (1971), at P. 373.

Transfer ▸ Assignment ▸ Conveyance ▸ Negotiation

以上單詞均有「轉讓」的含義。transfer 為通用術語，可泛指用一切方式（甚至包括遺贈）轉讓各種物品，包括財產及其所有的權益、票據或單據等[①]。assignment 多為民法或契約法上的債權「讓與」，且常指轉讓無體財產的權利，如：assignment of a contract、assignment of account、assignment of dower、assignment of income、assignment of lease、assignment of wages 等[②]。conveyance 多指不動產，如土地物權（title）等的轉讓，其也包括土地其他權利的轉讓或租賃（lease）、按揭（mortgage）或抵押（encumbrance），但不包括遺贈[③]。與該單詞相關的詞 conveyancer 也由此指專門從事不動產轉讓業務之律師（參見 lawyer）。negotiation 常指票據法上的權利轉讓，即票據之「流通」，最大特點是受讓人可不受前手產權瑕疵的影響[④]。

注

① "An act of the parties, or of the law, by which the title to property is conveyed from one person to another. The sale and every other method, direct or indirect, of disposing or parting with property or with an interest therein, or with the possession thereof, or of fixing a lien upon property or upon an interest therein, absolutely or conditionally, voluntarily or involuntarily, by or without judicial proceedings, as a conveyance, sale, payment, pledge, mortgage, lien, encumbrance, gift, security or otherwise. The word is one of general meaning and may include the act of giving property by will…Transfer is the all-encompassing term used by the Uniform Commercial Code to describe the act which passes an interest in an instrument to another." Cf. The Publisher's Editorial Staff, *Black's Law Dictionary*,

Abridged 6ᵗʰ Edition, West Publishing Co. (1991), at P. 1041.

② "transfer of an interest, right or duty", Cf. James E. Clapp, *Random Webster's Dictionary of the Law*, Random House, New York (2000), at P. 38.

③ "In its most common usage, transfer of title to land from one person, or class of persons, to another by deed." Cf. The Publisher's Editorial Staff, *Black's Law Dictionary*, Abridged 6ᵗʰ Edition, West Publishing Co. (1991), at P. 232; "transfer of an interest in property, especially real estate, by means of a deed or other instrument other than a will", Cf. James E. Clapp, *Random Webster's Dictionary of the Law*, Random House, New York (2000), at P. 107; "In law, the noun conveyance refers not only to the actual transfer of an interest in land, but also to the document (usually a deed) by which the transfer occurs." Cf. Bryan A.Garner, *A Dictionary of Modern Legal Usage*, 2ⁿᵈ Edition, Oxford University Press Ltd. (1995), at P. 221.

④ "The transfer of an instrument by delivery or endorsement whereby the transferee takes it for value, in good faith, and without notice of conflicting title claims or defenses." Cf. Bryan A. Garner, *Black's Law Dictionary*, 7ᵗʰ Edition, West Group (1999), at P. 1059.

Transportation ▸ Banishment ▸ Exile ▸ Deportation

　　上述單詞均有「流放」或「放逐」的含義,均為刑法上的一種刑罰。其區別在於 transportation 是英國舊時的一種刑罰,其所指的流放是罪犯不僅要被迫離開國家,而且是要被流放出境到一個具體指定的地方,多如美洲或澳大利亞的流放地(penal colony)等①。而 banishment 和 exile 則僅是將罪犯強制從其祖國或其長期居住地區驅逐到國外或國內某一邊遠地區而非具體之地點,其也是古時的刑罰，現在已經幾乎不再適用，兩者意思幾乎相當[②]。以上三個術語用於國民，而 deportation（驅逐出境）則是指將違法犯罪而不受歡迎的「外國人」（alien）而非國民驅逐出境[③]。

注

① "Transportation is usually distinguished from banishment or exile in that the criminal subject to the edict was not merely obliged to leave the country, but sentenced to be transported to a specific place.", Cf. James E. Clapp, *Random House Webster's Dictionary of the Law*, Random House, New York (2000), at P. 433.

② "exile: Expulsion from a country, esp. from the country of one's origin or longtime residence; banishment", Cf. Bryan A. Garner, *Black's Law Dictionary*, 7th Edition, West Group (1999), at P. 595.

③ "The removal under *Immigration Act* of a person from any place in Canada to the place whence he came to Canada or to the country of his nationality or citizenship or to the country of his birth or to such country as may be approved by the Minister under this Act." Cf. Daphne A. Dukelow, B.Sc., LL.B., LL.M., *The Dictionary of Canadian Law*, Thomson Canada Ltd. (1991), at P. 272.

Treason ▸ Felony ▸ Misdemeanor ▸ Summary offense

　　以上是英國刑法上傳統的四大犯罪分類（English criminal law has been classified as "treason, felony and misdemeanor" with a tentative fourth class described as "summary offense" [①]）。也有人將 summary offense 歸類於輕罪，認為它是輕罪的一個亞類。在美國，前三種犯罪的分類與英國相同，只是 summary offense 被有些人稱為 petty offense，即「簡易程序審判罪」，其完全等同 summary offense。在

這四種犯罪中，treason 為「叛國罪」，指以發動戰爭或勾結外敵之手段，陰謀危害國家主權、領土完整和安全，推翻國家政府的犯罪行為（The offense of attempting to overthrow the government of the state to which one owns allegiance, either by making war against the state or by materially supporting its enemies[2]）。treason 被視為最嚴重的犯罪之一，一般都處以重刑，也稱為 high treason、*alta proditio*。felony 為「重罪」，指最少處一年，最高刑可處以死刑（如在美國的路易斯安那州），且在普通法上可並處沒收其財產的嚴重犯罪，其最初甚至包括 treason，現主要包括諸如 murder、rape、arson、burglary 等犯罪，也稱為 major crime 和 serious crime[3]。misdemeanor 曾用於指除 treason 和 felony 之外的所有犯罪，misdemeanor 與 felony 適用之實體法原則和程序法原則曾一度差別極大，對 misdemeanor 的處罰多以 fine、penalty、forfeiture 或處短期監禁等（關押之場所為 jail 而非 prison）。在美國，其也稱為 minor crime 或 summary offense （而 summary offense 則被稱為 petty offense，參見上文）。相比之下，summary crime 則為「簡易程序審理之犯罪」，被稱為是從 misdemeanor 中劃分出的一種試驗性的分類（a tentative fourth class described as "summary offenses"，從上文可知，其原屬於misdemeanor 範疇），指因罪行較輕，而不用大陪審團之訴狀（indictment）即可起訴之犯罪（故程序可簡化），因此其不屬於 indictable 之犯罪。

注

① Cf. Li Rong fu/Song Lei, *A Course Book of Legal English*, Law Press, China (1999), at P. 10.
② Cf. Bryan A. Garner, *Black's Law Dictionary*, 7th Edition, West Group (1999), at P. 1506.
③ *Id.* at Ps. 633, 1506.

Trover ▶ Detinue

二者均是與動產被他人非法占有相關的普通法上的訴訟。區別在於 detinue 是指因動產為被告非法扣留而要求索回原財產之訴（a common law action for the recovery of personal property belonging to the plaintiff that is wrongfully detained by the defendant[①]）。而 trover（追索非法占用財產之訴）則指因財產被非法占用而要求得到原財產價值數量之補償，而非原物本身[②]，其也稱為 trover and conversion。

注

① Cf. Linda Pacard Wood, J.D., *Merriam Webster's Dictionary of Law*, Merriam-Webster, Incorporated (1996), at P. 137.

② "A common law action for the recovery of damages for the conversion of personal property, the damages generally being measured by the value of the property", Cf. Bryan A.Garner, *Black's Law Dictionary*, 7th Edition, West Group (1999), at P. 1513; "trover is an ancient French word meaning an action originally lay only against a person who happened upon property belonging to another and kept it for his own use instead of giving it back to its owner", Cf. James E. Clapp, *Random House Webster's Dictionary of the Law*, Random House, New York (2000), at P. 437.

Tutor ▶ Curator

二者均有「監護人」的含義。其區別在於 tutor 多在大陸法中指未成年人的監護人[①]，而 curator 可用在普通法中，指很久之前對已經達到 full age 和具有一切權利之人（尤指 males，稱為 a person who is *sui juris*）的臨時監護人[②]；在大陸法中，curator 則同樣可指對未成年人，即 minor 有監護權的監護人，只是其監護的對象已經到達一定年齡段，其所負的責任與 tutor 也有一定差異③。此外，其還指法院指定的對外出而不在住所或居所者（absentee）的財產之監管人④。

注

① "tutor: Civil Law. A guardian of a minor; a person appointed to have the care of the minor's person and estate." Cf. Bryan A. Garner, *Black's Law Dictionary*, 7th Edition, West Group (1999), at P. 1521.

② "One of the old monuments of Roman legislation placed all free males who were of full years and rights under the temporary control of new class of guardians, called *curators*." Cf. Henry S. Maine, Ancient Law, 17th Edition, 1909, at P. 134.

③ "The guardian of a minor past a certain age is called a curator and has duties somewhat different from these of a tutor." Cf. Bryan A. Garner, *Black's Law Dictionary*, 7th Edition, West Group (1999), at P. 1521.

④ "a person appointed to take care of the estate of an absentee", Cf. The Publisher's Editorial Staff, *Black's Law Dictionary*, Abridged 6th Edition, West Publishing Co. (1991), at P. 265.

U

Unfair dismissal ▶ Wrongful dismissal

二者在英國均是指雇主對雇員的解雇。區別在於 unfair dismissal（非公正解雇）是指無理解雇員工，如員工擬參加工會等[1]。wrongful dismissal（錯誤解雇）則雖然有解雇理由，但理由並非公正，而是一種違約行為[2]。就 unfair dismissal 而言，被解雇之雇員可向勞資爭議法庭（industrial tribunal）投訴；至於 wrongful dismissal，被解雇者可向郡法院（county court）投訴。

注

[1] "Removing someone from a job by an employer who appears not to be acting in a reasonable way (i.e.), as by dismissing someone who wants to join a union." Cf. P. H. Collin, *Dictionary of Law*, Peter Collin Publishing (1993), at P. 176.

[2] "Removing someone from a job for a reason which does not justify dismissal and which is in breach of the contract of employment." *Id.* at P. 176.

United States attorney ▶ District attorney

二者均是指美國地區（或地方，即 district）的檢察官。其區別在於 United States attorney 是指由總統任命的 lawyer，在刑事（或民事）案件中代表聯邦政府在聯邦司法地區（federal judicial district）進行檢控或擔任其他職責，其也稱為 United States District Attorney[1]，故譯為「美國聯邦地方檢察官」。而 district attorney

則指經任命或選舉的公共官員,代表州政府在特定的司法地區在刑事案件中作檢控,故譯爲「州地方檢察官」(a public official appointed or elected to represent the state in criminal cases in a particular judicial district[2]),也稱爲 public prosecutor、state's attorney、prosecuting attorney 等。實際上,在美國,檢察官的通用詞爲 public prosecutor,其分爲聯邦和州兩個體系,聯邦系統的 prosecutor 稱爲 United States attorney,而州體系的則稱爲 district attorney,而「檢察長」則稱爲 Attorney General,也分爲州檢察長(attorney general of a state)和聯邦政府的檢察長(attorney general of the United States)。目前有些法律詞典只將 district attorney 簡單譯爲(美)地方檢察官(又譯地區檢察官)[3],容易使讀者將該術語誤認爲是「聯邦地方檢察官」。在英國及威爾士,警方有 prosecutor 的作用,可用 information 提起刑事指控,其行爲應在檢察長的諮詢意見(advise)下進行。此外政府各部門或地方當局內的司法機構也可進行檢控(...many thousands of cases yearly are instituted by government departments and local authorities who have their own legal departments[4])。檢察長稱爲 director of public prosecutions,其一般由資歷在十年的沙律師或巴律師擔任,由內政大臣(appointed by the Home Secretary)任命,負責決定對疑難或嚴重犯罪的刑事指控,受制於總檢察長(Barrister General)或副總檢察長(Solicitor General)。

注

① Cf. Bryan A. Garner, *Black's Law Dictionary*, 7th Edition, West Group (1999), at P. 1533.

② *Id.* at P. 489.

③ 《英漢法律詞典》,法律出版社(1999),第248頁。

④ Cf. Li Rong-fu/Song Lei, *A Course Book of Legal English*, Law Press, China (1999), at P. 11.

Unlivery ► Unloading

二者均有卸貨的含義。區別在於 unlivery 是海商法（maritime law）中的專門術語，指船舶等到達貨運目的地後之卸貨（unloading of cargo at its intended destination[①]），因而嚴格講它應譯為「目的地卸貨」。相比之下，unloading 為一般術語而非嚴格的法律術語，其與「裝貨」（loading）相對，僅指「卸貨」（除 freight 外還可包括 passenger），並非一定指是在運輸的終點卸貨[②]。

注

① Cf. Bryan A. Garner, *Black's Law Dictionary*, 7th Edition, West Group (1999), at P. 378.

② "removal of load from (a vehicle)", Cf. Della Thompson, *The Concise Oxford Dictionary*, 9th Edition, Oxford University Press (1995), at. P. 1532.

Utility ► Nonobviousness ► Novelty

三者指美國等西方專利法（patent law）所規定的申請專利的三大基本要件（three basic requirements of patentability[①]）。其中，utility 為「實用性」，指能夠履行要求作為知識產權保護之發明主張的功能或達到其效果（Capacity to perform a function or attain a result claimed for protection as intellectual property[②]）。nonobviousness 為「非顯而易見性」，指發明必須不同於先前的技術，對發明領域具有通常技術的人而言其必須是非顯而易見的（The requirement that is quality must be demonstrated for an invention to be patentable. Nonobviousness may be demonstrated with evidence concerning prior art or with other objective evidence, such as commercial success or professional approval[③]）。novelty 則為「新穎性」，指發明在形式

（form）、功能（function）或性能（performance）幾方面必須新穎，且不能在先前已經取得專利或出版說明或爲他人所知或使用（If the invention has been previously patented, described in a publication, or known or used by others, it is not novel[④]）。

注

① Cf. Li Rong-fu/Song Lei, *A Course Book of Legal English*, Law Press, China (1999), at Ps. 119—121; "In patent law, utility is one of the three basic requirements of patentability, the others being nonobviousness and novelty", Cf. Bryan A. Garner, *Black's Law Dictionary*, 7th Edition, West Group (1999), at P. 1544.

② Cf. Bryan A. Garner, *Black's Law Dictionary*, 7th Edition, West Group (1999), at P. 1544.

③ *Id.* at P. 1079.

④ Cf. 35 USCA Section 102.

Vacate ► Reverse ► Overrule

三者均有使判決等作廢或失去效力的含義。其中，reverse 爲「撤銷」，多指上訴法院作相反判決，撤銷原判的排他性行爲（of an appellate court, to nullify the judgment of a lower court in a case on appeal because of some error in the court below[1]）。而 vacate 爲「廢止」，其可指上訴法院廢止下級法院的判決，此時它等同「撤銷」原判，但審理法院也可以自己廢止原判決，此時它便與 reverse 的含義有差異（to nullify a judgment or court order. This may be done by the court that issued the original judgment or order, or by a higher court on appeal[2]）。overrule 爲「推翻」，常用於法院推翻先例，使其不再具有拘束力（of a court, to overturn or set aside a precedent by expressly deciding that it should no longer be controlling law[3]），如：in *Brown v. Board of Education*, the Supreme Court overruled *Plessy v. Ferguson*（在布朗訴教育委員會一案中，聯邦最高法院推翻了普萊西訴弗格森案之先例）。

注

① Cf. James E. Clapp, *Random House Dictionary of the Law*, Random House, New York (2000), at P. 377.

② *Id.* at P. 451.

③ Cf. Bryan A. Garner, *Black's Law Dictionary*, 7th Edition, West Group (1999), at P. 1131.

Violent crime ▸ Violent offense

　　二者均是涉及使用暴力的犯罪的術語，極易被人混淆而認為是指相同的暴力犯罪。實際上，在刑法中二者的差異是很大的。violent crime 為「暴力犯罪」，泛指一般的暴力犯罪，即罪犯只要對他人的人身或財產之犯罪涉及到暴力因素，不論其是真正使用，還是企圖使用，或威脅使用，或實質上可能使用武力，都構成此種犯罪。其也稱為「暴力罪」（crime of violence）（a crime that has an element that use, attempted use, threatened use, or substantial risk of use of physical force against the person or property of another, also termed crime of violence[1]）。而 violent offense 則指一種極端暴力犯罪行為，諸如謀殺、暴力強姦、使用危險武器脅迫和毆打等之犯罪，故其應譯為「極端暴力罪」，也稱為「暴力重罪」（a crime characterized by extreme physical forces, such as murder, forcible rape, assault and battery with a dangerous weapon, also termed violent felony[2]）。

注

① Cf. Bryan A. Garner, *Black's Law Dictionary*, 7th Edition, West Group (1999), at P. 378.
② *Id.* at P. 1564.

Vocation ▸ Avocation

　　二者均有「職業」的含義。其區別在於 vocation 常指賴以為生的正業、主業（a person's regular calling or business[1]），而 avocation 則指賺外快等之副業（it's emphasis on something that is secondary to a person's livelihood, career or central concern[2]），如：Teaching is my vocation and writing is my avocation（教書是我的主業，寫作是我的

副業）。

注

① Cf. Bryan A. Garner, *Black's Law Dictionary*, 7th Edition, West Group (1999), at P. 1568.
② Cf. Reader's Digest Editors, *Use the Right Word*, The Reader's Digest Association Proprietany Ltd. (1971), at P. 272.

Wanton ▶ Reckless

　　二者均有無視後果而對他人造成傷害的含義。區別在於，在刑法中，wanton 經常有故意或惡意（malice）的含義，指完全不計後果的無理或有預謀的傷害行為（unreasonably or maliciously risking harm while being utterly indifferent to the consequence[①]），故其應譯為「放任（縱）的」。相比之下，儘管 reckless 遠不是一種過失，且其嚴重有悖於理性之人的正常行為，但其主要指魯莽和無視後果，而無惡意（malice），與 wanton 相比，一個 reckless person 有有意避免傷害的企圖，而 wanton person 則完全無避免傷害的嘗試，故 reckless 責任較 wanton 輕[②]，其應譯為「莽撞的」或「不顧危險後果的」。同理，與它們相對應的名詞 wantonness（放任性行為、放縱性行為）和 recklessness（莽撞行為、不顧危險後果的行為）在刑法上也有類似的區別。

注

① Cf. Bryan A. Garner, *Black's Law Dictionary*, 7th Edition, West Group (1999), at P. 378.

② "characterized by the creation of a substantial and unjustifiable risk to the lives, safety, or rights of others", Cf. Linda Pacard Wood, J.D., *Merriam Webster's Dictionary of Law*, Merriam-Webster, Incorporated (1996), at P. 409; "A reckless person is generally fully a ware of the risk and may even be trying and hoping to avoid harm. A wanton person may be risking no more harm than the reckless person, but he or she is not trying to avoid the harm and is indifferent about whether it results." Cf. Bryan A. Garner, *A Dictionary of Modern Legal Usage*, 2nd Edition (1995), at P. 924.

Winding up ▸ Insolvency ▸ Bankruptcy

三者均有破產的含義。在破產法（Bankruptcy Law）中，這些術語的用法因各國規定不同而各有差異。在美國，bankruptcy 可適用於個人與公司，可指作為資不抵債者，即債務人（debtor）或破產人（bankrupt）的個人或公司可據此調整債務，獲得重新開始機會之司法程序（a judicial proceeding under federal law by which a person or a corporation unable to pay its debts can have the debts adjusted and get a new state^①）。而在英國，bankruptcy 只適用於個人（不論商人或非商人），而從未適用於公司（... bankruptcy was never applied to companies, for which an entirely different regime was created, albeit one which incorporated many of the bankruptcy rules... The winding up of a company on the ground of insolvency may be effected...^②）。適用於公司（包括合夥等）的破產為另一套程序，即 winding up。正如上文所說，公司的 wining up 程序與 bankruptcy 有很多類同處，其差異僅在於 bankruptcy 最終是以解除債務人的債務為目的，而 winding up （或 insolvency）則導致公司解散（dissolution），終止其在法律上的存在。而insolvency是破產過程中的一個程序，即「資不抵債」，指債務人無力償還債務，法院宣布其為 insolvent，由此開始破產的正式程序。在表示「破產」時，其既可適用於個人的bankruptcy，也適用於公司的 winding up。在美國，以往不少州的破產法都稱為 insolvency law。

注

① Cf. James E. Clapp, *Random House Webster's Dictionary of the Law*,

Random House, New York (2000), at P. 47.

② Cf. Li Rong-fu/Song Lei, *A Course Book of Legal English, Principles of Insolvency Law*, Law Press, China (1997), P. 172—173.

索引

A

adopt Cf. foster

041 **adult**（條目）

adultery Cf. fornication

adversary system Cf. inquisitorial system

042 **advertisement**（條目）

043 **advice**（條目）**; Cf. legal aid**

advocate Cf. lawyer

043 **affiant**（條目）

044 **affidavit**（條目）

affidavit by process server Cf. proof of service

affidavit of service Cf. proof of service

045 **affiliate**（條目）

046 **affirm**（條目）**; Cf. assert**

affirmation Cf. allegation

affirmation of service Cf. proof of service

affirmative injunction Cf. mandatory injunction

047 **agency by estoppel**（條目）

agency by operation of law Cf. agency by estoppel

agency in fact Cf. agency by estoppel

agency regulation Cf. enabling act

aggravated damages Cf. damages

aggregation Cf. accumulation

048 **aggression**（條目）**; Cf. invasion**

049 **aggrieved party**（條目）

agreed costs Cf. costs

050 **agreement**（條目）

051 **aid**（條目）

air *attaché* Cf. diplomatic personnel

051 **alcoholic**（條目）

052 **alias summons**（條目）

053 **alimony**（條目）

All China Lawyers Society Cf. bar association

054 **allegation**（條目）

allege Cf. assert

054 **allegiance**（條目）

055 **allision**（條目）

allowance for depreciation Cf. depreciation reserve

ally Cf. associate

B

C

civil prison Cf. civil court
civil prisoner Cf. civil court
claimant Cf. plaintiff
claim preclusion Cf. former adjudication
claims made policy Cf. occurrence policy
clause Cf. pleading
close corporation Cf. public corporation
closed corporation Cf. public corporation
closely held corporation Cf. public corporation
collateral estoppel Cf. former adjudication
collateral fraud Cf. extrinsic fraud
collection Cf. accumulation
collision Cf. allision
combustio domorum Cf. arson
112 **commencement**（條目）
commercial Cf. advertisement
commercial company/corporation Cf. business company
(the) Commercial Court Cf. the Supreme Court of England and Wales
commercial impracticability Cf. impossibility
113 **commercial law**（條目）**; Cf. case law; law merchant**
114 **commission merchant**（條目）**; Cf. factor**
common barratry Cf. maintenance
common law contempt Cf. contempt
common law crimes Cf. crime
common law mortgage Cf. legal estate
common tenancy Cf. estate by entirety
114 **commutation**（條目）
116 **companies act**（條目）
(the) Companies Court Cf. the Supreme Court of England and Wales
117 **company**（條目）
company law Cf. companies act
comparative negligence Cf. concurrent negligence
compensatory damages Cf. damages
118 **competence**（條目）**; Cf. jurisdiction**
competency Cf. competence
competent Cf. able
complaint Cf. pleading; pleadings; commencement
119 **composition**（條目）

court of petty sessions Cf. courts in England & Wales; magistrate's court
court of summary jurisdiction Cf. courts in England & Wales; magistrate's court
court of record Cf. inferior court

136 **crib death**（條目）

136 **crime**（條目）
crime against nature Cf. bestiality
crime against property Cf. offense against property; crime
crime against the person Cf. crime
crime involving moral turpitude or not involving moral turpitude Cf. crime
crime mala in se Cf. crime
crime mala prohibita Cf. crime
crimes which are not infamous Cf. crime

138 **criminal assault**（條目）
criminal attempt Cf. inchoate offense
criminal complaint Cf. pleading
criminal contempt Cf. contempt
criminal intent Cf. motive
cross action Cf. counterclaim
cross-claim Cf. counterclaim
cross-demand Cf. counterclaim

139 **cross examination**（條目）

140 **Crown Court**（條目）**; Cf. the Supreme Court of England and Wales; courts in England & Wales**
cumulative evidence Cf. corroborating evidence
curator Cf. tutor

141 **currency depreciation**（條目）
currency devaluation Cf. currency depreciation

141 **curriculum vitae**（條目）
curtail Cf. abate

142 **custom**（條目）
customer Cf. invitee

D

143 **damage**（條目）**; Cf. injury**

(the) department of treasury Cf. finance ministry
depletion Cf. depreciation
deponent Cf. affiant
deportation Cf. transportation; exclusion; banishment

depository Cf. depositary
deposition Cf. affidavit; discovery
derogation Cf. abrogation
deserted child Cf. exposure of child
desertion Cf. abandonment
designate Cf. appoint
detainer Cf. detention
detective chief inspector Cf. detective
detective chief superintendent Cf. detective
detective constable Cf. detective
detective inspector Cf. detective
detective sergeant Cf. detective
detective superintendent Cf. detective
determinative judgment Cf. final judgment
deterrent Cf. arms
detinue Cf. trover
detinuit Cf. detinet
devise Cf. bequeath; testament; legacy
devolution Cf. decentralization
Diet Cf. Parliament
digamy Cf. bigamy
diminish Cf. abate

diplomat Cf. ambassador

diplomatic personnel（條目）

direct and proximate cause Cf. immediate cause

direct beneficiary Cf. incidental beneficiary

direct cause Cf. immediate cause

direct contempt Cf. contempt

direct examination Cf. cross examination

direct investment（條目）

direct liability（條目）

directors（條目）

disavow Cf. forswear

disbarment（條目）

disclaim Cf. forswear

disclosure Cf. discovery

discount Cf. kickback

discovery（條目）

discovery policy Cf. occurrence policy

disfranchisement Cf. amotion

disjunctive condition Cf. single condition

dismissal（條目）

dismissal with prejudice Cf. dismissal

dismissal without prejudice Cf. dismissal

disown Cf. forswear

disposition Cf. decision

dispute Cf. argue

dissolution (of marriage)（條目）

distress Cf. detention

district attorney Cf. United States attorney

district court Cf. inferior court

dsitrict registrars Cf. judicial officers

division Cf. affiliate

division bell（條目）

division lobby Cf. division bell

division of powers Cf. separation of powers

divorce（條目）**; Cf. dissolution**（of marriage）

divorce registry Cf. divorce

docket Cf. calendar call

doctor of juridical science Cf. doctor of law

doctor of jurisprudence Cf. doctor of law

179 **doctor of law**（條目）

doctor of laws Cf. doctor of law

document Cf. instrument

documentary discovery Cf. discovery

dodge a tax Cf. avoid a tax

180 **domestic company**（條目）

domestic corporation Cf. domestic company

180 **domicile**（條目）

dominant estate Cf. dominant tenement

dominant property Cf. dominant tenement

181 **dominant tenement**（條目）

dormant partner Cf. sleeping partner

double adultery Cf. fornication

182 **dower**（條目）

down payment Cf. deposit

dowry Cf. dower

183 **draft**（條目）

D reorganization Cf. spin off

drunk Cf. alcoholic

drunkard Cf. alcoholic

183 **due care**（條目）

due diligence Cf. due care

Duma Cf. Parliament

184 **duplicate**（條目）

duplicate original Cf. duplicate

E

earnest Cf. deposit

earnest money Cf. deposit

earnings report Cf. statement of income

easement Cf. servitude

ecclesiastical law Cf. canon law

186 **edict**（條目）

effective cause Cf. immediate cause

efficient adequate cause Cf. immediate cause

efficient cause Cf. immediate cause

efficient proximate cause Cf. immediate cause

186 **ejectment**（條目）

187 **elegit**（條目）

elemental fact Cf. evidentiary fact

embezzlement Cf. larceny; defalcation

188 **embryo**（條目）

emigrant Cf. migrant

emigration Cf. migrant

émigré Cf. migrant

189 **eminent domain**（條目）

emotional distress Cf. mental disease

emotional harm Cf. mental disease

190 **employ**（條目）

190 **enabling act/legislation/statute**（條目）

encourage Cf. abet

191 **engross**（條目）

192 **enlist**（條目）

enroll Cf. engross

193 **enrollment**（條目）

193 **enumerated power**（條目）

envoy Cf. ambassador; diplomatic personnel

194 **Equal Employment Opportunity Commission**（條目）

Equal Opportunities Commission Cf. Equal Employment Opportunity
Commission

195 **equitable action**（條目）

equitable estate Cf. legal estate

equitable fraud Cf. actual fraud

equitable mortgage Cf. legal estate

196 **equitable title**（條目）

equity Cf. law

error in vacuo Cf. fatal error

197 **escape**（條目）

escort Cf. convoy

198 **Establishment Clause**（條目）

199 **estate by entirety**（條目）

estate by the entireties Cf. estate by entirety

estate in common Cf. estate by entirety

200 **estate on conditional limitation**（條目）
estate subject to a conditional limitation Cf. estate on conditional
limitation
estate tax Cf. death duty
estoppel by judgment Cf. former adjudication
(the) European Court of Justice Cf. courts in England & Wales
evade tax Cf. avoid a tax
evaluation Cf. appraisal
eviction Cf. ejectment
201 **evidence**（條目）
evidential fact Cf. evidentiary fact
202 **evidentiary fact**（條目）
examination Cf. cross examination
exception Cf. demurrer
exceptions for insufficiency of a pleading Cf. demurrer
exchange Cf. barter
202 **excise**（條目）
203 **excise**（條目）
excise duty Cf. excise
excise tax Cf. excise
205 **exclusion**（條目）
exculpate Cf. absolve
executive Cf. government
206 **executive agreement**（條目）
executive appointment Cf. legislative appointment
206 **executor**（條目）
exemplary damages Cf. damages
exile Cf. transportation; banishment
exonerate Cf. absolve
expatriation Cf. banishment
207 **expiration**（條目）
208 **exposure of child**（條目）
express power Cf. enumerated power
expropriation Cf. eminent domain
expulsion Cf. amotion
expunction action/proceeding Cf. infringement of trademark
expungement action/proceeding Cf. infringement of trademark
464 extend Cf. renewal

extension Cf. renewal
extradition Cf. rendition
extradition warrant Cf. rendition
209   **extraordinary resolution**（條目）
211   **extrinsic fraud**（條目）

F

213   **factor**（條目）**; Cf. commission merchant**
faculty Cf. ability
faculty of Advocates Cf. bar association
false action Cf. feigned action
213   **false arrest**（條目）
false imprisonment Cf. false arrest
false oath Cf. perjury; false swearing
false pretense Cf. larceny
214   **false swearing**（條目）**; Cf. perjury**
215   **farm produce**（條目）.
farm product Cf. farm produce
216   **fatal error**（條目）
(the) Family Division Cf. the Supreme Court of England and Wales
217   **fault**（條目）
fault divorce Cf. divorce
favor Cf. benefit
fealty Cf. allegiance
Federal Parliament Cf. parliament
218   **federation**（條目）
219   **feigned action**（條目）
felony Cf. treason; high crime; non-arrestable offense; crime
fetus Cf. embryo
fidelity Cf. allegiance
fieri facias Cf. elegit
219   **filiate**（條目）
final appealable judgment Cf. final judgment
final appealable order Cf. final judgment
final decision Cf. final judgment
final decree Cf. final judgment

G

H

I

irretrievable breakdown of the marriage relationship Cf. irretrievable breakdown of the marriage

issuable fact Cf. evidentiary fact

J

jail Cf. prison, gaol

jailhouse Cf. gaol

286 **J.D.**（條目）

jetsam Cf. lagan

287 **job action**（條目）

jobber Cf. broker

joint adventure Cf. joint venture

joint and several liability Cf. solidary liability; joint liability

288 **joint custody**（條目）

joint legal custody Cf. joint custody

289 **joint liability**（條目）

joint party Cf. third party

joint physical custody Cf. joint custody

joint negligence Cf. current negligence

290 **joint resolution**（條目）

joint tenancy Cf. estate by entirety

290 **joint venture**（條目）

J.S.D.Cf. J.D.

291 **judge**（條目）**; Cf. arbiter**

judges in chambers Cf. judicial officiers

292 **judgment**（條目）**; Cf. decision; opinion**

judgment of court of last resort Cf. final judgment

judgment of last resort Cf. final judgment

293 **judicial aid**（條目）

293 **judicial officers**（條目）

judiciary Cf. government

295 **junior division**（條目）

jural cause Cf. immediate cause

295 **jurisdiction**（條目）

juris doctor Cf. doctor of law

472 jurisprudence Cf. case law

jus canonicum Cf. canon law
jus ecclesiasticum Cf. canon law
justice Cf. judge
justices of the peace Cf. inferior court; magistrate's court

296 **juvenile**（條目）**; Cf. delinquent child**

K

299 **kickback**（條目）
kidnap Cf. abduct
kidnapping Cf. abduct
killing Cf. homicide
(the) King's Bench Division Cf. the Supreme Court of England and Wales

L

labor reform Cf. forced labor
labor reform farm Cf. forced labor

300 **lagan**（條目）
lagend Cf. lagan
lagon Cf. lagan

301 **landed estate**（條目）
landed property Cf. landed estate
landlord Cf. landowner

301 **landowner**（條目）
Landtage Cf. parliament
Langdell method Cf. casebook

302 **larceny**（條目）
larceny by trick Cf. larceny

304 **law**（條目）**; Cf. act**
law agent Cf. lawyer
law-maker Cf. legislator

305 **law merchant**（條目）

306 **law of obligation**（條目）
law of property Cf. law of obligation
law of status Cf. law of obligation

law of the sea Cf. sea law
law society Cf. bar association; Legal Aid Board
Law Society of Scotland Cf. bar association
law spiritual Cf. canon law

307 **lawyer**（條目）
lay magistrate Cf. magistrate's court
leader Cf. boss

310 **leasehold**（條目）
leasehold estate Cf. leasehold
leasehold interest Cf. leasehold
lecture method Cf. casebook

311 **legacy**（條目）
legacy tax Cf. death tax
legal action Cf. equitable action

312 **legal adviser**（條目）

312 **legal aid**（條目）**; Cf. judicial aid**

314 **Legal Aid Board**（條目）
legal capacity Cf. ability
legal cause Cf. immediate cause
legal disability Cf. physical disability

314 **legal doctrine**（條目）

315 **legal estate**（條目）
legal fraud Cf. actual fraud
legal mortgage Cf. legal estate

316 **legal person**（條目）
legal principle Cf. legal doctrine

316 **legal representative**（條目）
legal rule Cf. legal doctrine
legal title Cf. equitable title
legate Cf. ambassador
legatee Cf. devisee
legislation Cf. act

318 **legislative appointment**（條目）
Legislative Assembly Cf. Parliament
legislative fact Cf. adjudicative fact

319 **legislator**（條目）
legislature Cf. government

legitimate Cf. filiate

Limited Cf. Ltd.

M

mail transfer(M/T) Cf. remittance

maintain Cf. assert

major crime Cf. crime

majority Cf. plurality

malfeasance Cf. misfeasance

malicious use of process Cf. malicious prosecution

maltreatment Cf. abuse

mandamus Cf. injunction

manslaughter Cf. homicide

marijuana Cf. hashish

maritime law Cf. sea law

marriage license Cf. marriage certificate

master Cf. boss

master of laws Cf. doctor of law

matricide Cf. parricide

maturity Cf. expiration

mayhem Cf. maiming

mediate fact Cf. evidentiary fact

333 **mediation**（條目）
medical examiner Cf. coroner
memorandum of association Cf. charter
mens rea Cf. motive
mental anguish Cf. mental disease
334 **mental disease**（條目）
mental disorder Cf. mental disease
mental illness Cf. mental disease
mental suffering Cf. mental disease
mental patient Cf. patient
merchandise broker Cf. commission merchant
merger Cf. acquisition
middleman Cf. broker
335 **migrant**（條目）
migration Cf. migrant
military *attaché* Cf. diplomatic personnel
336 **military court**（條目）
military law Cf. martial law
minister Cf. ambassador
minister counselor Cf. diplomatic personnel
337 **ministry**（條目）
338 **minor**（條目）**; Cf. adult; juvenile**
minor dispute Cf. major dispute
miscarriage Cf. abortion
misdemeanor Cf. treason; non-arrestable offense; crime
338 **misfeasance**（條目）
339 **mistake of fact**（條目）
340 **mistake of law Cf. mistake of fact**
mistreatment Cf. abuse
monogamy Cf. bigamy
moral fraud Cf. actual fraud
mortgage Cf. charge
340 **motive**（條目）
moveable Cf. heritable
341 **multinational corporation**（條目）
municipal court Cf. inferior court
municipal ordinance Cf. ordinance
munitions Cf. arms

murder Cf. homicide

N

name Cf. appoint
National People's Congress Cf. Parliament
naval *attaché* Cf. diplomatic personnel
naval court Cf. admiralty court
naval martial-court Cf. admiralty court
necessary party Cf. indispensable party
necessitous Cf. needy
342 **needy**（條目）
342 **negative act**（條目）
negligence Cf. fault; diligence; recklessness
343 **negotiability**（條目）
negotiation Cf. transfer
new contract dispute Cf. major dispute
344 **next friend**（條目）
(the) Noes lobby Cf. division lobby
no-fault divorce Cf. divorce; irretrievable breakdown of the marriage
nominal damages Cf. damages
345 **non-arrestable offence**（條目）
nonfeasance Cf. misfeasance
non-profit corporation Cf. business company
nonobviousness Cf. utility
not-for-profit corporation Cf. business company
notice act Cf. recording acts
notice of service Cf. proof of service
notice race statute Cf. recording acts
notice recording statute Cf. recording acts
notice statute Cf. recording acts
novelty Cf. utility
nuncio Cf. ambassador

·O

P

palimony Cf. alimony
palming off action Cf. infringement of trademark
panderer Cf. bawd
panel (of judges) Cf. full court
papal law Cf. canon law
pardon Cf. amnesty; absolve
parent law Cf. enabling act
parenticide Cf. parricide
355 **parliament**（條目）
partner Cf. associate
356 **parricide**（條目）
particulars of claim Cf. pleading; pleadings
partner in commendam Cf. special partner
partnership in commendam Cf. special partner
passing off action Cf. infringement of trademark
357 **passive breach of contract**（條目）
pat-down Cf. frisk
358 **patient**（條目）
patricide Cf. parricide
party aggrieved Cf. aggrieved party
(the) Patents Court Cf. the Supreme Court of England and Wales
payoff Cf. kickback
peace officer Cf. police officer
peculation Cf. larceny
peddler Cf. hawker
pederasty Cf. bestiality
pedlar Cf. hawker
pedler Cf. hawker
penitentiary Cf. prison
359 **pension**（條目）
performance Cf. act; satisfaction
359 **perjury**（條目）**; Cf. false swearing**
permissive inference Cf. mandatory presumption
permissive presumption Cf. mandatory presumption
persecution Cf. abuse

public order offence Cf. crime
public proclamation Cf. edict
publicly held corporation Cf. public corporation
punies Cf. damages
punitive damages Cf. damages
punitory damages Cf. damages
purchase Cf. buy
pursuer Cf. plaintiff

Q

qualified Cf. able
(the) Queen's Bench Division Cf. the Supreme Court of England and
    Wales
Queen's Bench masters Cf. judicial officiers

R

race act Cf. recording acts
race-notice statute Cf. recording acts
race statute Cf. recording acts
385 **raider**（條目）
real estate Cf. landed estate
385 **real estate agent**（條目）
real estate broker Cf. real estate agent
real-estate broker's agent Cf. selling agent
real property Cf. house property; property
reason Cf. opinion; argue
rebutter Cf. pleadings
receiver Cf. liquidator
recession Cf. depression
reckless Cf. wanton
reckless driving Cf. careless driving
386 **recklessness**（條目）
reconciliation Cf. mediation
recorder Cf. county court

representation Cf. legal aid
reprieve（條目）
reprisal Cf. retaliation; marque
requests for admissions Cf. discovery
request for entry of appeal Cf. originating process
requests for production Cf. discovery
rescind Cf. abolish
rescission Cf. abandonment
reserved power Cf. enumerated power
residence Cf. domicile
resident Cf. inhabitant
resign Cf. abdicate
res adjudicata Cf. former adjudication
res judicata Cf. former adjudication
respondent Cf. plaintiff; defendant
respondentia（條目）
restraint Cf. restriction
restriction（條目）
resume Cf. curriculum vitae
retain Cf. employ
retainer Cf. retaining fee
retaining fee（條目）
retaliation（條目）
retorsion Cf. retaliation
return of service Cf. proof of service
return receipt requested Cf. registered mail
revendication（條目）
reverse Cf. vacate; affirm
reversible error Cf. fatal error
revocation Cf. rejection
revoke Cf. abolish
right arbitration Cf. interest arbitration
right of rescission（條目）
right of termination Cf. right of rescission
right of way Cf. access right
right to rescind Cf. right of rescission
right to terminate Cf. right of rescission
riot Cf. rout

risk of jury doubt Cf. burden of proof
risk of non-persuasion Cf. burden of proof
road traffic offence Cf. crime
robbery Cf. hold-up

403 **rout**（條目）
royalty Cf. excise
ruling Cf. decision

S

405 **salary**（條目）
sales tax Cf. excise (or excise tax or excise duty)
sanction Cf. approval

405 **satisfaction**（條目）
satisfaction of debt Cf. satisfaction
save harmless Cf. indemnify

406 **sea law**（條目）
search Cf. frisk
secondary law Cf. enabling act
secondary legislation Cf. delegated legislation
secret partner Cf. sleeping partner
secretary Cf. diplomatic personnel
seizure Cf. apprehension; detention

407 **selling agent**（條目）
sentence Cf. decision

408 **separation of powers**（條目）

408 **serf**（條目）
serial bond Cf. series bonds

409 **series bonds**（條目）
servient estate Cf. dominant tenement
servient property Cf. dominant tenement
servient tenement Cf. dominant tenement

410 **servitude**（條目）
settlement Cf. mediation
sex Cf. gender
sexual assault Cf. indecent assault

sexual offences Cf. crime

split-up Cf. spin-off
spouse-breach Cf. fornication
spousal support Cf. alimony
(the) state department Cf. foreign ministry
state high courts Cf. inferior court
statement Cf. admission
statement of claim Cf. pleading; pleadings; commencement
statement of condition Cf. statement of income
statement of financial condition Cf. statement of income
statement of financial position Cf. statement of income

419 **statement of income**（條目）
statute Cf. act

420 **statute of limitation**（條目）
statute of repose Cf. statute of limitation
statutory arson Cf. arson
statutory crimes Cf. crime
sticking off the solicitor's roll Cf. disbarment
stipendiary magistrate Cf. magistrate's court

420 **stipulation**（條目）
stock Cf. share
stockbroker Cf. floor trader
stocks Cf. bilboes
strict confidential Cf. confidential

421 **strict construction**（條目）
strict constructionism Cf. strict construction
strict interpretation Cf. strict construction
strike Cf. job action

422 **structure of an act**（條目）
stub Cf. counterfoil
subjective theory of contract Cf. objective theory of contract
subordinate Cf. assistant
subordinate legislation Cf. enabling act
subpoena Cf. process
subsidiary Cf. affiliate
subsidiary corporation Cf. affiliate
succession duty/tax Cf. death duty
sufficiency Cf. admissibility

suit Cf. action

summary Cf. abstract
summary court-martial Cf. military court
summary dissolution procedure Cf. divorce
summary offense Cf. treason
summing-up Cf. instruction to the jury
summons Cf. process; originating process
superior court Cf. inferior court
superior force Cf. *force majeure*
supervisors Cf. directors
supreme court Cf. inferior court; court of appeals
423 **(the) Supreme Court of England and Wales**（條目）
suretyship Cf. guaranty
surrebutter Cf. pleadings
surrejoinder Cf. pleadings
surrender Cf. abdicate
swap Cf. barter

T

tacit mortgage Cf. legal estate
425 **tax avoidance**（條目）
426 **tax credit**（條目）
tax deduction Cf. tax credit
tax dodge Cf. tax avoidance
tax evasion Cf. tax avoidance
tax exemption Cf. tax credit
tax fraud Cf. tax avoidance
taxed costs Cf. costs
taxing masters Cf. judicial officers
technical error Cf. fatal error
tenancy by the entireties Cf. estate by entirety
tenancy by the entirety Cf. estate by entirety
tenancy in common Cf. estate by entirety
tenant Cf. plaintiff
telegraphic transfer(T/D) Cf. remittance
427 **testament**（條目）
testify Cf. assert

U

warrant of arrest Cf. bench arrest
warranty Cf. guaranty
weapon Cf. arms
weight Cf. admissibility
wherein Cf. herein
white knight Cf. raider
will Cf. testament
willful wrong Cf. recklessness

445 **winding up**（條目）
writ Cf. originating process
writ of fieri facias Cf. elegit
writ of mandamus Cf. injunction
writ of subpoena Cf. process
writ of summons Cf. process
wrong Cf. abuse
wrongful dismissal Cf. Unfair dismissal

Y

yield Cf. abdiacte
youth Cf. adolescent

國家圖書館出版品預行編目資料

法律英語翻譯指南／宋雷 編著.
—初版.—臺北市：五南，2005 [民94]
面；　公分
參考書目：面
含索引
ISBN 978-957-11-4072-8（平裝）
1.法學英語－翻譯
805.1　　　　　　　94015454

1Q99
法律英語翻譯指南

作　者－宋　雷
發 行 人－楊榮川
總 編 輯－王翠華
主　　編－劉靜芬
責任編輯－張婉婷　李楚芳　胡天慈
出 版 者－五南圖書出版股份有限公司
地　　址：106台北市大安區和平東路二段339號4樓
電　　話：(02)2705-5066　傳　　真：(02)2706-6100
網　　址：http://www.wunan.com.tw
電子郵件：wunan@wunan.com.tw
劃撥帳號：01068953
戶　　名：五南圖書出版股份有限公司
法律顧問　林勝安律師事務所　林勝安律師
出版日期　2005年10月初版一刷
　　　　　2015年 8月初版四刷
定　　價　新臺幣650元